The draconians started to hoot, hiss, and jeer. Their batlike wings, insufficient for true flight but able to hasten their speed in a charge, flexed and fanned, giving the moonlit horde a shifting, unreal quality, as if the monsters were not individual creatures, but parts of a blanket that was being fluttered horizontally in a light breeze. All the noises increased, until it seemed as though the forest itself was screeching and stomping at the elves. Finally the warlike sounds reached a crescendo, holding at this frenetic pitch for several taut heartbeats.

And then, is if a dam had burst, the entire mob spewed forward from the fringe of the trees. . . .

CHAOS WAR SERIES

The Doom Brigade
Margaret Weis and Don Perrin

The Last Thane
Douglas Niles

Tears of the Night Sky
Linda P. Baker and Nancy Varian Berberick
Available October 1998

The Puppet King
Douglas Niles

Reavers of the Blood Sea
Richard A. Knaak

The Siege of Mt. Nevermind
Fergus Ryan

The Puppet King

Douglas Niles

To Bénédict Niles Weber.
Welcome to a great life.

THE PUPPET KING
©1999 TSR, Inc.
All Rights Reserved.

Distributed to the book trade in the United States by Random house, Inc. and in Canada by Random House of Canada Ltd.

Distributed to the hobby, toy, and comic trade in the United States and Canada by regional distributors.

Distributed worldwide by Wizards of the Coast, Inc. and regional distributors.

Cover art by David Martin
First Printing: February 1999
Library of Congress Catalog Card Number: 98-8578
9 8 7 6 5 4 3 2 1

ISBN:0-7869-1324-X

21324XXX1501

U.S., CANADA, ASIA,
PACIFIC, & LATIN AMERICA
Wizards of the Coast, Inc.
P.O. Box 707
Renton, WA 98057-0707
+1-800-324-6496

EUROPEAN HEADQUARTERS
Wizards of the Coast, Belgium
P.B. 34
2300 Turnhout
Belgium
+32-14-44-30-44

Visit our website at **www.tsr.com**

Prologue

Year 25, after the Second Cataclysm

The elf made his way carefully down the steep, narrow trail. He ignored the massive waves crashing into the rocks so far below, concentrating instead on the placement of each foot, taking care to avoid patches of slick moss or crumbling gravel. A single misstep could send him plunging to certain death, yet his face was calm, unconcerned by thoughts of danger.

In his hand, he carried a long, slender lance, using the haft of the weapon like a walking staff to aid his balance as he moved along the treacherous trail. His clothes were rough, sturdy, and practical, showing the wear of long exposure to weather and time. He moved with speed and grace, skipping over a slippery patch of smooth stone, making steady progress until he came to rest on a rough promontory halfway down the precipitous bluff. There he remained frozen in place for a long time, as still as one of the crags jutting from the slope all around him. Intent on the base of the cliff, he stared, sniffing the air, searching with darting eyes for any sign of movement, of danger. He studied the empty gray sea, the line of waves rolling inexorably from the west to crash onto this continental shore. The lance he balanced upright, the pole rising a good three times his own height, capped by a barbed, lethal-looking head of shimmering silver.

Only after dozens of waves had crashed against the rocks did he move again, raising a hand and gesturing curtly toward the underbrush that draped the edge of the bluff over his head. Carefully, hesitantly, another elf came forward. This one's face blanched at the sight of the steep descent, and for a moment he turned a yearning glance back to the shelter of the woods. But then the first elf gestured again urgently, and the newcomer forced himself to follow in the footsteps of the other. His slender hands clutched at rocks and weeds, and his steps were short, tentative. Still, he came down the steep trail, staring wildly at his companion, at the raging surf, at the expanse of sea rolling unhindered to the west.

By the time he reached the ledge, he had regained some of his composure, disdaining the balancing hand offered by his companion. The second elf wore finer clothes and held his head high, looking over the seascape with an expression of wonder. Fastidiously he kept his boots out of the mud, though he, like the other, was dirty and unkempt, with the look of one who had lived, bathed, and eaten in the forest for a long time.

Ensuring that the youngster had a solid perch, a place that was dry and flat and offered secure footing, the first elf murmured some soft words, passing his hands in an intricate pattern around the other. When he had finished gesturing, he released a pinch of down, and the tuft drifted away on the breeze, dancing through the air, gradually settling toward the pounding surf. Only when the feather had vanished in the froth and foam did the elder return his attention to the descent.

Now he had to move carefully, turning to face the cliff, grasping for holds with his free hand while his toes sought resting places, then gingerly adjusting his grip slightly lower. He wedged the fingers of his left hand into cracks in the face of the cliff, and balanced his toes on narrow ledges or tiny shoulders of jutting rocks while he clung tightly to the lance with his other hand.

Though his progress was slow, his face betrayed no hint of strain or fear. If the great lance was an encumbrance, he did not allow it to slow him down. Instead, the expression of concentration remained fixed. He squinted slightly when it took him a long time to find the next toehold, but even so, his progress remained steady.

Finally the elder elf stood upon a seaside boulder, and here he leaned around a crag, looking into the large cave mouth that yawned darkly just a few feet above the reach of the waves at high tide. He balanced the lance in both hands now, head forward as he hesitantly advanced into the darkness, sniffing quietly, seeking to penetrate the darkness with his keen, almond-shaped eyes. The shadowy cavern dwarfed the warrior with its vast domed ceiling, but it did not seem to awe or intimidate him. Instead, an aura of soft light originated from the lance head, and an aura of confidence came from the elf himself.

The second elf, still waiting on the narrow shelf, looked down with unmistakable apprehension. It was a very young face, this elf's. Indeed, he was more a boy than a man. He tried hard to look unconcerned, to be brave, but there alone on the shelf, he seemed to shrink within himself. He leaned against the slope to grab any handholds he could find. When the elder reappeared at the base of the cliff and waved, the youth's face grew pale and his eyes widened in momentary fear. Firmly the elf below waved again, gesturing him down.

Taking a deep breath, the young elf stepped off the bluff, into the empty space yawning below. He floated gently, easily downward, no faster than the tuft of down that the elder elf had loosed into the wind a short time before. In half a minute, he came to rest beside his companion.

"Here. Put this on." The elder elf extended a thin fabric of green weave and assisted his companion in strapping the thing across his face. The mask covered the young elf's nose and mouth in a material that seemed to be woven from supple grasses.

3

"Don't you have one for yourself?" asked the youth, his voice naturally soft but unmuffled by the light screen. The elder merely shook his head and once more hefted the great lance.

Without further speaking, he led his young companion into the dark cave. The pair crept along soundlessly, moving gradually around a curving passage until they were cloaked in shadow. Here they paused, allowing their elven eyes to attune to the darkness. After a minute, they moved forward again. There was a strong smell, like bleach, that permeated the air. The floor of the cave was clean, except for small patches of moss and a channel where seawater rolled in during high tides.

Momentarily the young elf hesitated, but when his companion continued forward, he rushed after him, apparently preferring the dangers of the cave's interior to solitude close to the entrance. They moved farther into the darkness, the warrior holding the great lance at the ready. His eyes flashed back and forth, seeking to penetrate the shadows, alert to any movement, any sign of danger. Above the mesh mask, the youngster's eyes were wide, staring with barely concealed fear at his companion's back. Still cautious, the two crept around one more corner, and here again they froze as rigid as statues.

A massive shape coiled in this deep alcove, and the elder elf held his finger to his lips, an unnecessary gesture of caution as the youngster froze, horrified and silent, eyes widening while the visible skin of his face drained of all color. The scaled flanks of the huge shape rose and fell gradually. Huge wings of green membrane were folded along the back, while moss and lichen crusted along the great legs, even growing across several massive talons, an effect that appeared to merge the foot right into the cavern floor.

The lance-wielder approached the reptilian shape, holding the weapon pointed straight toward the snakelike head. The soft breathing, an exhalation from massive lungs, rasped around him with a stinging odor that brought tears to his eyes. The warrior winced, though his companion breathed through the mask without any appearance of discomfort. Still, the youngster's eyes widened over the green fabric, and he quickly moved back.

4

The lancer brought the weapon forward hard, stabbing the point into the sensitive skin within one of the massive nostrils. Leather lids rolled back, and golden eyes, the size of melons, came into focus with a growing sense of shock and rage. A cloud of green gas boiled from the gaping nostrils, but the elder elf stood to the side of the misty vapor. The younger elf, protected by his mask, blinked and coughed slightly but didn't recoil.

The warrior poked the snout again, and with a growl of anger and pain the dragon jerked backward, neck twisting, head rearing high above the two elves. With its massive jaws spread wide, the wyrm blasted a roar of fury.

Boldly the elder elf stepped forward and pressed the tip of his lance against the dragon's breast at the place where the sinuous neck merged into the emerald body. He pushed, and a green scale cracked. The dragon tried to recoil, but it was blocked by the side of the cavern.

"Be silent, Aerensianic, and heed me or you will die!" barked the warrior, his tone stern and unafraid.

"You know me?" growled the serpent, his eyes narrowing in confusion and surprise.

"It was twenty-five years ago that we met. You may not remember me," declared the elf calmly.

The wyrm fixed his gaze at the weapon poised for a killing thrust. But he made no move to attack.

"I could crush you with my jaws or in my talons!" growled the dragon called Aerensianic.

"You could try," the elf allowed, "but I'll take the chance that I could drive this dragonlance into your foul heart before you could move." He seemed utterly unconcerned.

"I have sheltered here for a dozen winters or more, bothering no one in all that time," the serpent replied in a tone of injured pride. "Leave me alone!"

"Not until we get what we have come for," replied the lancer, twisting and pushing his weapon slightly, drawing an insulted snort from his massive adversary.

"What is it you want of me?" the dragon finally demanded, his voice a deep hiss. "My treasures? My life? Take it and begone!"

"Not your treasures . . . nor do we have any wish to claim your life. Rather, the lad here has a simple request," said the elder, indicating his companion with a hunch of his shoulder.

Still staring, the second elf moved forward, eyes wide over the green mask as he stared at the monster rearing so high above.

"Make your demand!" spat the serpent.

Mustering all his courage, the young elf took another step. He glared into the dragon's face, trying vainly to suppress the trembling in his knees. Still, his voice, when he spoke, was firm and steady.

"I want you to tell me a story," he said.

PART 1

ELF WAR

Late Summer, 382 AC

Meeting in the Marsh

Chapter 1

The green wing curled gracefully, slicing the fetid air, bearing the great body through a shallow, banking turn. Aerensianic looked across the landscape of dark green, seeing the tracks of brackish streams like bright veins against a backdrop of verdant decay. Tall trees rose from the muck here and there, many draped with tendrils of stringy moss, while others loomed gaunt and skeletal, bereft of leaves and greenery. No breath of wind disturbed the air, and the landscape shimmered with a heat that was oppressive and unnatural even for this late summer day. Pale sunlight thickened the atmosphere, and vapors rising from the swamp were rich with the odors of decaying foliage, carrion, and the fishy, lizardy smell of scaly denizens.

Truly this swampland was a place of rot and death, and now it was the last such within the borders of the elven nation of Silvanesti. Beyond the delta of the silvered river, the Thon-Thalas, past horizons to the north and east and west, thriving forests rose from soft black loam. Sculpted as orderly, elegant gardens by the Woodshaper elves, these woodlands were places of precise order, carefully tended and schemed into regimented patterns. Aeren could see the lofty treetops waving in the balmy breeze, he could smell the hateful fragrance of vast, flowered meadows, and he could hear the relentless melody of a million songbirds as the feathered minstrels warbled their joy at the land's rebirth.

There was no place for a dragon, not in those tamed woods.

Only here, in the delta of the kingdom's great river, did decay and rot still linger in Silvanesti. Bordered by swift currents on all sides, an island inhabited by draconians, ogres, and other savage denizens, this murky fen was a stronghold of evil, the one such remaining within Silvanesti. Thirty years ago, the whole realm had been like this, but in that time, the elves had waged a relentless campaign of reclamation. Region by region, grove by grove, they had driven the monstrous denizens out, and the Woodshaper elves had then gone to work, sculpting and controlling and taming the wilds.

Aeren knew that the elves must inevitably be gathering their strength, preparing to clean out this last outpost of their enemies. In the thickets below were numerous bands of draconians, as well as ogres and two more dragons. Together they made a teeming, powerful force of savage and bestial warriors. But despite the might of the creatures gathered in opposition, it had seemed an unchangeable fact that the elves must prevail.

Until he had gotten the message, brought by a draconian who had once been a prisoner of the elves. The summons, too intriguing to ignore, drew Aerensianic from his moss-shrouded lair. Though he naturally suspected treachery, the green dragon had been curious in spite of his misgivings, and so he had come.

Now he saw the hillock at the southern end of the delta and tucked his wings, arrowing toward the slight elevation.

Beyond the mossy rise stretched miles of brackish salt flats, merging with an indistinct border into the Courrain Ocean far to the south. Meandering channels of water connected the low hill with the deep river waters to the west. No doubt the other party at this meeting would reach the hill by boating along one of those canals.

Aeren could remember a time when this delta had not existed, when the Thon-Thalas had flowed deep and clear all the way to the sea. In the past decades, the river had been sorely taxed by the elven efforts to restore Silvanesti. So much of the wracked landscape had been carried seaward as silt that this vast fen had developed at the mouth of the river. Naturally, all the surviving creatures of foulness and evil had collected here, and the marsh had become a stronghold of villainy within a realm that was, in all other respects, once more pristine and healthy.

A spot of whiteness showed at the crest of the hill, and the green dragon curled his lip in an unconscious sneer. How like a Silvanesti. Even on a mission calling for stealth and subterfuge, he could not divest himself of the elegant robe of his station. Under other circumstances, Aeren would have enjoyed punishing the elf for his disdainful lack of camouflage, but for now the wyrm contented himself with a snort of disgust as he circled lower, finally coming to rest on the crest of the mossy hill. A sidelong glance showed that, as he had suspected, a longboat was pulled into the rushes at the base of the elevation. Two elven polers, dressed in the humble leather tunics of servants, waited in the narrow hull.

The elf on the hilltop made no effort to hide his distaste. Indeed, he pulled a fold of his robe over his mouth and nose as the unmaskable stench of green dragon wafted across the ground. Aeren snorted again, enjoying the Silvanesti's discomfort as visible fumes drifted past his face. Then the dragon settled down, crouching like a cat and curling his neck around to bring his head down to the elf's level.

He studied the fellow, noting the gold-laced sandals, the gilt-trimmed robe, and the jewel-encrusted bracelets of precious metal. Looking more closely, Aeren saw the unconcealed hatred in the elf's narrowed eyes. Though he must be weakened by the effects of dragon awe, the Silvanesti was doing an admirable job of masking his unease.

"Audacious, don't you think, to wear these baubles into the presence of a known collector such as myself?" Aeren said, his voice a low, sibilant growl. "Those bracelets would look exceptionally nice atop my treasure mound."

The Silvanesti's eyes widened momentarily at the words, but his face quickly dropped back into its haughty scowl. "I have misjudged you badly if you yield to such a short-term inducement when I come to offer something much greater."

The green dragon huffed, affecting an air of great boredom. "I have come. I have not killed you. Speak."

The elf coughed—even that he did with casual elegance—and appeared to marshal his thoughts. Long pauses in conversation were nothing unusual to a dragon, so Aeren waited patiently.

"You realize that the Qualinesti elf, Porthios, has nearly succeeded in driving your kind from Silvanesti." The word "Qualinesti" rolled off the elf's tongue as if the very sound of it reeked of venom.

But Aeren was not prepared to concede this point. "My kind, as always, goes where it will. We are not driven anywhere we do not wish to go."

The Silvanesti made a gesture of impatience. "You know what I mean—draconians, that sort. They survive nowhere else in the kingdom but this island in the delta."

"Do not make the mistake, elf, of mixing draconians and dragons as the same 'kind.' I shall overlook your misstatement this once. Next time you are so careless, you will die and this meeting will be over."

With an admirable display of self-control, the elf showed no more reaction than a tightening of his lips. "Very well. The creatures of the Dark Queen have been exiled from all of Silvanesti except for this island. You must be aware that Porthios soon plans to clean out this last outpost."

"It is an obvious tactic," the dragon allowed.

"There are elves in Silvanesti who would be willing to see

your ki—that is, to see you and other green dragons, as well as such lackeys as you are inclined to allow, retain this small foothold in our kingdom. A peace offering, if you will . . . a testament to the end of war between dragonkind and the elves."

"There are such elves . . . and you are one of them?" Aeren replied, intrigued in spite of himself. Of all the things he had speculated that this elf might want to discuss, the notion of a truce had not been one of them.

"It is the reason I have asked to meet you here."

"And in return for your tolerance of our presence, you expect . . . what?"

"We expect that you will do Silvanesti a single favor—a great favor, it is true, but only one task. It is a thing that you will doubtless find satisfying on its own level."

"Continue."

"We want you to kill Porthios when he comes here, when he leads the elven army against you."

Aeren snorted, unmindful of the chlorine gas that again wafted past the elf's face. Despite the hasty raising of his silken robe, the Silvanesti coughed and gagged, stepping backward and wheezing in discomfort. And still the green dragon didn't notice.

"You want me to slay the hero who has restored your realm to the elves?" he asked curiously.

"He is not a hero. He is a Qualinesti radical who threatens our future, every bit as much as the mad king Lorac Caladon threatened our past!"

"Qualinesti . . . Silvanesti." Aeren had heard the terms, knew of the two nations, of course, but the distinction was vague in his mind. "Are you not both elves?"

"Bah!" The emissary's tone was scornful. "I do not expect you to understand, but the Qualinesti are ill-bred upstarts, unmindful of tradition, uncaring of the racial purity that is the gods-given gift of our race! We have sculpted our realm into a garden of precise, controlled beauty! Qualinesti is a place where the trees are allowed to grow as they will, in disorder and chaos. It is full of deep, trackless groves, and like their trees, the people of the western realm are untamed, utterly lacking in the decency, the refined sensibilities and regal legacy of Silvanesti!"

"But this upstart Qualinesti has you worried?" asked Aeren, privately thinking that the forest of the western elves sounded like a very fine place indeed.

"If Porthios is allowed to live, there is a very real danger that he will seek to unite the two elven kingdoms, and then the hallmark of purity, the legacy we have to offer our children through centuries to come, will erode to the point of uselessness."

Deep in thought, the green dragon lowered filmy membranes over the yellow, slitted orbs of his eyes. He could still see his surroundings and the elf, but the milky veil helped him to focus his mind, to consider all aspects of this proposed arrangement.

Truly he did not understand the elf's fears. Green dragons cared little for the fate of their descendants and generally sought to destroy and steal from their ancestors, so the notion of a legacy for future generations meant nothing to him. Still, the relevance of the argument to his own decision came down to one thing: Was the elf lying?

He considered the request, tried to imagine all the reasons the elf would come to him with such a proposal. Was it a trick, an attempt to lull the dragon into complacency before the attack? Aeren decided the elf would know that tactic was unnecessary. They had won every campaign Porthios had led them on. Nor could he see a way for the elf to make personal gain from this meeting. Instead, the dragon's intuition gave him a strong signal, and he decided that this elf was telling the truth. However mad the reasoning was from a dragon's perspective, the very presence of the Silvanesti on this hilltop, and the extraordinary nature of his bargain, persuaded Aeren to accept the fellow's sincerity.

The incentive, too, was powerful. Despite Aeren's bluster about dragons going wherever they wanted, he had faced the armies of Porthios. He had seen his clan dragons, greens that once had numbered in scores, fall to lethal arrows, deadly lances, and potent elven magic. He knew the elf's next campaign would be the last. The Silvanesti army would sweep this island as it had swept the rest of the realm, and the few green dragons remaining would either die here or be forced to migrate to new homes.

And that was not a prospect that appealed to Aeren. He liked verdant forest, he favored warm weather and thick vegetation. And even if this delta was a little too swampy for his taste, nowhere along this coast was he likely to find as hospitable a place for his lair.

He changed the tack of the conversation.

"You know that Porthios has fought and survived many campaigns. I know, too, that he has an able lieutenant who goes everywhere with him, and that this elf is the wielder of a deadly lance and is a master of magic. What makes you believe that, merely because you desire it, we will be able to kill Porthios when he makes his next attack?"

For the first time, he sensed the elf's hesitation, the difficulty he was having with this bizarre meeting. Long heartbeats passed without a word, and then finally the elf drew a deep breath.

"As to the lieutenant, he is an elf called Samar, and we have a plan to remove him from the upcoming campaign."

"What plan is this?"

"It is a distraction that will draw him away from Silvanesti, but the specifics are not your concern. Still, Samar is loyal to his queen—some say, excessively loyal—and it is this loyalty that will draw him away."

"And as to Porthios?" asked the wyrm.

Once again there was a long pause.

"There are those among the Silvanesti who have agreed this is necessary. Therefore, we will provide you with information about the nature and the timing of his offensive. This information will make it possible for you to arrange a lethal ambush."

Aeren's eyelids popped open. This was indeed a singular offer!

"You realize, of course, that during such an ambush it is very difficult to slay with precision . . . that is, it is likely that more elves besides this general, Porthios, are likely to lose their lives."

14

Again the Silvanesti waited a long time before replying.

"Yes. My fellow patriots and I recognize that this is unavoidable. Of course, our own Silvanesti fliers were decimated in the first ten years of this campaign, so now Porthios's flying troops are a bodyguard of Qualinesti elves. His chief lieutenant, Tarqualan, is as much a radical as his master; it would be good if you could kill many of the griffon riders. But it is true that he will lead a large contingent of Silvanesti warriors as well. Losses among them are . . . regrettable but necessary to the greater good."

The green dragon regarded the elf coolly. "It may be, Silvanesti, that there are not so many differences between your people and mine as both of us have imagined."

Again the emissary's features drew into haughty disdain. "I shall not dignify that remark with a reply, except to say that you would not understand the priorities that lead us to make such a sacrifice for those who will come after us."

Aeren's smile was crocodilian. "It seems to me that the greatest sacrifice will be made by Porthios, if the plan works as you propose."

"It will work. It *must* work!" Now the elf was all earnestness. "The campaign will not begin for at least a fortnight. Porthios will need time to rest and reorganize his armies from the liberation of the Tarthalian Highland, the thick forests in the eastern niche of our kingdom."

"How will I identify Porthios?"

"He rides a griffon called Stallyar. The creature has silvered feathers at each wingtip. It is quite unique. Also, Porthios and Samar tend to remain aloof, above the bulk of the troops. With Samar drawn away, the prince will probably be alone."

"And how will you get word to me?"

"I will come here one more time, to this hilltop."

"You will come again in person?" Aeren's tone was subtly mocking, but the elf was too serious to perceive the sarcasm.

"Yes. It is very dangerous for me to be gone from the capital. Even this mission is fraught with risk, but I had to see you face to face so that you would know we are serious. I cannot trust this matter to others."

"I believe that you are serious, elf, even though you do not tell me your name, nor the names of your co-conspirators."

"I tell you, we are patriots!" insisted the Silvanesti. "There is no alternative to ensuring the security of our future!"

"No other alternative save killing Porthios yourself," the green dragon couldn't help but observe.

"We are not assassins!" Again the elf's shock was palpable, though Aeren was utterly mystified by the distinction. To him, whether the elves arranged for a dragon to kill their marshal or did the murder themselves seemed very much the same, morally speaking.

Not, of course, that he had any moral qualm about implementing the death of Porthios. Indeed, that warrior elf had been creating vexing problems for the green serpent since he had first come to Silvanesti, and his deathæwhoever brought it aboutæwould be a very good thing for Aerensianic and his clan dragons. He was only too willing to accept the elves' assistance in doing the deed. In fact, the advance intelligence about Porthios's attack would be crucial, since the elven commander had demonstrated a knack for striking his enemies when and where they least expected. It would be a pleasure to turn the tables on him for a change.

"Then I shall be your assassin," Aeren declared finally, striving for a soothing tone that was, despite his best intentions, a little beyond his grasp. Still, the elf seemed content with the resolution, not to mention eager to get away from this hilltop.

"Look for the information here. I will get you word as soon as Porthios makes his plans known."

"I shall check this hilltop every day, within an hour of the sunset. But there is one more thing, before you rush off. . . ."

The elf, who was about to do just that, hesitated suspiciously.

"How do I know that you will honor your word once Porthios has been removed? It may be that you will still decide to eradicate my clan and our 'lackeys,' as you called them, from this corner of Silvanesti."

"You have the word of a Silvanesti general, an elf of House Protector . . . that is my bond."

Aeren snorted. "That, and one other thing," he growled ominously.

"What is that other thing?"

"Without the leadership of Porthios, your army may come after us, but they will surely die."

The elf may have wanted to dispute that argument, but he thought better of his urge to reply. Without a backward glance, he stalked down the hill toward the boatmen, who were already making ready to depart.

Aerensianic, in not so much of a hurry, squatted on the mossy hilltop, watching the elves pole through the brackish fen toward the silvery river glinting on the horizon. Even when the robed figure had dwindled to a tiny spot in the distance, he stared and pondered.

In the end, he knew that it had been a good day's work.

* * * * *

"This elf who wanted to kill Porthios . . . he claimed that he was Silvanesti?" asked the younger of the pair who had entered the green dragon's den.

The serpent sniffed derisively. "Elves are all the same to me, but, yes, that was his claim. And I knew that was the elven name for the place where I dwelled, so his assertion made sense."

"Why did he hate Porthios so much?" The youngster was perplexed, deeply troubled by the tale.

"How would I know the follies of elvenkind?" retorted the dragon, who then yelped as the elder elf pushed and twisted the lance.

"Why do you think he would betray his country's hero?" asked the lancer.

The dragon shrugged disdainfully. "I suppose I can guess. There was a time, a mere eye blink ago by the reckoning of my life, when the whole realm of Silvanesti, all the forests and hillocks and streams, was a swath of delicious corruption. It was a time when Lorac Caladon was king of that elven land, and he was maddened by the power of a crystal sphere . . . a dragon orb. His darkest nightmares were whispered into his ear by the mighty green dragon, Cyan Bloodbane, a wyrm even greater in age and power than I. For years Lorac was caught in the spell of that orb, and he writhed under the grip of powerful and ancient magic. All the realm had withered under the influence of massive corruption. Trees bled, monsters skulked in the shadows, and the elvesæthose who survived the scourge—all fled to distant lands."

"That is ancient history. Silvanesti is not like that anymore!" insisted the young elf. "The forest has been restored, and the elves have returned!"

"True . . . because of the leader called Porthios."

"But first," interjected the elder of the pair, "Lorac died, and the Silvanesti General Konnal tried to vanquish Lorac's nightmare. But he failed abysmally. His campaigns led to the decimation of the Windriders, the Silvanesti griffon riders who were once a feared force across all Krynn. The Kirath scouts penetrated parts of the realm, but Konnal's army was thwarted at every turn."

"I remember those days," the dragon resumed. "And I knew that only after ten years of Konnal's failures did the proud Silvanesti call for help, seeking a leader from their kinsman in the west. Pcrthios came, and he was a ruler in effect as well as name. Under him, the elves reclaimed their land, scouring the madness from forest and glade, slowly, inexorably restoring the pristine woodlands that had ever been the hallmark of this ancient kingdom. For years Porthios had led his elves on relentless campaigns, with armies of warriors attacking the denizens of the Dark Queen—denizens such as I myself—until we were cornered in a small corner of that once vast realm . . ."

"Who was the traitor?" the elder elf asked, his lips taut across his teeth and his finger tight around the hilt of his sword.

"That," the dragon said, with a smug tightening of his scaly lips, "is a question that will be answered in good time."

A Marshal of Elvenkind

Chapter 2

"Hail, Porthios! Long live Porthios!"

The chants and cries rang from the balconies, from the lofty towers and the elegant, narrow windows of Silvanost, as the general led his weary troops on a triumphal march into the elven capital. Using the giant turtles that served as ferries around this island city, the army had just a few hours earlier crossed from the mainland into their capital. After forming into companies and divisions at the waterfront, they had straightened with practiced discipline and then started on this parade.

The file of elves, four thousand strong, was mud-spattered, dirty, and exhausted after months of war. Yet for all their fatigue, these troops gave no sign of anything other than jubilant good spirits. They marched with crisp precision, and if a few uniforms showed the rents of draconian claws and ogre spears, if a few boots were patched or worn from the rigors of a long march, none of these cosmetic flaws gave any pause to the elves who paraded for their people in serene, righteous pride.

The banners of the infantry companies were bright, twenty colorful pennants held high, floating in the gentle breeze. They marked the Red-Tails, the Gray Foxes, the Cardinals, and the Silver Heads, and all the rest of the units that had fought under Porthios during the long, bloody years of the campaign. Together, they made up the Wildrunners, the army of Silvanesti that had been protectors of the kingdom for more than three thousand years.

And those people who had lined the streets to see the triumphal parade, elves who were normally reserved, dignified, and quiet, let their joy show in unison. Cheers rocked the air, cries of adulation for the marshal and for the long file of his troops that followed. Horses of the four cavalry companies, their bridles shined to gleaming silver, pranced in tight formation. The griffon mounts of Tarqualan's Qualinesti scouts, fierce fliers who had to be tightly reined on the ground, reared and snapped, their eagles' beaks clapping loudly as they struggled and stalked along. And the Silvanesti throng cheered as lustily for their brother elves from the west as for the bold sons of their own realm.

The column proceeded through the city of marble, passing between the lofty spires and graceful mansions. Gardens, formal and precise, flanked them on all sides, and fountains sprayed at the larger intersections. As the march continued, the troops relaxed and soon were cheering back at the enthusiastic crowds.

Alone at the head of the column, Porthios rode on his proud griffon Stallyar, allowing the creature to set the pace for the march. He was the military governor of Silvanesti, commander of the Wildrunners, and had been accorded the exalted rank of marshal in the field. Garlands and blossoms flew from the crowd to land before the prancing animal, while maidens and elderly dames blew him kisses. Elven men of all ages saluted as he passed, their posture rigid and eyes bright with pride.

Through it all, the hero of these throngs held his face high, his expression a careful mask of cool acceptance. He could not bring himself to acknowledge the crowd, to wave or to smile, for there were dark thoughts raging in his head, and it was all he could do to keep those grim emotions from marring his visage. He knew that this parade was good for his troops, as it was good for the elves of Silvanesti. Every year had seen another part of the realm reclaimed from the nightmare of Lorac Caladon's madness, and every year brought more elves forth to cheer for the return of their realm.

He felt sorry for his troops even as he loved them. He knew that he would call on them again, and in the near future. For three months they had campaigned against a nest of draconians and ogres, battled three treacherous green dragons, and finally cleared the Tarthalian Highland of its hateful denizens. Even now elven priests and naturalists of House Woodshaper were restoring the last of the diseased groves, bringing beauty back to a part of the realm that for more than thirty years had languished in the deepest depths of nightmare.

But to Porthios, it was merely another part of an odious task that was now, finally, almost done. It was a task that had kept him from his wife for much of the past two decades, a separation that had become increasingly difficult, knowing that they were expecting their first child.

Behind him came bold Samar, the great warrior-mage walking amid the company of House Woodshaper elves. He carried the long-shafted weapon that was his trademark, a footman's dragonlance with which he had personally slain more than half a dozen dragons. Now this famed hero, champion of the Silvanesti queen and the marshal's chief lieutenant, strolled along with the weapon upright, bowing and waving in response to nearly as many cheers as greeted Porthios himself.

The parade curled around the marble-paved streets—no straight avenues in this elven capital!—and soon the marshal caught sight of Silvanost's most stunning feature. The Tower of

Stars rose from the center of the city, a spire nearly a thousand feet tall. The structure's outer surface was a facade of brilliant white marble across most of its expanse, highlighted by crystal polished to a mirror sheen in others. Gems sparkled from the many window frames, and ornate battlements twirled gracefully outward from the lofty central spire. Several smaller spires jutted from the main structure, balanced as if by magic over the city so far below.

Under the bright sunlight of this early spring afternoon, Porthios felt a chill, remembering that tower as he had first seen it some two decades earlier. It had been winter then, a bleak and chilly season made even more hateful by the madness that had corrupted the forest, the city, the very land itself. Abandoned by its elven population, the city of Silvanost had been a ghastly ruin of destructive vines, pavement-cracking thistles, and odious deformity that had extended throughout the buildings and streets.

And nowhere had this blight been more obvious than on the Tower of Stars. That magnificent spire had withered and curled until it resembled a gnarled, weather-beaten tree trunk. It had been there that the task of rebuilding this land had begun by the magical restoration of horrific corruption. From that tower, the slow, painstaking process had expanded across all of Silvanesti, a campaign lasting thirty years until, a few days ago, it had reached the high, rugged territory at the farthest corner in the northeast of the kingdom. And soon it would extend to the south, where one final stronghold of corruption claimed a festering island at the terminus of the Thon-Thalas River.

The balconies of the tower were now lined with lords and ladies of the Sinthal-Elish, the city's ruling council. The males were clad in the white robes of their station, while the women wore gowns of silk that shimmered and dazzled in an array of bright colors. From there, too, the cheers rained down on Porthios and his army, though he couldn't help noticing that the esteemed members of House Advocate, one of the oldest of the elven realm's clans, were faint in their praise and haughty in their expression as they looked down upon this elf who, in their eyes, would always be an unworthy foreigner.

Suddenly Porthios felt very tired. He was sick of the celebration, and he had a headache from the noise. His mind wrestled with age-old questions, problems that had plagued him all his life and still threatened to drag him down in despair.

Why can't they see the truth? We're all elves—Qualinesti and Silvanesti. The future belongs to both of us! He thought about a secret that he shared with only Samar among all the elves in the city, the knowledge of a treaty that might change some of this, and he wished that he could tell them about it. With that thought came memories of his wife, and he felt the familiar pang. He missed her terribly.

Finally the long procession curled along the quarter of House Protector, where most of the military elves dwelled. Here the troops dispersed, Samar making his way to the marshal's side as Porthios stood before the gates of the Palace of Quinari and the warrior made ready to turn toward his own home.

"Another splendid campaign, my lord," he said, clasping the marshal's hand.

"Thanks to you and all the rest. Now go and get some well-deserved rest."

Finally mustering a wave for the crowd that was gathered around his royal residence, Porthios passed through the gates, which quickly, smoothly closed to mask the sounds and sights of the city. In the courtyard, he was greeted by a dozen servants, all sincerely overjoyed to see him return. His steward, Allatarn, led him into the marbled anteroom and informed him that a bath was already drawn, awaiting his pleasure.

"Thank you . . . in a moment," Porthios replied. "First I need a few moments of rest and reflection."

Porthios shrugged out of his leather cuirass, and Allatarn helped him out of his boots. With a golden goblet of wine in his hand, Porthios slumped into a chair, unmindful of his faithful servant's discreet withdrawal.

This ancient palace was his residence, but it could never be his home. As with every part of this realm, he felt like he didn't belong here. Sometimes he viewed himself as a conqueror, at other times an unwelcome guest . . . but never as a true citizen of Silvanesti.

And why should he? For the thousandth time, he thought of the arrogance, of the hidebound tradition and mindless fealty to house name and noble status that were the twin hallmarks of this, the oldest continually surviving nation on Krynn. Even as he risked his life to restore their land, as he slept on the ground, ventured through nightmare-racked forests, battled draconians and ogres in their name, the Silvanesti elves consistently viewed him as one who wasn't good enough to rule them. He could help them, he could even give them sound advice, but he could never be of them.

Not, if he was really truthful with himself, that he wanted to be. His mind drifted back to the pastoral woodlands of Qualinesti, the trees that were somehow more vibrant, more fragrant and more beautiful than the ancient and hallowed, the *regimented* trunks of this eastern realm. He remembered the Tower of the Sun, the place where he really was a king, and–though the Tower of Stars was far older–he savored the opinion that the great spire in Silvanost was but a pale and lifeless imitation of the crystalline obelisk that was the dominant feature of Qualinost. Touching the medallion that he wore over his heart, he thought of the office that disk symbolized. Speaker of the Sun, exalted master of Qualinesti, it meant that he was revered by his people there. As military governor here, he would never be more than a caretaker. Instead, he looked forward to the day when he could go home and stay there.

It's ironic, he thought, that his wife—who was a queen in this place—should be working so hard in Qualinesti while he labored here. They were each, of course, embarked on important tasks. Alhana Starbreeze, together with trusted allies that included Porthios's sister and his half-elf brother-in-law, was striving to bring about a treaty among the Unified Nations of the Three Races. At first Porthios had been a reluctant observer to that treaty process, but lately he had come to see the pact as offering the best hope for a peaceful future across Krynn.

"Allatarn . . . I would have more wine," Porthios said, and the servant was there in an instant to refill his glass. The warrior noticed the emblem on the bottle, the diamantine star that was the sigil of his wife's family. The vintage was good, he thought idly, but his mind drifted inexorably toward deeper concerns.

"Tell me, has there been any word from Lady Alhana?" asked the general, swirling the blood-colored liquid around the bowl of the golden goblet.

"No, my lord. The last letter was the missive that arrived before you embarked on your recent campaign." The servant's face was neutral, save for a tightening around the corners of his mouth.

"I see. Leave the bottle, if you please."

With a formal bow, Allatarn withdrew to leave his master alone with his thoughts.

Restless now, Porthios rose from the chair to pace the study, the silken hose on his feet gliding soundlessly across the slate flagstones of the floor. For a few minutes, he stared out at the Garden of Astarin, beautiful and precisely ordered. The place was a work of art, he knew, but he couldn't help thinking that it was merely sterile.

His mind drifted further, and he thought of the golden elven princess, the bride he had accepted so unwillingly. . . and he reflected on how his feelings had changed over the decades of their marriage. She, like himself, had come to the bond out of a sense of duty. Alhana was a Silvanesti princess and only daughter of Lorac Caladon, the promise of her people's future. Porthios, one of three children of Qualinesti's Speaker of the Sun, was the acknowledged heir to the leadership of his own homeland.

In so many ways, the marriage of Alhana and Porthios had been a bond of great promise to both elven realms—especially now that his wife had become pregnant. Each an heir to a throne, between them they created a hope of bonding the two elven realms, a hope with a greater chance of success than anything since the Kinslayer War had torn a bloody gap between the kingdoms more than two thousand years before. With the promise of a baby on the horizon, there was at last concrete hope of a ruler who could begin to unite the two tradition-bound nations of elvenkind.

The memory of Alhana's pregnancy brought a new quickening of Porthios's concern. How was she? How fared the unborn child? And why hadn't she written to him? Her work on the treaty was important, but surely she would take time to rest, to care for herself! For the first years of their marriage they had pursued separate lives, each dedicated to the cause of elven unification, though not so terribly dedicated to each other. Finally there had come respect between them, and then a measure of affection—not passion, not love, certainly, but enough warmth to bring about the promise of a child. But now there was ominous silence from the west.

Porthios turned on his heel, unconsciously pacing faster as he remembered the circumstances of their separation. Since he had been tied down by matters in Silvanesti, she had gone in his name to see to matters in his own homeland of Qualinesti. At the time, it had seemed like an eminently sensible solution. After all, if they hoped to install their child as a uniter of the two nations, then it was only natural that the peoples of Qualinesti have a chance to see Alhana among them much as the Silvanesti had become used to the presence of Porthios here in their own capital.

Of course, Alhana had help. In particular, Tanis Half-Elven, who was married to Porthios's sister, was a staunch ally, but because of his mixed lineage, he was unable to work effectively in the elven kingdom. Instead, he served as a liaison between Alhana and the humans who lived all around Qualinesti. For a long time, Porthios had been suspicious of the half-elf's motives, but grudgingly had come to trust him as a benign influence and a man with the wisdom to see what was best for the world. Still, the negotiations had remained secret for the most part. The senate of Qualinesti, like the Sinthal-Elish of Silvanesti, was a close-minded body, certain to be resistant toward any substantial change.

Now Alhana had been gone for nearly two seasons. He had one letter from her, received four months ago, in which she had declared that she missed him and that she found things in Qualinesti "strange." This in itself was not surprising, but he had expected more information to follow.

In the early years, of course, he would have had no such

expectations. Indeed, he had once thought of her as his "Ice Princess," a prized possession that was important to him politically, but who bore little significance in the day-to-day functioning of his life. There had been neither hatred nor resentment in this reality—in fact, he knew that she had felt pretty much the same way about him.

Yet somehow, as the years had passed and they began to know each other, some of that ice had begun to thaw. At first there had come a certain sense of kinship, an awareness that each of them was a prisoner of birth and had gone to marriage from a sense of duty, nothing more. He had learned that Alhana had loved a man—a human, ironically—during the days of the War of the Lance. That man, a famed Knight of Solamnia, had died a hero, and there were times when his wife still grieved for him.

Porthios could track his own feelings for his wife by remembering the changes in his reaction to that grief. At first he had been mystified, wondering how a mere human could have captured this proud elf woman's heart. Then, as he became more conscious of his own prerogatives, he had grown resentful. How could she feel such pain over the loss of this man, when she barely seemed to muster any interest whatsoever in Porthios, a splendid elven prince?

For a time, he had even been jealous, and it was then that he realized that he was beginning to care for her. He had resolved to try to understand her, and that had formed the seed of true affection between them. He had learned—from many sources, for the knight's exploits were legendary—about Sturm Brightblade, and he admitted his own respect for the warrior's death, standing alone upon a fortress rampart to face a powerful blue dragon and its masked rider. And finally he had realized that he would never replace Sturm Brightblade in Alhana's memories, but that there was room for him and those memories in her life. He began to see the things about Sturm that Alhana had admired, and instead of begrudging that admiration, he began to show her subtly some of the same features about himself.

Porthios had always been a warrior, an elf who understood

that force sometimes provided the most effective means of resolving a dispute. He was smart, quick, and strong, but perhaps even more importantly, he had learned that he possessed a natural instinct in battle. He could see what an enemy's course of action was likely to be, and he readily perceived the steps he should take with his own forces—first, to encourage the enemy to behave in the way that Porthios desired, and second, to strike him in such a way that his will and ability to fight were shattered with the sudden violence that so often broke the morale of an army and sent its troops to rout, its commanders seeking terms of surrender.

He thought of the day she had told him she was pregnant. Her own trepidation had been obvious, but he knew her well enough to see that she was especially worried about his reaction. And Porthios, from some well of emotion he had not even realized he possessed, had thrown back his head and laughed with pure, contagious joy. He had hugged his wife of thirty years, held her like a bride, and she had shared his joy and his laughter. For a few minutes, the world beyond themselves had ceased to exist, and they savored an embrace that bound them together just as they both hoped their child would be able to bind the two disparate nations of elvenkind.

But why hadn't she written?

Porthios's further pondering of that disturbing question were interrupted as Allatarn hesitantly knocked on the door to his study.

"Yes?" asked the marshal curtly, deciding against another glass of wine. He put the goblet on the table and turned to the portal.

"General Konnal is here to see you, sir. He says it is a matter of some urgency."

Rethinking his decision, Porthios poured himself another glass of the splendid wine. "Send him in," he said sourly. Out of a sense of duty, he reached for another vessel and poured a drink for his guest.

"Your Lordship . . . congratulations on your victory," declared Konnal, striding through the door as if he owned the house.

"Thank you, General." Porthios replied, suspecting that the elf's pleasantries were merely an initial salvo designed to put him off his guard.

The two elves stood only a few paces apart, but neither made any effort to initiate the ceremonial kiss that would normally formalize a greeting between two such colleagues. Ungraciously, conscious of the stiffness of his manner, the host gestured his guest to a chair, then offered him the glass of wine before settling into his own seat.

Porthios found himself sizing up the general, who was his own age, and—if not for the Qualinesti Speaker's presence—would doubtless still have been leading the Silvanesti army on its campaigns against the nightmare that had so long scourged the realm. Konnal was much beloved by the nobility and the senate of Silvanost, but his face and hands betrayed none of the hardness of soldiering, the grim weathering that had etched lines around Porthios's mouth, toughened his fingers and palms with rough callus. For ten years he had led the Wildrunners, but his leadership had resulted in significant disasters, including the decimation of the nation's griffon riders. Now Konnal's generalship consisted of recruiting troops, of garbing them in splendid uniforms and equipping them with gleaming armor and sharp blades, and then of training them to march in precise file and drill.

"I have the Keys of Quinarost," the general said, handing over the ring of golden icons that gave access to the Tower of the Stars.

"Thank you. I will keep them until I leave again on the next campaign," Porthios replied.

"It is true, then . . . the Tarthalian Highland is reclaimed?" asked General Konnal.

"There are some matters for the foresthealers to attend, but, yes, the last of the dragons and their minions have been expelled from that part of the elven lands." Porthios took some small pleasure in his geographical terminology. He had long made it known that he envisioned all the domain of the elves as one great land, not two eternally divided nations.

"Your troops made quite a parade of their return. Was that

really necessary?" Konnal's tone was just short of insolence.

"Stallyar had a strained wing, or I would have flown him in victory circles low over the city," Porthios replied with a straight face. The savage griffon, loyal flier who answered to the elven warrior's will, was well known to the people of Silvanost.

Konnal sighed, as if he were dismayed but not really surprised by the Qualinesti's display of humor. "I thought we had agreed that demonstrations of a martial nature were to be curtailed now that the populace has, for the most part, accepted that our land has been reclaimed from the nightmare."

Porthios felt his temper slipping but held on to his self-control with a powerful effort of will. "You will recall, General, that it was your suggestion that such demonstrations should be abolished. I never agreed to any part of it. Furthermore, these elves have fought bravely, under difficult conditions, and they were doing nothing more than returning to their homes for a brief interval preceding the next campaign. Surely you don't expect that I would have them slink into the city after dark, like fugitives seeking to avoid notice?"

"The fact is, you know how the people get stirred up by these displays. They cheer themselves hoarse, and then they are surprised to learn that there is one more battle to fight. There's always one more battle to fight!"

Porthios was feeling very tired, and his fatigue shortened his patience as much as Konnal's words. "Ah, but this time we might be finished after one more battle. I trust that even you can see the truth of that!"

"You speak of the Thon-Thalas delta, I presume."

"Unless you know of some other district where the nightmare has suddenly blossomed resurgent, yes."

"I know of no such place . . . the delta, then. When do you presume to launch your so-called 'final' campaign?"

"Perhaps I won't go at all!" Porthios snapped. "Maybe I should turn my back on this city and let you handle a campaign in the field!"

Konnal's eyes widened momentarily, but he was too shrewd to reveal much of his alarm at this prospect. Instead, he merely shrugged. "If that is your wish, I shall make my preparations at once."

"It's not my wish, and you know it! My men need some time—a fortnight, at least—with their wives and their families. Time to let the nightmares settle, to remember why we embark on these battles."

"Two weeks, then?" Konnal suggested. "Then you will move against the delta?"

"Two weeks, and then the last battle begins. Now go away, General Konnal." Porthios had lost all pretense of politeness; this conversation had left a foul taste in his mouth. "I am suddenly reminded that I need a bath."

* * * * *

"I admit, through it all, that Porthios was a worthy foe," the dragon said pensively. "Much more capable than that imbecile he replaced, Konnal."

"Yet you promised to kill him!" accused the younger elf.

The wyrm sniffed. "He was a foe, after all."

"And the traitor?" asked the elder elf, still holding the lance pressed firmly against the dragon's scaly breast. "He carried through with his promises?"

"He was as good as his word," admitted the green dragon.

A Council in Silvanost

Chapter Three

"And so I place the matter before you, esteemed nobles, honored lords, and all Silvanesti who take an interest in the future: The island in the Thon-Thalas delta is the last remaining outpost of Lorac's nightmare. It is a broad place, flat and festering, but it is surrounded by water and thus isolated from the rest of the land."

Porthios looked across the ranks of gowned and robed elves gathered in the great chamber at the base of the Tower of Stars. This was the Sinthal-Elish, the ruling body of Silvanesti. He had their attention, and he knew what he needed to say.

"Isolated though it is, it cannot be allowed to stand. The island morass blocks trade, barring all seafaring traffic between us and other realms. Too, it stands as a symbol of the nightmare that has been our legacy for too long. I ask you now, the elven citizens who are the true rulers of this hallowed land,

32

to authorize one more campaign. The Kirath, our bold scouts, have reconnoitered the place. The leader of the Kirath, Aleaha Takmarin, has reported to me personally.

"The delta, like all the rest of the realm that had languished under corruption and evil, is vulnerable to a combined operation. We will use troops and wizards and the healers of House Woodshaper, employing the three-pronged approach that has served us so well throughout the past three decades. We will root out the corruption at its very foundation and use the skills and artistry of our greatest minds to restore the fen to the pastoral grove that it once was."

"Hear, hear!" The stamping of feet came from all around, and other elves whistled softly to indicate their approval. The clamor, as was the way with elven outbursts, quickly faded as a young, handsome elf clad in a robe and the silver sandals of an ancient noble house stepped forward.

Porthios bowed toward the proud Silvanesti. "I recognize you, Dolphius. Please share your words with the Sinthal-Elish."

Dolphius returned the bow with serene dignity and turned on the steps just below the dais where Porthios stood. The lord looked at the gathered elves, waiting with the patience of a born speaker until the room had grown absolutely still.

"I offer a resolution of commendation for our esteemed marshal, Porthios of House Solostaran. Not only has he selflessly devoted his life toward the restoration of a land that is not his native realm, but he has also done so in a manner that we can only label as impeccably proper and selflessly devoted. Therefore, good lords and ladies, all elves of Silvanesti, I suggest we declare that upon his return from this last campaign, we declare a holiday and that our greatest artists and musicians prepare an homage to an elf who must be regarded as a great hero of our people."

Again came the foot-shuffling applause, this time maintained for a surprisingly—and, to Porthios, embarrassingly—long time. As Dolphius returned to his stool and the sounds again faded, the marshal found himself compelled to speak.

"You do me great honor, people of my wife's homeland.

And I shall be grateful for the acknowledgment—*after* our campaign is successful. But I beg you not to forget that the restoration of Silvanesti has been a task faced by countless numbers of Silvanesti as well. Indeed, without the use of the dedicated and capable army that the nation has raised and supported, none of these campaigns would have even been possible."

"And it is worth noting—" General Konnal's voice came from his seat high on the side of the chamber; he rose from his stool and stood straight and tall, allowing all eyes in the chamber to locate him—"that this final campaign has yet to be fought and the results determined. It is on this matter that I have a proposal to make."

"Speak, General, please," Porthios declared, his own dignity highlighting the other elf's lack of manners in his interruption.

"I join my esteemed colleague, the lord Dolphius, in expressing our gratitude toward the royal elf of Qualinesti who has devoted so much of his time to our problems," Konnal began. His tone was free from irony, but somehow he still managed to state the name of the western realm as if it were a distasteful word.

"At the same time, we have reached a point where we can begin to assess the end of the long war of reclamation that has so long been the focus of our populace, our army . . . and, not least, our treasury."

Konnal sighed, an exaggerated gesture that emphasized the weariness brought about by the long years of war. "Naturally we must insure the success of this last venture, the expedition to annihilate the final, lingering corner of the nightmare from our realm. With the esteemed Marshal Porthios leading the way, we can be all but certain of success."

"Get on with it, Konnal," called Dolphius, gently mocking. "Where do you want to pinch pennies this time?"

"My honored colleague, the lord, has brought us to the heart of the matter, as usual, without wasting time on the niceties of formal debate. Naturally I am grateful." Konnal bestowed a dazzling smile on Dolphius, who frowned and gestured in irritation.

"My proposal is this: Since the impending mission is, for once, directed against a part of the realm that is, by our marshal's own admission, water-bound and isolated from the rest of Silvanesti, we suggest that the campaign function with the use of but ten companies of the Wildrunners, instead of the twenty that have generally formed the backbone of Porthios Solostaran's army. The savings in steel coin will be significant, not to mention that it will begin to allow many of our brave warriors, those who have given so much over the last three decades, to commence a return to the routines of normal life."

Inevitably there were murmurs of protest and several outright shouts of derision. Porthios himself kept his expression bland. He was grateful for the support of so many of these elves, and he knew that it was politic for him to allow them to make his objections for him. Not surprisingly, it was Dolphius who rose, waited for Porthios to acknowledge him, and then turned to address the council in stentorian tones.

"The esteemed general, scion of an ancient house, proud bearer of Silvanesti standards handed down through long generations, has, as usual, failed to grasp the necessary prerequisites of modern day operations. His logic, where it is not utterly flawed, is so misguided as to represent a significant departure from rational thought. Perhaps, as is not inconceivable, he spoke without *any* such cogitation and would even now like to retract his remarks, remove his proposal from the table?"

Dolphius looked at Konnal, as if certain that the general would indeed take advantage of the lord's generous offer.

Konnal smiled and waved good-naturedly. "No! Continue, by all means, honored lord and renowned Defender of Logic."

With a bow and a modest shrug, Dolphius did just that, though he turned to address a question to Porthios.

"Honored Marshal, could you share with us an estimate—your best but most cautious assessment as to how long this campaign in the delta might take?"

Porthios nodded. "It seems likely that it will require perhaps a month, not very much more, to sweep and clear the island that remains in the grip of nightmare. Naturally the work of the healers and wizards charged with restoring the landscape will continue for many months longer. But for the army, a month."

Dolphius turned back to Konnal, and now he spoke in tones of utter astonishment. "Did I hear correctly? Our colleague, the esteemed general, proposes that the army be cut in half so that some warriors who have bravely fought for thirty years can now turn to peacetime pursuits, instead of partaking in a last campaign, a venture that will extend their duties by so long as another whole *month*?"

The senator shook his head, doing a fine impression of a man who just couldn't believe what he was forced to say. "And as to the matter of the treasury . . . naturally we are all concerned with the future of our realm. And, of course, a sizable fund of currency is a part—a *small* part—of our planning for the future. We wish to leave our children with the means to fund those necessities that, we all agree, must be taken care of by the nation's financial reserves."

Warming up now, Dolphius raised his voice. "But I ask you, elves of Silvanesti! Have we reached the point where a few steel coins in the treasury mean more to us than the purity of the forests, the sanctity of the waters and the woodland creatures of our homeland? Have we reached the point where a matter of financial bookkeeping shall be rendered more important than the task to which so many of us have devoted our energies, our courage, our blood and tears, and, yes, our very *lives* over the last three decades?"

With a sigh, the senator seemed to shrink. Suddenly he looked weary far beyond his relatively youthful years. "I ask you this, in all seriousness, my fellow elves. And I must warn you: If the answer is yes, then the future of Silvanesti is already lost, and no mountain of silver or steel in the treasure chamber is going to change that fact!"

"No!" The cry came first from General Cantal-Silaster, a female leader of noble descent who had fought in all of Porthios's campaigns. Lately she had commanded one of his two divisions of troops. Her objection was quickly echoed by a score, then a hundred, voices.

"Send the full army! Finish the campaign! Only then will we turn to the future!" The shouts and whistles came from all over the chamber but quickly died down as Porthios raised a hand.

The marshal looked at the general, who stood calmly by his stool on the martial side of the chamber. "I ask you, General Konnal, do you wish to put your motion to a vote?"

"The will of the people is made clear," Konnal said graciously. "I withdraw the motion. But I would ask just one question, if I may."

Porthios watched him warily but gestured that he should continue.

"Have you made a decision that you can share with us, honored marshal, as to when you plan to launch this next campaign? It would only be fitting for the people to turn out and send you off in style."

Though he wondered what the general was getting at, Porthios couldn't see any harm in sharing the decision he had made just that morning. "This is the Day of First Gateway, in the month of Summer End. My expedition shall embark onto the river in twelve days, at dawn on the Day of Second Dream Dance."

"Very well," Konnal replied with a bow. "And you will have the entire army with you. I am certain that we can look forward to nothing but another unqualified success."

* * * * *

"Why did he make that motion?" Samar asked Porthios later as the elves dined in the Palace of Quinari.

Also present was Aleaha Takmarin, the scout who had reported about the state of the delta, and the two generals of the Wildrunners. These were Lady Cantal-Silaster, the elegant patrician, and her counterpart, the one-eyed Karst Bandial, veteran of every Silvanesti campaign fought over the last two hundred years. Crystal windows spilled bright moonlight onto a linen-draped table spread with pyramidical loaves of bread, cheese, jars of honey, a variety of fresh fruit, and a small haunch of venison.

The five veterans had been discussing plans for the upcoming assault in the delta, but naturally enough their conversation had come around to the debate that had gone on in the Sinthal-Elish that day.

"I'm curious," admitted the marshal. "It's not like Konnal to speak out for something that he knows has no chance of passing."

Porthios felt at ease, knowing that these were his four closest allies among the Silvanesti. Samar, of course, was relentlessly loyal to Queen Alhana, and, by connection, to her husband. Aleaha had been an invaluable ally as she and her Kirath scouts mapped out the realms of nightmare and gave him solid information on the necessities of each campaign. Bandial and Cantal-Silaster had proven themselves capable subcommanders, and Porthios couldn't imagine embarking on a campaign without their able assistance.

"At least he went down to defeat graciously," suggested the scout.

"And that, too, is not like him." Porthios's droll remark drew smiles all around. Still, the thought darkened his own mood. "The only reason that popinjay talks from two different points of view is that his mouth has only two sides," the marshal declared sourly. "Imagine, suggesting that the Sinthal-Elish is doing us a favor by allowing us to extend our campaign through the summer!"

"I don't think he speaks for most of Silvanesti," Samar noted with an easy smile. "The people know what you've done for them."

"What we've done," Porthios corrected. "I tried to make it clear that these campaigns have been joint efforts between Qualinesti and Silvanesti companies."

"You did." Lady Cantal-Silaster voiced her approval. "And then Konnal somehow made it sound as though the Silvanesti have been treated with disrespect by your own guards."

"Bah! He's a fool!" snapped Porthios, wishing it were true. In fact, however, he was concerned because he knew that Konnal was not a fool. He had given his inflammatory speech to the elven council for a reason, and so far Porthios had not been able to figure out what that reason was.

"In any event, you know that the people are behind you. There must have been ten thousand of them cheering our arrival back home," noted the female general.

"As they should," Aleaha noted wryly. "For ten years, Konnal tried to wage this campaign without you, and we all know what happened."

"Aye," Samar agreed. "I can remember when the Windriders were the proudest force of griffon riders in Krynn. After Konnal was finished, we had to import our flying troops from Qualinesti!"

"And now we're on the brink of victory," Bandial observed, sounding almost wistful. But he quickly brightened. "Still, there's one more battle, and we'll get the job done right!"

"You know, I sought to find out a little more . . . went to Konnal's house, as a matter of fact, to see what he was trying to accomplish," Samar said. "And oddly enough, he wasn't home. His servants didn't know where he'd gone, but they were told he was attending an important meeting."

"That is odd," Porthios agreed. "You'd think with supplies being drawn, an expedition mounted, he'd want to keep an eye on everything I'm doing. I'm just glad he didn't start talking about the cost of boats."

"We're going to take the army down the river, I presume?" Cantal-Silaster asked.

The marshal nodded. "My Qualinesti will fly on their griffons, of course, but we'll have no need of cavalry on the island, so I figure that the bulk of the troops will land on the upstream shore. We'll make it a thorough sweep and gather around that low hill we noted down in the south."

"I think your estimate of a month might even prove generous," observed Aleaha. "From the few tracks we saw, there won't be many draconians. I'm surprised, though, that we didn't see any sign of ogres."

"Me, too, though I admit that I'm grateful for the fact. And you saw no sign of goblins? Nor of dragons?"

The scout shook her head. "We Kirath went over the place as thoroughly as possible, though we had to be careful. There are, after all, plenty of draconians there."

"I would have thought that place would be irresistible to green dragons," Samar said. "Not that I'm complaining, of course."

"No, naturally not. Still, there's something strange about this whole operation." Porthios couldn't hide his misgivings. "I'm more glad than I want to admit that foolishness about only going down there with half an army was so quickly overruled. I have to admit, I was also a little surprised by the support I got."

Samar grinned. "I keep telling you, most of Silvanesti is behind you. These elves recognize all the good things you've done, and the fact that you're from the west doesn't make any difference to them. Those are very old grudges you're worrying about."

"The trouble with our people, my friend, is that they have long, long memories. And even if most of Silvanesti is for me, those who oppose me include some very influential people among their numbers."

"That, sadly, is true," Cantal-Silaster noted. "Still, you have many allies, even among those of us in the Sinthal-Elish."

"What word from Princess Alhana?" asked Samar, dipping a honey-smeared piece of bread on his plate to sop up the last morsels of the dinner.

Porthios shrugged. "None . . . and truth to tell, that lack has me a little concerned."

"Surely you would have heard from her if there were problems. . . ." The warrior-mage shook his head, embarrassed. "That is, with the baby, I mean."

"I would have to think so, but I know the Qualinesti. They're my own people," the marshal said grimly. "There are some of them—Senator Rashas and the rest of the Thalas-Enthia, for example—who are as distrustful of her as Silvanesti like General Konnal are of me."

Samar glowered across the table. "Old habits die hard. It grieves me now to remember my own rudeness when first you came to help us."

Porthios laughed finally, his mood lightening. "I think you

did everything you could to provoke me into a duel. But I couldn't accept. You probably would have killed me!"

Samar's own chuckle was rueful. "At the time, none of us could see why Alhana agreed to wed you. And furthermore, I think every male Silvanesti was a little bit in love with her—myself included." With a faint grimace, the warrior looked down at his plate, averting his gaze from the marshal.

"With good reason," Porthios agreed, taking little note of his companion's awkward pause. Instead, he was wondering, Why did it take *me* so long to figure out her worth?

Cantal-Silaster spoke. "But we can all see it now: a child born to you both will offer a promise for the future that the elven nations haven't known since the Kinslayer War. Why doesn't the rest of Silvanesti recognize that?"

"I think because they have hated the Qualinesti for so long, they can't imagine life without that hatred. And for generations, we elves have been raised to believe that change is dangerous, something to be feared."

"But, still," Aleaha noted, "there are those among us who can see the way toward change . . . who recognize your worth. And not just warriors like Samar, or the scouts of my own Kirath, who have served with you and know what kind of man you are. Senator Dolphius, for example, is firmly in your camp."

"You're right about that, but for every one like Dolphius, it seems that there are two or three Konnals."

"And you think Alhana is meeting the same kind of resistance in Qualinost?" Samar pressed, trying unsuccessfully to conceal his deep concern.

"I know it. Though she has spent more than half of the last thirty years there, she is still viewed as an outcast, an interloper, by many. They might not be the majority, but with Rashas and other conservative senators among their number, they wield a lot of influence."

"Even now, when she carries your child . . . the child who could grow up to become Speaker of the Sun and Stars?"

"That's exactly what they *don't* want to happen, and that, my friend, is why I'm worried."

Further discussion was interrupted by the sounds of commotion from the outer courtyard. Servants shouted, and they heard the unmistakable keening cry of a griffon, followed by a moan of pain.

"Who's there?" demanded Porthios as he and his guests bolted from the dining room into the courtyard of the Garden of Astarin. Though it was surrounded by a verdant hedge, the yard was open to the sky, and there was indeed a griffon there. The creature's haunches were streaked with blood, and its flanks shook like bellows as it tried to regain its breath. It was saddled, but there was no rider in sight.

"My lord!" cried Allatarn. The servant was on the far side of the griffon, and Porthios raced over to find him standing over a motionless, bleeding figure. The griffon eyed him warily but seemed to realize that he meant the fellow no harm.

"Who are you?" asked Porthios, kneeling, seeing an elf whose shallow breathing indicated that he still lived, though barely. The stub of a broken arrow protruded from his flank, and the marshal suspected that this wound was the source of the blood that had streaked the griffon's sides.

"My . . . my name is Daringflight," said the wounded elf. "My lord . . . I am a loyal Qualinesti, your faithful servant. . . ." His back arched in sudden pain, and Daringflight gritted his teeth, breathing harshly through his mouth.

"Of course. I know you," Porthios declared calmly, recognizing the man through the fear that was suddenly surging in his gut. "Now, gather your strength for a moment, then speak."

Daringflight groaned, still trying to speak.

"Rest now. Don't injure yourself further. Allatarn, fetch the healer!"

"She's already been sent for, lord."

"Urgent . . . Lady Alhana . . ." gasped Daringflight, drawing all of Porthios's attention into tight focus. He heard Samar gasp behind him.

"What is it? What word of my queen?" he asked, fearing the answer.

"She is taken. . . . Captured by the Qualinesti and held in the

42

house of Senator Rashas. They did not want you to know. . . . Tried to kill me when I left to bring you word."

"That bastard!" snarled Porthios, his tone furious. He knew and hated Rashas. Leader of the Thalas-Enthia, he was a Qualinesti as utterly opposed to change and unity as were the reactionary Silvanesti such as Konnal. He turned back to Daringflight, his concern for his wife overriding his consciousness of the man's wound. "Has she been harmed? Have they mistreated her?"

Daringflight shook his head. "She is treated well . . . called a 'guest,' in fact. But she is not allowed to leave, nor to send or receive messages."

"Did she send you?" asked Porthios

Again the wounded elf shook his head. "I came on my own. . . . It's important that you know, my lord. There are others, too, who hate what Rashas is doing . . . who despise the way he wants to close our land against all contact with the rest of the world."

"I will deal with Rashas in good time," Porthios declared grimly. He wanted to mount Stallyar, to fly to Qualinesti and to storm the Tower of the Sun. Unconsciously his hand went to his medallion, the badge of his rank as Speaker. His temper flared as he tried to imagine the arrogance of those who would work so hard against his will.

Only gradually did reality intrude. He remembered the imminent campaign, the last stage of an unfinished task. He knew that he would have to carry that matter through to its finish. The marshal looked at Samar, who, like himself, was kneeling over the wounded man.

"Damn Rashas and all his ilk!" Porthios growled. "I'd like to go and deal with him right now . . . but you know I can't."

"I understand," Samar said grimly. "And you should know that all Silvanesti is grateful for your sense of duty."

"I also know you cherish your queen, my friend. I must ask you to go to Qualinesti, to see what aid you can offer her. And to tell her that I will be coming very soon."

"As you command, lord. I could wish to do no less."

* * * * *

"It was Konnal, then. He was the traitor," declared the young elf.

"Yes," the dragon replied. "He returned to my island to give me the date of Porthios's attack."

"The bastard!" hissed the lancer, his voice a growl of pure rage.

After a momentary hesitation, the dragon squinted carefully at the older elf.

"Samar . . . I thought it was you. And so Konnal conspired to draw you away?"

"With the help of Rashas of Qualinesti, yes. It's hard to think of two more vile traitors, nor more natural conspirators, than that pair."

"Still," interjected the young elf, addressing the dragon. "I know you didn't kill Porthios. The ambush failed, of course!"

The serpent shrugged. "Yes, apparently you know that he lived. Still, the ambush was not without some success. Porthios was careless."

"He was," agreed the elder elf. "But it was because he was worried about his wife."

Battle in the Delta

Chapter Four

Porthios completed the preparations for his campaign like an automaton. With every free moment, he thought of his wife, held prisoner in his own homeland. For every minute he spent planning his battle against draconians, he spent an hour plotting the vengeance he would take against Senator Rashas of the Thalas-Enthia in Qualinost.

He drew his only comfort from the knowledge that Samar had gone to Alhana. The loyal warrior-mage, carrying his dragonlance and riding his fleet griffon, had no doubt made the long journey as quickly as possible, though even at an exhausting pace, the flight would take a week. And Samar's devotion to Alhana was legendary. Hadn't he even blushed in embarrassment over the matter at their last dinner together? And there were other allies close to Qualinesti. Much as he distrusted his brother-in-law, Porthios had hope that Tanis

45

Half-Elven would also come to the aid of the queen.

Furthermore, Porthios felt quite certain that Rashas wouldn't dare to harm Alhana. Most of his misgivings arose from the fact that he knew his wife would be frightened and anxious about her detainment, and he wanted to be able to alleviate her concerns. And there was the matter of his unborn child. How wrong it was that the future king of elvenkind might enter life as a captive of his own countrymen!

Yet he tried to force himself to attend the matters of his duty, to finish the task toward which he had devoted the last three decades of his life. The preparations went well. His was a veteran army, and under Generals Bandial and Cantal-Silaster, he had many reliable officers who tended to the mundane matters of readiness. As the departure date for his sweep against the delta approached, Porthios found himself increasingly distracted by his hope for a letter, for any kind of message, from Qualinesti. But the time slipped away without any word, and finally the marshal resolved himself to focus on this one last campaign.

At least Konnal stayed out of his way. The Silvanesti general had been gone for several days after the meeting of the senate, but then he had returned to lend his considerable organizational skills to the preparation for the expedition. Thanks to Konnal, Porthios didn't have to worry about getting the boats he would need to transport his force down the Thon-Thalas. Furthermore, the general organized a full array of provisions, wheels of hard cheese, barrels of salted fish, and crates of elven warbread that were gathered at the dock several days before the army was due to depart.

The standard component of replacement weapons was also delivered promptly. There were boxes upon boxes of deadly, steel-headed arrows, as well as a hundred or more replacement swords. Even though the elven weapons were of splendid quality, a few of them inevitably were broken or lost during the course of a campaign. Other crates contained shields, buckles, straps, sandals, and bedrolls, all the equipment necessary to keep his warriors safe and as comfortable as possible.

Delivered to the docks at the last minute were two long wooden crates, secured by thick hasps and shiny steel locks.

These were the storage cases for precious dragonlances, each holding a pair of the lethal weapons that could be borne by elves on foot and used against the event of draconic attack. Though Porthios was not expecting to encounter dragons on this campaign, he had requested that the weapons be added to his inventory as a standard precaution; he would assign one pair of lances to each of his two divisions.

The twenty companies of Silvanesti warriors boarded the boats with the first light of dawn on the Day of Second Dream Dance. Despite the early hour, thousands of city elves turned out to cheer their heroes' departure. Carried more by the current than by the languid efforts of the polers, the wide, flat riverboats slowly drifted away from the dock and meandered down the stream. The warriors gazed back toward Silvanost, looking at the towers and gardens bright in the morning sun, enjoying the cheers that remained audible until the force made its way around the first great bend of the river.

The Qualinesti archers, all of whom would ride their griffons through the air, departed from their bivouac outside the city. Though they could make the journey in a fraction of the time required by the sluggish riverboats, Porthios had ordered that the two forces would travel together. He considered it a symbolic gesture, but an important one. Under his command, the elves of the two nations had learned to function with cooperation and reliance upon one another. He wasn't about to let some notion of favoritism color the impressions of his Silvanesti warriors.

It was for that same reason that Porthios rode along on river barges. Stallyar would carry him into battle, of course, but for the river voyage, the griffon flew above the boats, gliding back and forth while his master met with Bandial and Cantal-Silaster and planned the specifics of the campaign on the open deck.

During the voyage, the plan evolved from its simple beginnings. Instead of a single landing at the broad clearing located by Aleaha Takmarin, the army would be split into two divisions and would land in two places, on the northeast and northwest ends of the island. In each place, the ground troops would quickly establish a large, fortified encampment. The Qualinesti, on their griffons, would fly back and forth, maintaining communication between the two divisions, and the Silvanesti would quickly venture forth to clear the ground between the two camps of draconians and other dangerous inhabitants. Once the two forces were securely united, the Wildrunners would commence a southward sweep, spanning the width of the island and forcing all unfriendly denizens into a south corner at the bottom, where—if any survived—they would be confronted in a battle of annihilation.

With the griffons wheeling back and forth overhead and the sure knowledge that this was the last outpost of the nightmare that had plagued their realm for three decades, the Silvanesti elves on the boats treated the four-day journey down the river almost as a holiday outing. The splendid woodlands around them were sculpted as perfectly as any formal garden, with groves neatly arranged, framed by trimmed hedges, often complemented by regular, reflecting pools. At night, no worm was safe anywhere near the army encampment, and all day fishing lines drooped into the water from stem to stern of each boat. The elves ate well—fresh fish morning, noon, and night—and the crated provisions hadn't even been touched as the army finally came within sight of the festering island.

These were veteran troops, of course, and now all vestige of holiday excursion vanished from the members of the expedition. The stench of decaying swampland thickened the air around them, and the sight of the bleeding, tormented trees provided a strong reminder of the purpose that had brought them down the river. A shrill whistle sounded from the shore—this was the atrakha, the unique horn used by the Kirath to communicate among themselves—and the anchors were dropped. Under the full control of the boatmen now, the rivercraft waited a mile north of their destination.

Here Aleaha Takmarin came over for a last conference before the elves went ashore. She paddled a slender canoe from the thicket on the shore and quickly found Porthios to give her report.

"The island remains quiet," she informed him. "Still, don't

abandon caution. We've seen signs of many draconians, and I still don't like the way that they've stayed away from their villages."

"You know we'll be careful . . . and thanks for your report," Porthios replied. "Do you still think the two clearings are good places to land?"

"Yes, if you want to risk dividing your force," she said cautiously. Almost as an afterthought, she reached into a pouch at her waist and drew out a small packet of woven grass. "Here—a greenmask. It's a gift from the Kirath. Wear it when you go into battle, and it will offer some protection from noxious gases, smoke, and the like."

"You still suspect there might be green dragons?" he asked.

She shrugged. "We haven't seen any sign of them, but it's like Samar said, this seems like a perfect place for them."

"I'm afraid of the same thing," he admitted. "I appreciate the gift."

"My scouts will be on the island. We'll make contact later, try to keep you posted on the enemy's movements."

"Thanks. Be careful."

Minutes later, on the bow of the lead boat, Porthios met with Tarqualan, who commanded the company of Qualinesti flyers, and the two Silvanesti division commanders, the scarred veteran, Bandial, and the aristocratic noble, Cantal-Silaster. Also present were several of the nature priests of House Woodshaper, who would be charged with beginning the long, slow healing process of the woodland, and two of the white-robed elven wizards who would be entrusted to lending magical might to the Silvanesti ground forces.

"We'll time the landings so that both divisions come ashore simultaneously," Porthios clarified. "The Qualinesti archers will fly overhead, giving protection against attack from the air and keeping watch for any reaction on the ground. I want both camps established by nightfall, completed with palisades."

"Shouldn't be difficult," Bandial said, with a look at the sun, which had not even reached its zenith as yet. "Can we move out as soon as we have a wall up?"

Porthios shook his head. "I want to keep a sense of coordination between the divisions. Even if one of you gets the camp established ahead of time, you're to wait within the palisade. I'll be flying back and forth and will put together orders for an attack with the dawn."

"I thought you said you only expected a few draconians," Bandial countered, adjusting the eye patch that he wore proudly. "Why all the caution?"

With a sigh, the marshal tried to make sense of his answer. "It's just a feeling I have. We could have some trouble with this one. True, Aleaha looked the place over and didn't see any sign of dragons or ogres, and not many draconians, at that. Maybe it was their villages. Too many of them looked abandoned, as if perhaps they still lived there but were hiding out in the woods."

"If the denizens of nightmare are there, we'll find them," Cantal-Silaster promised. "You know that, my lord marshal."

Porthios looked at these elves with real affection. "I do know that, my brave men and women. And it is my sincere wish that every elf with us survives this campaign to make it back home again. But these woods are thick, even for Silvanesti forests. It will be hard to see what's happening from the air, and in the event of a surprise, I want all forces ready to defend themselves."

"Understood, sir," agreed Bandial cheerfully. "Now, good luck to you!"

"And to you all!"

Stallyar and another griffon came to rest on the boat's upper deck, and Porthios and Tarqualan took to their saddles. The great, winged creatures leaped into the air, and the prince of elvenkind, Speaker of the Sun, and Military Governor of Silvanesti once more made ready to lead his troops into battle.

* * * * *

Aerensianic watched the elven deployment with keen interest. The green dragon was coiled through the limbs of three massive trees, just below the upper canopy of tattered leaves, the barrier that would probably have masked his supple green body from the prying eyes of any of the elven scouts on their cursed griffons. However, Aeren was not relying on mere camouflage for protection. As he had when the elven scouts had first scoured this island, he was concealing himself behind a spell of invisibility.

If his features could have been seen, they would have been creased by an obvious frown as he watched the elven riverboats divide into two separate flotillas. One group of the long, flat craft glided to the dragon's right, while the other floated toward the shore not far from the dragon's concealed vantage.

The green dragon was remembering his second meeting with the Silvanesti traitor, the elf who hated this Porthios so much that he had bargained his own army—and a portion of his ancestral homeland—away so that this bold marshal might be killed. The elf's information had been useful and accurate, so far as it went. The elven army appeared on the river exactly on the day the general had predicted. The mob of creatures lurking in the woods below—ogres, goblins, and draconians, all held together under the tenuous reins of Aerensianic's lordship—was emplaced, ready to strike at the landing forces. They, too, had hidden from the scouts, ignoring their almost irresistible compulsion to attack early.

But the traitor had said nothing about a landing in two places. Secure in the knowledge that the elves were too far away to smell him, Aeren snorted a cloud of deadly chlorine gas, irritated with this new development. Unlike the disciplined elven army, the unruly creatures who had answered the green dragon's call to arms were far too disorganized to perform any complicated offensive maneuvers. He would have to leave them where they were, letting the battle develop as it would.

Aeren could make out the form of the elven marshal, mounted upon his silver-feathered griffon, as the commander flew back and forth between the two portions of his army. The green dragon took careful note of the elf, resolving that, when the battle began, he would seek out that particular enemy and give him the honor of a hero's death. Unfortunately, this meant that the green dragon would not be there to help with the main attack. Instead, Aerensianic would have to rely upon a simple plan and on the natural aggressiveness of his troops.

Yet there were other things, too, about the impending fight that would work in his favor. The traitor had informed him that elven tactics had evolved into a predictable approach to a new campaign. Porthios would land his force and quickly build a fortified wall around it. Once sheltered behind that palisade, the elves would be virtually unassailable.

But before then, they would be vulnerable. This was the same tactic the marshal had developed over long experience during the cleansing of Silvanesti. On occasion, Aeren had learned, the elves had been attacked by resentful denizens of the nightmare before they had a chance to complete their defenses. In those cases, the elves had survived by a rapid withdrawal, with a sudden return and a construction of their fort in a new place.

None of those attacks had been landed on a hostile shore, however, and it was this fact that gave Aeren hope. The current would press the boats hard against the riverbank, making any withdrawal exceptionally difficult. Instead, the invading army would be forced to fight where it was, ill-prepared and unfortified. And they would have no idea that a major force was lurking in these woods, alerted to the elven approach and prepared to launch a deadly ambush.

Watching as he tried to suppress his natural impatience, Aeren saw the elven boats pull up to shore, their blunt prows driving into the muddy bank, hull to hull across a breadth of three or four hundred paces. The invading warriors leaped onto the ground and quickly spread out, axes ringing into tree trunks within a minute after the first troops had landed. The second flotilla, off to the right, had drifted out of sight behind the curve of the island's shore. The green dragon suspected that those boats hadn't reach shore yet, so he refrained from making any move, giving any sign of the ambushing force lurking in the shelter of the woods. He wanted to make sure the other force had landed, their boats grounded in soft muck so they would be unable to come to the aid of their beleaguered comrades.

But soon it would be time to attack.

Very, very soon.

*   *   *   *   *

Porthios scanned the broad shore of the island, trying to reassure himself that things were developing according to plan. He saw that the First Division, in the west, was already drawing up to shore. The Second Division was still a mile or more from its designated landing zone but was closing fast, borne by the current and by the diligent efforts of the elven polers.

Stallyar banked along the shore, flying low and parallel to the riverbank. The marshal wore the greenmask as a precaution and was pleased to find that he could breathe quite easily through the gauzy material. Still, he was nervous and edgy. He squinted into the dank vegetation, trying to reassure himself that there could be no real threat there. After all, he and Samar had thoroughly scouted the island. A few hundred, even a thousand or more, draconians would be no match for either one of his divisions, even supposing that the disorganized monsters could somehow muster the coordination to attack together. It was far more likely that individual bands of the creatures would try to offer what resistance they could and would be slaughtered by the elven phalanxes. Porthios even allowed himself to hope that this might be a relatively bloodless campaign for his own troops. The elves had skilled healers, and all but the most grievous of wounds could be magically healed so long as there weren't too many injured all at the same time.

The First Division was well on the way toward clearing a swath of shore. Already axemen were working on sharpening the trunks of felled trees, while the cutters worked their way farther and farther inland. Half his griffon-mounted Qualinesti, under the command of Tarqualan, soared in circles over the troops, keeping alert eyes on the woodland, with arrows ready to shoot if any target presented itself. Unfortunately, Porthios knew that the dense undergrowth created little chance of seeing a target that didn't want to be seen.

With a mild tug on the reins, Porthios pulled Stallyar around, then urged the griffon to hurry as they flew toward the boats of the Second Division. Coming around the bend at the northern point of the island, he saw that those boats were finally drawing near to shore. A hundred griffons wheeled overhead, archers studying the bank where the vessels would make their landing.

Porthios joined these fliers, allowing Stallyar's powerful wings to stretch into an easy glide. The boats, driven by strong pushes on the poles, churned up little wakes of white water, then nudged firmly into the soft muck of the banks. In another minute, the elves of the Second Division were swarming ashore, attacking the corrupted trees with as much vigor as had their comrades two miles away along the shore of the island.

The thin notes of a trumpet trailed through the wind, so faint that at first Porthios thought he must have imagined it. But then the call was repeated, the distinctive, ascending three-note cry that meant only one thing: We are being attacked!

Even before Porthios could pull on the reins, Stallyar banked and dived, picking up speed as he carried the marshal toward the sound of the alarm. They swept just above the trees, cutting over the island rather than taking the longer route over the water.

It was this detour that undoubtedly saved his life.

As the griffon flew at a frantic speed, Porthios had eyes only for the elven troops of the First Division. The first thing he noticed was that the griffons and their archers, who had been circling over their comrades on the ground, were now diving toward the woods. Arrows were showering down into the trees, clear enough proof that his soldiers were being attacked.

The second thing to catch his attention was a writhing, shimmering shape twisting through the treetops directly below. His mind registered the identification—this was a dragon, and a big one.

The blast of poisonous gas erupted upward from widespread jaws, a green cloud boiling and churning into the air. The seething mist swirled just beyond Stallyar's right wing, and Porthios saw that the dragon had tilted its sinuous neck all the way over its back to spew its lethal breath at the flying elf. The attack was awkward, and that enabled the griffon to dive away from the deadly cloud. Stallyar cawed angrily as the tendrils of mist burned his eyes, while Porthios blinked and gagged, grateful for the protection of the mask.

Even as branches lashed his face while Stallyar ducked below the top layer of the forest, Porthios was thinking about that attack. The dragon had been invisible—he had seen the effects of the spell fade as the monster burst into motion—and it had been waiting for him. If he had been flying over the river, along the bank, as he had been since the first boats landed, he would inevitably have glided directly into his death.

The griffon's foreclaws, powerful eagle talons, seized a limb and pulled, the leonine rear legs pushing off the same branch to catapult the creature back into the skies. Porthios risked a glance and saw that the dragon, a massive green wyrm, was disentangling itself from the treetops. Enormous wings beat, crushing branches and leaves, but the monster's own size worked against it.

In moments, the marshal was flying over the encampment, and Porthios was appalled to see the chaos reigning below. More than a thousand winged humanoids, many bearing hooked swords, while others attacked with their talons and crushing jaws, had swarmed from the shelter of the woods to strike the elven work parties. His first glance showed at least a hundred torn, bleeding bodies lying in the wake of the initial attackers, while more of the axemen were falling back to the boats.

From the flanks of the forest, a great, lumbering line of creatures emerged. These were ogres, bashing with huge clubs, some wielding long spears, others carrying sticks like tree trunks as they struck the unprepared elves on the right and the left. Massive feet thudded across the ground as growls rose thickly over the field. The first elves to meet this charge were instantly smashed down, crushed lifeless beneath the brutal onslaught.

The veteran warriors of the First Division were making a valiant effort to handle the shock. Already they had a semblance of a line formed, a barrier of silvery swords that blocked the draconians' advance and forced the savage creatures to hit their enemies head-on. In line, each elf relied on the presence of his comrades to right and left, and there were no warriors on Krynn more skilled with the long sword than a veteran elf.

But the problem with the line came from its flanks. The ogres rolled against both right and left sides, and without supporting formations to screen, the tenuous line was inevitably being chewed away. One after another, elves turned from the frontal attack to face the threat from the flank, only to perish beneath the weight of the monstrous, club-wielding humanoids.

Porthios gave a quick glance behind him. The green dragon had broken from the trees and was winging after him, but it was slow to accelerate and somewhat clumsy in the cramped quarters. Still, it seemed to pursue him with singular, deadly purpose The elf reckoned that he had about a minute to issue orders and take action before he would once more have to flee for his life. He pulled back on the reins and Stallyar climbed, winging desperately toward the Qualinesti on their griffons. These elves were busy shooting arrows into the attackers, but their efforts were uncoordinated. Many shot at the draconians, while a few directed their lethal missiles at the ogres on the right and left flanks.

Porthios saw Tarqualan trying to make order of the chaos.

"There! Concentrate your fire on the near flank!" shouted the marshal. "We've got to stop the ogres or the whole division is lost!"

"Yes, lord!" shouted the captain, immediately turning to signal his disorganized flying troops.

Again the marshal stole a glance, and he saw the green dragon bearing down. The yellow eyes were unblinking, the slitted pupils fixed unerringly on him. With an anguished look down at the battle, Porthios knew that he was needed down there. His leadership, and his sword, might give some hope of stabilizing that brave but crumbling line. Yet there was no mistaking the serpent's purposeful pursuit, and if he flew down to join his army, the commander knew that the dragon would bring its indiscriminate attack down there as well.

Instead, Porthios pulled the reins to the left. Stallyar, with a momentary squawk of confused protest, obeyed, driving his powerful wings through the air, veering away from the battle and the river, carrying his master over the dank forest of the island. Roaring in fury, the dragon followed, cutting the angle on the inside of Porthios's turn, closing the distance between hunter and quarry as the massive monster built up more and more speed. Wind scoured the elven marshal's face and stung tears from his eyes as he laid his head flat along the griffon's powerful neck.

The elf knew he would never outdistance the dragon in straight, level flight, but he had to put some distance between the serpent and the desperate battle. He looked over his shoulder, fighting off the inevitable quiver of dragonawe as he saw that the beast was closing rapidly.

"There! Dive!" shouted Porthios, pointing to a gap between a couple of tall, leafless tree trunks.

Stallyar responded instantly, tucking his wings, veering through a turn that would have pulled the elf out of the saddle if he had not been firmly seated. Again branches lashed his skin, and Porthios buried his face more firmly in the soft feathers of the griffon's neck. He felt them drop swiftly through the brittle limbs of the dead tree, plunging out of the sky with precipitous haste.

They landed with a thud hard enough to knock the wind out of the rider, but the griffon, unfazed, used the ground to pounce directly sideways. Scampering catlike through a maze of thick, dead limbs, the creature raced through an arc that carried them back to the north. Porthios hung on with desperation, knowing his only chance for survival rested with the griffon's quickness and natural instincts for escape.

With a bellow of rage, the dragon dropped into the trees.

Massive trunks snapped like twigs, including a forest giant that crashed to the ground directly before Stallyar. Without hesitation, the griffon leapt the barrier, then used the branches and his powerful wings to lift mount and rider back into the sky.

The dragon smashed to the ground, and once again green gases spumed upward. This time the cloud was far behind Stallyar's tail, and without any urging from Porthios, the griffon sped toward the battle raging on the riverbank. The great dragon was left below and behind them, roaring in frustration and splintering trees to right and left as it fought to free itself from the tangle.

Two or more miles away, the battlefield was nevertheless easy to mark, since Tarqualan's Qualinesti still wheeled on their griffons over the site of the elven landing. But as Porthios drew closer and looked down into the clearing on the riverbank, he groaned under an onslaught of disbelief and despair.

The elven line was a shambles. The draconians had broken through in the center, and though the arrows from the flying archers had slowed the ogre onslaught on the left, they had done nothing to check the hammer blow against the right flank. Now scattered parties of Silvanesti fought to reach the boats, or at least to give a good account of themselves in their last fight. Draconians swarmed over the hulls of two or three riverboats, while a fourth was already smoking. More sooty plumes marked the progress of torches as the attackers raced from boat to boat, obviously intending to put the whole fleet to the torch.

Even worse, Porthios saw that two more green dragons—not as huge as his pursuer, but formidable monsters nonetheless—had slithered from the woods to join in the slaughter. Disdaining to use their lethal breath weapons against this disorganized and scattering foe, the wyrms pounced on individual elves and tore them to pieces with their jaws and talons. Each of the dragons left a trail of blood and gore in its wake and was given a wide berth by the ogres and draconians that also continued the slaughter.

The sight of the serpentine killers was too much for Porthios's already frayed emotions. In the midst of all the horror, of the knowledge that this expedition had already turned into a disaster, he saw a young green dragon bite a fleeing elf in two. His self-control and sense of reason snapped, and he put his heels hard into Stallyar's flank, pushing the griffon's head down toward the hateful lizard.

Nothing loath, the bold flier sensed his master's intentions and willingly obeyed, even to the point of biting back the shrill cry of challenge that would have automatically accompanied such a swooping attack. Instead, as silent as a wisp of wind, the griffon and the elf plunged toward the back of the rampaging dragon. Porthios had his slender long sword in his hand, the blade of purest elven steel gleaming like cold fire in the late afternoon sun. It was a hallowed weapon, blessed by the gods of goodness and borne by three generations of elven heroes. Stallyar's talons were extended, as if the creature were eager to reach the dragon, to wring the life out of that hateful, scaly shape.

They dropped like a missile, wind rushing through Porthios' hair and pulling tears from his eyes, though he never lost sight of the dragon, which was now coiling for another pounce. At the last minute, the griffon's feathered wings spread wide, slowing the dive just enough to spare them injury from the crash. The rush of air became audible, and the dragon lifted its head fractionally, undoubtedly sensing the presence overhead.

But it was too late for any other reaction. Stallyar's talons seized both sides of the wyrm's head, the force of the griffon's weight smashing downward to drive the monster against the ground. The lion's paws of the griffon's rear legs tore at the green dragon's shoulders while the serpent lay stunned and writhing on the ground. Swiftly the eagle's beak jabbed down and tore a great gash in the top of the wyrm's broad, flat skull.

Still, it was the silver sword that did the real damage. As soon as they struck the creature, Porthios drove the blade deep into the snakelike neck. Withdrawing the weapon with a wrenching twist, he slid from the saddle to land on the ground next to the dragon. While the beast squirmed in the grip of the powerful and enraged griffon, Porthios looked for the spot where the hard skull merged into the supple neck. In one powerful, unerring thrust, he jabbed the keen steel deep and severed the monster's spinal cord.

Shuddering reflexively, the dragon died, oozing blood from its wounds and puffing a small gout of greenish gas from its wide nostrils. Porthios was already scrambling back into his saddle, barely straddling the griffon's broad back before Stallyar launched themselves into the air again. He saw the second young serpent lift its head above the chaos of the battlefield, yellow eyes flashing with hatred as it saw the fate of its clan dragon. More menacing by far, the elf also saw the massive green monster that had pursued him so relentlessly. Having broken free of the trees, it was once again winging toward the fight, head twisting back and forth as it looked for the elven marshal.

Wicked jaws curled into a mockery of a grin as the beast picked out the lone griffon struggling for altitude. But now many of the other Qualinesti, heartened by their leader's heroics, were spiraling down to fly with Porthios and Stallyar. A glance showed the marshal that their quivers were nearly empty, but that each still had enough arrows left for a few shots.

"Archers—we need a volley!" he shouted, his voice powerful enough to easily carry through the air above the fight. "On my mark!"

Nearly a hundred griffons were soaring along with him, and as he pointed his sword into the southern sky the target was obvious to them all. Porthios would have liked to launch the barrage from a little more altitude, but there was nothing to be done about that. They would have to shoot well, these brave Qualinesti who were inevitably shaken by the rising nausea of dragonawe.

No single arrow was going to kill a monster like that, of course, but the marshal hoped that the concentration of scores of painful hits would be enough to drive the dragon away, if not seriously injure it. The elves nocked their arrows, the griffons shifting in flight instinctively to make sure that no flier blocked another's shot.

If the dragon perceived the danger, it gave no sign. Instead, it bored in closer with each beat of its massive wings. Porthios knew he had to shoot at the last possible minute, but he also understood the need to give the order before the beast was close enough to exhale a gout of that lethal gas.

"Archers, now! *Shoot!*"

Ninety-four arrows arced outward on his command, and more than half of them struck the target. Many drove deep into that hateful head, pricking the sensitive nostrils, a couple even stinging the yellow eyes. Others scored gouges into the monster's neck or tore through the soft membrane of the dragon's wings.

The flying elves instantly dispersed in all four directions, insuring that the dragon had no concentration of enemies upon which to spew its killing breath. But it became immediately apparent that the monster had lost all interest in pursuing the attack. Instead, with a howl of elemental anguish, it curled its wings and dived away from the fight, gingerly coming to rest at the fringe of the forest while the flying elves jeered and insulted the proud monster.

That danger temporarily alleviated, Porthios turned his attention to the battle raging on the ground, and with a heartbreaking ache of dismay, he knew the tragic fight was all but over. Every one of the large riverboats had been seized by attacking draconians, and the few surviving elves of the First Division were being hacked down and cut to pieces before his eyes.

General Cantal-Silaster organized a last stand, shouting orders frantically, her own blade red with blood. Porthios dived to help, but could only watch in horror as her plumed helm vanished beneath a press of draconians.

The ambush was a disaster unprecedented during his career as a marshal of Silvanesti, and the loss of life was all the more appalling because those elves, like himself, had fancied this war so close to its end. He had sent these warriors ashore into the very teeth of a powerful enemy, a force that had somehow been perfectly positioned for an ambush.

But there was no time for grief nor self-recriminations right now, not while the Second Division was still ashore on this nightmarish piece of land. Later Porthios would try to decipher how he could have been so wrong about this place, and how this normally disorganized and chaotic enemy could have been so well prepared for the arrival of his legion. Now, however, he had to see to the survival of the rest of his men.

Mounted on their griffons, the Qualinesti archers circled around their leader, exchanging grim looks or staring in horror at the carnage below. With the exceptions of a few riders who had been felled by boulders or spears cast by ogres, these western elves had survived the fight, but they shared the universal knowledge that the battle had been an utter, catastrophic defeat. Still, Porthios wondered if perhaps he and his Qualinesti could exact some measure of vengeance before they departed this bloody field.

The large green dragon was some distance away, enlisting the aid of many draconians who gingerly plucked arrows from the monster's head and wings. Every so often one of these unwilling nurses would tug too roughly, and the enraged serpent would cuff the offending creature so hard that it tumbled across the ground. Sometimes these battered draconians got up again, and sometimes they didn't. It obviously made no difference to the wounded wyrm.

The third dragon, the youngster who had continued to fight on the ground, was now busy worrying elven corpses, pulling apart pouches and packs in its relentless pursuit of shiny coins. Already a small mound of the precious metal glittered in the mud beneath the protective, whiplike lash of the dragon's tail.

"Kill it," Porthios declared, pointing his sword at the avaricious wyrm.

Instantly a volley of arrows showered downward, razor-sharp heads plunging deep, drawing shrill screams of pain from the dragon. The creature, whose scaly hide was nowhere near as tough as its elder's, writhed around in pain, its tail and neck lashing as it reflexively fought against the sudden attack.

A dozen griffons swooped low, while other elves shot arrows at any ogres and draconians who ventured too close.

Fortunately, these other creatures had already been inclined to stay back because of the dragon's possessiveness about its plunder, and they showed no eagerness to help it now as elven swords sliced in and quickly finished the work that the volley of arrows had begun. Unscathed, the twelve elves remounted, and the fliers spread across the sky, leaving the bloody remains behind and winging toward the encampment of the Second Division.

* * * * *

"You were driven off by a volley of arrows, then?" asked the young elf, all but sneering in contempt.

"You have the story in my words," the dragon replied, with a shrug of his great wings.

"Are you not ashamed of your cowardice?"

The serpent growled and shifted his posture, an elaborate gesture that rippled along the full extent of his scaly shape. He remained pressed against the wall by the dragonlance but managed to turn a disdainful glare on the two elves. "I do not like pain. But at the same time, I lived through that fight—and you should know that the battle was not over, not by any means."

The Second Division

Chapter Five

The marshal assigned a score of griffon-mounted elves to observe the monsters that were busily plundering the wreckage of the First Division's landing.

"Keep an eye on that dragon," he warned them. "Get out of here in a hurry if it shows any signs of coming after you."

"Aye, Lord Marshal," pledged a Qualinesti captain, an archer who had put one of the arrows into the serpent's eye. "But may I beg permission to give it another stinging before we go?"

"Granted," Porthios agreed. Then he led the rest of the fliers across the island, toward the surviving elves of his once mighty army. He thought fleetingly of Samar, missing the warrior-mage's steady courage, not to mention his skill with the lance. Perhaps the ever alert Samar would have even discerned the ambush before it was too late. He could only hope that same alertness and competence were being employed to protect and serve his wife.

As the formation of griffons came into sight of the second landing zone, Porthios saw that the construction of the fortifications was progressing well. Already the elves had cleared a large swath of ground at the riverbank, and the spiked palisade that would surround the camp was more than half completed. Frameworks of towers had been made, marking the sites of the four battle platforms that would soon rise thirty feet into the air. Everywhere General Bandial's Silvanesti were working hard, certainly worried about their comrades, but not allowing themselves to be distracted from their task.

In obedience to his orders, the other half of the griffon-mounted Qualinesti had remained with the Second Division, flying circular patrols overhead and scouting the environs of the camp. Now these fliers pulled into formation besides their brethren from the west, shouting for news.

Porthios let Tarqualan's elves mingle with their fellow Qualinesti. While all the fliers continued to circle over the camp, the marshal guided Stallyar to a landing in the midst of the Second Division's camp. He was vaguely pleased to note that, despite the added distraction of his arrival, the elves remained busily working at their assigned tasks. Sadly he suspected that the fortifications here would be tested, and very soon.

General Bandial met him as he landed, and the one-eyed veteran listened grimly as Porthios quietly told him of the First Division's fate.

"They were waiting in ambush?" Bandial asked in disbelief.

"As certainly as if they'd known the time and location of our landing," the marshal replied. Once again that circumstance rankled at the back of his mind, but he knew he had to attend to more urgent matters. "As soon as you get the fence up, get your men working on a ditch on the outside of the walls. And we'll want double the usual number of towers. Also, you had two of the dragonlances in your boats, right? Get them out and place them in the hands of a couple of your biggest, steadiest warriors."

"And Lady Cantal-Silaster?" asked Bandial, his eye narrowing.

"She fell leading the defense, overwhelmed by draconians."

The one-eyed general blinked, silently grieving at the news even as the tough commander's thoughts turned to the next matter. "What about news of the First? Do you want to try to keep their fate a secret?" asked Bandial, shrewdly eyeing his commander.

Porthios shook his head. "You know as well as I do that won't work. No, it's best to give them an announcement, let the troops know where we stand. You can spread the word that I'll talk to them as soon as the wall's done."

"All right, Marshal. I think you know that these are good warriors, men and women as steady as you could want in a fight."

"I know that, General," Porthios said with a sigh. "But we both could have said the same thing about the First Division."

Five minutes later the marshal got his next dose of bad news. He and Bandial were looking into the case that held— was *supposed* to hold—two dragonlances. Instead, they saw only bare shafts of wood. The barbed, razor-sharp heads of the enchanted weapons, the lethal metallic killers forged by Theros Ironfeld and the Hammer of Kharas, were missing. Scuffs showed where they had been pried off the hafts.

"Stolen?" asked the general, gaping in disbelief. "I can't believe any elf would do such a thing!"

"They would be worth a lot, but even so, I'm inclined to agree with you," Porthios said. "They were obviously taken off the shafts, but I doubt—I can't *believe*—that the motive was personal profit."

Again suspicions whirled in his brain, but like his questions about the ambush, none of these thoughts would do them any good in their current predicament. Still, he resolved that they would be addressed in the future.

"We'll have to stop the green dragon with arrows," Porthios declared. "At least, we already gave him a stinging to remember."

Despite his bold words, he was remembering the dragon's single-minded pursuit of him. That was yet another suspicious thing about this campaign, a question that would eventually demand some answers. But for now, the dragon's motivation, like everything else, must simply be accepted as a fact of the battle.

Perhaps an hour of daylight remained as the last stakes of the palisade were driven into the soft ground. Now the Second Division was protected by a semicircular wall of stout posts, with the river—and the landed boats—at their backs. Towers rose every fifty paces, each a squat, sturdy platform for a score of archers.

At about the same time, one of the Qualinesti scouts landed to report that the horde of draconians and ogres had marched into the woods, bearing on a line toward this camp. The green dragon had taken to the air, and the other scouts were giving it a wide berth. The wyrm, for its part, seemed content to remain well beyond the range of the elven archers.

Knowing it would take several hours, at least, for the file of creatures to make its way through the tangled undergrowth of the island, Porthios had Bandial gather his division around the center of the camp, though he didn't neglect to have plenty of pickets posted on the wall tops and towers. The white-robed wizards among the elven force cast spells of detection and alarm through the woods for a quarter mile in every direction, so the warriors were fairly confident of notice prior to the enemy's approach.

The marshal stood upon a broad stump in the middle of the camp, high enough that he could see across all the elves ranked before him, but close enough that he could project his voice across the entire gathering.

"Elves of the Second Division," Porthios began, "you have already heard rumors of the disaster that has befallen our comrades in the First. It grieves me to tell you that those rumors are true. Their camp was overrun before the palisade was built. The boats were taken, and casualties were many."

He paused to let that sink in, pleased to note that the faces before him remained stoic. The changes, where he did note them, were not expressions of fear or resentment. Rather, these elves were getting angry, becoming grimly determined to exact revenge.

"We now know that a force of denizens, including ogres and draconians and one dragon, is on its way to try to repeat that victory over us. But you should know that your comrades did not yield their ground without a bloody fight. Nor did they turn and run, even when disaster was certain. Two green dragons lie dead there, fodder for maggots and worms, and more draconians than you can easily count spilled into acid, burst into fire, or froze into stone as they gave up their lives on the swords of the First Division.

"I do not try to mislead you into thinking that the fight will be easy, or the result certain. But you men of the Second Division have a sturdy palisade, and you know how well these walls of wood have served us over the last thirty years. Not once—remember that, not *once*—has an attacker breached the walls of a fortified elven camp.

"But we will let them try, my bold elves; we will let them try. And we will kill them at the borders of the palisade. We will let their force break itself on our ramparts. And when they are broken, then we will sweep out with steel and blood.

"And only then, my elves, will the First be avenged."

There was no cheering following his speech, nor did Porthios expect to hear any. But he could tell by the looks on the faces that his warriors had taken his words to heart. They would fight with confidence and fury and, the gods willing, the First Division would be avenged.

Two hours later, well after darkness had settled over the mist-shrouded island, the woods erupted with sounds of musical bells as the magical alarms set by the wizards were tripped by the approaching horde. Immediately Porthios sent his Qualinesti, whose griffons had been resting within the palisade, aloft. They had strict orders to keep alert for the dragon and to shower the creature with arrows if it appeared.

The Silvanesti of the Second Division took their posts along the walls, with two companies detached to watch the riverbank in case the attackers somehow found a way to slip around the barrier by water. The main defensive line consisted of archers on the ramparts and towers who would shower the attackers with deadly missiles and oil-soaked bundles of flaming rags. Steadfast swordsmen lined the entire inside of the wall. The palisade was made of stout tree trunks, but there were gaps of several inches between each pair of posts, and the elves had learned through experience that the enemy would press close to the wall in an attempt to get at the defenders. This very proximity would make the denizens vulnerable to elven counterattack through the gaps of the palisade.

The white moon, Lunitari, was waning but still more than half full, and though low in the western sky, she cast enough light to aid visibility. Porthios was fairly certain that the dragon wouldn't be able to approach unseen. As an additional protection, he had posted a wizard atop each of the eight towers. They would cast spells to aid the defense on the ground, but were also charged with scanning the sky, through eyes magically charmed to detect invisible attackers.

Soon the clanging of the alarm bells gave way to the grunting and cursing of thousands of creatures. Tree limbs snapped, and heavy boots and taloned feet tromped loudly on the ground. The horde of island denizens broke from the woods a hundred paces from the palisade wall, and there they waited. Their numbers continued to swell as more and more of the beasts emerged from the woods, until it looked as though the clearing was fringed with a dark and deadly border.

"Stand to, there," Porthios called to his elves from the wall top. "Don't shoot until you've got a good target."

"Aye, Marshal!" came a cheerful reply. "I'm going to pluck me an ogre eyeball!"

"Get one for me as well," shouted General Bandial from a different tower. "I need something to wear under this patch."

The elves raised a quick hurrah, and the commander was heartened by the evidence of his warriors' high morale.

Stallyar remained on the ground, prancing and fluttering nervously in the center of the fortified shore. Porthios knew that this fight would be won or lost on the ground, so he had decided to stay here among the Silvanesti, at least for the time being. The Qualinesti, two hundred strong, were all flying overhead, and he just had to rely on them to prevent the big green dragon from getting into the camp.

The mass of creatures emerging from the woods had grown to a horde by now, spreading in an arc to face approximately half of the total length of the palisade. With a rhythmic tromping of heavy feet, the ogres began to count a cadence that would build their excitement and inevitably compel them to make a charge at the elven camp. Porthios had seen and heard this many times before, but the steady beat and rising volume still brought a queasiness to his stomach. He wished they'd get the preliminaries over with and start the damned fight.

The draconians started to hoot, hiss, and jeer. Their batlike wings, insufficient for true flight but able to hasten their speed in a charge, flexed and fanned, giving the moonlit horde a shifting, unreal quality, as if the monsters were not individual creatures, but parts of a blanket that was being fluttered horizontally in a light breeze. All the noises increased, until it seemed as though the forest itself was screeching and stomping at the elves. Finally the warlike sounds reached a crescendo, holding at this frenetic pitch for several taut heartbeats.

And then, as if a dam had burst, the entire mob spewed forward from the fringe of the trees. Some draconians burst into the lead, galloping on all fours, using their wings to propel them as fast as a galloping horse. These were dangerous, Porthios knew, for their momentum—coupled with the sharp, gripping talons on their hands and feet—could help these creatures to scale all the way to the top of the wall in the first impetus of their charge. His veteran elves had seen this before, however, and he noted that the archers along the top of the wall all had their swords close at hand.

The ground shook from the impact of heavy boots, and the impossibly loud noise seemed to swell even more as the horde closed rapidly on the camp. Arrows began to dart out from the elven positions as archers picked off the leading draconians. Here the natures of the magical creatures worked in the elves' favor. The slain kapak draconians dissolved into pools of caustic acid, while the occasional bozaks among their number died in explosions of sparks, smoke, and fire. These fatalities inevitably created obstacles, slight falters in the momentum of the thundering charge.

And even if a draconian wasn't killed outright, the impact of a steel-headed missile from fifty paces away was enough to break the pace of the creature's charge, to send it rolling and tumbling to the ground. As often as not, the wounded monsters were quickly trampled by the mob rushing along right behind.

The survivors among these first draconians, still racing at breakneck speed, used their wings and their powerful legs to fling themselves into the air. They crashed heavily into the timbers of the palisade, but the sturdy posts held. Some of these attackers were felled by sword thrusts through the fence, cuts that gouged into exposed bellies and necks. Others, however, leapt too high to be struck from the ground, and now they scrambled up the rough posts, clawing to climb over the spiked parapet at the top.

But now the elves on the ramparts had their swords out, hacking and stabbing at the scaly, crocodilian faces. One elf was seized by the arms and, clutched in the grip of a dying draconian, pulled over the wall to tumble into the frenzied creatures now smashing into the base of the parapet. A couple of the winged monsters actually scrambled over the top of the wall, but these were quickly cut down by the elves manning the upper parapet. The rest of the beasts were knocked back, bleeding, to tumble into the chaotic press below.

The elves on the towers maintained a steady rain of arrows into the horde, and now, with the last of the first wave repulsed, the archers atop the walls again took up their bows. There was no pausing to aim now; the attackers were so closely packed that any arrow sent downward was likely to plant itself in monstrous flesh.

On the ground, killing frenzy raged on both sides of the parapet. The elves stabbed with their long swords, cutting any creature that pressed close to the barrier. Some ogres wielded huge spears, and they used these with grim effect, sticking the long weapons through the gaps in the fence and twisting them about to gouge into any defenders within reach. Many elves tumbled back, bleeding, but others seized the spears behind their crude iron heads and tried to wrestle them away from the brutes.

In places, the wall of posts rocked back and forth, straining under the impact of thousands of bodies. Some of the elven archers on the rampart staggered under the shifting footing, and a few fell back into the encampment. But the Second Division had done its work well, planting the timbers deep, and nowhere did the palisade show signs of imminent collapse.

The marshal risked a quick look around the battlefield. There was still no sign of the green dragon, and the two companies he had posted at the waterfront were, with commendable discipline, paying careful attention to their duties instead of watching the distraction of the great battle raging behind them. Likewise, the elves posted on the large portion of the wall that wasn't currently under attack kept their eyes on the dark forest instead of turning to watch the carnage occurring on their flank. Stallyar, near the base of the commander's tower, had settled down, though he kept his eyes, unblinking, on his rider. Overhead, the Qualinesti still circled, some shooting into the battle, but most of them keeping their eyes alert for any sign of the great green dragon.

Looking back to the battle line, Porthios saw that the pace of the arrow fire was slackening. Many of the archers had nearly empty quivers.

"More arrows! Get them up to the walls," shouted Porthios to the elves of his reserve company.

Immediately fresh ammunition was passed up the ladders, and the desultory barrage once again became a furious shower. Everywhere along the base of the wall lay dead and dying monsters, though the living took no notice of the casualties, trampling them mercilessly as they fought for positions adjacent to the palisade. Though Porthios had seen it before, he was amazed to witness ogres with huge clubs, weapons that were far too big and clumsy to fit through the gaps in the palisade, and draconians armed with nothing more than the talons on their clawed hands pressed eagerly up to the fence.

There, easy meat for elven swords, they were cut, wounded, and killed.

Screams of alarm pulled the marshal's attention around to the rear, and he was stunned to see the huge green dragon tearing through one of his companies on the riverbank. Like some horrible apparition from the deep, it was draped in muck and weeds from the river. The sinuous form scattered a glittering cascade, spraying droplets of muddy water as it tore and clawed and bit through a dozen helpless elves. A massive cloud of green murk drifted through the palisade, and Porthios groaned at the knowledge that many of his warriors must have died in that first, lethal exhalation.

He knew that green dragons were excellent swimmers. Why hadn't he thought of that obvious tactic? The elven commander was infuriated by his own carelessness, at this evidence of one more mistake that had cost lives among his loyal elves.

The Qualinesti on their griffons were diving now, sending dozens of arrows showering into the great wyrm. Rearing high on its rear legs, the dragon spewed another blast of gas into the air, dropping many of the fliers right out of the sky. Lashing with its foreclaws, striking like a snake with its head on its long, supple neck, the creature ripped other elves from their saddles or knocked griffons to the ground, each time leaving a trailing plume of fluttering white feathers.

And then there was another alarm, and Porthios saw that a bare stretch of wall was faced by a new attack. This force, a band that had been held back from the main attack with admirable discipline, was made up entirely of draconians. The creatures raced across the stumpy field, hurling themselves up the palisade with flapping wings. At the same time, more of the creatures spiraled down from the sky to land atop the parapet. These were sivaks, the marshal was certain, the one kind of draconian capable of true flight.

Now his reserve was entangled by the sudden rush of the dragon, and the weary troops along the palisade were still engaged by the original attack. He was appalled to see elf after elf knocked from the parapet by the sivaks, who carried massive, jagged-edged swords that they wielded with both of their hands clutching the hilts. Other draconians swarmed up and over the wall, while elves on the ground struggled up the ladders to reinforce their comrades overhead. But now, for a change, it was the monsters who held the higher position, and the elves found themselves battling up narrow ladders, precariously balanced as they tried to wield their swords against the hulking creatures overhead. One after another of the elves was bashed from the ladders to plummet hard onto the unforgiving ground.

Porthios absorbed the changes in the battle over the course of ten or twelve heartbeats, and then he knew what he had to do. Sliding down the ladder from the tower rampart, he whistled for Stallyar and saw the griffon race over to meet him. Leaping into the saddle, the marshal was shouting orders as the creature lifted him into the air.

"Elves on the towers—give them support over there!" he shouted, directing the archers to shoot at the draconians who had claimed a portion of the wall top. He glanced over and saw that the dragon was still wreaking terrible havoc in the camp, but that the Qualinesti on their griffons had circled up and away and were seriously distracting the creature with their vexing missile fire.

Stallyar knew where his master was needed, and as soon as he was twenty feet off the ground, he flew on a level course directly at the big sivak who seemed to be directing the battle on top of the wall. The monster looked up briefly, jaws gaping wide as it saw the vengeful griffon, and then the crushing beak tore a great gouge in the draconian's scalp. Stallyar's eagle talons picked the screaming creature up and dumped it over the wall,

The griffon came to light on the narrow parapet, and Porthios slid over his mount's tail. The silver long sword reached out almost of its own will to cut the arm off of a charging sivak, and on the backstroke, the elf chopped the draconian hard to the side, knocking the dying creature onto the ground inside the palisade. There the body burst into oily flame, the dying pyrotechnics of a sivak.

More draconians closed in, and the sword became a whirling blur of bright steel and slick blood. Behind him, Porthios heard the griffon crowing savagely and knew that Stallyar was rending creatures limb from limb with his beak. Back to back, the two stood in the middle of the parapet and dared any of the attackers to close with them.

Despite the gory wounds scored by his elven long sword, many of the draconians accepted the dare. One after another, they lunged along the narrow platform, stabbing, clawing, seeking to drag him down. The marshal's arm grew numb from wielding his weapon, but his mind was clouded by a battle haze that banished any thoughts of fatigue, of despair. He lunged, cut, and parried, stepping inexorably forward and driving the press of draconians back. Taloned hands reached for him, and he sliced through scales, laying flesh open to the bone. Jaws snapped, and his blade whipped downward, carving nostrils, gouging eyes, even hacking right through skulls, cutting into wicked brains. His face, his hands, and his arms were scorched by the flames spouting from these dying monsters, but always there were more ready to lunge over their fallen comrades, eager to attack and kill.

A massive sivak stood in his path, wings flexing like a great battle cloak. The draconian wielded a huge sword, and it brought the weapon straight down, like an axeman trying to split a solid stump. Desperately Porthios raised his sword, blocking the blow with a clang of steel that echoed across the battlefield. The force of the attack numbed his arm, but when the sivak pulled back for another strike, the elf darted with serpentine quickness, driving his bloody blade into the sivak's belly. The draconian howled in anguish even as flames crackled around the fringes of its body, and as it died and burned, the marshal kicked it off of the parapet and lunged forward, still seeking new foes.

When at last the draconians started to back away, to see that there was no point in attacking this infuriated elf, it was Porthios who carried the attack forward. On his own, he charged, swinging his blade with an apparent wildness that frightened even the savage denizens of the nightmare island.

Only the elven marshal knew that the wildness was a sham, that each cut was carefully calculated to injure and kill his foes, and yet leave the elf in position to recover quickly, to insure that he didn't leave himself open to any daring retaliation.

More elves were coming from the towers now or pressing up the ladders, and slowly the parapet was being reclaimed by the elves of the Second Division. It was the draconians inside the wall who were being sorely pressed, finally bunched into little pockets here and there. Even the sivaks, with their mighty two-handed swords, could not hold the onslaught of elven steel at bay, and now they were too tightly packed to spread their wings and take to the sky. Most of them died, though a few hurled themselves back over the wall to limp and crawl toward the imagined safety of the woods.

With a look into the camp, Porthios saw the dragon disappear into the river, dark water closing over the sinuous tail with a slight splash. The ogres and their allies had withdrawn from the parapet, slinking back to the woods in admission of defeat. Many of the retreating denizens were limping or leaning on the arms and shoulders of comrades. The more badly injured lay among the corpses of their companions, a gory swath marking the base of the wall where the initial attack had slammed home.

As always, the sudden silence after battle seemed surreal to Porthios. He heard a scream from a wounded elf as the warrior was gingerly carried from the wall by his comrades. It was not truly silent, he realized as he heard the soft voices of elves asking each other how they had fared or inquiring if anyone had seen the fate of this or that bold warrior. The base of the parapet was a seething mass of dull sound as well, hellish with the pitiful moans of wounded draconians and ogres. Somewhere an elf called for his lady, the voice a bubbling gasp that ended in a sickening gurgle of blood.

Griffons began to land in the middle of the palisade, and Porthios saw that most of his Qualinesti had survived the battle. The healers in their silken shelters were busy with the wounded, but it saddened the marshal to see that many of the injured were being shunted off to the side, their injuries judged too serious to waste the limited powers of the elven clerics.

Porthios found Bandial on the shore of the river, where dozens of elves lay dead. They were not marked by wounds, but each face was distorted by an expression of monstrous horror. Tongues protruded from gaping jaws, and eyes bulged with the knowledge that death had come, had reached into lungs with tendrils of green mist and torn away life from the inside.

The boats along the riverbank were still intact, and for a moment the marshal and the general looked at them longingly. Bandial, Porthios suspected, was feeling the same urge that was influencing him.

Yet then he looked back toward the dark forest, toward the corrupt island that sprawled beyond this bloodstained parapet, and his decision—if there had ever been any doubt—was cemented in his mind.

"We march after the bastards tomorrow?" Bandial guessed, his tone grim but not the least bit hesitant.

"Aye, General," Porthios replied. "There's still a job to be done."

* * * * *

Three weeks later, the warriors of the Second Division closed in on the lone hillock on the southern terminus of the island. Behind them lay a forest that was slowly being restored by the nature priests who followed in the warriors' wake. And it was a forest divested of dangerous denizens, for the division's sweep had been thorough and deadly. Porthios knew there wasn't a draconian or ogre anywhere on this island, except for the band that had now gathered on this one outpost of high ground.

It was not a prepossessing force, this remnant. Perhaps two hundred ogres and twice that many draconians had formed a ring on the grassy slopes. Weapons pointed outward, they waited as the companies of elves emerged from the forest to gather in a large circle around the base of the rounded hill.

They had been herded here like cattle, and now they were gathered for a last fight, a battle with a predetermined outcome, but which still must be fought before the conclusion of the campaign.

"They're up on that hill, my lord . . . all of them," Aleaha Tamarkin reported for the Kirath, having skirted the entire elevation since early that morning.

"This is where it ends, then," Porthios said. He felt no elation, so sense of accomplishment as he contemplated this last attack, the culmination to a campaign that had lasted thirty years, had been his own quest for the last two decades.

"And . . . my lord?" Aleaha hesitated but obviously had something else to say.

"What is it?"

"I . . . I wish I could tell you how sorry I am about the ambush. It was my failure and that of my scouts that led to—"

"No, it wasn't!" Porthios cut her off, speaking sternly. "It was my own fault more than anyone's—and how could any of us have known?"

"It's just that we missed them, we Kirath," she insisted. "If we had looked more carefully, stayed on the island longer . . ."

"Then the Kirath would have been killed, just like Cantal-Silaster and the First Division," Porthios shot back. "No, we all did our jobs as best as we could, and that one time, the enemy was ready for us."

His face softened as he acknowledged that his anger was directed at himself, not at this bold scout, nor at any of his brave warriors. "We have to be grateful, at least, that we've brought the matter to a close."

"Aye, my lord," Aleaha replied. Still, her head was low, her eyes downcast as she backed away.

But now there was the last battle to fight. Porthios swung onto Stallyar's back, and the creature's wings pulsed downward as, with a smooth leap, he carried his rider into the sky. Griffons spiraled overhead. Stallyar and Porthios rose to fly in the middle of the formation. The marshal looked over his enemies arrayed on the hill and wished he could take some pleasure from this final battle. He remembered the brave elves of the First Division and knew that they would be avenged here today . . . but even that knowledge was no consolation. It was time for the killing to be over, time for the elven veterans to go home.

Twisting in his saddle, he scanned the horizon, saw the ocean waters gleaming dully to the south. All across this broad marsh, lined with the now healing forest to the north, there was no single sign of the enemy he really sought, the green-scaled horror who, he felt certain, was behind the initial ambush and the subsequent long and bloody campaign.

He felt another pang of regret as he saw the thin ranks of the Second Division companies. These veterans had fought boldly, driven by duty and by a powerful desire to avenge the slaughter of their comrades. They had relentlessly pushed through the fen, butchering the denizens wherever they were encountered. But at the same time, they had suffered casualties, more than would have occurred if the two divisions had been able to work together.

As a result, the remaining Silvanesti elves in his force were significantly less than half of the total that had departed Silvanost a month earlier. The losses were greater than he had suffered on any of his previous campaigns, and it seemed exceptionally tragic that they had come on this, the last march in thirty years of war.

Looking at the ground for this final confrontation below, Porthios knew that still more of his warriors would have to die if they were to charge up that hill. Inevitably the Silvanesti numbers and discipline would carry them through the surrounded rabble, but just as inescapably, brutish ogres and savage draconians, holding the high ground, would be able to exact a horrific cost in blood from their attackers.

Yet there was a way, perhaps, to change that toll. It was not a method that would assuage elven honor, or aid in the thirst for vengeance, but Porthios viewed these two considerations as far less important than saving elven lives.

A gentle nudge with his knees guided Stallyar downward, and the griffon came to rest in the field before Bandial.

"The troops are ready, my lord marshal," reported that

erstwhile general. "Would you care to give the orders to charge?"

"We'll attack, General . . . but not with a charge."

Bandial looked surprised but said nothing. He waited for an explanation.

"Call up your archers," Porthios said. He turned to squint into the sky, looking at the monsters arrayed on the open hillside. "We're going to finish this off with arrows."

* * * * *

"And so they fell without fighting, killed to the last by elven arrows." The dragon spoke without passion, as if describing the extermination of an anthill, or the removal of a nest of mice.

"And you—you lived, but you didn't help them?" the young elf demanded accusingly. He stalked a few paces away, then turned back and glared at the creature.

"Why should I?" retorted the wyrm, his tone genuinely curious.

"They were your comrades!"

"They were nothing! The battle was lost, and there was nothing for me in Silvanesti. Instead, I decided to go away."

"Yes," Samar noted wryly. *"And perhaps that was not such a bad idea."*

"But in Silvanesti, what happened next?" asked the young elf. *"I must know!"*

"You should know—but it is a tale of elves, not dragons," replied the serpent.

"I was not there, not until much later, but I can tell the story," said Samar softly. *"It is not a pretty tale, nor one that should make any elf feel even a twinge of pride."*

"You must tell me!" demanded the other.

"And so I shall. . . ."

Trial in the Sinthal-Elish

Chapter Six

"Two hundred and seventeen Qualinesti flew with this army . . . and two hundred and one of them came back!"

Konnal's voice boomed through the chamber in the Hall of Balif, which was crowded with Silvanesti nobles and high-ranking commoners. The gathering, occurring the day after the Second Division's return to the city, was so large that it was occurring here in the palace, rather than in the smaller council chamber at the base of the Tower of the Stars.

Now Konnal had the rapt attention of every elf present. Porthios sat on the marshal's chair at the front of the rostrum, steeling his face to show no reaction as he listened to this elf's words. He knew what was coming, hated the words, even the speaker, but he had no reply.

For Konnal spoke only the truth.

"More than four thousand Silvanesti sailed down the river . . .

four thousand of our bold sons, warriors we entrusted to the command of this—" the general groped theatrically for the term, making it apparent that he couldn't bring himself to repeat the name of the other nation of elvenkind—"this prince out of the west!"

He paused again, looking at a small piece of paper he held in his hand. On that paper were numbers, though Porthios suspected that the general was fully acquainted with each figure on the sheet. Still, Konnal made a great show of studying the information, and, like the rest of the nobles, generals, and lords, the marshal waited without making a sound.

When Konnal spoke again, his voice was barely a whisper, yet still it carried to the far corners of the marbled chamber.

"Fewer than seventeen hundred of them returned."

"Shame!" The word was hissed by a Silvanesti noble, the elf anonymous among the throng of his fellows. All of them sat on their stools, rigid and stern, their looks cold and accusing. The charge was repeated, picked up, carried with sibilant force throughout the chamber. None shouted it, but every voice, it seemed, echoed it, until the sound washed over Porthics like waves pounding against a beach of sand, driving into his soul, twisting and tearing and flensing his flesh away.

"Shame . . . shame . . . shame . . . shame."

Konnal, the master of timing, allowed the sound to be repeated for a long time, until the resonance had been drilled into every ear, repeating in the depths of every mind, universally condemning the marshal who stood alone on the rostrum. The golden images high on the walls glared down, silent and accusing. Only then did Konnal raise his hand. As if trained to wait for the cue, the elves ceased the chant.

"This is a tragedy . . . a catastrophe . . . a failure," he said grimly. "These facts are apparent to us all, and these facts alone suggest that action is required. But I submit, honored nobles, esteemed senators, brave generals, that this is more than a tragic, catastrophic failure."

He whirled, his cold eyes resting on Porthios, and suddenly, with utter clarity, Porthios saw where Konnal was going. And there was nothing he could do to prevent it, save to feel an insignificant twinge of satisfaction as, with his next words, the general proved that the marshal's instant of foresight was correct.

"I say to you, elves of Silvanesti, that this is nothing less than *betrayal!*"

The hiss of agreement came from all over the hall, a nearly universal sentiment that surprised Porthios with its passion and depth. His first reaction was to flush with anger and scorn. Could these Silvanesti elves really be that *stupid?* He drew a deep breath before he stood and cursed them, knowing that such a course, however gratifying, would only fan the flames of a very dangerous situation.

Instead, he rose from his stool to stand, his expression mild as he regarded the array of hostile glares around him. He spotted a few sympathetic faces—Lord Dolphius shook his head in dismay, while General Bandial's one-eyed visage was locked in an expression of dignified outrage at his fickle countrymen.

Like his expression, Porthios kept his voice calm as he began to speak. Ignoring the undercurrent of muttering, he spoke quietly, thereby forcing the elves in the hall to fall silent in an effort to hear.

"General Konnal is right about a number of things." His opening statement provoked some startled astonishment, though all too many elves nodded in arrogant agreement, as if he could have said nothing else. Grimly he resolved to ignore the prevailing mood, to speak his piece deliberately, carefully, accurately.

"The events on the delta island were catastrophic and tragic. Far too many brave warriors lost their lives. The plan of attack was mine, and the responsibility for its execution lay with me as well." He paused to draw a breath, fairly certain that his calm and reasonable approach would begin to reach these elves. After all, weren't they famed as the calmest and most reasonable people on all Krynn?

"The opposition on the island was well prepared, and our initial—"

"You killed my son!" shouted a noblewoman from the back of the house, and abruptly the Sinthal-Elish rang with echoed cries of outrage. Once again Porthios was shocked by the depth of emotion, and for the first time, he worried that the outcome might indeed go badly for him. Furthermore, it was harder than ever to retain his self-control, to master the rising temper that sought to burst from his expressions and words.

"I did not kill your son. In point of fact, I did everything in my power to save him, just as I have done everything in my power to restore Silvanesti from the effects of Lorac Caladon's nightmare!"

There was still an undercurrent of muttering, and Porthios felt his voice rising as he struggled to be heard. "Is there an elf here who does not remember the state of this nation twenty years ago? Who does not know that I have dedicated those years of my life, that I have worked with my wife—your queen—to wrest this hallowed land from the corruption that, some claimed, would forever make Silvanesti a place of ruin and death?"

"Qualinesti scum!" came another shout, this one in an elder's stern and unforgiving voice. "Your own people lived, while ours died!"

"This is not the fault of Porthios!" interjected another voice. For a moment, the noise in the hall settled to a rumble as the esteemed personage of Aleaha Tamarin stood and spoke. "If you must lay blame, then call out the name of myself and my Kirath scouts! We looked over the island, and we failed to spot the ambush."

"But Porthios was in charge!" shouted another anonymous voice, and the bold scout was shouted down by more elves joining in a chorus of condemnation.

"We're all elves—can't you see that?" demanded Porthios sharply. He shouted in the forceful voice that had carried across a score of battlefields, but even so, the rising swell of noise almost drowned his words in a force of outrage and recrimination.

"Death to the Qualinesti scum!"

"Exile to the traitor!"

More cries, a disjointed volley of rare invective and hateful vituperation, came from all over the hall. Porthios glared at Konnal, who sat calmly on his stool, saying nothing, but expressing his smug satisfaction in a sneer he returned to the marshal. When he realized that he wished he had his sword, Porthios recognized that his own temper was fraying far beyond the boundaries of self-control.

"Elves of Silvanesti, listen to me!"

Somehow Lord Dolphius's voice penetrated the angry crowd, and once again the shouts subsided to a murmured undercurrent. Dolphius, who sat near the front of the Sinthal-Elish, took three strides forward to climb onto the first steps of the rostrum. He turned to address the crowd, first sweeping a hand in an elegant gesture that seemed to encompass every elf in the crowded chamber.

"My people . . . my esteemed elves . . . let us remember who we are. Should we trample over dignity and heritage like a mob of enraged humans? I think not."

With a slight inclination of his head, Dolphius acknowledged the presence of Konnal, high on the side of the chamber. "Our general has made some charges . . . highly inflammatory charges, it is true. But they are just that: accusations. We are not a lynch mob, nor would it serve us any purpose to allow justice to be short-changed by an explosion of rage that belittles us even more than it does the target of our anger."

Dolphius took a breath, and the throng waited for him to continue. "The charge of treason is not one to be leveled lightly. I, for one, do not believe that charge—not for a minute, not for a single heartbeat. I, for one, remember the sacrifices that Porthios of House Solostaran has made during the course of the last thirty years, of the work that he has led . . . that he has followed through to its most bitter conclusion. Yes, my elves, this . . . 'Qualinesti' "—he said the term with a perfect sense of mockery, a scorn that belittled the pretentiousness of those Silvanesti who would use the word as an insult—"deserves credit for the restoration of Silvanesti. I do not think, nor should any rational elf think, that he would have worked so hard only to plot base treachery at the conclusion of his labors."

Konnal's sneer had turned from Porthios to Dolphius, and, watching that haughty expression, the marshal felt a grim foreboding, a sense that this meeting had not heard the last of the general's charges.

"I do not suggest," the senator continued, in a tone of utmost rationality, "that we merely dismiss the charges. They must be examined, debated with thought and foresight, considered with dutiful care. Indeed, there are other charges—tales of missing dragonlances, and of faulty intelligence—that deserve scrutiny as well. But this is not the time, nor is the Tower of Stars the place, for such a trial. I urge you, elves of the Sinthal-Elish, not to act with haste but to consider with wisdom the weighty matter that has been placed before you today."

The hall was mostly silent as Dolphius returned to his seat, but then all eyes turned to the side as Konnal once more rose to his feet. His manner was sorrowful, his expression full of regret, as he began to speak.

"Our esteemed senator is correct. This gathering is not the suitable venue for consideration of such charges. It grieves me, therefore, to declare that circumstances leave me no choice. But under the glare of my erstwhile colleagues' pleas for reason, I must now reveal that there is more to my accusation than I was at first prepared to reveal."

Even Porthios was curious, and though he knew he wouldn't like what he was about to hear, he waited in silence with all the other elves to hear what Konnal said next.

"I have proof, noble elves, that Porthios Solostaran has engaged in the negotiation of a treaty that is a betrayal of our sovereignty, a relinquishment of our heritage, and a seditious mortgaging of the futures of our children and their children."

"That's a lie!" snarled the marshal. "You are a liar, Konnal, and yours are the words that reek of treachery!"

"You say this," Konnal retorted with maddening calm, "but do you deny the existence of the Unified Nations of the Three Races treaty?"

Now the silence was absolute, and Porthios had no idea what to say. He could not deny that he knew about the treaty. He and Alhana had been negotiating the pact with representatives of dwarven Thorbardin and human Solamnia for more than year. Nor could he claim that the treaty wasn't a secret, for the two elves had known that there would be elements in both elven realms who would fiercely resist the notion of such an agreement.

But the pause was growing, and he was acutely conscious of the need to say something even as his mind reeled with the knowledge that Konnal had somehow learned of the document, and that the general's words right now stood a good chance of dashing into ruin all the carefully laid plans and negotiations of the past year.

"That treaty holds promise of peace and safety for the future of all elvenkind." Porthios spoke slowly and carefully, hoping against all fear that his calm demeanor would help the Silvanesti to see reason. "It has been negotiated for many months, with the full knowledge of elven leadership as well as with elements of the dwarven and human realms. When the terms have been established, the document will of course be submitted for study and ratification by the Sinthal-Elish and the Senate of Qualinesti!"

"And there's the catch, esteemed listeners," Konnal cried before the echoes of the marshal's words had begun to fade. "The ruling councils of *two* elven nations, linked, locked under *one* treaty. Well, I have seen the terms of this document—much to the displeasure of our Qualinesti prince, I assure you all—and I can tell you that there is a key component Porthios Solostaran has neglected to mention!"

All ears were hanging on his every word, and now Konnal took the time to relish his pause. Finally he finished with his damning accusation:

"This treaty calls for nothing less than the merging of our august body with that of the upstarts to the west. It makes Silvanesti, my honored listeners, nothing less than a subject territory, a mere *colony* of Qualinesti."

"That's not true!" Porthios shouted, but now his voice was swamped in a massive tide of outrage. Elves were on their feet, stools knocked over, fists waving, foam-speckled lips decrying this foul treachery. Even Dolphius was gaping in shock, while many of the nobles and ladies were surging toward the rostrum, eyes wild, tempers flaring beyond all vestige of control.

The drumlike pounding of the vast bronzed doors some-how cut through the chaos in the chamber, and Porthios looked up in surprise to see scores of elves charging into the chamber. They wore leather jerkins and carried bows and arrows with missiles nocked onto the strings, drawn back and ready to shoot. The room fell into stunned silence as fully two hundred armed warriors poured through the door and arrayed themselves on the outer ring atop the deep well of the senate chamber.

It was with a mixture of shock and relief that Porthios recognized Tarqualan, his Qualinesti captain. These were his elves, the deadly archers who had flown griffons into battle and now marched to the marshal's aid on a different kind of battlefield.

"There's the proof!" Konnal cried, his voice shrill and frenzied. If he was afraid of the archers, he gave no sign. "Armed Qualinesti in the Hall of Balif, the audience chamber of our capital city. I rue the darkness of this bleak day."

One of the archers raised his bow, his silvery arrowhead fixed on the general's breast. Konnal sneered, then pulled his robe aside in what even Porthios had to admit was a magnificent gesture of contempt. "Shoot me if you will. You cannot, either with arrows or words, slay the legacy and future of a magnificent elven nation!"

"Hold!" Porthios cried as the archer's taut fingers showed that he was fully prepared to take the general up on his challenge. "There will be no blood shed in this chamber!"

For a moment, he feared the Qualinesti would shoot anyway, and with a clarity that astounded him, Porthios saw into the future, realized what effect that arrow would have on the peoples of the two elven nations.

It would be the beginning of another Kinslayer War, another conflict the equal of that epic and ultimately tragic struggle. Occurring nearly twenty-five centuries ago, that violent strife had first divided elvenkind in the days of Kith-Kanan and Sithas, the twin sons of the Silvanesti king. It had led to the sundering of the nation, to the creation of Qualinesti as a separate realm. The scars of that war lingered still today, though it had been Porthios and Alhana's sincere hope that the treaty of the three races would have begun the long process of healing at last.

Now, clearly, those hopes were dashed. Porthios felt a stab of gratitude for the loyalty of Tarqualan and his elves. They had risked much, he knew, to invade this chamber. He even wondered if they had saved his life. Certainly the elves here, during the last seconds before the Qualinesti's entrance, had been enraged to the point where murder had become a definite possibility.

"So, Prince of Qualinesti?" It was Konnal again, mocking him with his words. "Is this your will? Shall it be war?"

From the mutterings in the great hall, Porthios knew that a great many of these Silvanesti hoped that the answer would be in the affirmative. Perhaps he made his decision in order to spite those hopes, though in truth he knew it couldn't do that even if he tried. Rather, he had the power right now to influence the futures of the elven peoples.

And he couldn't doom that future.

"Tarqualan, I thank you for your courageous assistance, but I must ask that you put up your weapons. The matters under debate here will be resolved through reason and discussion, despite the attempts of some to bring about a frenzy." He tried to freeze Konnal with an icy glare, but the general, in the full flush of his victory, merely smiled with that haughty condescension that brought Porthios's blood to a boil again. Only with great difficulty did he control his temper.

"I bid you to take your men to your camp . . . and there to wait for word from me. You will offer no harm to Silvanesti, of course. We must show that these inflammatory remarks have no basis in fact. However, neither will you allow General Konnal or any of his lackeys to disrupt your camp and your right to stay there. That is, defend yourselves with such force as you deem necessary."

The Qualinesti captain looked miserably unhappy. He had relaxed the tension on his bow, but the arrow was still ready, and Porthios knew it wouldn't take much to cause the bold warrior to shoot any one of these Silvanesti right through the heart. The marshal drew a deep breath and held up both of his hands.

"Please, my good warrior, I beg you to consider the good of both our peoples. We have both spent many years fighting to remove one nightmare from Silvanesti. The cost has been high, and too much has been lost for us to replace that scourge with another. There will not—there *cannot*—be another Kinslayer War."

"Very well, my lord marshal," Tarqualan said stiffly. "But rest assured that we will be waiting and will pay careful attention to events in the city."

"I understand . . . and again, I thank you."

The archers marched out of the chamber. Through the open doors, Porthios caught sight of fluttering, white-feathered wings and knew that the griffon-riding Qualinesti would follow his orders. Safe in their camp, they would be watchful and ready, and he hoped their presence would help restrain the Silvanesti from any truly rash behavior.

As to events within this chamber, and in the city as a whole, he would have to see what happened.

"You stand charged of a high crime, Prince," declared Konnal smugly. Porthios noted that he was no longer using the Silvanesti-appointed rank of marshal. "And it must be insisted that you be placed in a secure location until those charges can be examined."

Porthios felt again the rising of his outrage, but there had been too much rage already expended in this chamber. He would not add fuel to those fires.

"I look forward to an honest examination of those charges," he said agreeably. "And until then, General, I shall consider myself your prisoner."

*   *   *   *   *

"A treaty?" The dragon was quizzical. "That was the source of the traitor's hatred, the thing that would mean the doom of Porthios?"

"Indeed," replied the elder elf. "That was Konnal's great charge, the accusation that brought Porthios to imprisonment."

"But . . . but why?"

"You'd have to be an elf to understand," declared the younger of the pair.

"And even then," said his companion, "it is a tale with twists and turns aplenty, a story that makes itself hard to believe. . . ."

A Gilded Cage

Chapter Seven

Konnal declared that Porthios would be incarcerated in one of the upper chambers of the Tower of Stars. Since his accuser already held the keys to that sanctified spire, the marshal was immediately marched there under an escort of armed Silvanesti, though Konnal took care to select the guards from the city garrison troops. Porthios was not surprised to see that none of his Wildrunners were allowed anywhere near the detail.

They marched him through the city streets, the same winding lanes that had been the scenes for many of his triumphal returns. Now those avenues were lined with hostile faces, including many elves who jeered or cursed him. Here and there he saw a friendly or pitying face, but he dared not acknowledge these loyal elves. He suspected that, in days to come, such sympathies could cost decent citizens their freedom, property, or more. Instead, Porthios took pride in maintaining a contemptuously aloof manner, refusing to show any reaction to the constant vituperation.

At the base of the tower, Konnal made a great show of withdrawing the Keys of Quinarost from his pouch. He opened the door, then led his prisoner through the quiet Sinthal-Elish chamber to the stairway. They climbed for many minutes, stopping frequently to catch their breath, until at last they halted before a golden door. This was unlocked by one of the guards.

"In here," Konnal ordered with a peremptory wave of his hand. "You will be comfortable, at least until we decide what to do with you."

Porthios passed through, and the metal door slammed shut behind him.

Only then did he start to think about the choice he had made and the predicament he was in. Alhana! His pride had prevented him from fleeing this city, even when Tarqualan would have rescued him. But now he realized that his decision might have cost him any chance of seeing his wife, of witnessing the birth of his child.

Still, he had to face his accusers, to show them that he was right! In a trial, his wisdom, his patience would surely prevail. The more he thought about it, the more he knew he had done the proper thing, that it had been smart not to yield to the promise of Tarqualan's violence. Indeed, Alhana would have wanted, expected, such restraint of him. In the end, he would make her proud.

But he was forced to admit that the Unified Nations of the Three Races treaty was doomed. His wife had worked so hard on the pact, with the help of his sister Laurana and her half-elf husband. Now that word had leaked, Porthios knew that the Silvanesti would never accept the terms of the prospective agreement. As far as these elves were concerned, the treaty was dead.

Surprisingly, he found himself wondering what Tanis Half-Elven would have suggested. He had never been friendly with the man—indeed, when they were youngsters, Porthios had gleefully joined in the cruel teasing that had forever marked Tanis as an outcast from his mother's land of Qualinesti. The prince had even scorned his sister for her choice of "that mixed–race bastard" as her husband. But somehow, over the years, he had been forced to see the strengths that lay so subtly beneath his brother-in-law's skin. Now he almost wished that Tanis were here, that he could ask the half elf's advice or merely share the quiet competence of his presence.

Yet that was just one more thing he couldn't change. With a sigh, Porthios decided instead to take stock of his surroundings, and he immediately noticed that his accommodations were in fact quite comfortable. The chambers were spacious and included a sleeping room with a huge bed, a mattress of soft down draped with a canopy of bright silk. He had a large sitting room, a balcony with a splendid view across nearly two-thirds of the horizon, a good-sized dining room with windows looking across the other directions, and a private cooking chamber. The only structure anywhere around that was higher than his prison was the main summit of the tower, which rose another hundred feet overhead. From his complex of apartments, he could look out of any of several windows and take in the vista of Silvanost in all four directions, observing almost all corners of the island city sprawling across the landscape eight hundred feet below.

He crossed back through the main room, went to the door, and was not surprised to see that it was locked. Porthios knocked loudly, and it opened.

A pair of burly Silvanesti axemen stood beyond the outer door to the apartments, maintaining constant vigilance and presenting uncompromisingly stern aspects. Inevitably the guards were veterans of House Protector, but Porthios noted that neither of them had served him during the recent campaigns to restore Silvanesti. Obviously General Konnal was not taking the chance of assigning to guard duty an elf who might have conflicting loyalties. Furthermore, the tower's top chamber was accessible only by a single flight of stairs, and Porthios had no doubt that there were more guards waiting at the bottom of the tower.

Not that I would try to escape, he argued to himself during one of his many hours of solitude. After all, didn't I come here willingly? Didn't I *stop* Tarqualan when he would have used violence to free me? Still, his reasoning rang hollow as he looked out at the city turning to the bright shades of autumn. He wondered how soon his baby would be born . . . and how was Alhana faring?

He settled into a comfortable chair, somehow drifting off into a sleep so deep that he was surprised when the door opened to reveal one of his guards.

"A visitor," the elf said coldly, stepping back to reveal General Bandial. That venerable warrior wept to see his old commander so mistreated, tears pouring from the elf's one good eye until an embarrassed Porthios bade him to please control his emotions.

"How can they do this to you?" moaned Bandial. "Don't they understand what you've done for them . . . for us all?"

"At this point, I think Konnal has them more concerned about what I'll do to them in the future. But what did he have to say after he had me locked up here?"

"Funny thing, that," Bandial admitted. "Konnal left the city again right after you were brought here. No one knows where he's gone, though there's a rumor he traveled all the way to Palanthas!"

Porthios shook his head. "That makes no sense at all. Not that I miss the arrogant wretch. I could use a few more days to calm myself down. It wouldn't do any good to throttle him, not with his bullyboys standing outside my door."

"D'you want me to take care of those fellows?" growled the loyal general. "I could bring a few veterans of the Second Division with me next time. . . ."

Porthios chuckled, a dry sound more bitter than humorous. "Tempting as it is, I have to ask you not to. I've gone this far without resorting to violence against my own kind. No, it's best to let this matter play out in the senate."

Bandial looked as if he didn't exactly agree with that sentiment, but he said nothing.

"What of Tarqualan and the Qualinesti? Have they been

left alone?" Porthios worried about the two hundred griffon riders from his own nation. They weren't as numerous as a Silvanesti army, but with their fierce fliers, they were highly mobile, and he had convinced himself that they would be able to take care of themselves.

"As much as could be expected. The Sinthal-Elish has discontinued food shipments to their camp, but with their griffons, they of course have no trouble taking all the deer they can eat. Konnal posted several companies of Silvanesti to keep an eye on them, but there hasn't been any trouble."

"Good—and I say that more for the sake of the Silvanesti than Tarqualan's bunch. I daresay it wouldn't take much to set him off."

"I know," Bandial agreed. "But you've got to realize that there are a lot of us Silvanesti on your side, too. We don't like what's happened to you, or to our comrades on the griffons."

"That means a lot to me, old friend."

The two old warriors talked for a little while longer, but in the end, Bandial left without persuading Porthios to try to escape.

And in all truth, as his old comrade made his farewells, Porthios was not disappointed to be left alone with his thoughts, his brooding. He found himself remembering many things, with thoughts of his wife growing strong among the tangle of his feelings. How had he let so many years pass during which he'd viewed their marriage as a cold alliance? Now that affection had blossomed between them, now that the miracle of a child was before them, he feared that he'd wasted too much time.

He worried about her status in Qualinesti, wished for some word from Alhana or Samar. With autumn advancing, he knew that her pregnancy was well advanced. The baby would be born in another month or two, maybe even sooner. But still the west was silent.

Several more days passed, and the Prince of Qualinesti finally got some clue as to his accuser's whereabouts when General Konnal came to visit him, accompanied by an elf in the regal white robes of a Qualinesti senator.

"Rashas!" snarled Porthios, immediately recognizing the pinched features of the elf who had long led the most conservative faction of the Thalas-Enthia, the senate of Qualinesti. This body had long been opposed to a merger between the nations; indeed, it had been in resistance to the Thalas-Enthia where Alhana and Porthios had first found common cause.

"I see you are learning some of the virtues of elven cooperation," the haughty noble said with a sneer. "This is the end of your foolish dream. Ironic, isn't it, that you meet the same fate here that your wife has met in your own homeland?"

"You bastard!" Porthios threw himself at Rashas, but somehow one of the axemen from the door interposed himself. With a casual swing of the haft of his weapon, the warrior knocked the Speaker of the Sun backward, and Porthios tumbled heavily to the floor.

"Oh, and you may be interested to know that Alhana's man, Samar, has also been arrested and imprisoned, charged with spying and sentenced to die. I anticipate that the sentence will soon be carried out."

Porthios growled, slowly rising to his feet. Only the presence of the keen-edged axe prevented him from once again rushing at the hated senator.

"Patience, my prince," said Konnal, clucking his tongue. "How do you think it looks . . . two Qualinesti squabbling like children here in the hallowed tower of Silvanost? Surely you have a greater sense of heritage than that."

"This . . . this *mongrel* does not deserve to be called Qualinesti," Rashas said in scorn, leaning forward as if he'd like nothing more than to spit upon Porthios. "He married outside of his clan. He would devote his life to knocking down the barriers that the gods have seen fit to raise."

"There are some things, Senator, upon which we can agree," Konnal noted with a stiff bow. "Now, as to the matter that brings you here? . . ."

"Yes." Rashas straightened, with visible effort arranging his facial features into a bland mask. "I have made this journey for a single purpose, Porthios. I require that you relinquish the Medallion of the Sun."

His hand going instinctively to the golden disk that he wore beneath his tunic, Porthios gaped at the senator. "You're mad!"

"Hardly . . . rather, I am a voice of sanity in a world grown increasingly unbalanced."

"Yet you expect to become to become the Speaker of the Sun, just like that?"

Rashas looked horrified. "Me? Speaker? Of course not!"

"Then what do you want with the medallion?"

"I shall bestow it upon the elf who will become our next Speaker, the elf who will insure that Qualinesti purity remains untainted!"

Konnal looked angry at these words about "Qualinesti purity." Porthios realized that it was a sign of both men's fanaticism that they were willing to work together to insure that their two nations remained ever separated. He could only shake his head at such insanity and then stare mutely at the gloating Rashas.

"Surely you are curious. You must want to know who your successor will be!"

"I shall have no successor. Not yet, for surely *you* know that the medallion must be given willingly in order for the new Speaker to wear it as a sign of office."

"Oh, you will give it willingly, believe me."

Porthios felt a chill at the words, and immediately he thought of his pregnant wife, held in Qualinesti under the orders, undoubtedly, of this madman.

"Your time in Silvanesti has perhaps worn heavily on your memory," Rashas went on, his lips tightening slightly as he failed to arouse a response from Porthios. "You do recall that you have a sister?"

"Lauralanthalasa? *Laurana?* She's a remarkable person, a credit to all elvenkind to be sure, but I can't believe that a stickler for tradition such as you would consider placing a woman on the Speaker's throne."

Rashas looked properly horrified again. "Of course not. But are you so out of touch that you failed to hear that she has a son . . . a strapping youth, almost fully grown by now."

"Gilthas?" Porthios almost laughed out loud. "*He* will be your new Speaker of the Sun?"

"Do not underestimate the lad. I think he will do a splendid job . . . with plenty of guidance from the Thalas-Enthia, of course."

"Guidance from you, you mean!"

"However you care to phrase it, I'm sure you begin to see the circumstances. It is quite an ideal solution, in truth."

His jaw clenched, Porthios could barely spit out the words. "I know Gilthas. I have seen him. But he is still a child! And his father is Tanis Half-Elven. Your new speaker would be one-quarter human!"

"It has been many years since you have seen him. He is no longer a child. As to that last matter, it is a trifling thing, especially since the pure blood of House Solostaran runs in his veins, thanks to his mother's excellent lineage."

This was too horrifying. The walls spun around, and the room seemed to cant crazily under his feet. Porthios wanted to sit, to gasp for breath, even to vomit. But he wouldn't give Rashas the satisfaction of witnessing his discomfort. Instead, he masked his inner turmoil with a glare of pure loathing.

"The fact remains that I wear the medallion. You would have to kill me to get it. And if you do, if you steal it off my body like a ghoul, the power of the Sun enchantment will be broken and a curse will fall up the realm."

"My dear Porthios, what do you think I am? A barbaric human? I would never jeopardize the future of Qualinesti thus," Rashas protested, with a great air of wounded dignity. "As I said before, you will give it to me willingly."

"You *are* mad!"

"I tell you, no!" The senator's voice was a snarl, his face suddenly distorted by anger, and Porthios knew that his remark had struck very close to the truth. Laboriously Rashas struggled to regain his composure. He drew a deep breath.

"I do, however, hold your wife and your unborn child under guard in conditions of relative comfort in Qualinesti. If you would like to see Alhana again . . . if you would have your child breathe his first of the sweet air of Krynn, then you will relinquish the medallion."

"You dare to threaten the queen?"

"I do what must be done. If harm comes to her, the fault will be yours!"

Porthios looked at Konnal, who was watching the exchange stone-faced. "Alhana is the princess of your people, heir to the throne of Silvanesti!" he exclaimed. "Yet you would be a party to this extortion?"

"It is for the greater good," Konnal replied, his eyes like ice. "I can see that with the utmost clarity, though I would not expect you, who was arranging a treaty that would betray all the elven realms, to understand such a lofty purpose!"

"I understand the purposes of greed and corruption, of blind ambition and the pure, selfish lust for power. I see those purposes here in you both!" Porthios felt his self-control slipping, and for once he didn't care. He pointed at Rashas, at Konnal, allowed his voice to rise to a shout that thundered through the chambers, rocked the door on its hinges. "I see the talons of the Dark Queen sinking into you both, pulling you in ways that will doom the elven nations to repeat the mistakes of the past. You are sickening in your sanctimonious posturing, your talk of 'the greater good'! Shame! Shame on you both!"

Konnal recoiled as if he had been struck, then stepped forward, his hand reaching for his sword. Porthios wished the general would attack him. Even bare-handed as he was, he would have relished the physical release of a fight.

But it was Rashas who remained cool, who laid a hand on Konnal's arm—a hand that the Silvanesti regarded with disgust, as if it were a venomous spider—and halted the general's rush toward violence.

"See . . . see how thick? How he refuses, is unable to see? It's tragic, really. He was once a wise man."

The senator stared at Porthios, his expression haughty and contemptuous. "I assure you that I am not bluffing. I will not enjoy causing harm to your wife, but I will do so if you make it necessary. So please, for Alhana's good and for the well-being of your child, relinquish the medallion."

The elven prince put his hand to the golden disk he wore

on his chest. As he had countless times before, Porthios sensed its unwelcome weight, felt again the burden that came from its presence. How many times he had wanted to give it to someone else, or even to cast it away, let it sink into the murky waters of some trackless swamp.

Yet now, strangely, he found himself coveting the Sun Medallion as he never had before. He would give it to Rashas—he had to, for he knew that the senator's threat was sincere—but he would hate to part with it.

And for a single terrifying instant as his fingers wrapped around the curved disk of ancient gold, his eyes saw down the winding tunnels of the future. There were many paths there, many tracks his life could take. But there was a certainty along them all:

He knew that he would never wear this medallion again.

With a wrenching pull, unmindful of his own gasp of physical and spiritual agony, he tore the thing away, snapped the golden links that held it around his neck. Porthios staggered under the assault on his senses as he reached out his hand, didn't feel the medallion fall from his nerveless fingers to roll across the floor, trailing its chain with soft clinks as it curled to a rest underneath a couch.

Quickly, but with a gesture of distaste, Rashas dropped to his knees and reached under the divan to seize the medallion. His eyes might have flashed as he raised it to his face, stared at the intricate facets that winked and sparkled like the disk's namesake, but Porthios saw none of that. His eyes blurred with tears, he slumped at last into a chair and buried his face in his hands.

When he finally looked up, the two elves were gone.

* * * * *

Another week dragged by, a time when autumn roared into full fury. This was a season that came forcefully to Silvanesti, and these were days of unrelieved rain and chill. Porthios looked from his balcony across the city of Silvanost, noting the bleak swath of the gray Thon-Thalas, the shivering quality of the once splendid gardens.

It was as this early cold wave reached its nadir that General Konnal and an escort of axe-wielding elves again came to see Porthios in his chambers atop the Tower of Stars.

"You're looking well," the Silvanesti of House Protector declared with apparent sincerity. "You must be getting some sun on your balcony. I had feared that your skin would fade to a wintery pallor, but you still have the healthy tan of an outdoorsman."

"Praise the gods for small favors," Porthios replied wryly. "Tell me why you're here."

"Such abruptness. Not very elven, wouldn't you agree?" Konnal looked around archly. "Are you too busy? You have no time for pleasantries or civilized conversation?"

"There's little either elven or civilized about treachery, coercion, and betrayal," snapped the prisoner. "And in the glaring presence of these significant traits, I see no need to place a layer of frippery over our interaction. I ask you again, what do you want?"

Konnal shrugged away the insulting tones. "I know you have your sources of information—even a one-eyed elf can read the writing on the wall—but I thought for once I would bring you fresh news."

Porthios glowered but didn't respond. Konnal continued as if he had been invited to speak.

"For obvious reasons, you are no longer able to function in your command role. I thought I would be the one to tell you that the senate has appointed a new Military Governor of Silvanesti."

"Yourself, of course."

Konnal merely nodded, a mild, polite bow of his head as if he were accepting sincere congratulations. "The baton of rank was found in the Palace of Quinari and bestowed upon me with the proper ceremony. I thought, since the action affects you so directly, that you should be told right away."

If Konnal was expecting to goad Porthios into an outburst, the Qualinesti resolved to disappoint him. Instead, he asked a question that had been lingering in his mind as the days of his imprisonment had grown into weeks.

"What are you going to do with me? In the Tower of Stars, you made lots of noises about a trial—and I warn you, General, I will welcome the opportunity to air my situation in a public hearing." Porthios derived some small satisfaction from his failure to address Konnal by his official rank.

But the new governor apparently took no notice. "My dear Porthios, of course there will be no trial. Those remarks were all for show, for the benefit of the senate and the nobles—and, of course, to highlight the differences between us."

"I'm not surprised. You servants of darkness have good cause to fear the light that always shines from the truth."

For the first time, Konnal revealed a glimmering of his temper. "It is you who serve the darkness, you fool—you who would tear down the legacy of thirty centuries of culture and civilization!"

Porthios smiled, enjoying the flush that darkened Konnal's stiff features. Casually he asked again, "You didn't answer my question. What are you going to do with me?"

The Silvanesti lord drew a deep breath, calmed himself with visible effort.

"I have prepared a document. You will read it and affix your signature. After that, you will be free to leave."

Porthios laughed. "A confession, no doubt? An admission of this treachery you've dreamed up?"

Konnal shrugged. "It's an admission that you sent Silvanesti troops into a massacre, knowing that you would weaken us and leave us vulnerable to control by Qualinesti."

"You're insane!"

"No . . . I'm just determined. And I assure you that your signature is the only thing that will earn you your freedom."

"You can't hold me. No walls could hold me without my cooperation! I can see no reason why I should stay here, and thus I inform you that I shall make arrangements to leave at the earliest opportunity."

Konnal smiled. "I think the guards might have a little to say about that."

"If you think I have remained here because of your guards, then *you* are the fool. If departing means escaping, then I assure you that I will escape and return to my own homeland and my own wife."

"There is another thing you should know. We have received word from Qualinesti—after all, you have good cause to know that the barriers between our two peoples are not as impenetrable as the typical elf might assume. The Thalas-Enthia has been active during this season."

"I assume Gilthas Solostaran has been sworn in as Speaker of the Sun and Stars."

"Naturally—but that is not my information."

"Go on." Porthios once again felt that sickening nausea, a premonition that he was going to hear some very bad news.

"The Thalas-Enthia, under the leadership of your young nephew, has endorsed the authority of the Sinthal-Elish of Silvanesti regarding the matter of your imprisonment. You are to remain here as our guest for as long as we deem it necessary in preparation for your trial."

"Which trial, as you told me, shall never occur."

Konnal shrugged. "A detail, but, yes, I can see where you might deem it important."

"And if your guards can't stop me, what force does an edict from a thousand miles away have to hold me in my cage?"

"Just this: The Thalas-Enthia has agreed that if you come to Qualinesti without signing the confession, you will be branded an outlaw. Your property will be forfeit, your legacy forgotten."

"And if I have signed, then I will be seen as a weakling and a traitor," snapped the prince.

Konnal shrugged. "Still, you will be free to go anywhere else, do whatever you want. Sign this and be away from here."

Porthios glared without speaking.

"Here is the document." The usurper laid the hateful parchment on the table, but Porthios didn't even look at it. "Sign it and leave with our permission."

"A traitor only to myself," Porthios declared bitterly.

"I repeat, it's the only way you'll leave."

"Unless I escape."

Konnal appeared to think about this response. "I don't think I can allow that to happen." With a meaningful gesture, the new governor nodded to the elves who stood at each of his sides.

Porthios looked at the two elves flanking Konnal. Each was a huge, strapping warrior and held his axe as if he knew how to use it—and was more than willing to use it right now. He couldn't resist a goad.

"Did you only bring two of them? Not very careful, for a cautious politician such as yourself."

"Two will be enough," Konnal declared grimly.

"What did he promise you?" Porthios asked the question of the axemen in a tone of idle curiosity. "Jewels? Whores? What's the price for assassinating an elven prince?"

There was no answer, though the pair of warriors stiffened visibly.

"Your names will go down in history, you know. Did he tell you that? Of course, you might think you'll be heroes—certainly this craven being, this so-called governor, would want you to think that. But in the end, Astinus Lorekeeper will write the truth. You will be known assassins, murders, wretches. . . ."

Konnal drew a deep breath. "There is the paper. Sign it and live. I give you the night to consider. Tomorrow I shall demand an answer, and I assure you that my tactics will not be so gentle."

* * * * *

The dragon looked puzzled. "Why didn't he just kill Porthios right then? A dragon would have done so."

Samar turned to the younger elf. "Do you know why?"

"He did not dare to take the political risk. Konnal was, and still is, based on a very treacherous foundation of support."

Samar nodded. "So he wanted that confession. It would give him legitimacy."

"And you—did Rashas really have you imprisoned and sentenced to die?" asked the dragon.

"For a short time. I had good help—a mage of black magic and

Tanis Half-Elven helped me to escape. It was the three of us who rescued the queen and made our way out of Qualinesti."

"But you did not return to rescue Porthios?" stated Aerensianic.

"That was our plan," Samar declared, "but we could not proceed—my queen's pregnancy was too far advanced. Indeed, we had barely passed the borders of Qualinesti before her labor began. . . ."

Flight Into Exile

Chapter Eight

Porthios found himself pacing slowly around the large room. He knew beyond doubt that he faced assassination on the morrow. He would never sign the shameful confession, and Konnal couldn't afford to let him live. Yet despite his bluster to Konnal, he did not have an actual plan of escape. Given time, he could have come up with something, but events were moving faster than his own ability to control them. Therefore, it seemed a certainty that Konnal would have him killed.

He found the prospect depressing and spiritually draining, though, surprisingly enough, he wasn't frightened. He thought of Alhana and missed her more poignantly than ever before. Wondering about the baby, he tried to guess if his child would be a boy or a girl. His despair darkened at the awareness that he would never know.

Still aimless, he drifted from the doors onto his balcony.

The autumn chill was bracing, invigorating, and he started to think about trying to live. Escape. . . He needed a plan.

The ground was eight hundred feet below, and the sides of the tower were sheer marble. There was no way to climb down. He needed time to think, to contact his allies outside the city, but his time was running out.

Below him, Silvanost was a vast, ghostly white vista. The pure marble and crystal of myriad structures absorbed the starlight, softly reflecting upward. Even the gardens had their sources of brightness, as phosphorescent waters trilled from small fountains and blossoms of luminous flowers glowed and shimmered in precise, artistic patterns.

It should have been a soothing vista, but it had the opposite effect on Porthios. He found himself pacing the length of his balcony, wishing for wings. The ground below seemed an unattainable goal, distant and aloof. The shifting patterns of brightness and starglow taunted him even as he scorned them for the false quietude they portrayed.

Silvanost was a hateful city, he suddenly saw, and it was emblematic of this whole benighted nation. These elves hid behind a facade of grace and mastery, but it was merely a shell for prejudice and arrogance that had been nurtured beyond reason for more than three thousand years.

He laughed bitterly at an image that flew into his mind: He should hurl himself from this height and smash himself against the city as a last, futile gesture of his scorn. No doubt several haughty Silvanesti would be physically sickened by the sight of his corpse. But the notion instantly faded, and not from any impulse of self-preservation. Instead, he pictured the young workers of House Gardener, elves he had known and befriended over the last two decades. They would find his body, and they would be affected by the horrible sight for the rest of their lives.

It was odd, he thought, how when he looked at the city as a whole, all he saw was a blanket of oppression and self-righteous blindness. Yet when he thought of these elves as individuals, as commoners like his servant Allatarn or the hard-working gardeners, nobles such as Dolphius and Aleaha, they were good and decent people. Not so very different from Qualinesti, if he was truly honest with himself.

"Then why do we work so hard to hurt, to kill each other?" he whispered, feeling his voice swept away into the vastness of the sky. He leaned forward, laying his head on the rail, too tired to do anything else.

Silver shimmered in the night, a flash of movement beyond the balcony, and at first he thought the starglow had swelled into a flare of brightness. But then the motion solidified, and he saw a griffon gliding past, wings spread and motionless.

"Stallyar!" he gasped, his voice loud in the vast silence of the night.

Once again thoughts of escape, of freedom, rose within him. He watched in joy as the magnificent creature reached the edge of the balcony, used eagle talons to grasp the rim of the wall, then land his full weight on the powerful, feline rear legs. Soundlessly the griffon laid his wings flat, easily slipping over the wall to crouch on the ledge. Bright yellow eyes, reflecting more than starlight, fixed upon the stunned elf's face.

And then Porthios rushed forward, wrapping his arms around the feathered neck, feeling the gentle beak over his shoulder, nudging and scratching his back. He allowed himself a moment of profound emotion, trembling, feeling stinging moisture in his eyes. "How did you know, old friend? How did you know to come for me?"

Only when he opened his eyes did Porthios see movement beyond Stallyar. Another griffon came to rest on the balcony, and this one had a rider. The prisoner came around the side of his faithful steed, then paused as he saw that the newcomer was bearded. He carried no sword, though the ends of a bow and arrows jutted over his shoulder.

Porthios halted in shock, momentarily speechless as he recognized the griffon rider.

"Hello, Prince," said Tanis, his voice as level as his gaze.

Not "my prince," Porthios reflected . . . not from the husband of his sister, the grown man who had been tormented and scorned by royal Qualinesti as a lad.

"Hello, Half-elf," he replied. He felt a rising wave of anger but forced himself to bite it back. There were too many questions, too much urgency, for him to yield to old rivalries. Yet he had to wonder, why Tanis?

"I bring word of your wife," the half-elf said by way of answer.

"What about her? Did you see her? How is she? *Where—?*" His old prejudice was forgotten as the elf's mind instantly focused on impending news.

Looking around at the wide, silent view, Tanis nodded toward the doors behind Porthios. "Hadn't we better go inside?"

"Yes, but be quiet. There are guards."

"So I gathered," whispered the half-elf. "I come from Tarqualan's camp outside the city. He told me about your status."

"Alhana—where is she? Did Rashas—"

Tanis held a finger to his lips, and Porthios realized that, in his agitation, he was starting to raise his voice.

"There's a great deal to tell, but know that when I left her she was well . . . and out of Qualinesti. Samar and I were able to spirit her away. She would have come to see you herself, except that her pregnancy has become too advanced. Indeed, brother of my wife, I expect you might become a father any day now."

"Where is she? *Where?*"

"In Solace, at the Inn of the Last Home. She was showing signs of early labor when I departed, and that was just yesterday."

"I must go to her!" Porthios said.

"That's why I came," Tanis said. "Samar and I talked to Alhana. We decided that he should stay with her and I'd come for you."

"Yes, yes, of course." Practical considerations had been pushed far to the side of the prince's brain, but Porthios raised an eyebrow at one thing the half-elf had said. "You were in Solace yesterday? But that's more than a week's flight, even on a fast griffon!"

"I had magical help, both with the escape and with my journey to Silvanesti."

"But what mage has that kind of power?" asked Porthios.

Tanis maintained a grim silence, looking directly at the prince, and then Porthios began to understand. "A dark elf?"

"One of the Silvanesti," Tanis agreed with a slow nod. "One who took up the magic of the black robes and so was banned from his people forever."

"And one whose name may never be uttered among elves," Porthios said, even as his mind voiced the word: *Dalamar*.

He pointed to the sheet of parchment from Konnal, still sitting on the table. "Your timing is very good. That is my death warrant, signed for tomorrow."

"They wouldn't dare!" Tanis declared, appalled.

"You'd be surprised at what they dare."

The half-elf nodded grimly. "Maybe I wouldn't be. In many ways, it's the same in Qualinesti—the Thalas-Enthia ruled by isolationist fools, my own son forced to don the medallion of Speaker."

"And the treaty of the three races . . . it is finished there as well?" asked Porthios, veering away from the subject of the throne that had once been his.

"Yes—killed by Rashas. And you should know that you would be in danger if you return there."

"I realize that. But—"

The doors opened with a crash, and four Silvanesti guards spilled into the room. They halted halfway across the entryway, and Porthios was impressed to realize that Tanis had dropped his bow off his shoulder, nocked and drawn an arrow, and taken aim in the instant that had passed since the guards entered. The steel-bladed arrowhead was fixed toward the heart of the first sentry, whose face had blanched into a deathly pallor.

"No—don't kill him!" Porthios declared, sensing that the half-elf was about to release his missile.

"I won't, but they should know that I could," Tanis replied grimly.

Porthios addressed the Silvanesti, his voice harsh and demanding. "Tell your master that I'm going . . . and that my vengeance will take time. But he should take care never to relax his guard."

The first guard nodded. One of the others, partially shielded by his companion, replied, "We'll tell him."

In another instant, the two men, different in race and temperament but united by ties to a sister and wife, had ducked onto the balcony, mounted the two griffons, and taken to the air.

PART II

QUALINESTI

Prologue

"They flew for many days," Samar said, "leaving Silvanesti that very night."

"And they came to the Inn of the Last Home," said the young elf. "I know this, for my mother told me that my father arrived in time to see me born."

"You are Silvanoshei, the son of Porthios?" The dragon seemed genuinely surprised.

"The name means 'the Hope of Silvanos,' " explained the young elf.

"Then why do you come to me for the tale of your father's life?"

"There is much I already know—my mother and Samar have taught me. But there are other details about that tumultuous year that are vague, and some of those are facts that you can fill in." Silvanoshei looked at the dragon with a pensive

114

expression. "I know that it was at the end of the year three hundred and eighty-two that you decided to fly west as well . . . and I know that you came to Qualinesti. But why?"

"I will explain, but . . ." The dragon turned his slitted yellow eyes to Samar, allowing his leather lids to droop disarmingly. "Do you know that it is very uncomfortable sitting upright with my back pressed against the wall? Let me relax. I will not attack you. After all, I myself am curious as to where this tale is going. I should like to hear the ending of the story myself."

"Very well." The warrior relaxed his hold on the dragonlance, allowing the great serpent to settle more comfortably onto his bed, which consisted of scattered coins, bits of jewelry, and assorted boots, belts, and other articles of clothing. It was a relatively pathetic hoard for a dragon of Aeren's size and age, but he merely shrugged.

"This was a place that called to me when I knew that I would at last have to move. Of course, I would miss my home in the south. In many ways Silvanesti was perfect for me. When I first came there, trees were thick and verdant, and the woodlands offered plenty of food. Water was everywhere, and for a long time, I was free to do whatever I wanted.

"I had dwelled there for the thirty winters after the Draconian War—the war you two-legged people call the War of the Lance. Those were good years, but those times were over. Your father was finished reclaiming the land, and my offspring were all slain, killed through the years by elven arrows and by those horrid dragonlances. If I had wished to remain, I would have had to skulk through the tamed gardens and keep my presence secret from the elves.

"And I remembered this place, the forest called Qualinesti, for it had been described to me by the elven traitor. It was a place in the west, and the elf had claimed that it was a wild woodland, very unlike the subdued and formal setting that Silvanesti had become. There were great trees, he had said, and vast realms of forest.

"And so I came here to live out my years in peace."

"But peace is not what you found," Silvanoshei noted

wryly. "After all, as I said, I know much of the story of my first year of life. My mother has told me many times how she saw Tanis for the last time on the day after my birth as he turned toward his wife and his home . . . and his destiny in a war that had yet to begin. And how, when I was only a few months old, she swaddled me in the *tai-thall* that she wore on her back and we took flight on the back of a griffon, flying beside my father as we made for the forests of his homeland. "

"I remember that flight," Samar said. "We flew with Tarqualan and his two hundred scouts, all of us spurning the authority of the Thalas-Enthia, bound for a life as outlaws in the forest."

"The elves of two lands had made my father an outlaw." Silvanoshei shook his head in disbelief.

"That much is true," Samar noted. "But the land, the elves, the entire situation in Qualinesti was nothing like the place we had left behind. . . ."

Speaker of the Sun

Chapter Nine

Spring, 383 AC

He looked out from the top of the Tower of the Sun, his view encompassing the place that he knew to be the most beautiful city in all Krynn. Ivory spires jutted from the pastoral groves that sprawled like a carpet across the landscape a thousand feet below. From his lofty vantage, he could see three of the four elegant bridges that bordered Qualinost, strung like tendrils of crystal and silver across the sky. Below, in the center of the city, he could see the top of a rounded hill, the great Hall of the Sky, with its mosaic map of Qualinesti and the surrounding lands.

The dominant buildings of the city were towers, some paneled with wood and resembling the shapes of living trees, others splendid structures of rose quartz rising amid the groves so that just the summits were in view, narrow spires jutting above the canopy of foliage. Though elsewhere the woodlands were browned and crispy, suffering under the onslaught of this season's unnatural heat, here in the city everything was green, carefully watered and tended by skilled elven gardeners.

Beyond the eastern and western boundaries of the city, the view from the tower almost masked by the thick growth of trees, the landscape plunged into a pair of deep ravines, wherein flowed the waters of the two branches of the Elf-stream. Deep and shadowed within its gorges, the brooks trickled and meandered to a confluence at the north of the city. Those ravines, so well screened by foliage, were more effective than any moats in blocking unwelcome intruders from reaching Qualinost.

To the south, in between the branches of the stream, the ground rose in a series of steep hills, and from this high vantage he could see all the way to the snowcapped whiteness of the High Kharolis. That was dwarven territory, he knew, foreign lands, though at a time not very long ago a treaty had been negotiated, a pact that would have sealed the peace between dwarf and elf as the Pax Tharkas had done a millennium before. It grieved him to know that the events that had brought him here, to this high tower, had also shattered the chance of that treaty's ratification. With his ascendancy had come retrenchment for the races of Krynn, elves and dwarves and humans withdrawing unto themselves, waiting, watching . . . and fearing the events that the future might bring.

He was Gilthas Solostaran, Speaker of the Sun, ruler of mighty Qualinesti, the greatest elven nation on Krynn.

And he was a mere figurehead, a puppet controlled by the elves who had placed him on this high throne and who could knock him off of his exalted seat with the casual ease used to swat a meddlesome insect. He was a tool of the Thalas-Enthia, the hidebound senators who had schemed and plotted and fought to insure that nothing in the world would ever change.

His mother was an elven princess, daughter of the revered Speaker Solostaran, who had guided his people through exile during the War of the Lance. She was a heroine of the world, the Golden General who had led armies against the dragon highlords. And his father was Tanis Half-Elven, a Hero of the Lance, a leader in that same war.

Ah, but there was so much more to his father. . . a half-breed bastard, an elf who had proudly grown and maintained a beard as a symbol of his half-human parentage! Tanis, who was banned from his son's kingdom, had been branded an outlaw, threatened with death should he dare come to Qualinesti again. Gilthas uttered a sharp bark of laughter as he thought of the irony. He was one quarter human, yet for the purposes of the Thalas-Enthia, he was regarded a purer elf than his uncle Porthios.

It was Porthios whom Gilthas could not help thinking of as the rightful Speaker of the Sun. Porthios, who had given up his medallion of leadership under coercion, because his wife and unborn child had been a hostage of the Thalas-Enthia. And Porthios, who had at last escaped from Silvanesti and disappeared into exile.

Yet his power had disappeared with him. Gilthas knew that he had none of the influence, none of the might that was the rightful accessory to the crown that fit so uneasily upon his young head. But even now, when that knowledge dragged him down, threatened to mire him in a swamp of despair, he felt at least a glimmer of pride, of acceptance, and of destiny. There was no longer an arrow pointed at Alhana Starbreeze's heart. He could walk away from this place, throw down his medallion of office and, if he so decided, just leave.

He would not do that.

"Damned griffons—the beasts should have their wings plucked, their loins roasted on a slow fire!"

Senator Rashas, esteemed leader of the Thalas-Enthia and the elf who had placed Gilthas on his throne, wiped the sweat from his brow as he entered the lofty tower chamber. He looked at the Speaker crossly. "Why don't you stay on the lower levels, where you can be reached when you're needed?"

Gilthas shrugged, keeping his expression bland. "I like it up here."

"Well, it's a damned nuisance, you staring off into space all the time instead of attending to matters of your office."

"You mean such matters as you leave for my consideration . . . what color of roses to adorn the banquet tables, that
sort of thing?" The young speaker was feeling bold and
allowed his words to show the fact. He feared Rashas—well
he knew the punishments the senator was capable of inflict-
ing, when the elder's fearsome temper was released—but
Gilthas had enough of his mother's and father's sense of
pride that he couldn't entirely bite his tongue even when
silence was the politic choice.

Apparently today Rashas was not going to bother with a
rebuke.

"You need to be ready in two hours. There's an emergency
meeting of the Thalas-Enthia called for noon today."

"And how could the senate meet without their Speaker to
preside?" Gilthas noted sarcastically.

Now Rashas looked at him with narrowed eyes, and the
young elf felt a stab of fear. Perhaps he had gone too far. He
tried to force himself to stand straight, to meet the cold glare of
that icy gaze, but after a few seconds, Gilthas found himself
looking sheepishly at the floor.

"Such a childish attitude does not befit an elf of your high
station," Rashas declared. "No doubt it's that human blood
again. I'd hoped you'd begin to outgrow it by now."

Gilthas knew that Rashas was, in fact, grateful for his
human blood. He assumed that it was an ancestry of weakness, that it would help make the Speaker malleable to the will
of the Thalas-Enthia. There was a time when the younger elf
would have agreed with him. But now, after he had had long
days to reflect on his father's courage and had learned more
about the reputation Tanis Half-Elven had earned throughout
Krynn, he was not so sure.

"What is the purpose of the meeting?" he asked.

"There is word from the western frontiers, just confirmed
by messenger this dawn. Our trade routes with Ergoth and
Solamnia are being plagued with banditry."

"Then the reports last week were not just rumors?" Gilthas
asked, unable to keep a twinge of triumph from his voice. He

had urged that the senate act when they had first learned of a plundered steel caravan, but the Thalas-Enthia had disbelieved the elf who reported it because he was a mere woodland elf who had been traveling in the company of humans. Gilthas had suggested that the humans be interviewed as well, but the senate would not allow the men into the hallowed chamber at the base of this lofty tower.

"They have been confirmed by reliable reports. Now it is appropriate that the senate consider some action."

By "reliable," Gilthas knew that Rashas meant either his own spies or the word of some wealthy elf of high caste and unimpeachable reputation.

"If the griffons weren't being so uncooperative," the senator continued, "then we would have had word days ago!"

"I see." Gilthas refrained from saying the remark that rose to the tip of his tongue: If the Thalas-Enthia had treated Alhana Starbreeze with respect, instead of with extortion and imprisonment, the griffons would not have been offended. As it was, the beasts that had ever been loyal helpmates to the elves of Qualinesti had abandoned their ancient masters, returning instead to a life in the wild. Now they dwelled free and unsaddled among the lofty peaks of the high Kharolis.

"As it was, a rider had to make his way on horseback, through the roughest part of the kingdom. And even so, he brings more questions than he does answers!"

"Perhaps we should invite the princess back. Maybe she could talk some sense into the griffons."

Rashas's glare was pure malevolence. "You should be a thousand times glad that the bitch is gone!" he snapped. "She was feeding you lie after lie, and you were too naive to see through her!"

"I enjoyed talking to her," Gilthas admitted, feeling bold again.

"She, and your father as well, would have been the ruin of this kingdom! I should think that now you'd start to understand what that damned half-breed bastard was trying to do!"

"Sometimes I think that the 'half-breed bastard' has more courage and honor in his little toe than any elf left in Qualinesti!"

snapped the Speaker, flushed out of his reticence by the senator's insults.

"You're still a fool!" Rashas raged. "Now get ready. I told you, the Thalas-Enthia meets in two hours, and you'll be there! Don't even think about getting one of those headaches. You should be ashamed, claiming they keep you closed in a dark room! I think they're just an excuse to keep you from doing your duty."

The senator stormed away, and Gilthas sighed, turning back toward the pristine view from his balcony, knowing that he had to do as he had been told.

But it was so unspeakably hard!

He thought of his last meeting with his father, probably the last time in his life he would ever see Tanis Half-Elven, who had been exiled from his homeland of Qualinesti. Only later did the son come to see what that sentence had meant to his father. At the time, the young and newly appointed speaker had been too concerned with his own future to worry about Tanis's past. They had met at the edge of the kingdom—in fact, when Tanis had taken a step toward the border, elven sentries had shot arrows at the half-elf's feet to underscore the rigidity of the banishment. Father and son had embraced for too short a time, and Gilthas had promised to honor the legacy that had brought him to this throne and to do what he could to block the most shortsighted and mean-spirited acts of the Thalas-Enthia.

Yet so far his presence had been almost entirely symbolic. It seemed that the senate did whatever Rashas wanted, and the presence of Gilthas Solostaran only added legitimacy to their acts.

His musings of self-pity were interrupted by a hesitant knock at the door.

"Enter."

His mood brightened as he saw the beautiful, golden-haired wild elf who shyly pushed the door open and stood just outside the Speaker's chamber.

"Please, Kerianseray . . . come in."

With a deep bow, the young slave stepped hesitantly forward, keeping her face downcast.

"You can look at me, you know. The sight of me won't

burn your eyes," Gilthas said gently. As always, he was discomfited by the honors shown him by the palace slaves—and by this slave in particular.

"I was told that the Speaker would be wanting his robes of office," she said hesitantly, and Gilthas saw that Rashas, as usual, was not being subtle about pointing his young king in the direction he was supposed to go.

"I guess you're right . . . I should put them on," he said with a sigh. "But I still have a little time before fussing with all of that."

Kerianseray looked at him in confusion. The wrinkling of her brow did nothing to diminish her beauty. In fact, Gilthas found her appearance utterly beguiling. His mind searched, groping for something to say that would keep her here.

"I slept very well last night," he declared. "That bark tea was soothing. I was fully rested with the dawn."

Though Gilthas didn't want the fact widely known, his sleep had been plagued by nightmares—fierce, dire episodes of violence and tragedy—ever since he had assumed the mantle of his office. Even more than the headaches, these episodes had tormented and weakened him. So far as he knew, Rashas didn't know of these disturbances, nor did anyone except a few of his royal slaves. He was ashamed by what he perceived as his weakness, but the images were so frightening that, when once he had awakened to find Kerianseray soothing his fevered brow with a cool cloth, he had willingly accepted her ministrations. Finally she had grown bold enough to suggest that he sip a brew before retiring, a bitter tea that she had learned to make from her Kagonesti ancestors, a mild medicine that might serve as a balm for just the kind of distress he was suffering.

For some days, he had refused to yield to her suggestion, and she had let the matter drop. The night before last, however, he had awakened with his mouth locked in a rictus of horror, his mind reeling with the image of his mother impaled on a stake of burning wood. All around him this city of crystal and gold had been crumbling, consumed by flames that swept upward from the very ground beneath his feet.

That experience had been so frightening that at last he had gone to Kerianseray and sought her help.

"I am happy I was able to serve the Speaker," she said, casting her eyes down to the floor. "His suffering is my own," she added, almost in a whisper.

"There is another thing you could do for me," Gilthas said. Still Kerianseray held her eyes downcast. "Stop speaking of me as if I'm not here. Refer to me as 'you,' not 'the Speaker.' If you could do this, it would please me very much."

"If the Spea—if you wish, I shall try," the young slave replied. Despite her bronzed skin, Gilthas noticed that a blush was creeping up her cheeks, and this was an expression he found strangely attractive.

"Has my robe been sent for?" he asked.

"Yes. The matrons are starching it and will bring it up shortly. I shall go to help them . . . that is, unless the . . . unless you want something else."

I do, Gilthas thought. I want you to stay here with me. But for reasons he didn't fully understand, he dared not put those thoughts into words. Instead, he cast around for some excuse, any excuse, that would cause her to remain.

"The matrons will be able to starch the robe by themselves. Perhaps you would be good enough to brush my hair while we're waiting?"

"Of course!" Kerianseray brightened at the suggestion, and Gilthas felt unaccountably pleased by her reaction. He arranged himself in a comfortable low-backed chair, where he still had a good view of the city sprawling beyond his window. The Kagonesti slave picked up a golden brush and slowly, carefully began to stroke the locks of his long blond hair.

He was soothed by her touch, calmed by her gentle strokes. There were times, he reflected with a sigh, when his life was not so utterly, terribly bad.

* * * * *

Gilthas stood upon the rostrum in the center of the Tower of the Sun. Around him, standing attentively—there were no seats in this hallowed council hall—the robed senators of the Thalas-Enthia waited for him to bring the meeting to order. Though he did not look to the rear, the Speaker knew that Rashas would be very near, standing unobtrusively off to the side but close enough that he could reach the center of the rostrum in a pace or two should events begin to develop in a way he did not desire.

Looking around the uncrowded chamber, Gilthas saw that several dozen of the younger senators were not in attendance. These, for the most part, had inherited their seats during the last forty years or so, following the untimely death of a noble parent. As a rule, they had tended to be more open to change than the staid elder members of the group, many of whom had held their seats for upward of four centuries. When Gilthas had been appointed Speaker, in a ceremony that, for all its rigid legality, had carried the taint of threat and extortion, many of the young senators had stalked out of the chamber. Some of them had refused to return.

But there were still a hundred or so elves here, more than enough to make a quorum. In truth, the only thing that the young hotheads had accomplished was to deprive themselves of a voice in these councils. Gilthas truly regretted their absence. He knew that they despised him, but he hoped that if they could but see what went on in here, they would begin to see that he could offer some real hope to the future of the realm.

The outer doors, portals of solid gold, were closed with a loud clang, sealing off the chamber from the rest of Qualinesti. Immediately Gilthas felt stifled. He wanted to throw the doors open, to admit sunlight and air, but Rashas had informed him that the volatile nature of today's topic required that the meeting be held in secrecy.

"I call the Thalas-Enthia to order on this day of Fourth Gateway in the month of Spring Dawning, in the year of Krynn three hundred eighty-three years after the Cataclysm."

The murmuring of the senators in the room died away, and many of them looked at him expectantly, curious as to the topic that had brought them here on such short notice. It irritated

Gilthas to see that some elves looked past him to Rashas, but he was determined to conduct this meeting in a way that would give the reactionary senator no cause to intervene.

"We have just received an urgent report from the western wilds of the kingdom. General Palthainon has ridden for three days over forest trails to deliver this important message. I now call upon him to make his report known to the Thalas-Enthia."

Palthainon, still wearing his mud-stained boots and travel-worn tunic, stood at the foot of the rostrum. The costume was for effect, Gilthas knew. He had been in the city for at least six hours since making his report to Rashas at dawn. Nevertheless, the garb served to focus the attention of the senators on the urgency of his mission. Every eye was on the general as Palthainon climbed four steps to take a position on the highest step, save for the rostrum itself. His back to Gilthas, he turned to address the gathered elves.

"You have perhaps heard disturbing rumors out of the west, stories of banditry and robbery dating from the beginning of this summer. They have been regarded as tall tales, for the most part. Who would dare to challenge the mastery of the Qualinesti in our own domain?"

The general's remarks were greeted with mutters of astonishment: "Who indeed?" As Palthainon went on to describe his own mission of investigation, begun at the insistence of Rashas, of course, Gilthas tried to remember what he knew of this tall warrior who was so unusually broad-shouldered for an elf.

Palthainon had been an appointee of Rashas, so Gilthas assumed that the warrior's loyalty lay firmly with the elder senator. He had captained a company during the War of the Lance, when the Qualinesti elves had fled to exile on Ergoth while the unstoppable dragonarmies had claimed their homeland. Palthainon had grown rich in the practice of war, though, perhaps because he had never actually fought against the hordes of the Dark Queen. Instead, his campaigns had been limited to subjugating the Kagonesti, the wild elves, who had roamed free across Ergoth before the coming of the Qualinesti. According to his reputation, Palthainon's company had never been beaten in battle . . . and if the number of wild elf slaves he had sold in the markets of Qualimor and Daltigoth was any indication, the reputation was well earned.

Gilthas's attention snapped back to the present as the warrior continued his story.

"At first I was skeptical of the tales, but then I interviewed two noble elves, high lords of unimpeachable reputation, and their tale was the one that convinced me. They were both part of an overland caravan, journeying south from Caergoth with a load of gemstones and spices, having set forth to barter good Qualinesti steel and leather goods. They were not overly cautious—only a dozen guards—for they had already passed the border stones into Qualinesti. Naturally enough, they felt quite secure with the sanctity of our nation.

"I grieve to tell you, elves of the Thalas-Enthia, that their caravan was attacked in the middle of the night. The bandits number many—the nobles estimated two hundred or more, but experience has shown me that even the most perspicacious of witnesses is untrustworthy on matters such as this. Still, the guards were overwhelmed, the cargo stolen, and the bandits made their escape into the darkness of the woods."

There were cries of outrage throughout the chamber, and several elves stomped their feet as they agitated for action. Gilthas held up a hand, but the gesture wasn't enough to calm the gathering into silence. Instead, he spoke loudly, asking his question in a voice that carried over the grumbling.

"Good general, you interviewed both of these noble elves?" he asked.

"Yes, Honored Speaker, and their tales matched in every detail. It may interest you to know that I spoke with them separately, so that they did not have the advantage of each hearing the other's testimony."

"A splendid precaution," Gilthas agreed. "But I take it that, since they were able to talk, neither of them met with harm during this episode?"

"No, Honored Speaker. As a matter of fact, neither of them showed the mark of a single wound." Palthainon's tone was a little scornful as he shared this information.

"And the guards . . . were many of them killed?"

"Their testimony included no remarks as to the state of the guards," the general said with a shrug.

And you didn't think to ask! Gilthas wanted to voice the rebuke but decided that it was more politic to bite his tongue. "Still, we can assume that if great bloodshed was wrought among the escort, the nobles would have mentioned the fact as part of their testimony."

"It is a logical assumption," agreed the warrior.

"I fail to see what difference the relative wounding of the victims bears upon the facts here," Rashas interjected. "Clearly a crime has occurred."

"Very clearly," Gilthas agreed genially. "I merely wish to establish the exact nature of that crime."

"The crime is robbery, theft of legitimate imported goods!" declared Palthainon. "We have evidence and testimony to that effect."

"Yes . . . in fact, we've had testimony to that effect for a week, if I recall correctly."

"But this is testimony from reliable sources!" the general retorted.

"To be sure . . . and since this testimony is the same as we heard days earlier, doesn't that prove that the other sources were reliable as well?" Gilthas was actually enjoying himself.

"Enough!" Rashas snapped the command, and the Speaker felt as though a leash had been jerked tightly around his neck. The senator continued, obviously doing his best to speak in a level and reasonable tone. "We now have the proof we lacked before. Doesn't this suggest that the Thalas-Enthia proceed to the consideration of some sort of action?"

"It does," Gilthas agreed, forcing himself to reply in kind.

Senator Fallitarian, a doddering elder known to be a fervent supporter of Rashas, made the motion. "We should send a company of warriors to the west . . . patrol the trails, bring the rascals to justice!"

"Here, here!" The suggestion was echoed throughout the chamber.

"A single company?" Rashas interjected, with a deliberative scowl. "Two hundred elves to hunt down and capture a band that might be their equal in numbers, if we are to believe the words of the witnesses?"

"We should make it at least three companies," Gilthas suggested. "That way, they can patrol a larger area and will be readily available to reinforce each other should the bandits prove to be numerous."

"Excellent idea," Rashas concurred.

Gilthas was paradoxically annoyed with himself to find that the senator's praise pleased him.

"Three companies it is!" Senator Fallitarian fell into rank. "I submit that General Palthainon should be appointed their general."

That motion, too, passed with a mere voice vote. Palthainon was authorized to raise six hundred Qualinesti warriors from the clans in and around the city and to outfit them with armaments from the city armory. He was given a week to organize his three companies. Then he would embark for the west, where he was granted full authority to decide how to deal with the bandits. The senate suggested that he try to bring the leaders back to the city for trial, but even this notion was couched in polite terms, and very few of the gathered nobles ever expected to see any of the bandits in Qualinost—at least, not alive.

Gilthas was about to suggest the meeting be adjourned when the chamber was rocked by a violent pounding on the great golden doors. The noise reverberated like a drumbeat, and a steward immediately looked through the spyhole, then turned to announce to the chamber:

"It is the scout, Guilderhand. He says he has information of urgency to the senate, relevant to the matter being discussed here today."

"Admit him at once," Gilthas said, knowing that Rashas would have spoken the same words if he hadn't. Guilderhand was one of the senator's trusted agents—"scout" was a euphemistic term for an elf who was widely regarded as a spy. His arrival at such a climactic juncture was typical, for he had a way of drawing attention to himself when he wanted to be noticed.

The scout came into the room, and if Palthainon had looked travel-worn and scuffed from the road, Guilderhand looked as if he had crawled through a muddy sewer to reach this exalted council. His hair was plastered to his skull, his face was filthy, and his dirt-green cloak was thick with brambles and leaves. Apparently unmindful of his unkempt state, he stalked down the aisle and climbed the steps toward the rostrum. He offered a perfunctory bow to Gilthas and a longer genuflection toward Rashas before turning and sweeping his gaze across the rapt audience of elven rulership.

"Elven nobles, esteemed senators, honored elders," he began. He paused, a long delay even by elven standards, but no one spoke. No elf's attention wavered even slightly from the bedraggled figure.

"I come with grim news from the west . . . news that would brook no delay. I have traveled day and night to reach the city and came at once to the chamber where I knew our nation's wisest leadership would be gathered."

Again he paused for dramatic effect. Gilthas wanted to urge him to get on with it. Why should news that would brook no delay be delivered with such tantalizing deliberation? But he knew the ways of Rashas's spy, and so he held his tongue.

"The honorable Palthainon is correct in reporting to you that the bandits number at least two hundred," Guilderhand said, with a bow toward the general, who stood proudly aloof as he accepted the praise.

That statement begged another question, at least to the Speaker, who was listening with a certain amount of skepticism: How did Guilderhand know the substance of Palthainon's report? Gilthas knew then that the spy had been waiting outside, eavesdropping on the meeting, waiting until the moment was right for his dramatic entrance.

"My own investigations carried me right into the bandits' camp, and it was there that I gained my startling information. I have learned the nature of these outlaws and the identity—though it grieves me to know it—of their leader."

Again he paused, but this time there came urging from the Thalas-Enthia. "Speak—say the name! Who is it?"

"The bandits that have come to prey on our western highways are not, as we all expected, mere human wastrels, scoundrels who seek to enrich themselves off of elven labors. No, my honored leaders, I tell you that these bandits are themselves elves, traitors against their nation and their people!"

"Shame!" The sibilant curse rose from the Thalas-Enthia and was followed by uglier cries and demands for further information. "Who is their leader? Who draws elves into treachery?"

"Their leader is a dark elf, one who is well known to these chambers and to this very rostrum. I grieve to tell you, members of the Senate of Qualinesti, that these outlaws represent an insurgency, and that they are led by none other than Porthios Solostaran, the former Speaker of the Sun and current traitor to his people."

Gilthas felt weak in the knees and had to exert all of his discipline to keep himself from falling. Porthios! Turned against Qualinesti, violating the exile that he had chosen as he made his escape from Silvanesti!

Suddenly it seemed to the young Speaker as though the entire world was going insane, torn by a hurricane of uncontrollable events . . . and that he, Gilthas Solostaran, somehow stood at the center of the whirlwind.

* * * * *

"And this was the place you now came to live?" Silvanoshei asked the green dragon.

"Yes. For my part, I flew westward for many days. It was not the purposeful flight of a journey to a specific destination. Instead, I spiraled north or south as the spirit moved me, stopping to hunt whenever I chose. Once I killed a whole herd of cows just so I could feast on delicacies—tongues, hearts, udders—that were most pleasing to my ancient palate.

"I flew past the snowcapped High Kharolis, for I was seeking a vast woodland—and, too, there were more griffons there than I could abide. I remember a mountain that loomed high, in the ominous shape of a human skull, but the environment was far too dry for any

green dragon. The mountains beyond showed more promise, for they were forested, but they were also well populated with settlements of humans, hill dwarves, and elves. I had had enough of war for a while and knew that any attempt to settle here would be met with ruthless violence.

"And thus I continued westward, skirting to the southward of an elven city of arched bridges and a lofty, golden tower. Finally I found myself over a woodland that at last reminded me of Silvanesti, for here the trees stretched in a blanket from one horizon to the other. Of course, I did not make my lair near the great, crystalline city, nor near any concentration of elven habitations. Instead, I continued over the limitless forest, allowing my wings to glide through the air, bearing the one I fancied to be the new master of these skies.

"Eventually I came into sight of a vast ocean, the western terminus of this realm, and a perfect coastline for a dragon lair. It was not flat and marshy, like so much of Silvanesti's southern border. Instead, the forest continued right to the ocean's edge, where in many places the land plunged down steep and craggy bluffs to meet a rocky and inhospitable shore. There were caves in these cliffs, and some of them even smelled of ancient dragon spoor.

"I found this large cavern . . . as you can see, a place where fresh water trickles warmly from springs in the bedrock, where moss grows thick across the flatness of smooth rock. And this is the place where I made my new home."

"So you, too, had come to live in the path of war," Silvanoshei said, and his voice was almost sympathetic.

Chapter Ten

"Can you believe there was a time when all elves lived like this?" Porthios said, leaning back in his hammock, pushing with a sandaled foot to sway the garland-draped net easily in the clearing.

"Sometimes I wonder why we felt it necessary to move into cities," Alhana agreed, likewise swaying beside her husband. Silvanoshei was drowsing quietly at her breast. The baby seemed content to eat and sleep, for the most part. Porthios had just chuckled softly with the realization that, for the first time in his life, he was happy with the same regimen.

The three of them were not alone. They were never alone in a camp of more than two hundred warriors, many with spouses and children. Still, they shared a sense of sublime solitude, the late afternoon broken only by the sounds of murmured conversation and the pleasant, swooshing sound of the gentle wind through the trees.

In many respects, this camp was more comfortable than the nicest houses in which they had ever dwelled. Despite the relentless heat of the early summer, they were close enough to the coast that they were eternally soothed by an offshore breeze, a wind that was channeled between two towering bluffs so that it always flowed up the valley.

A pleasant stream meandered right through the middle of the encampment, and numerous waterfalls trilled from the heights on either side. A canopy of lofty trees—ironwood, oak, and an occasional towering cedar—provided constant shade, as well as screened the camp from observation by anyone overhead. Yet the tree limbs were so high that the effect was not stifling. Instead, it was more like a vaulted ceiling that kept them cool with its lofty, heavy boughs.

Of course, the elves had done some work to improve the comfort of the settlement. Dozens of small huts had been erected near the walls of the gorge, and guard posts had been established on the two trails leading into the ravine from the upper walls. Several small caves were used for food storage, and early efforts at establishing a vintner's yard had been made at the lower end of the gorge. This area of Qualinesti was rich in natural grapes, and the elves had been diligent in their collection, so that now several large casks of mash were slowly fermenting into wine.

It was Tarqualan who had led them to this gorge. The Qualinesti captain had remembered the place from his childhood. The entire band, led by Porthios, had flown here after bidding farewell to Tanis before they had reached the borders of Qualinesti. The half-elf had journeyed northward, returning to his wife. He had been concerned by the rumors of an impending war in the far north, stories that remained unconfirmed but that Tanis had been determined to investigate.

Here in the forest glade, such reports seemed distant and insignificant compared to the easy pleasures of daily life and parenthood. Porthios was glad that he could be with his baby so much. Silvanoshei spent most of his time in the comfort of his *tai-thall*, the leather cradle that Alhana, or sometimes Porthios himself, wore over the shoulders to support the infant on his parent's chest. The Qualinesti warriors had crafted the traditional baby carrier during the days after Silvanoshei's birth, and the *tai-thall* had supported the newborn infant during the remainder of the flight to his father's homeland.

As the band of fliers had crossed the border, Porthios had felt a twinge of melancholy and misgiving, knowing that he was now an outlaw in his own homeland. Still, his outrage against that perceived injustice was powerful enough to easily overcome any misgivings he may have had over defying the exile. Now that they were here, he felt like a king again—an outlaw king, perhaps, but that role was well suited to his current mood.

Only recently they had raided another caravan bound southward from Caergoth, and their plunder had included many woolen cloaks as well as iron implements that greatly enhanced the band's cooking process. Their diet consisted thus far of venison and fish, supplemented by the natural fruits and berries that were blooming throughout the woods. Wild grasses were being harvested and shucked, though so far the outlaws had not gathered enough grain to make a mill or bakery worthwhile. Still, Porthios was determined that, before the coming of winter, they would be cooking a variety of breads.

White-winged shapes flew overhead, and he looked upward from his hammock to see griffons wheeling and gliding in the wide spaces between the trees. He was grateful that the creatures had come with them and had decided to continue to cooperate with the outlaw elves instead of the civilized Qualinesti, the so-called masters of this domain. Porthios knew that, so long as the griffons were with them, his force was much more mobile than any warriors the Thalas-Enthia or their figurehead Speaker could put into the field. With their sentinels posted on the trails and the griffons ready to carry the outlaws into battle, the prince was certain they were safe from surprise attack. Too, the griffons gave them the ability to move quickly, to strike the caravans as they entered the elven kingdom, and to get away with their plunder.

So far, they had managed to make their attacks without any killing, which had been one of Alhana's most urgent desires. Porthios himself was not terribly worried about the prospect of slaying fat merchant elves. As far as he was concerned, they were working hand-in-pocket with the Thalas-Enthia, and that shortsighted body of conservatives was bad for elvenkind, and consequently his enemy.

He thought a little about the young elf who had replaced him as Speaker. Alhana had gained the measure of Gilthas Solostaran during the short time when they had both been imprisoned in Senator Rashas's house. Though Porthios was inclined to dismiss the youngster as a mere puppet of the Thalas-Enthia, his wife had cautioned him that Gilthas was in fact made of sterner stuff. She had reminded him that the blood of Tanis Half-Elven and Laurana Solostaran, Porthios's sister and the famed Golden General of the War of the Lance, flowed undiluted in his veins.

Gilthas, however, had been raised in a sheltered environment, for his parents had foolishly wished to protect him from life in the real world. But now the young elf was fast gaining an education during his tumultuous term as the Speaker of Sun. While on the surface he acted unfailingly to enforce the will of Rashas and the other senators of his faction, Alhana had suggested that Gilthas was in fact his own master and was working toward a future of his own, not the Thalas-Enthia's, design.

In a sense, Porthios hoped that was true. He thought about his mixed feelings for Tanis, the half-elf who had helped him escape from Silvanesti, yet who had taken his sister to a marriage so far beneath herself. The old animosity still lingered, the rage at this bastard who, Porthios was convinced, had grown a beard to offend elven sensibilities, to audaciously flaunt his humanness. Was it any wonder that a prince of Qualinesti had teased him mercilessly during their shared youth? There were times when Porthios even wondered if Tanis had wooed Laurana merely as a means of gaining vengeance on her brother.

Of course, he had to admit that his sister seemed content,

even happy, with the union. He felt sorrow for Laurana, who had, because of her marriage, sentenced herself to virtual exile from Qualinesti. Still, if her son proved to be a true leader of the elves, if his wisdom could begin to guide the two realms toward an eventual reconciliation, then the future might not be as bleak as the outlaw leader sometimes feared.

His musings were interrupted by the rattling call of a crane, the sound reverberating down the sides of the gorge. This was the prearranged symbol of warning from the guards at the head of the trail, and Porthios was immediately out of his hammock, striding through the encampment as he girded on his sword and saw that Alhana, Silvanoshei, and the other nonwarriors were safely hidden in the nearby caves.

Around Porthios were mustered more than a hundred of his fighting elves, while the griffons were thick in the trees overhead. The hooting cry had been a warning, but not the urgent symbol that indicated an imminent attack, so the prince merely waited, his eyes on the winding trail that led down the bluff and into the clearing before the camp. This was the one path into the glade, and it was covered by many archers and blocked by a line of swords. He noted without surprise that Samar had come to Alhana's side and held his weapon ready while the woman sheltered her baby in her arms.

Even with their watchfulness, however, the outlaws didn't see the movement along that trail. Instead, there were suddenly elves around the tree trunks at the base of the bluff, silent people who had slipped right down the slope without being seen. Despite his astonishment, Porthios retained enough composure to bow in polite greeting as the first of the elves stepped forward from the band of several dozen that regarded the outlaws from the fringe of their camp.

These were Kagonesti, Porthios saw immediately, a fact that went a great way toward explaining how they could have slipped down the trail without notice. Naked but for girdles and loincloths of soft deerskin, the wild elves were covered all over with the spirals, whorls, and leafy patterns of black tattoos. They were bronze of skin and, for the most part, dark of hair, though a few of the wild elves were blond or even red-haired.

Partially because of their camouflage, and partly because of their natural affinity for the woodlands, they could move almost invisibly through dense foliage or across nearly barren ground.

"Welcome to our village," Porthios said formally. "We greet you in peace, as our cousins of the forest."

"Welcome to our forest," replied the leading Kagonesti, who was a strapping warrior, even taller than the lanky Porthios. "We accept your greetings, as our cousins from beyond the woodlands."

Porthios couldn't help but notice the wild elf's reference to "our" forest. He knew that there were tribes of the Kagonesti throughout Qualinesti, though he had thought them to be pretty well subjugated by the civilized elves. Obviously here was a band that thought of its existence in more independent terms.

"We did not want to startle you, so we allowed your sentries to spy us as we passed them at the summit of the trail," the leading Kagonesti went on. "The call of the crane was not unskilled, coming as it did from the throat of one raised in the city."

Porthios flushed. Daringflight, the scout who had hooted the warning, was widely known as one of the most skilled elves at imitating animal sounds. Still, he did not want to offend this visitor, and so he held his tongue.

"I am Dallatar, chieftain of the White Osprey Kagonesti," the wild elf intoned.

"I am called Porthios Solostaran. Once I was Speaker of all Qualinesti. Now I am chieftain of the Westshore Elves." He made up the name on the spot, conscious that he didn't want his band to seem less civilized than these forest-dwelling primitives.

"We have seen that you fight the city elves," Dallatar noted. "It is curious to see you attack those that we see as the same clan."

"It is curious to us as well," Porthios said, unwilling to go into a full explanation. He told himself that this savage would never understand the intricacies of interkingdom politics, though in fact he realized that he was suddenly ashamed of the fractiousness that had driven him to take up the outlaw's life in the forest.

"We have made ourselves happy here," he added, feeling even as he spoke that the explanation sounded a little lame.

Dallatar nodded sagely, as if Porthios's statement was the most logical thing in the world. When next the wild elf spoke, it was to reveal a startling change of topic. "You should know that the city elves are marching from Qualinost to come after you. They have a force of six hundred swords."

"That's news." Though he had expected something like this, Porthios was in fact surprised to hear that the Thalas-Enthia had already put a plan into motion. "Have you seen this force? Is it close?"

"No. They will not depart the city for several days yet. But training is under way, under the captainship of one called Palthainon."

"General Palthainon . . . I might have known," the outlaw leader declared in disgust. Palthainon's reputation for brutality and bullying had been established, and well earned, during the exile on Ergoth. Now he seemed like a logical choice to send after a group of bandits in the western forests.

Only then did another, very obvious, question occur to him. He asked Dallatar bluntly. "You say they won't leave for days, yet you know their timetable, even the name of their captain. What's the source of your intelligence?"

"We Kagonesti have brothers held as slaves in the city of gold. There are many ways we can learn of events in Qualinost without the Qualinesti suspecting that news is traveling back and forth."

Porthios had to admit to the logic of this statement. He had spent many years in the city and had never suspected that the wild elves who worked as house slaves for some of the more arrogant nobles had maintained any kind of contact with their brethren in the forests. Still, he was now grateful for the fact and said so.

The wild elf chieftain shrugged. "We have heard of you, of course . . . the one who was once Speaker of the Sun. You were always fair and generous with our people. That is different from the manner of many noble elves."

Porthios was immediately glad that he had always made a practice of treating the Kagonesti as his equals. He knew what Dallatar meant about the arrogance, even cruelty, of some city elf slave owners, though doubtless they, like he, had never attributed such resourcefulness to the clan that had always been casually dismissed as a bunch of painted barbarians.

"Will you join us in the humble sustenance of our camp?" asked the outlaw who was once a king. "As we are neighbors in the woodlands, I would like to think that so we will also be friends."

"That is our wish as well," agreed the tribal chief. At a signal of his hand, many women of his tribe came forward, carrying two freshly killed does, baskets of fish, and satchels full of fruits and berries of varieties that the Qualinesti had only rarely seen. "The woods are a full larder at this time of year, and we have brought gifts of food to share with you."

The shade was thickening in the gorge as the smells of sizzling deer and roasting fish wafted through the air. Porthios and Dallatar sat beside each other around the large central fire pit. Alhana, with Silvanoshei in his *tai-thall*, was at her husband's side, and a beautiful Kagonesti maid, her black hair streaked with startling splashes of silver, joined the wild elf chief.

"This is my bride, Willowfawn," boasted Dallatar proudly. "She has been mine for more than one hundred winters."

"And together we have made two children," the woman said frankly. "It was our son who slayed the largest doe, using only his knife."

"A mighty hunter is Iydahar," agreed the chief easily.

"And who is your other child?" Alhana asked.

Porthios noticed a darkness come into the chief's eyes. "She was taken from us as a young girl during the years on Ergoth. She was sold to a Qualinesti lord. Now she works as a slave in his house."

Porthios and Alhana exchanged a look of guilt and remorse. They had both grown up around wild elf slaves, but somehow they had never considered the origins of those unwilling workers. Now Porthios thought it seemed unutterably barbaric to remove young children from their parents' family merely because their tribe was judged to lack civilization.

"And I see that you, too, have a child," said Willowfawn.

"Our first—not a full month old yet," Alhana said with a smile. Her eyes twinkled. "Of course, Porthios has only been 'mine' for thirty winters."

If Dallatar thought the juxtaposition of the possessive was remarkable, and undoubtedly he did, he made an exceptional pretense of masking his surprise. "I wish the best of health and happiness to your child," he said solemnly.

Alhana's hands were suddenly tight around Porthios's arm. "Thank you," she said softly. "Thank you very much."

* * * * *

Bellaclaw came to rest in the clearing before Porthios and his outlaws. Samar dismounted, dropping easily to the soft loam of the ground.

"Palthainon is a fool," snapped the warrior-mage, shaking his head in disbelief. "He has his elves marching four abreast, one company following right on the heels of the next. They're making more noise than a drunken dwarf in a chime shop."

"What about the warriors in his companies? Was Dallatar's information correct?" Porthios wondered.

"As far as I could tell. It doesn't look like more than one in ten of them is a veteran of any kind of campaign. Maybe that's why he's holding them in such a tight formation—he's afraid the novices will run away if he's not looking over their shoulder every step of the way."

"So he marches them like swine going to the butcher. . . ." The outlaw leader was still amazed. Every elf who'd ever held a sword knew that a loose formation, flexible and supple, was the best marching order for thick woodlands. That way, if part of a column was attacked, the rest of the elves could circle around and strike the attackers in the flanks. But a dense, short formation such as Samar had just described meant that it was quite possible for the entire force to wander into an ambush.

"Remember, he's never fought Qualinesti before. His victories were against small tribes of wild elves, who could rarely muster more than two- or threescore warriors against him. I daresay he's in for a nasty shock."

Porthios nodded grimly. He felt none of the excitement that normally preceded a battle, but he knew he had a job to do and was determined that his own forces would suffer very few casualties. He turned toward Stallyar, who was prancing eagerly under the nearby trees, when he was stopped by a gentle pressure on his arm.

Alhana stood there, sweat standing out in beads on her fair skin. Her huge eyes were dark with concern.

"Please, my husband, isn't there some other way? Do you have to kill them?"

Porthios sighed, at once angry with her persistence and at the same time grieving for the necessity he perceived in this situation.

"When we robbed from them, we were able to do it without killing. We outnumbered the caravans, and the guards were easily scared away. But this is an armed force sent to find and attack us! You know they won't hesitate to use their weapons against us. Furthermore, they outnumber our warriors by three to one. There is no longer any room for gentleness."

"Can't you just avoid them?" She used the same argument she had been pressing for the last week, ever since the Kagonesti had reported that Palthainon's force had departed Qualinost.

"You know that's impossible—unless we want to abandon our camp, to be ready to move at a day's notice wherever we settle."

Through a combination of the wild elves and his own outlaws mounted on griffons, Porthios had kept careful tabs on the advance of the Qualinesti force. For a time, it had looked as though Palthainon might blunder southward along the coast, which would have taken him away from the camp for another month or two. But a day earlier, the general had made a fateful guess, veering his force to the north on a bearing that, within another few days, would lead him right into the gorge where Porthios had made his camp. To counter, the outlaw prince had brought his elves out of the encampment and gathered them in this clearing in the deep forest. He had studied the general's route of advance and planned his battle accordingly.

"I ask you again, can't you try to frighten them away? You have to see that, up until now, many elves perceive you as the true leader of their people, someone who has been wronged by the Thalas-Enthia. But if you draw elven blood, you suddenly prove to them that you *are* an outlaw, a threat not only to their pocketbooks but also to the lives of their husbands and sons, to the very fabric of Qualinesti society!"

"Why should I care about the fabric of Qualinesti society?" Porthios demanded harshly. "Isn't that the agency that stole my crown, that cast me into exile—called me a dark elf?"

"No!" Alhana was annoyingly insistent. "You know that was a few hateful old men in the Thalas-Enthia. *They* are your enemies, elves like Rashas and Konnal. I beg you, my husband, don't make this into a war that you'll regret for as long as you live!"

"Lord Porthios!" cried the scout, Daringflight, who was landing in the clearing. "They're only a mile away, and they've picked up the pace of their march."

"The decision has been made," Porthios declared to Alhana, trying for a stern tone but knowing that he merely sounded petulant. "Now I'll have to ask you to get away from here. The battle is about to begin, and nothing anyone does can change that fact. You'll be safe here, though if you'd like, I can ask Samar to stay with you."

"It is not my safety I'm worried about!" she snapped. "I wish you could see that, could understand what you have to do!" Her tone dropped, her words pointed and hurtful. "It's not enough, husband, merely to send Samar to take your place."

Her jaw set, Alhana stepped back. Porthios was stunned by the depth of her anger and deeply hurt by her rebuke. He wished she would turn and march away, but instead she kept her eyes fastened upon him, her glare harsh and unforgiving as he stepped to Stallyar's side and lifted one foot into the stirrup. Samar, nearby, looked away awkwardly. Finally Porthios whirled to face her, his own face distorted by anger.

"I don't have any choice!" he shouted. "Don't you see that? Why can't you see that?"

"I see you, husband, and I see the choices that you make," she said calmly. "And I grieve for those choices, even as I know that you do the same."

Only then did she turn and walk away, melting into the woods that made her invisible within a dozen paces.

"Why does she do that?" Porthios growled to himself, kicking Stallyar with unnecessary harshness. The griffon cast a reproving glance over his shoulder as he spread his wings and sprang into the air. "Sorry, Old Claws," the bandit leader said in chagrin, patting the softly feathered neck.

Within a minute, the sky over the clearing was filled with griffons, the savage fliers silent as they took to the air, bearing Porthios's company of elite fighters toward the approaching file of Qualinesti. He had picked the site for the ambush carefully, knowing that Palthainon's force would have to cross a wide clearing and then ford a deep stream. The obvious crossing was a tangle of broken tree limbs that would serve as a makeshift bridge but would allow only one or two elves to cross at a time. The far side of the stream was thickly wooded, and this was where Porthios had decided to conceal his force.

As they flew the short distance, Porthios reflected more on his wife's accusations. Did she really think that he sent Samar to be with her to take his place? Yet, in honesty, he knew he had relied on the warrior-mage for a lot of help, and he was always willing to attend his queen. A glimmering of suspicion sparked in his mind, but he roughly pushed that poisonous thought aside, though it didn't vanish entirely.

But now the flying elves were settling into the trees just before the stream. The griffons gathered in several small clearings, a few hundred paces back from the scene of the ambush, while the elves crept forward to take up hiding places in the underbrush to both sides of the prospective crossing. Within a few minutes, all of the bandits, nearly three hundred strong, had secured hiding places for themselves in the tangle. Arrows were laid beside bows, and swords were loosened in scabbards, though if the plan worked as Porthios intended, there would be little need for the bloody combat of a close-ranks melee.

Soon the Qualinesti companies broke into the clearing on the far side of the stream. They marched, as Tarqualan had reported, in tightly packed ranks. Many of the recruits shuffled with weariness, while a few veterans shouted harshly at their comrades, even jabbing and slapping with swords to move the recalcitrant warriors along. Clearly this was a raw and dispirited group of elves.

Porthios's military mind admired the perfection of the setting, even as his elven conscience railed against Palthainon's stupidity. Oblivious of the danger, the general marched his column almost to the river's edge on the far side of the stream. Scowling, the commander stalked along the bank, finally pausing to study the tangle of trunks that spanned the otherwise rock-filled and treacherous gorge.

"Stand alert there!" Palthainon called to his warriors, some of whom had settled to the ground as they waited for orders. "We'll cross here. No rest until we're all on the other side."

"Perfect, you fool," whispered Porthios. These troops, already ragged with weariness, would be denied a chance to rest before they marched into the ambush. The outlaw leader found himself wondering how Palthainon had earned his reputation on Ergoth. Perhaps it was true that all of his battles had involved attacks against peaceful villages, brutal raids with the primary objective of taking slaves.

The first of the Qualinesti started awkwardly along the makeshift bridge, and now events really did move beyond Porthios's control. He had set his ambush, given his troops orders, and there was no way to countermand those instructions without revealing himself to the enemy across the waterway. The outlaws were to wait until half the city elves were across the stream. Then they would attack with lethal volleys of arrows, killing most of the hapless invaders before they even knew that battle had been joined.

After several volleys of arrows, the biggest of the outlaws were to fall on the survivors with cold steel, while the rest of Porthios's force would race back to their griffons and sweep against the remaining Qualinesti from the air. Probably some of the elves on the far side of the river would escape, but the carnage over there would be savage as well. And it served Porthios well to have a few survivors make it back to the city. He wanted the Thalas-Enthia to think twice before they sent another army after him.

The first elves to cross the bridge collapsed in exhaustion on the near bank, while others slowly, painstakingly made their way across. They made no attempt to spread out, to scout the thick woods on the far side. Instead, they were all too grateful to have the chance to rest and to be momentarily beyond the range of Palthainon's temper and authority.

Porthios looked down at his bow and arrows. He had four steel-tipped shafts ready to shoot, and he pictured each of them puncturing elven flesh, drawing elven blood and piercing elven hearts. He felt sick to his stomach, suddenly horribly reluctant to fight this battle. Alhana had been right after all. It would be a great mistake, an unspeakable tragedy, to lead his countrymen into battle against their own people.

But already the first company of Palthainon's three units had crossed the stream, and the elves of the second were starting to pick their way across the bridge. At any moment, the first arrows would dart from the trees, and the killing would begin.

When he heard the shouts of alarm from Palthainon's elves, Porthios at first thought, with perverse relief, that his ambush had been discovered. "Run, you fools!" he whispered fiercely, certain that the Qualinesti would race back across the stream and he would have an excuse not to commence this butchery.

But he quickly realized that Palthainon's troops still had no clue as to the outlaws' presence. Instead, the Qualinesti were pointing toward the northern sky. Those troops on the opposite bank were running along the stream, heading for the cover of the nearest copse of trees, a quarter-mile downstream. The elves who had already crossed were standing, staring upward, trying to discern the cause of their comrades' alarm. Then, with shouts of dire panic, they turned and dashed into the woods, falling and tumbling among the outlaws who lay there in ambush, too panicked even to react to the surprise.

Yet the ambush never occurred, for now the elves of Porthios's force could see the sky, and none of them cared to raise a weapon against the Qualinesti. Instead, they could only stare, knees turning to jelly, eyes goggling from their heads, as they watched a wing of blue dragons soar downward. The dragonawe permeated even into the woods, and Porthios felt his own bowels grow loose as the massive serpents swept past.

Even so, he had to admire the military precision of their flight. Each dragon was ridden by a mounted knight, and the creatures flew wing tip to wing tip, a dozen of them spanning the full breadth of the wide clearing. Ignoring the elves who had crossed the stream, the serpents dived in pursuit of the Qualinesti who fled along the far bank of the gorge.

Lightning spat from their gaping jaws, blasts of powerful fire that tore elves into pieces and threw up great clods of dirt from the ground. The explosive volley was repeated with ruthless cruelty, changing the pastoral meadow into a scene of carnage, nightmare, and death. The thunder of the deadly attacks reverberated through the trees as dozens, then scores, of Palthainon's Qualinesti were cut down.

Finally the dragons landed in the midst of the fleeing elves, and the slaughter was tremendous, horrifying, unreal. Jaws snapped, crushing warriors between daggerlike teeth. Wyrms pounced and clawed, tearing other elves to pieces. Knightly riders stabbed with their lances, chopped with their swords, and shouted in glee as the helpless Qualinesti were mercilessly butchered and harried from the field.

All during the massacre, one dragon flew overhead, its rider trailing a pennant, a banner bright with the colors of a five-headed wyrm. Porthios knew that these dragons were part of an army, and that the army fought in the name of Takhisis, Queen of Darkness.

And he knew that war had come once more to Krynn.

* * * * *

"Ah, yes, the blues," said Aeren. "Their coming was not welcome in any part of the forest."

"But surely they are not hateful to you. Do you not all serve the same Dark Queen?" asked Silvanoshei.

"Bah," Aeren said scornfully. "I've always hated blue dragons—not as much as I hated elves, of course, or the serpents of gold and silver and their other metallic kin-dragons, but I hate blues nonetheless."

"Why?" asked the young elf.

"They're forever currying the Dark Queen's favor. And they're too precise, too willing to give up their freedom to answer their goddess's call. Once, as a young wyrmling, I was seared by the bolt of a blue's lightning breath. I still have the scars," the dragon stated sternly.

"I know they came to the forest and the city. Did they come to your lair?" asked Silvanoshei.

"Not at first, but I knew the blues had come with every intention of taking my new territory away from me. My first clue was an acrid scent carried by the southward breeze, a hint of char and ozone reminiscent of a nearby lightning strike. I emerged from my lair to watch the blues from the shelter of the leafy forest. I saw them fly over in precise formation, four ranks of five dragons each.

"Even worse was the sight of the long banner that trailed from a lance borne by one of the riders. The five-colored heads of evil dragonkind, here worked in a pattern around a white flower that looked like a death lily, could only mean that these serpents were flying under the sanction of Takhisis, the Queen of Darkness."

The Siege of Qualinost

Chapter Eleven

"My lord Speaker, the dragonarmies have come again! We must flee!"

"Stop . . . speak a little more carefully." Gilthas sat up in bed, looking at the excited Kagonesti slave who had burst into his bedchamber. "What's this about dragonarmies?"

"They have come. The Blue Wing returns!" cried the slave, an elder male who had been a part of the migration westward thirty years ago.

By now the young Speaker was fully awake. He climbed from the bed and went to look out the window. Qualinost, to all appearances, was a city in peaceful slumber. The sky was clear, and he saw no sign of any dragon or other attacker. He turned on the slave, irritated at being so rudely awakened.

"What are you talking about—dragonarmies? It's not possible! Who told you this, and where are they supposedly attacking?"

"They have swept southward from Solamnia and crossed the Newsea. Already they have struck the outposts on the borders!" continued the servant, his eyes wide. "Oh, lord, there is no stopping them! We're all going to die!"

Gilthas was sliding into his boots, shrugging his robe over his shoulders. Once more he looked out the window. His house—the official dwelling of the Speaker of the Sun—was located directly beside the Tower of the Sun, and that lofty spire blocked his view to the northeast, but even so, he assumed he would see some sign of trouble if there was in fact an invasion occurring.

Still, he couldn't suppress a sense of alarm as he left his house and started across the wide garden leading to the tower. He noticed other nobles gathering, a strange urgency gripping the city, considering that it was the middle of the night. They came from all directions, silent, exchanging worried glances and frightened looks. Gilthas felt a flash of worry, a thought of his mother and father in their house so far to the north. If war came, they were sure to be in the middle of it—and he couldn't help feeling that he should be with them to offer whatever help and comfort he could.

At the base of the tower, he found Rashas, and Guilderhand as well. The nobles and senators filed into the chamber with unseemly haste. Torches and magical lanterns lit the great council hall at the base of the tower, light reflected and magnified by the burnished gold of the walls and the numerous mirrors set into alcoves. The gathering was a startling and motley collection. Some of the elders were barefoot, while others were wearing wrinkled or even dirty robes.

Voices rattled and screeched as rumors were exchanged, questions asked, fears aired.

"What's going on?" one matron was demanding of anyone and everyone within earshot.

"I heard Haven is burning!" a well-fed merchant declared, wiping sweat from his brow and staring wildly around the chamber.

"An army—blue-skinned troops, big as ogres—crossed the border this evening!" This came from an orange grower who owned many groves.

And more cries chimed in, universal in their notes of hysteria and certainty:

"They fly the banner of the Dark Queen!"

"Their general rides a blue dragon!"

"Thousands of troops . . . they butcher anyone in their path!"

Gilthas climbed the steps to the rostrum and glanced over a sea of anxious faces. Elves looked from him to Rashas and back again. They both raised their hands to try to quiet the crowd, but the gesture had little effect in damming the stream of frightened words.

The Speaker shouted, somehow finding the depth to roar his voice across the chamber. "Elves of Qualinesti! Gather and attend! We need to learn what's happening, not stampede under an avalanche of rumors!"

The elves grew still, nervously looking back and forth. There remained a dull rumble of whispers, but this was mainly due to hasty explanations passed to the new arrivals who kept filtering through the partially opened doors. Gilthas noted the presence of even some of the youngsters who had typically avoided the meetings of the Thalas-Enthia, radicals such as Queralan, a young captain of archers who had held his seat in the senate for only a few years, and Anthelia, mistress of a clan of prominent artists and glassmakers. These two now looked just as afraid as everyone else.

"Is there anyone here who has seen these invaders?"

"I have!" a voice shot through the circular chamber. Guilderhand had spoken loudly. He stood near the back, and now he held up both hands in a gesture that was both contemptuous and soothing.

"Please give us your testimony," Gilthas said quickly.

The spy was dressed in his usual traveling garb, right down to the muddy boots and stained, torn cloak. Still, he strode up the steps of the rostrum as if he belonged there as much as the highest noble. He turned to the crowd, and with a sweeping gesture of his hands, drew the attention of every elf to himself.

"I am sorry to report that the rumors are true, right down

to the worst of the tales. The war in the north, about which we have heard fleeting reports, has swept southward to draw Qualinesti into its tendrils. Right now there is a force approaching our fair city, an unstoppable army of brutish warriors, Dark Knights, and blue dragons. They breached the borders of our realm during the night and march with remarkable haste."

Gilthas drew a deep breath, trying to absorb this incomprehensible news. "What do you know of their numbers . . . of the makeup of the force?"

"Their legions are huge, my lord Speaker," replied Guilderhand with a bow that somehow seemed like a mockery. "They filed past me on the Haven road for many hours, and still I could not see the end of the column. As to the warriors that make up the bulk of the force, they are like nothing I have ever seen. Huge, blue-skinned, and all but naked, they march toward battle with jeers and laughs. Truly, they seem monstrously cruel."

"And the knights and dragons?"

"With my own eyes, I saw twoscore dragons take wing and fly back and forth over the army on the ground. All were blues, and each was ridden by an armored warrior. They flew with discipline, these wyrms, and seemed ever watchful and vigilant.

"As to the knights on the ground, these might have been armed and armored from Solamnia, so like those human warriors did they seem, save that they ride under the banner of the Dark Queen."

The mention of that hateful goddess brought another bubbling of concern through the chamber, and like a master speaker Guilderhand waited for the whispering to die down.

"They rode in companies. I saw ten companies of forty or fifty knights each. All wore heavy armor, and their horses were huge, monstrous creatures that could crush an elf with one hoof. Many of the knights were lancers, while others had great swords and shields. From the order of their road march, I deduce that they would have no difficulty launching a precise charge. They could ride down any rank of warriors who dared to stand in their path."

"And they are now in the kingdom, on the roads to Qualinost?" Gilthas pressed, his heart sinking at the thought of such an onslaught.

"I predict that by tomorrow they will reach the bridges leading to the city itself. I have also heard rumors, tales claiming that more of these invaders have entered the western parts of the realm. Naturally we have not been able to confirm those tales."

"Of course not," the speaker agreed dejectedly. Oh, why had the griffons abandoned them? If the elves had the services of those once loyal fliers, he knew that at least they'd be able to get word back and forth through the kingdom. As it was, they were feeling their way blindly, could only hope that they acted before it was too late.

"Were you observed?" asked the young senator Quaralan, speaking to Guilderhand. "Did you spy on the army from concealment or move about in disguise?"

"Oh, great lord, it was a harrowing time," replied the spy. "I tried to hide myself in the undergrowth, where I watched the army pass for some time. Ultimately I was observed and captured by the blue warriors—brutes, they were called. Much to my horror, they took me to see the general commanding this army!"

Cries of horror and sympathy rose from the elven crowd, but Guilderhand raised his hands again, gesturing for silence, for calm.

"Shortly before I was to enter his presence, they held me near a wagon of the Dark Knight sorcerers—Knights of the Thorn, they are, and they wear robes of gray." The spy held up his hand, in which he gripped a ring of bright gold. "It was from there that I made my escape, stealing this ring of powerful magic. It gave me the power to teleport away, and so I made my way back here. If not, I would certainly have been put to death!"

More shouts of outrage and fear echoed in the chamber.

"We must activate the rest of the city militia," Gilthas declared, trying to mask his own despair. "Get elves standing at each of the bridges, ready to defend Qualinost against the first sign of attack!"

"What good will that do?" Rashas demanded vehemently, contemptuously. "Weren't you *listening?* This is a force that can trample anything that stands in its path! Would you send every young elf in Qualinost to his death?"

Gilthas spun around, at first too surprised even to speak. He gaped at the senator in astonishment, finally shaking his head, forcing out the words. "What would you have us do, then? Flee to Ergoth again, the second exile in thirty years? And even if we wanted to, you know there's no time for the city's population to get away!"

"Now is not the time for us to lose our heads," Rashas replied, his tone calm and soothing. The Speaker realized that somehow Rashas had again made Gilthas appear to be an excitable youngster. Now the elder senator addressed the crowd of elves in general. "What else do we know of this army, these 'Knights of Takhisis'? Who leads them?"

"I was able to learn a few things during my brief captivity. Their leader is now in Palanthas, a man called Lord Ariakan," Guilderhand explained. "He is said to be the son of the Dragon Highlord Ariakas, who was once the Emperor of Ansalon. His mother is unknown, though there are those who claim her to be the goddess Zeboim."

"A lackey of the Dark Queen's . . . I admit that the tale makes a certain amount of sense," Rashas mused.

"I know that these Dark Knights have already conquered Kalaman and much of the north—without bloodshed," claimed one noble elf, who was a regular importer of marble quarried near that fabled city on the northern coast. "Even allowed the Lord Mayor of Kalaman to hold his seat. Business there has been better than ever."

"The Kalamans didn't *fight?*" This question was asked by Quaralan, who seemed to be making himself spokesman for the young hotheads who had scorned Gilthas's appointment to the Speaker's throne.

The noble merchant shrugged. "Perhaps there'll be a battle at the High Clerist's Tower, where the Solamnics are trying to hold off the invaders. Of course, if that tower is lost, Palanthas itself would be pretty much defenseless. I would expect that they would let the invaders march in. It would be foolish to let the place get burned down when they don't have enough troops even to man their own walls."

"And they have the proof before them, for it's a fact that Ariakan's army spared Kalaman!" shouted another elf. "I know this from my brother, who is a seller of silk there. The mayor maintains his station, and the council, too. Indeed, he says that these knights have been a boon in some ways. They've stopped the thievery that was always such a problem near the docks."

Gilthas felt he had to take some steps to control this discussion. He stood straight and assumed his sternest glare as he looked around the chamber. "Am I to assume that the attitude of the Thalas-Enthia is that we welcome these invaders with open arms, that we invite them into our capital and perhaps hope that they will help us solve some recurring problems regarding merchandising and crime?"

His sarcasm was heavy and apparent. After all, Qualinost had no crime to speak of, and virtually every elf in this chamber was rich beyond the dreams of even the most avaricious human noble. Even so, his scornful remarks were greeted mostly with silence, a few elves exchanging nervous glances.

"It seems logical that we should at least meet with the leader of this army," Rashas said. "There can be no harm in diplomatic negotiations, in finding out what his intentions are." He addressed Guilderhand. "Is this Lord Ariakan himself leading the troops that are marching on Qualinost?"

"The best information I could gather is no, Esteemed Senator. The commander of this army is called Lord Salladac. He is reputedly a trusted lieutenant of Ariakan's and has been given complete command of the campaign in Qualinesti."

"At the very least, we should arm ourselves and make ready to fight!" Gilthas declared, surprising himself with his own vehemence. He heard several shouts of agreement, though they were scattered far and wide through the crowded chamber.

"Who will command?" asked Rashas. "Our most experienced general, Palthainon, is in the west, trying to solve the bandit problem."

"Then I shall take charge of the troops," Gilthas said coldly, ignoring the looks of astonishment he saw on many faces. He was prepared to challenge for his right to do so when, to his surprise, Rashas spoke in support.

"I commend the Speaker for his excellent suggestion," declared the senator. "He has the necessary authority to bring together such recruits as we can gather in a short time."

"Hear, hear!" Cries of support came from here and there in the chamber, though it was nothing like a universal acclamation.

"At the same time," Rashas continued, "we have to realize that there is no profit in excessive bloodshed. The honorable members of the Thalas-Enthia must consider the minimum terms that we would require to arrive at a nonmartial solution."

Gilthas shook his head in astonishment. "You'd be prepared to abandon the defense of the city, of the kingdom, before the first arrow is loosed?"

"I make the suggestion merely because I know that it will make sense for us to be prepared for every eventuality. We all applaud our young Speaker's courage and the rightness of your intentions. But bear in mind that war is serious business, and that we are facing a great force, well practiced in the arts of subjugation and conquest. Courage and honor are worthy concepts for any elf, but foolish sacrifice is nothing more than a waste."

"Where are the Dark Knights now?" Gilthas asked, turning back to Guilderhand. He wondered how the spy had so easily escaped from these ruthless and efficient attackers, but there was no time to follow up on that question.

"They crossed the border after marching along the Southway. I predict they will be no more than five miles away by the dawn."

"Then we really don't have any time to lose," the Speaker declared. He addressed the group at large. "I urge you all to go home, to arm your servants and to take up weapons yourselves. Armed elves should congregate . . ." Where? Suddenly Gilthas felt overwhelmed by the task. He didn't even know how to bring his armed elves together! He thought fleetingly of his father, missing Tanis with a powerful sense of longing. Surely the heroic half-elf would know what to do.

"The Hall of the Sky?" suggested Rashas smoothly. The suggestion was perfect. The "hall" was in a fact a huge clearing in the center of the city, large enough to accommodate a good-sized force.

"Yes—meet at the hall, and spread the word!"

The agitated crowd began to disperse, but Gilthas took Rashas aside before the senator left the hall. "I need to send a message," said the young Speaker. The thought of his father had brought to mind another concern, something that he was determined to address.

"A message? Where?" inquired Rashas, irritated at the delay.

"I want to send for my mother. With war threatening the land, she should come to Qualinesti. I know that my father will be fighting, and it would be best to have her return here to her homeland." Where she'll be safe, Gilthas wanted to add, but he didn't say it, for he knew that it wasn't true.

Surprisingly, Rashas thought for only a few seconds and then nodded sagely. "An excellent idea," he replied. "By all means, send for Laurana. Encourage her to come with all haste."

Watching the senator's back, Gilthas tried to fathom the elder's response. He had expected some resistance, even an outright refusal. Now he was worried that Rashas had agreed so easily.

Still, he would send the message by fast courier, then turn to the matter of raising a defense force. Relieved to have reached some course of action, Gilthas left the hall, followed by many worried elves. But he took little notice of the throng around him as he made his way back to his house, wondering what he should wear, where he would find a weapon. And what would he do with a weapon if he had one?

Shaking off his concerns, he stalked away, knowing that he had an army to raise . . . and just a few hours during which to do it.

* * * * *

The dragon snorted derisively. "So the elves thought they could resist, could stand against the onslaught of blue dragons?"

"Yes!" Silvanoshei insisted. "And some elves, such as my father, did manage to give Lord Salladac pause for thought!"

"Indeed," Aeren said, "I had heard something about that. . . ."

A Night of Glory and Blood

Chapter Twelve

The outlaws found Palthainon on the muddy field. His hair had been seared off by a dragon's lightning bolt that had also knocked the warrior elf unconscious, but other than that, the general was unharmed.

The same could not be said for two of his three companies of recruits. Nearly four hundred elves had been caught in the clearing when the blue serpents had flown over, and nearly three-quarters of them had been slaughtered by dragon breath or by the talons of the monsters and the swords of their riders.

Only the elves of the first company—the group that, ironically, would have been the first to suffer the lethal strike of Porthios's aborted ambush—had survived unscathed, by taking shelter in the thick woods that would otherwise have been their undoing. Though these city elves had tumbled among archers who had been prepared to attack them, both bands of the sylvan folk had been so startled by the arrival of the greater foe that their initial conflict had been immediately forgotten.

Fortunately the dragons hadn't stayed long after working their butchery on the field. Neither had they discovered the outlaws' griffons, who had been sheltered in small clearings very near the site of the intended ambush. Now these savage fliers had been gathered, and the survivors of the Qualinesti force had joined with the bandits preparatory to falling back into the forest. General Palthainon was still dazed and disoriented, so Porthios had assumed command of all the elves.

"Get the wounded back to our camp," he directed. "See that the general is made as comfortable as possible, but don't waste any time."

"Lord Porthios!" The cry came from the skies, and the shadow of a griffon's wings momentarily passed over. One of his Qualinesti warriors gestured wildly as the creature came to rest before him.

"There's a whole army to the north. It's a full-scale invasion!"

"All under the banner of the Dark Queen?" he asked, dumbfounded.

"Knights, and columns of marching troops as well—great, blue-skinned brutes, they look like they could crush an elf's skull with their bare hands. It looks like the dragons are winging back to rejoin the infantry."

Porthios didn't know where this army could have come from, but the attack on the elven formation made its objective clear enough. "How far away are the ground troops?" he asked, trying to think, to plan.

"Twenty miles. They're finding slow going in the woods, but they're coming this way."

"Let's get away from here, then. We'll make plans as soon as we reach the gorge."

Together with about three hundred survivors from the Qualinesti militia, the outlaw band made its way back to the encampment. Because so many elves had to travel on foot, the journey took quite a bit longer than the one-hour griffon flight that had led the band to the ambush site. The wounded were loaded onto litters, which further slowed down the party's progress, and it wasn't until well after sunset that the weary elves marched down the trail into the deep darkness of the cool gorge.

Once back at the camp, they learned—from Dallatar's Kagonesti, not surprisingly—that another force of Dark Knights had invaded the eastern end of the kingdom and was even now drawing up against Qualinost itself. Flying scouts had given Porthios an idea of the size of the army marching along the coast. It seemed likely that at least five thousand troops were headed almost directly toward his camp.

The wild elves had come with another fifty or so warriors—"braves," as they called themselves. With this addition, Porthios found himself with a force of some six hundred elves, but nearly half of them were unblooded recruits, fresh from the streets and courtyards of Qualinost. Furthermore, he had serious questions about whether or not those elven warriors would have the stomach to battle a truly dangerous foe.

The bandit leader met with Dallatar, Samar, and Tarqualan around the firepit in the center of their encampment to discuss a course of action. They were warmed only by a low bed of smokeless coals, for with dragons abroad, the elves knew the need for camouflage and concealment was drastically heightened.

"We can stay here and hope they pass us by, or we can pick up the camp and move," Porthios began. "Or we can choose to fight a battle against outrageous odds. We have to discuss the question. It's too important for me to make a decision by myself."

"I say we attack them from ambush," Samar urged. "They won't be expecting it, and we can hit them hard while they're marching, then use the griffons to get away."

"My braves fight on the ground," Dallatar declared. "We have befriended griffons through the years but would not ride them into battle. They should be free to make their own choices."

"Believe me, these griffons are choosing their allegiance,"

Tarqualan said. "They have refused to serve the elves of Qualinesti ever since the Thalas-Enthia ordered Alhana Starbreeze imprisoned."

"Be that as it may," Porthios interjected, "there are a little more than two hundred griffons allied with our band. That's not enough to move all of us anywhere. If we fight, two-thirds of us will have to go into battle on the ground."

"Still, an ambush is the only way—hit them as they march, then fall back into the woods," Samar urged. "We've spied on these brutes. They move like ogres, and they'll never catch an elf in thick terrain."

"I agree," Dallatar said somberly. "We cannot just move away from them, and my pride will not let them take our woodlands without a fight. We wild elves have already decided—we will attack the invaders. What the rest of you do is a matter for your own councils."

"I applaud your courage," Porthios replied with equal sincerity. "And I urge you to remain with us. Surely you can see that, together, we can strike a much harder blow than any part of us working alone."

"Then you, too, are determined to fight?" the Kagonesti chieftain asked.

Porthios looked at his companions. Samar nodded curtly; he had already made his opinion known. Tarqualan drew a deep breath, then spoke. "Neither I nor my scouts could ever sleep well again, knowing we had turned our backs on such a menace. Even if it leads us to the endless sleep of death, such a battle is preferable to flight."

"Then we are unanimous," the outlaw who had once been Speaker of the Sun declared. "For I, too, cannot bear the thought of this incursion passing without a fight. If we are fortunate, Qualinost will stand against the attack from the east, and we can sting this western army hard enough that they will have to rethink their strategy. At the very least, they will know that they have attacked a proud, brave enemy."

"What of the elders and the little ones?" asked Dallatar. "As a rule, they do not fight beside the male and female braves."

Porthios thought of Alhana and Silvanoshei. He had a fleeting wish that his baby could have been born into a time of peace. Such eras, he realized grimly, were all too rare. "Nor is that the case with us," he replied. "I suggest that we choose our battleground as far from this camp as possible. Perhaps by doing so we can keep this gorge safe. If the worst happens, the new mothers, the elders, and the children will learn of our defeat, and then they will have to make a quick departure."

"Madness! What are these crazy ideas you discuss?"

The shrill voice came from out of the darkness, and then the Qualinesti General Palthainon, his head bandaged where the lightning bolt had seared his scalp, shambled into view. He was waving his arms, looking wide-eyed from one elf to another.

"They have dragons—surely you saw that! They cut my companies to pieces, wiped us out almost to the last elf! The only solution is to take to the woods and try to make our way back to the city. Once there, we can sue for peace!"

Dallatar looked at the Qualinesti general with ill-concealed scorn. Porthios kept his expression neutral but rose to his feet and gestured that the commander of the troops from the city join them at the low fire.

"I am glad to see that you are recovering from your wounds," he said graciously. "But you have been unconscious. Perhaps you don't know that more than half of your troops survived the attack."

"Survived? How?" demanded the general.

"They joined us in the woods," Samar said curtly. "We know that your mission was to find and attack us. We were prepared to ambush you as you crossed the stream. You might say that the dragon attack actually saved the lives of a good number of your warriors."

"Madness!" cried Palthainon again. "I—I *order* you, as the duly appointed commander of Qualinesti forces, to cease this insanity!"

All intentions of civility vanished in the rush of anger that swept through Porthios. He whirled on the general, his hand going to the hilt of his sword, knuckles whitening as his grip tightened. Frightened by the gesture and by the expression on the dark elf's face, Palthainon stepped hastily backward.

"I remind you, General—" Porthios's voice was heavy with scorn —"that you were appointed to the command of a force with the task of seeking and attacking my band. Also, that you failed dismally in that task. You led your companies into the perfect site for an ambush. If the blue dragons hadn't come along, you would have been cut to pieces! Now you speak of tactics that any loyal elf can only describe as treasonous!"

"You are the traitor!" hissed the Qualinesti commander, apparently deciding that his life wasn't in immediate danger. "You hide here in the forest, taking the rightfully earned goods of loyal elven merchants! How dare you–"

With lightning quickness, Porthios reached out a hand and slapped the general, spinning him around, sending him tumbling to the ground.

"You will not address me with contempt," he growled, standing over the cringing elf. "Nor will you ask how I dare to do anything. You have drawn your own sentence. I would have willingly treated you as an ally against the greater menace of the Dark Knights, but now I can only see you as a craven coward. You will be treated as a prisoner, and even that is a role of higher honor than I think you deserve."

Palthainon looked as though he wanted to speak, but he gulped and reconsidered his words.

"Guards!" shouted Porthios. Several of his warriors came running. "Bind this elf securely, hands and feet, then tie him to a tree. I want him watched at all times!"

The elves quickly did as they were told. In the meantime, the outlaw leader looked around the encampment, seeing that all of the elves had observed the confrontation between the two leaders. Porthios also considered the problem of the general he had just ordered bound to a tree. There were not enough elves in his band to spare any for guard duty, and as long as he was here, Palthainon was an obvious irritant and distraction.

He decided that this was the time to address the issue of

the band's past and future loyalties.

"Elves of Qualinesti," he declared, speaking loudly. His words were directed at the warriors who had marched with Palthainon, though all the elves in the camp listened attentively. "I offer you a choice—a choice that you must make now, tonight.

"My loyal scouts and the braves of the Kagonesti will strive to resist this new invasion of our homeland. Our opponents are many, and include blue dragons among their number. But we are elven warriors, and we are fighting for our own forests, so I promise you that we will give these invaders something to think about. We will let them know that Qualinesti is not a nation to be violated with casual arrogance.

"There is at least one among us who feels that this is a doomed course, that we should crawl back to the city, and there try to make peace with these invaders. He has not said what he is prepared to pay for this peace . . . his treasures? His woman? Who knows—and who cares? I only know that such a choice is repugnant to me.

"But know this, also: I intend to release General Palthainon, to allow him to make his way back to the city and to sacrifice whatever he feels is necessary to save his life. He will be taken into the woods before dawn and pointed in the direction of Qualinost."

Here Porthios drew a deep breath. He was about to make a tremendous gamble, and he could only hope that he had judged these elves properly.

"I offer this opportunity to any of you who would accompany the general back to the city . . . back to his negotiated peace, or whatever that course holds. For the rest, I ask you to sharpen your swords and make ready your souls. In the morning, we march to war."

After a few minutes of deliberation, only about two dozen of Palthainon's original company elected to desert the band in the gorge. The outlaw leader had these elves escorted southeastward from the camp. They were divested of their swords—"You won't be doing any fighting," he pointed out with inescapable logic—but allowed to keep their bows and a few arrows for hunting.

As he was led from the encampment, the general tried to bluster some threats about returning with a new army, but the outlaws took the sting from his words by laughing in his face. While a strong escort of Kagonesti insured that these refugee elves kept going, Porthios met with his other chieftains and discussed a plan for the attack on the Dark Knights.

"We have seen the strength of the enemy, and we know something about the heart of our own troops," he began as Dallatar, Tarqualan, and Samar all listened intently. "It has been suggested that we strike the Dark Knights while they are on the march, then melt back into the woods. This is a tactic that has some chance of success, but I would like to propose something else."

"Speak," Samar said earnestly. "We have all seen the wisdom of your battle plans."

"Very well. Instead of an ambush while the enemy is on the move, I suggest we strike their camp during the quiet, dark hours before dawn. They will be weary and unsuspecting, while many of them will be sound asleep. We, on the other hand, will be able to make our escape under cover of darkness."

And so it was decided. The battle was planned for the middle of the following night.

* * * * *

The Dark Knights marched with military precision, and the elves who spied on them from the woods soon saw the wisdom of Porthios's suggestion. Outriders on horseback preceded the column, and skirmish companies of the blue-skinned brutes were scattered far and wide. As a result, any ambushing party of elves would have been discovered long before the main body of the enemy force was in range.

Furthermore, the blue dragons ranged before and to the flanks of the marching column, always within hailing distance. Any attacking force would have been hammered hard by the lightning breath and crushing weight of the massive, deadly wyrms.

Not that the army's evening camp would make an easy target, of course.

The Kagonesti, who were the most adept among the elves at moving silently and unseen through the woods, kept close to the force and periodically brought reports back to Porthios. The outlaw captain was waiting with the main body of his force ten miles north of the encampment in the gorge and very near to the line of the enemy's march. Together with two hundred griffons, he had fewer than six hundred elves to attack a formation that numbered at least ten times the number of his own warriors.

"They have stopped marching for the day," Dallatar reported as the sun neared the western horizon. "They will make their camp on the slopes and summit of a large, steep hill."

Further reports indicated that the Dark Knights would apparently keep one dragon in the air all night, alternating in one-hour shifts so that the flying serpent wouldn't get overly tired. Though the invaders didn't build a palisade around their camp, the steepness of the hill gave them a measure of defensibility. Some thickets of brush and stumpy pine trees extended up the slopes, but the crest of the hill was bald, providing the knights with good visibility and easy movement from one side of the elevation to another.

As soon as they learned that the enemy had stopped marching, the elves moved out. Like a file of ghosts in the forests, they moved silently toward the hill. The Kagonesti led the way, with the volunteers from the Qualinost recruits in the middle and the scouts of Porthios's original force bringing up the rear. The griffons came with them, padding along on the ground in order to prevent any chance of being discovered in flight.

Full darkness had settled around them by the time they drew near to the hill.

"Do they have pickets in the forest?" Porthios asked Dallatar, gesturing to the fringe of thick woods around the base of the hill.

"Not enough," replied the Kagonesti. "Those who are there we will kill in silence."

"Very well." The dark elf looked upward, seeing the shadowy form of the circling dragon pass across a pale wisp of cloud. "We'll take to the sky and try to get that fellow at the same time."

The rest of the battle plan was formed on the spot, taking into account the terrain, the relative abilities of the Kagonesti and the ill-trained recruits from Qualinost. Fortunately each of these elves had a flint and a steel, and these were ingredients of a key aspect of the impending assault. The wild elves left immediately, relying on their natural stealth as they embarked on the difficult task of removing the Dark Knight pickets.

It was nearing midnight as the rest of the elves dispersed, two bands slipping through the woods to different places at the base of the hill, while Porthios and two hundred of his original Qualinesti waited with the griffons to make up the final part of the attack.

The minutes seemed to drag by like hours, but he knew that they had to wait. Timing was a crucial element of the attack, and each formation would have to make its presence known at the appropriate time. Finally he judged that the moment was right, and with a gesture of his hand, the prince sent two hundred elves into their saddles. White wings fluttered through the clearing, and he had a brief impression of a reverse snowstorm as the fierce griffons swarmed around and slowly lifted themselves and their riders into the sky.

Once they had reached the top of the trees, the elven formation strung into a long line, flying swiftly away from the Dark Knights' camp. Porthios was grateful for the absence of moonlight as he gradually led the group higher and higher into the air. Puffy clouds wafted past, blocking out many of the stars, and he hoped that these, too, would work to the elves' advantage.

Gaining altitude steadily, Porthios led the flying formation around a large mass of cloud. Here, screened from the invaders' view, they spiraled into a rapid climb and finally headed toward the enemy's camp. They flew at an altitude far above the monotonous spiral of the flying dragon. Maintaining utter silence, they winged closer and closer, veering only enough to keep one or more clouds between themselves and the Dark Knights.

Finally the outlaw prince and Stallyar emerged from a gap between two clouds, and far below he saw the outline of a large blue dragon. The serpent was gliding, wings lazily out-spread, with the dark outline of a rider on the saddle between its shoulders. Both dragon and Dark Knight had their attention focused on the ground, which was just what Porthios had been hoping for—indeed, had been counting on.

The griffons tucked their wings, one by one other plummeting after their leader. Porthios drew his sword in a silent gesture while Stallyar, who knew the plan as well as any of the elves, targeted the neck of the monstrous serpent. Wind whistled past, rasping against the prince's skin, and he felt certain that the knight must soon hear his approach. But even as the target grew larger, until the dragon's wingspread seemed to span the full width of his vision, both dragon and rider held their attention on the still, dark hilltop below.

Just before the two fliers collided, Porthios leapt from his saddle, landing hard on the back of the dragon. The wyrm uttered a startled gasp as Stallyar's talons scraped his head, while the elf's sword, a weapon toned and hallowed by generations of the finest elven artisans, was darting toward the back of the armored knight.

But perhaps that dragonrider had heard his attacker an instant before contact. In any event, the man twisted away, grunting as the sword scraped past his shoulder. He had a short-bladed sword in his own hand, and he made a powerful thrust, rocking Porthios back on the rough spines of the dragon's backbone. At the same time, the wyrm ducked into a dive, and the elf felt himself sliding toward a broad, leathery wing.

Frantically he reached out, grasping at anything he could touch. His hand closed over the back of the knight's saddle, and his sword slashed wildly. Steel clanged as the two weapons met, and then the dragon tilted back, twisting and hissing as it tried to pull the griffon off its neck. Porthios was pushed forward with the shift in momentum, and he thrust unerringly, feeling the sharp blade punch through the man's breastplate, then cut through gristle, flesh, and bone.

Without a sound, the knight toppled away, and now more griffons were plunging past. Elven swords sliced the wyrm's wings, hacking scales from the supple neck, gouging deep into haunches, flanks, and tail. Still grasping the saddle, Porthios leaned forward and stabbed downward, slicing deep into the wyrm's shoulder, feeling the dragon twist convulsively. Eyes wide, the elves saw gaping jaws, a neck twisted impossibly as the creature lashed around to bite at him.

But then Samar was there, the warrior-mage riding Bellaclaw and bearing the slender dragonlance. The keen silver edge sliced through the dragon's neck, gouging deep, nearly severing the hateful head. Porthios was washed by a warm spray, and he realized that blood was gushing from the deep wound on the monster's neck.

And just like that, the dragon died, never uttering a sound louder than the irritated hissing that had greeted the first attack. The massive wings swept upward, pushed by air pressure as the lifeless shape tumbled toward the ground. Sheathing his sword, Porthios flung himself into the air, flailing wildly, grasping at Stallyar's reins as the griffon dived past. Pulling himself into the saddle, the prince jabbed his feet into his stirrups and looked around with a sense of exhilaration. The rest of the griffons were diving with him, wings tucked, though they weren't dropping as fast as the slain dragon.

Still, the camp on the hilltop was now growing underneath them. His eyes skimming the trees, Porthios spotted a glimmer of flame, then several spots of brightness, like living sparks that danced and sparkled in the dry woods. He heard shouts of alarm, saw agitated activity, and knew that the timing of the attack was working perfectly.

Dragons bellowed, and knights shuffled out of their bedrolls, cursing and grunting as they hastily slapped on their weapons. The blue dragons were gathered at the hilltop, and they huffed and snorted impatiently. All of their attention, as far as Porthios could tell, was focused on the fires that were now growing to encompass an arc around a third of the base of the hill.

The slain dragon crashed to the ground in the middle of a bivouac of the army's brutish warriors, and these blue-skinned creatures bellowed and howled in fury and surprise. Some of them even turned on the corpse, stabbing with monstrous spears or hacking with swords, obviously unaware that the creature was dead.

Then the griffons plummeted like deadly hailstones into the middle of the dragon camp. Abruptly the night was split by the flash of lightning, though the first bolt missed the attackers to cut deeply into the flank of another blue dragon. Porthios wielded his sword from Stallyar's saddle, striking down a knight who tried to raise a massive, two-handed sword. The silvery griffon galloped forward, ripping into the wing of a dragon with his sharp beak and claws. The elven captain slashed the keen steel blade, cutting another rip out of the wing.

The griffon pounced quickly away, just a hairbreadth of space before the wyrm's massive talons smashed into the ground. Instinctively Stallyar darted to the side, and a moment later a blast of lightning scored through the night, streaking past, crackling through the air and sizzling the skin on the back of the elf's neck. Porthios ducked, already feeling the imminent, killing blast of the next lightning bolt, but now the dragon was distracted by other griffons and whipped about to slash at new attackers that worried its wings, flanks, and tail.

Stallyar spread his wings and leapt high, while Porthios had a sickening impression of another griffon's wing, torn from the bleeding body and floating grotesquely in the air. An elf screamed, the sound hideous as a dragon bit down and gored the unfortunate warrior in two. But dragons and knights were howling, too.

Another man stood in the griffon's path, and Stallyar reached down, tearing away the fellow's scalp with a single, vicious bite. Another knight charged in from the right, and Porthios chopped hard, feeling his sword cut through a steel helmet to gouge deep into the skull below. The man screamed and tumbled away, dropping his sword to clasp both hands to his bleeding head.

Flames flickered across the hilltop, the lingering effects of lightning sparking through the air, while other sparks, scattered from campfires and fanned by frantic wings, tumbled across the ground and ignited tufts of dry grass. Dragons still roared, and here and there griffons shrieked in pain as they were caught by massive talons or reptilian jaws. Bodies twitched, and men and elves moaned in pain. The scene was nightmarish, a chaos of horrible sounds, garish fires, and gruesome injuries whirling across the dusty hilltop. Out of nowhere, a hot breeze arose, fanning the little fires into furious blazes, swirling the thick dust through the air until it clogged mouths, eyes, and nostrils.

A dismounted elf tumbled past Porthios, and a blue dragon head lashed like a striking snake in pursuit. The prince's sword chopped down, gouging the flaring nose, but the wyrm bit down and the fleeing elf was cut in two. The dragon shook its head like a dog worrying a rabbit, and Porthios stabbed upward, carving deep into the blue-scaled neck. Now the serpent reared back in surprise, bloody jaws gaping for another strike.

From the flank, another griffon dived in, tearing at the monster's face, and Porthios saw Samar slip from his saddle, sliding down the dragon's side, stabbing deep with his lance. The two elves charged in as more griffons clawed and snapped at the wyrm's face. With a powerful stab, the prince thrust his blade through the scaly breast, twisting with all his strength. A gout of chill blood soaked him as, with a convulsive shudder, the great serpent tumbled forward.

Porthios tripped, falling on his back as tons of slain lizard pressed him down. He felt strong hands on his shoulders, and he kicked frantically, barely squirming free before the monstrous form crashed to the ground.

"Thanks," he gasped as Samar let him go and turned to face the attack of a charging knight. "That's twice you've save my life."

The other elf had no time to reply as he parried the human's savage blow. The knight's face was twisted in an expression of grief, and Porthios wondered for an instant if this man had been the dead dragon's rider. If so, his sorrow only increased his fury, for his second blow knocked Samar's lance from the elf's hand. As the loyal Silvanesti fell backward, Porthios lunged in from the side, piercing the man's flank and then pushing the blade upward to cut the blood vessels around his heart. Soundlessly the knight fell across the foreleg of the dragon, his own warm blood mingling with the cool fluid that still gushed from the blue's torn chest.

A bolt of lightning crackled through the air, knocking Porthios flat and blasting a griffon and its rider into charred flesh. Stirred by the dry wind, white feathers whirled past, bright in the firelight and deceptively gentle as they settled to the ground. Another dragon pounced, shaking the ground with its weight as it bore an elf and his mount to the ground. With savage bites and tearing claws, it instantly reduced its helpless victims to gory flesh.

"Fall back!" cried Porthios, realizing that the dragons had recovered from their initial surprise and were now making a methodical attempt to eradicate their elven attackers.

The cry was repeated from every elven voice within reach as the warriors leapt into their saddles and griffon wings pulsed, aiding the powerful legs in vaulting the creatures into the air. Some of the elves flew overhead, and these shot arrow after arrow at the dragons, aiming for the sensitive eyes, desperately trying to hold the pursuit at bay long enough for the attackers to take to the air.

Porthios found Stallyar, seized the reins, and then heard a groan of pain from underfoot. He looked down to see an elven warrior, missing one of his arms at the elbow but desperately trying to push himself to his knees. The captain grabbed the fellow by his good arm, pulled him across the griffon's withers, and silently urged Stallyar into the sky.

Burdened by the extra weight, the griffon didn't try to leap straight up. Instead, he raced across the hilltop, hurling himself into the air at the edge of the crest, straight into the teeth of the hot wind. Immediately white wings spread wide, catching the air.

Then, with the keen instinct that had so often saved his

own and his rider's life, Stallyar banked hard to the side and
dived. Porthios leaned flat across his mount's shoulders, clinging to the wounded elf with both hands as a lightning bolt
hissed through the air over his head. He felt the searing heat
on the back of his neck, sensed the world canting crazily as the
griffon leveled out his flight, and then the hilltop was behind
them. Another bolt spat outward, but sizzled into nothingness
before it could reach them.

Laboring hard to gain altitude, Stallyar banked through a
wide circle, and then dived into a thick column of smoke that
was rising from the woods at the base of the hill. Ignoring the
searing heat, blinking the tears from his eyes, Porthios looked
down as the flier broke from the other side of the massive
cloud.

He saw that the Kagonesti attack had ignited a great conflagration. Like his griffon riders, those elves were falling back
but leaving chaos in their wake. Bellowing brutes raced back
and forth, batting at flames that singed their skin, striking at
shadows that seemed to move with living purpose in the light
of the dancing, shifting plumes of fire. Casks of oil exploded
with billowing towers of roiling heat, and from a stack of burning crates came the stench of charred beef as the army's food
stockpiles were incinerated.

Here and there a wild elf lay on the ground, his bloody
corpse hammered with mindless violence by the brutes, and
Porthios felt a stab of grief as he realized the horrific toll of this
battle. But the wind whipped the flames higher, carrying the
fires across the dry grass of the hillside, and everywhere the
light showed an army disrupted by chaos. As Stallyar's flight
took him around the hill, he looked back to see saw Dark
Knights turning their weapons against brutes, and other
brutes smashing at their own comrades.

On the far side of the hill, he saw the effects of the third
prong of his attack. Here the Qualinesti recruits, their numbers
stiffened by a few of his bandit veterans, had waited until the
rest of the camp was assaulted before they struck. A few fires
flared here and there, and he saw that many brutes lay dead in
the ruins. From the arrows and cuts in their backs, he suspected

that—as he had planned—this part of the camp had been taken by surprise, ambushed while they looked toward the distractions of the first two attacks.

Finally the griffon was flying over the dark forest. Around him, Porthios saw other winged shapes, more of his Qualinesti who had escaped from the hilltop. Wondering what toll the morning would bring, the elves swept away from the Dark Knights toward their rendezvous in the deep woods.

* * * * *

"So that's why they were so angry?" Aerensianic said with a ground-shaking chuckle.

"Who?" asked Silvanoshei.

"The blue dragons. You see, they came sweeping down the coast the next day. They were blasting the trees with their lightning, doing everything they could to find the elves. And they were in a most foul state of temper."

"Did they find your lair?"

"In fact, one of them poked his nose in here . . . not as far as the first bend. I gave him a blast of poison, and he backed right away, albeit with some very unfriendly words."

"Didn't he come back with more blues? Surely they had you out-numbered," Samar suggested.

"Indeed . . . but by then, I think they were concerned with business farther to the east . . . in the city of the elves."

A Day of Shame and Tears

Chapter Thirteen

By evening, after one day of trying to recruit, Gilthas had concluded that the elves of Qualinost had no stomach for defending their city against the incursion of the Dark Knights. After sending a message to his mother, pleading with her to come to Qualinesti, he had spent the day going from house to house or speaking loudly at the intersections of the city's main streets. In most cases, the elves were far more concerned with their own fate than in anything they could do to help the nation as a whole.

Rumors of the invasion, of course, had spread like wind through the city, and the Speaker was met with many panicked questions, demands for protection, and a level of fear that seemed likely to grow into hysteria. Everywhere he went he found people hiding their valuables, boarding up their splendid houses, disguising beautiful wives and nubile daughters as filthy hags. The mood among almost all of the elves was that if the Dark Queen's army was drawing close to the city, there was no hope of preventing Qualinost's fall.

A few, including some of those who still had pride in their homeland and a sense of the elven role in Krynn's history, had scorned Gilthas's proposal that they join him in fighting the invaders. One of them, the young Senator Queralan, had almost spat in his face, declaring that the young Speaker lacked the honor to sit upon the throne of Qualinesti and that, as such, he was unsuitable to serve as the city's military leader. Instead, Queralan had said, he was making plans to flee with his family and household servants into the forest. There he would resist the occupation in whatever manner he could devise.

Shamed and humiliated, Gilthas had almost wept as he left the young noble's lofty crystal mansion. How could they misunderstand him so? Why wouldn't they even give him a *chance* to show that he could be a leader?

Indeed, almost no one had been willing to take up a sword and gather with the Speaker at the Hall of the Sky. Now, at sunset, the appointed hour for the meeting, barely threescore Qualinesti had gathered, and nothing about these volunteers gave him confidence even in this small fighting force. A few of them were veterans of the War of the Lance who had fought with Gilthanas and Laurana against the armies of the Dark Queen thirty years before. They were still young, though several had been so grievously wounded that they moved like cripples, or were missing an arm. And one of them was blind!

Dejectedly Gilthas thanked them for answering his appeal and told them that he would summon them again if they could be of use to the city. After sending them home, he trudged wearily through the city until he came to the Tower of the Sun, where—as he had expected—many members of the Thalas-Enthia were gathered, awaiting news.

Gilthas learned that Rashas's spy, Guilderhand, had returned to the tower just before the Speaker's arrival. Feeling more like an eavesdropper than the nominal ruler of this august gathering, he pushed through the doors and stood near the wall of the chamber.

Rashas stood atop the rostrum, and Guilderhand had just been led to the second-tier step. For once the spy was dressed decently—in the robes of an elven senator, as a matter of fact!—though the garb could not conceal the man's essentially furtive and clever demeanor.

"Elves of the Thalas-Enthia," Guilderhand began, "I have met with the leader of this army, a bold Knight of Takhisis called Lord Salladac. I have been able to learn, through observation and surreptitious interviewing, that he is regarded as a man of integrity and honor, of great pride and of utmost savagery in battle."

"Terms! Did he give you terms for our surrender?" cried an elderly senator near the back wall.

Guilderhand nodded and allowed himself the shadow of a smile—a smile that Gilthas thought distorted his ratlike features into something resembling a smug, self-satisfied, and well-fed weasel.

"Can the city be spared a sacking?" cried another elf anxiously.

"I believe that our courageous agent can set your worst fears to rest," Rashas declared smoothly, thus confirming Gilthas's suspicion that the senator had spoken to the spy before he made his report to the Thalas-Enthia as a whole.

"Indeed, I hope that I can," Guilderhand declared. "Fortunately this ring of teleportation allowed me great freedom to move through the enemy camp. After learning all that I could about him—to my considerable reassurance, I promise you all—I presented myself to the lord as an emissary of this hallowed body."

Of course you did, Gilthas thought bitterly. You didn't have to wait for that role to be confirmed. You knew your master would support you as long as you did his bidding! He felt himself growing nauseous but forced his feet to remain in place, unwilling to attract attention to his presence here. Also, he had to admit that he was morbidly curious to see what sort of terms the enemy general had proposed.

"Lord Salladac received me most graciously. He is, as you may know by now, currently encamped on the road approaching the north bridge, less than a mile from the city's gates. His troops, including many blue dragons, are bivouacked in the woods, but they have done so with obvious respect to the hallowed trees of our forest. Only a few trunks have been felled, to clear space for the dragons to sleep, and they are building no more fires than are absolutely necessary for comfort and cooking."

Gilthas wondered how fires could be necessary for "comfort" in this sweltering summer. Nevertheless, Guilderhand's information was greeted with quiet murmurs of appreciation throughout the crowd.

"The lord informed me that terms for Qualinesti were identical to those terms offered to Kalaman, a city that has yielded to the Knights of Takhisis, yet still functions with pride and identity intact."

"How can you call that pride—to hand over your city and your people, to allow a foreign army to occupy and rule you?" demanded a female elf sarcastically. Gilthas recognized her as a radical young senator, Anthelia.

"Nevertheless," Rashas intervened sternly, "all reports show that the people in that city have been able to maintain their possessions, their freedom, and even most of their significant rights!"

"Except rights such as the freedom to criticize the city's rulers!" Anthelia retorted angrily.

"In my opinion, the right to criticize one's ruler is a privilege that all too often lends itself to abuse," snapped Rashas. "Now I must beg that you remain silent, so that our agent may conclude his report!"

"Let the silence linger here, then!" she shot back. "You're all very good at that as long as your precious wealth and status remain intact!"

"Guards, remove that woman!" Rashas commanded, and several Kagonesti slaves moved forward from the doors.

"Never mind. I shall remove myself," Anthelia replied. "I need to get some fresh air. The stink in here is already unbearable, and I have a feeling it's going to get worse!"

Gilthas stepped out of the way as the slender female stalked through the crowd, which parted like magic before her haughty gaze. She glanced once at the young Speaker, then tossed her head and looked away. Feeling the full brunt of the contemptuous gesture, Gilthas once more withered under the combined onslaughts of guilt and shame.

At the portals to the great chamber, Anthelia spun around and regarded the gathered elves with wild eyes. Her blond hair was unkempt, scattered across her face and shoulders. Her face was twisted with an expression like pain, but it was an agony on a deep and spiritual level.

"I spit on your concept of honor! I spit upon your pretentiousness and your cowardice. Elves of Qualinesti, I spit on you all!"

Shocked, the Thalas-Enthia recoiled in mass as she did just that. The chamber erupted in outraged mutters and angry shouts as the doors slammed behind the departing woman.

Rashas, however, merely shook his head theatrically, a gesture that managed to imply benevolent tolerance for an immature girl and scorn for her radical notions. Once more Gilthas felt his temper rise, and yet once more he knew he was incapable of doing anything to prevent the march of events. Still, he started to push his way through the crowd, determined at last to make his way to the rostrum.

Surprisingly, the elves stood back to let him pass, and a wide avenue opened through the council chamber so that he was able to ascend the steps with relative ease. As he took his place on the rostrum, Rashas indicated to Guilderhand that he should keep speaking.

"As I was saying," the spy resumed, somehow managing to affect an air of wounded dignity, "we have been assured that personal property, including slaves, will be respected. The Thalas-Enthia will continue to meet in this chamber and to have full authority over matters relating to Qualinesti, except when they conflict with matters of the Dark Knights' security."

"And what do the Dark Knights get out of this conquest?" Gilthas asked. "Why have they come here?"

"Perhaps I can answer that," Rashas said. "For, shrewd and observant as our loyal agent is, these were facts he did not discern. However, as I hear more about the developments of this recent 'war' "—he said the word as if the elves should realize that the conflict was in reality nothing more than a big misunderstanding—"the more I realize that the coming of the Dark Knights may, in fact, be a good thing for Ansalon."

Murmurs of astonishment greeted this statement, but they were muted by those who found some cause for agreement with the senator's startling remark. The young Speaker of the Sun found nothing agreeable in the statement, however, and turned his eyes upon Rashas with a cold glare.

"Can you explain yourself?" Gilthas asked. "Does this mean that you have chosen to embrace the worship of the Dark Queen?"

"Certainly not!" Rashas was indignant. "Nor, as I understand the terms of this occupation, is the worship of Takhisis a matter that the knights intend to advocate. But think about it, wise elves . . . think about the events that have marked our world in the last years." He spoke reasonably, turning his back to Gilthas as he addressed the elder senators in the front rows of the council.

"Haven't we seen an increase in banditry and brigandage? All across Ansalon, and even here, in Qualinesti? And has there not been a tendency among the youth to scorn the time-honored ways of their elders, to abandon the wisdom that has evolved through centuries, through *millennia* of life and culture?"

Now his words were greeted with nods of agreement, and Gilthas knew that the senator had them.

"We have all seen the signs of this cultural erosion . . . the lack of respect shown to those of high rank. Too many fortunes are made easily today, and as a consequence, the hallowed traditions of generations-long dynasties are replaced by upstart youngsters who would as soon spit upon this great tower as honor it with appropriate fealty."

Who could argue with this eminently reasonable statement? After all, the memory of Anthelia's angry departure was still at the forefront of everyone's mind.

"Then, too, there are matters of sedition, such as the treaty our former Speaker and his Silvanesti wife were attempting to impose upon us. They would have broken down the time-honored barriers that make us our own unique people!

"Elves of the Thalas-Enthia, it seems to me that the coming of the Dark Knights is not necessarily the tragedy that we first perceived it to be. Surely they will take steps to guard our highways from bandits, and perhaps, where we are inclined through benevolence and tolerance to put up with outrageous behavior, the knights will see that such outbursts are punished in a way that will prevent them from happening again."

Once more the lingering shame of Anthelia's diatribe worked in Rashas's favor. No elf had been bold enough to lay a hand upon her as she stormed out, but there were many here who would have relished the prospect of seeing her imprisoned, whipped, or even worse.

"Finally, there is the matter of practicality, the knowledge that we simply do not have a force to resist this imminent onslaught. Or, forgive me Honored Speaker." Now Rashas turned to Gilthas, who stood, white-lipped, behind him. "Did you have success in gathering an army to defend our city."

"You know very well that I did not," replied the young Speaker tightly.

Rashas did not even bother to acknowledge the response. "Then I make the following resolution. That we send an emissary to Lord Salladac, empowered to treat with him, and that we make a pact to accept his terms. We will welcome him into our city and treat him with the honor a conqueror deserves, and we will hope that Qualinesti is allowed to flourish under the same circumstances as Palanthas and Kalaman.

"I will ask for a voice vote. Speak if you are in favor of my resolution."

There was a mutter of assent—not a shout of acclamation, but still a nearly unanimous grumble of elven voices.

"And opposed? . . ."

Gilthas wanted to shout his own outrage, but he knew there was no use. In truth, what good would it do to resist, when the elven nation could not muster an army, when the people did not have the will to defend themselves? And so he held his silence.

"It is decided, then," Rashas declared. "The Speaker of the Sun and Stars and I myself shall go to see Lord Salladac on the morrow. With luck, by tomorrow night, we will again be a nation at peace."

At peace, perhaps . . . Gilthas's thoughts were bitter, and tears stung his eyes.

But peace at what price?

* * * * *

Lord Salladac was an imposing figure, taller than an elf and broad-shouldered and massive in a way that was unmistakably human. Gilthas quailed at a momentary image: It was not difficult to imagine this man picking up an elf in his hands and breaking him in two.

But in contrast to his bearlike physique, the lord's face and words were geniality personified. The two elven emissaries were ushered into his command tent, and he greeted them warmly. Servants offered small glasses of iced wine before withdrawing to leave the trio alone. Seated in comfortable chairs of wood that were ingeniously designed to fold for easy transport, Gilthas and Rashas faced the leader of the invasion force.

"Your terms have been relayed to us," the senator began without preamble.

"Ah, yes, your emissary . . . Guilderhand, I believe he was called. He seemed impressed by my display of strength."

"Would you really have sentenced him to death had you caught him sneaking around your camp?" Gilthas asked.

Salladac chuckled. "Why? In fact, he was quite useful to me. Though I doubt that he suspects the fact, I myself arranged for him to steal that ring of teleportation. I knew that if he had freedom of movement around my camp, he would come to the conclusion that resistance would be futile."

Gilthas flushed, embarrassed and shamed by the knowledge of how easily the elves had been manipulated.

"After considerable debate," Rashas said, with a sidelong glare at Gilthas, "the Thalas-Enthia has voted to accept your more than generous terms."

"Splendid!" declared Salladac, in a manner that reminded Gilthas of a person agreeing to a pleasurable social outing. "I must say that I was fully confident elven wisdom would see the logic of our proposal."

"Indeed," Rashas said in the same polite tones. "I am sure, as events transpire, it will become apparent that there are advantages to all sides in this arrangement."

The young Speaker felt his face flush with shame, but as always when he was in the presence of Rashas, he seemed unable to find the words to articulate his feelings. Better, he decided, to let the senator speak, to let him prostitute his nation and his pride for the sake of this invader's ambition. Even so, Gilthas felt the history of the moment and knew that he was witnessing a shameful day in the long life of a proud race.

How could Rashas not feel that same humiliation?

But instead, the senator was cheerfully discussing the arrangements for the army's entrance into the city, promising that splendid lodgings would be made available for Salladac and his chief lieutenants, offering to procure venison for the dragons and fruits and breads for the Dark Knights.

"And the brutes?" Gilthas suddenly asked. He had seen the ranks of blue-skinned, virtually naked warriors arrayed before the general's command tent. Their appearance had been savage in the extreme, and he had noticed that even Rashas had quailed at their scowling expressions and hulking size. "What do they eat?"

Salladac shrugged. "They are not particular, as you might imagine. Indeed, it is not my intention to lodge them in the city. We have learned that they do not mix well with the nations that we are trying to unite across Ansalon. Of course, they are useful in battle, but we are grateful for occasions such as this, when a nation sees the wisdom of joining our ranks without the need for gratuitous bloodshed. And fortunately much of the land has thus acceded to our inevitable advance."

"It's true, then . . . places like Kalaman have also surrendered to the Dark Knights without fighting?" Gilthas had not fully believed the stories that Guilderhand and Rashas had presented to the senate.

"For the most part, yes. It's true that the Knights of Solamnia look to put up a good fight at the Tower of the High Clerist. In the end, however, I have no doubt that Lord Ariakan will prevail. Indeed, the outcome of the fight is inevitable." For the first time, the lord's genial facade cracked slightly, and his look gave Gilthas a suggestion of the iron-thewed warrior that lived beneath the pleasant exterior. "As it would have been inevitable had you elves been so foolish as to offer resistance."

Gilthas thought of his father and knew that he would have joined the Knights of Solamnia in their heroic defense. He wondered what would happen to Tanis, but he didn't want to ask the human knight for information.

"Merely a few young hotheads," Rashas was saying smoothly. "I assure your lordship that the bulk of our population gave no consideration to impulses toward useless violence."

"I regret to say that is not the case in the western part of your nation," Lord Salladac said, his tone still stern. "There dwells a horde of elves in your forest that has caused serious harm to the other branch of my force."

"Porthios?" Gilthas blurted without thinking. "He attacked you?"

"Ah, the rebel of House Solostaran," the lord replied. "That explains a great deal. Yes, in fact, he led many thousands of elves in a night attack against a legion of Dark Knights. His warriors killed hundreds of troops and destroyed most of the army's provisions. Not to mention that they slayed three dragons as well."

At last Gilthas felt some salve to his elven pride. He didn't know how Porthios could have gained an army of thousands, nor how elves and griffons could hope to kill dragons, but here was proof that the entire race was not craven and cowardly. He strained to keep his face bland, but his heart pounded with the thrilling news.

"Of course," Salladac continued, "that army was commanded by a lesser lord. He has been summoned back to Lord

Ariakan, and has probably already paid for his failure with his life.

"Even so, it is a distressing matter and will command my attention during the next few days. I must attend to this Porthios before I embark for Silvanesti, where I fear that your fellow elves will not prove as wise and accommodating as have you Qualinesti. I trust that such incidents of violence and intractability will prove exceptionally rare, for I must warn you both that although I pride myself on my tolerance, I can only be pushed so far before I start pushing back. And that will lead to consequences that none of us want."

"Porthios is an outlaw!" Rashas declared. "At the time of your inva—er, arrival—he was the subject of a campaign by our leading general, Palthainon, and hundreds of Qualinesti warriors. In fact, General Palthainon has only just returned to the city. It occurs to me that he may be able to furnish you with information about the location of the outlaw camp."

"Good. Send General Palthainon to me at once."

Rashas nodded eagerly, despite the human's tone of peremptory command. "I assure you that when he is caught, the elves of the Thalas-Enthia will wholly support whatever punishment you deem appropriate."

"Splendid!" Lord Salladac was again all happiness and geniality. "I can see that this is the beginning of a fruitful alliance, a relationship that will bring prosperity—and profit— to all sides."

"Your wisdom obviously is as great as your military acumen," said Rashas, standing and bowing deeply. "Now, if you will forgive us, we should return to the city and make ready to offer you a fitting welcome."

Salladac and Gilthas rose, too. The human was effusive in his thanks to the senator, including the Speaker almost as an afterthought. "Shall we say noon tomorrow for our official entrance?" he said in conclusion.

"That is more than enough time," Rashas agreed.

With an escort of braying dragons and prancing horses, the two elves were led back to the bridge and were finally left by the humans only as they started across the elegant span leading to

Qualinost. Gilthas looked down, saw the white rapids churning through the gorge so far below, and had to forcibly shake away an impulse that urged him to leap over the railing and end his life and his shame on the jagged rocks in the deep ravine.

* * * * *

"Does that feel better?"

Kerianseray's hands massaged the Speaker's scalp, smoothly combing through the long, golden hair, pressing with soothing pressure against the throbbing points of pain beneath his temples and brow.

"Yes . . . it helps more than you can know," Gilthas murmured, allowing his head to roll loosely from one shoulder to the other.

The Kagonesti woman stood behind him at the low couch where he half-reclined, trying to shake off the lingering distaste of his meeting with the Dark Knight lord. The afternoon had been spent in discussion with various senators and nobles, and he faced the prospect of more meetings tonight. But for now, at least, during the hour before sunset, he had been able to retreat to his own house for some much-needed solitude and recuperation.

"Would you like some tea to help you sleep?" she asked.

"No, I'm afraid sleep is a luxury that I'll have to postpone," Gilthas murmured, thinking how pleasant it was to have Kerian speak to him as a friend, instead of with the deep formality of a slave to a master. "There are matters to arrange, houses to procure for the lord's residence in Qualinost."

"Will the dragons come into the city?" Kerianseray asked. Though all the elves were frightened of the monstrous serpents, she spoke in cool, level tones.

"No . . . not the brutes, either." Gilthas sat up, forgetting the pain in his skull as his indignation flared anew. "I tell you, this whole thing is just too damn *civilized*. It was like Rashas and Salladac were making arrangements for a tea party, not a military occupation—certainly not the surrender of a proud nation!"

"Sometimes pride gets lost behind wealth and comfort," Kerian observed, startling the speaker with her insight. "Those such as Rashas are more concerned with keeping what they have than with leaving anything for the future—or showing any honor to the past."

"Sometimes I think Porthios is right," Gilthas admitted. "Did you know he attacked a Dark Knight army with thousands of elves? Even managed to kill three dragons!"

Kerianseray was quiet for a little while, and Gilthas thought she was surprised by the news. Instead, it was he who was startled when next she spoke.

"Actually, he only had about five hundred elves. But it's true about the dragons . . . though many elves were killed as well."

He sat up abruptly and turned to face her. "How do you know that?"

She shrugged shyly, allowing her golden hair to fall across her eyes. Then, with a proud gesture, she pushed it back and met his accusatory glare.

"Some of his elves were Kagonesti, of my father's tribe. They have allied themselves with Porthios and share his village in the forest."

"Really?" Gilthas was surprised, and a little thrilled, by this revelation. He took it to mean that Kerian trusted him, or she certainly would not have let him see the extent of her information. Then he thought further about what she was saying.

"Your father's tribe, you said. You know where they are, where they live?"

Now her pride was unmistakable. "My father is Chief Dallatar, scion of Dallatar, one of the Kagonesti who saw our tribe survive the Cataclysm. I have been a slave since I was a little girl, but I have never forgotten who my family is."

"And you are in contact with him . . . or with your tribe," Gilthas said in wonder. "Yet you stay here, in the city, as a slave? Do you ever think of escaping, of going to him?"

"Every day," Kerian replied frankly. "But I serve a purpose in Qualinost, and it is an important cause . . . reason enough for me to stay in the city."

"You're a spy?" The Speaker was truly astonished.

She shrugged. "If you want to call it that. We long ago learned that it is important for us wild elves to know what the city elves are planning, especially in relationship to the Kagonesti. I was taken from the tribe together with twelve other children by a Qualinesti raiding party, elven butchers who murdered our nursemaids and carried us off to Daltigoth. If we had known that General Palthainon was on the way, it is quite possible that we could have taken shelter, avoided his raid, and spared the lives of those he killed."

Gilthas hung his head again, fighting the tears that rose to his eyes. How much shame would fall on him today? He blinked, looked up at Kerianseray with awe and affection.

"You're very brave. Do you know that?"

She shrugged. "I do what must be done. It is what my father does, too . . . what he taught me."

"And what Porthios does. What *all* elves should do!" Bitterly he recalled the reaction of the city elves when they had learned of the army's approach . . . the fifty volunteers he had been able to muster, a pathetic fragment of a company to defend a city that should have raised a proud army!

Gilthas rose from the couch and stalked to the window. He looked out at the pastoral city with its floating lights dancing like fireflies among the crystal towers and golden manors. There were unusually few people in sight, but other than that, there was no indication that this was a place facing the occupation of a hostile army with the dawn. Doubtless most of the elves were busy hiding their treasures, he thought scornfully, or making arrangements to sell food, wine, and other goods to the human knights.

With a sudden sense of decision, he turned to Kerianseray. He looked at this slave woman with new eyes, seeing her as much, much more than the meek and servile person who had been able to soothe his sleep with her bark tea.

"I must speak to Porthios," Gilthas said. "I will go to him in the forest, talk to him, show him that not all of us in the city are cowards."

"You would do this?" she said, her eyes wide. "But the

Thalas-Enthia—"

"Are fools!" he snapped. "And I want Porthios to know that we're not all like that!"

"How will you do it?" she asked pragmatically.

"First I have to find him. Can you get a message to him, ask if he will see me?"

She considered his request for only a few heartbeats, but it seemed to Gilthas as if time dragged by, as if his entire future, the hope for himself as a man and for his nation as a whole, hung on the decision she would make in those few seconds.

"Getting a message to him is simple, and I will do so," she finally said. "But I fear that it will not be easy to persuade him to see you."

"I'll take that chance," Gilthas said.

"Then we have to try," Kerian agreed with a nod.

* * * * *

"And so my uncle agreed to come to see my father," Silvanoshei said. "It would seem that such a meeting should have held much hope for the future of the elves."

The dragon's eyes had drooped shut, and he breathed deeply, puffing long exhalations from his huge nostrils. The two elves, however, were wide awake, and the elder nodded sagely in response to his companion's remark.

"So it would," Samar agreed. "But then, as now, there were many forces abroad in the world, and only a very few of them can be influenced by the actions of we mere mortals. . . ."

Rage

Chapter Fourteen

Bellaclaw glided through the treetops and came to rest in the center of the encampment. Porthios recognized Samar's urgency in the way the Silvanesti dropped his dragonlance and leapt down from the saddle even as his griffon pranced and settled on the bare ground.

"The blue dragons have broken camp and flown. They're coming this way!" declared the scout. "Straight for the gorge."

"Time to move!" shouted the outlaw prince, and instantly the encampment was transformed by a wave of frantic activity.

Elves picked up their babes and a few necessities of clothing and tools. Warriors ran into their huts, grabbed weapons, bent strings onto bows and checked quivers to make sure they were full of straight, sharp arrows. The cookfires were smothered by quick scoops of loose dirt, while a few tanned hides were pulled off the drying racks and employed to wrap supplies into bundles. Other racks, those where the hides were still fresh, would be left behind, as would the crude huts that had served as the band's shelters for the last few weeks.

Despite the baby slung over her back in his *tai-thall*, Alhana moved adeptly as she wrapped a cooking kettle, several knives, and the small amount of spare clothing that she and Porthios had into a soft velvet blanket, the only concession to comfort they had allowed themselves as they had flown to this primitive lifestyle. Watching her, Porthios felt a pang of regret. She was a princess, heir to a great throne and the leadership of a proud people, and yet, out of loyalty to him, she had followed him into exile.

And now the exile had brought a taste of real danger.

Samar ran past, holding his lance again, urging the elves to haste.

"How long until they get here?" Porthios asked.

"Not much time," the warrior-mage replied. "They must have found us somehow. They were flying on a beeline toward the camp."

Porthios knew that ever since the raid on the Dark Knight army, the invaders had been vigorously searching the forests, seeking the location of the elven encampment. Dragons in flights of four or five had winged across western Qualinesti, though they had been able to see little through the leafy canopy. Their searches might have been more efficient if they had flown individually, but the elves took pride in the fact that the powerful serpents obviously feared being caught alone.

Parties of brutes had stomped all through the woods as well. Several of these had met stinging ambushes, but the savage warriors seemed undeterred by the danger. Indeed, the prospect of fighting seemed to make them all the more enthusiastic in their searches. Over the last few days, several of these bands had swept close to the gorge, and despite the precautions taken by his outlaws, Porthios had known that inevitably the location of the camp would be discovered.

Now Samar's warning seemed to indicate that the worst had happened—that the camp had been discovered and word had been taken to the army without the elves knowing that their secret was out. If the dragons flew fast, they could get here in less than an hour, and everyone in the camp knew the elves had to be long gone by then.

"Take the inland trail!" Porthios reminded those elves who would be traveling on foot. The band had planned their flight in advance, knowing that if they headed toward the coast they would be more easily trapped against the barrier of the sea. "Split up as soon as you get into the deep forest. Remember to rendezvous at Splintered Rock in two nights!"

"Good luck," declared Tarqualan as he and a number of griffon riders prepared to fly west. The sea was no obstacle to them, and they planned to take a long route before circling around to the meeting place, a bluff that had been repeatedly struck by lightning and was characterized by the broken, jagged spires that jutted from its face.

Porthios and two other warriors, each of whom was accompanied by a wife and a newborn babe, would ride three griffons through the forest. The creatures would not be able to fly as fast as Tarqualan's single-mounted warriors, so that small party planned to take a more direct route to the rendezvous. They would be escorted by two skilled archers on griffons of their own.

"I'll fly with the queen," Samar said decisively.

"No!" Porthios surprised himself with his vehement reaction. "You need to help with the main body," he added.

Samar looked at Alhana, and the prince felt a startling pang of resentment. "Very well," replied the warrior-mage, turning to Porthios calmly. "Good luck."

"Good luck to you—and hurry," the outlaw added unnecessarily.

He took Alhana's hand and joined the file of elves following the steep trail out of the gorge. Because of the extra weight the griffons would carry, the three mothers with their babies and mates would climb the bluff on foot and mount up only when the flying creatures could launch from a high altitude. Atop the elevation, they were to meet the two other warriors who would escort the couples to safety.

The back of the outlaw captain's neck prickled anxiously, and he had to resist the notion that at any moment the sky would erupt in a cloud of blue wings and a barrage of lethal lightning bolts. Fortunately two of the babies slept, and Silvanoshei looked around in silent, wide-eyed wonder.

Soon they were out of the deep ravine, and here the trail branched into many winding paths. Porthios found Dallatar waiting for them there. He stopped to talk to the Kagonesti chieftain as many of the Qualinesti elves filed past and dispersed into the forest.

"We will go east," the wild elf said. "There may be word from my daughter. I have heard nothing from the city in many days and will try to make contact before joining you at the Splintered Rock."

"Have a care," Porthios replied. "The brutes will likely be everywhere."

"Indeed, but they do not have the woodcraft to track a Kagonesti who does not wish to be followed. It is yourselves who should take care. Though you have made these woods your home, they are not your natural surroundings. I bid you good fortune and speed, and hope to see you in three days."

With a firm handclasp, the wild elf turned off the trail and, in an eye blink, seemed to vanish into the undergrowth. Porthios and Alhana, together with the other members of the little party of refugees, continued on the path, moving as quickly as the burdened women could walk.

It was not too many minutes later when they heard a violent splintering of wood followed by the explosive crackling of blue dragon lightning breath. The sounds came from the rear, a mile or so away. Porthios could imagine the havoc as the wyrms swept down into the gorge, blasting the huts, knocking down the trees that had given the band such good shelter and concealment. He was grateful that the ravine had been moist even in the midst of this dry summer. With any luck, the wood was wet enough that it wouldn't develop into a conflagration.

Despite their successful escape, the outlaw chief had to fight back the tears that forced their way into his eyes. He felt a powerful sense of anger and futility—rage at the knowledge that the sacred vale was being ravaged, and impotent fury at his failure to do anything to counteract the threat.

They met Stallyar and the four other griffons at a bare ridge of rock along the escarpment over the gorge. From here, they could see down into the site of their camp, though the elves and their flying mounts remained screened by trees and underbrush from the rampaging serpents below. They saw blue heads on snaky necks rise from the forest, jaws gaping to spit out bright flashes of lightning. In places, sooty smoke rose from the verdant canopy, and here and there they saw a lofty tree topple, pushed by the monstrous force of a destructive dragon.

As the trees were thinned, Porthios caught frequently glimpses of the knights who rode those serpents. Dressed in their black armor, which must have been stiflingly hot, they stalked back and forth, knocking down what remained of the ruined huts, kicking through the debris of elven lives with their heavy boots, or hacking at furs and fabrics with their great swords.

Porthios wanted desperately to launch an arrow or two into that vale, to punish these arrogant humans for their transgressions, but his sense of discipline was too strong. He and the others had come here to make their escape, and it made no sense to announce their position by such a gratuitous attack.

Unfortunately neither could they launch into the air from this high vantage, for to do so would have carried them clearly into the sight of the dragons and Dark Knights wreaking their damage below.

"Come on," he whispered bitterly, his voice unnecessarily harsh as he moved the other elves and the five griffons along the winding path. They were deep in the woods now and had left no spoor that could be followed from the ruined camp, but he felt a growing sense of alarm, a need to move even faster to get away from this place.

For more than an hour, they walked along the narrow trail, the griffons prancing in agitation, occasionally hissing or fussing as the sharp rocks wore against their tender forefeet. But like the elves, the creatures understood the need for stealth, and despite their impatience, none of them tried to spread wings and fly. The elf women, too, were suffering. All three were carrying infants too small to walk, which was why they had planned to make their escape in the saddle. And here, where the warriors needed to be combat ready at a moment's notice, they dared not burden themselves with babies or supplies. But the females bore their fatigue and discomfort without complaint, though it tore at Porthios when he looked at his wife's drawn face, at the rivulets of sweat than ran through the dust caked across her skin.

Discomfort was further aggravated by the stifling heat that penetrated even into the normally cool floor of the forest. The summer had been growing increasingly warm, and now the wind seemed to have died away to nothing. The sun blazed above the trees, and the stuffy air pressed close, drawing perspiration freely from each elf's skin.

Finally they reached a place Porthios had remembered, a low bluff on the opposite side of the ridge from the escarpment over the camp. They had moved several miles closer to the coast, and with that distance behind them, he felt safe in exposing themselves for as long as it would take for the griffons to spread their wings and start to gain altitude.

"Mount up here," he said tersely. The griffons went to the edge of the precipice, and the warriors helped their women into the saddles. The escorting archers took to the air, circling overhead. The two warriors with wives and babies were veterans of Porthios's company in Silvanesti, and now they waited for his signal with the same discipline and patience that had carried them through decades of nightmarish campaigns.

"Good luck to you all. Let's fly!" he said, sliding over Stallyar's rump to rest as firmly as possible behind Alhana and the deep saddle.

With a spreading of silver-feathered wings and a flexing of powerful haunches, the mighty griffon pounced into the air, catching the wind and immediately driving them forward and away from the looming cliff. The treetops seemed to rush up from below, and Porthios held on tightly, wincing as a dizzying vision of the forest swept underneath.

With powerful strokes, Stallyar first held them at level altitude, banking slightly to get around the tops of the tallest trees. Then, very slowly, the griffon started to climb.

Still clinging to his wife and the reins, Porthios looked around and saw that the two other heavily laden griffons had likewise managed to bear their precious passengers aloft. The final two, bearing their escorting archers, flew just above them. With Stallyar in the lead, the creatures trailed slightly behind to the right and left, and the little formation winged its way along the valley. Far ahead of them, in the western distance, they could make out the glint of the sea.

"Bear southward," he said to Alhana, who tugged gently on the reins. Anticipating the direction, Stallyar veered slightly, wings stroking powerfully as he lifted them gradually higher. With just enough altitude to clear the neighboring ridge, the griffon once again allowed them to glide, descending slightly while the valley floor dropped quickly below.

Now they had two ridges between themselves and the wing of blue dragons, but even so, the elves did not relax their vigilance. Porthios guided them along the course of this deep valley, making sure that they flew below the summit of the ridges that ran in serpentine crests to either side. Slowly the vista of the sea grew before them, with the brightness of the setting sun reflected in almost painful brilliance from the broad swath of water.

It was out of that brightness that death came seeking, a blue dragon and its black-armored rider plummeting right out of the sun. Porthios suddenly sensed menace there, vaguely saw the terrible wings extending to right and left out of the blazing sunset. He shouted an alarm, but Stallyar had perceived the threat at the same time. The griffon banked to the left hard and dived toward the treetops.

"Fly, Lord Porthios!" cried one of the other elven warriors, an archer who was alone in his saddle.

"And you—try to escape!" shouted the outlaw prince, sensing his loyal man's intentions.

But the elf's course had been chosen. Somehow he had his bow out and shot an arrow straight into the snout of the beast.

The subsequent bellow of rage seemed to shake the air in the sky, a forceful onslaught of sound that rocked the griffons sideways and threatened to press the elves out of the saddle.

Next came the blast of lightning, and Porthios didn't have to look to know that his bold warrior had been slain. The stench of burned flesh carried instantly to his nostrils.

Now the treetops were whipping past, and Stallyar was gasping with the effort of flying with his double load of riders. The two other couples were nearby, their mounts, too, showing the effects of the burdened flight. All three infants were squalling loudly, frantic and afraid. With a quick glance backward, Porthios saw that the remaining warrior of their escort was angling upward and away, shooting arrows and attempting to draw the dragon after it.

From the thunderous bellows of rage, it seemed likely that the monster was going after the pesky archer, but the elf also heard the harsh commands of the knight, who was struggling to bring his serpent after the greater concentration of enemies. He looked again, saw that the wyrm was reluctantly wheeling, preparing to dive after the three griffons and their riders now gliding right through the lashing branches of the trees.

It was a pursuit that could only have one outcome, and Porthios desperately sought some tactic that would give them a chance of survival.

"There, land!" he shouted as a tiny patch of clearing opened before them. "We've got to go on foot!" he shouted to the others.

All three griffons plunged to the soft ground, and the warriors and their women tumbled from the saddles, the men frantically cushioning the falls of their children and wives.

"Now, go!" shouted the outlaw captain, waving frantically to urge the riderless griffons into the air.

The dragon roared again, and Porthios looked upward. He saw that the knight was now slumped in the saddle, an elven arrow jutting from his back. The four griffons swirled about the azure serpent until those horrible jaws gaped again, spewing a lightning bolt that shattered one of the brave creatures with a direct hit. The elves groaned, and Porthios felt a sickening lurch in his heart. Because of the sun's glare, he couldn't see if the stricken griffon had Stallyar's distinctive, silvery sheen on its wingtips.

"Into the woods! We've got a slight chance, nothing more!" he said, propelling the three women and two warriors ahead of him. They stumbled onto a narrow deer trail and jogged away from the clearing as quickly as the females could move. The babies, exhausted and numb, had again fallen silent.

After ten minutes they paused, gasping for breath, and Porthios scrambled up a lofty pine tree. He saw the distant figures of the dragon and at least two griffons, the smaller creatures leading the wyrm on a frantic chase. They were heading west, toward the sea, and the elf murmured a silent prayer to Paladine, thanking the god for their escape and begging his aid to help the brave griffons to escape.

Finally he dropped down from the tree to report on what he had seen. He looked at the somber, strained faces of his companions and knew that the course of their flight had been drastically changed.

"We're going to have to reach Splintered Rock on foot," he told them. "If we set an easy pace we should be able to do it in two or three days."

With the fortitude born of months of living as outlaws, the others quickly agreed. Porthios led and one of the other warriors brought up the rear as the elves continued through the forest. Where the deer trails worked in their favor, they followed them. For a while, a shallow streambed gave them a path. When the underbrush finally closed in, the men took turns hacking with their swords to open a path.

As night fell they found a large willow tree, with a trunk that had been hollowed by years of decay. Using their swords to expand the makeshift cave, the elves managed to make a shelter that allowed all three women and infants to sleep with some degree of protection from the elements. The men hunkered down outside the entrance and took turns staying awake during the dark, silent night. A short rainstorm washed over them sometime before dawn, and though the warriors were sodden, their wives emerged from the shelter dry and at least partially rested.

One of the warriors took time to collect some wild berries, and these provided at least minimal sustenance before they once more started on their way. Their luck seemed to be improving, however, for within an hour, they stumbled upon a wide path that seemed to bear more or less in the direction they wanted to be going. Porthios led the way again, holding his wife's hand in his own as he held his weapon at the ready, trying to peer into the shadowy forest that pressed close to each side.

The first clue of the ambush came from a waft of wind that brought the scent of stale, acrid sweat to his nostrils. The other elves sensed it, too, and instinctively looked in alarm at their leader.

Porthios had his sword in his right hand, while his left still gripped Alhana's tense fingers. He stared into the woods to both sides. He realized that the shrubbery was very thick here, and that the ground sloped up both to the right and to the left. Intuitively he sensed a trap and was about to turn to order the elves to backtrack when the first brutes crashed from the woods.

In a moment of frozen panic, he saw a male elf go down, skull crushed by a massive club. The warrior's woman screamed and bent over her man, only to be cut in two by the brutal sweep of a massive sword. Dozens of the monsters charged, coming from all directions, and in a moment of crystalline clarity, he saw his wife and child beneath the threat of those crushing blows.

His perceptions, his whole world, twisted violently in that instant. Caution and practicality vanished in a cloud of pure fury.

Like a whirlwind, he flew past Alhana, stabbing one brute through the belly, then cutting the throat of another with the backslash. A club slashed at him from the side, and instinct warned him to duck. He felt the gust of air as the blunt weapon whipped past his scalp and tore at his hair. Lunging to the side, he drove his blade into the flank of the club wielder, sending the creature tumbling backward with a ragged bellow of pain.

Alhana's scream galvanized him, and he whirled to see a brute's blue hand wrapped around her wrist. Silvanoshei was swaying in his cradle, crying again. Before the attacker could pull his wife into the underbrush, the prince's weapon came down and Alhana screamed again, this time at the sight of the dismembered paw still clutching her arm. Clutching her baby, the elf woman fell back, leaning against a stout tree trunk, flailing her arm until the gruesome remnant broke loose and fell into the underbrush.

Porthios lunged past his wife, the bloody blade flashing in a deadly dance, driving several brutes backward with such haste that they tumbled over each other. The sword of his ancestors flashed, drawing howls as he gouged his enemies' massive legs, but then the prince retreated to stand before Alhana. She was sheltered against the tree trunk, two broad limbs reaching around almost as if to fold her in a protective embrace, and Porthios drew several ragged gasps of breath as he looked at the circle of looming figures.

He was vaguely aware that the other elves had disappeared, slain or captured by the blue-skinned attackers or perhaps escaping into the woods during the initial confusion of the ambush. At least a dozen of the monstrous warriors now faced him, forming a ring that closed off any hope of escape.

"Porthios . . . get away—over them, through the branches of the tree," Alhana whispered behind him, her voice taut as a bowstring. "They'll take me prisoner . . . you can come for me later."

In a flash of emotion so strong that it all but burned through his heart, he saw how much he loved her and this child, this son who was the hope of the elven nations through the coming years.

His eyes were clear, his body immediately restored by the power of his emotion. The brutes were all panting, and some of them held hands over cuts and gouges that dripped blood and smeared streaks of blue along their limbs. With a sense of vague detachment, he saw that the creatures were actually covered with paint, that their natural flesh was more like a human's. They loomed as tall as he was but much more solid, and the growls and barks emerging from their throats showed that they were angry and ready to take their revenge. Clubs were raised, swords readied, as the brutes cautiously closed in.

Porthios did the one thing they didn't expect. He attacked, throwing himself bodily toward the center of the ring of blue-skinned horror. His sword flashed out like the flicking tongue of some metal-mawed dragon, and in a whistling flash, tore open the bellies of the two nearest brutes. Groaning piteously, hands struggling to contain their spilling guts, the creatures staggered backward and collapsed. The other brutes gaped, momentarily astonished at the audacity of this elf who had charged them so recklessly.

Porthios continued his attack, whirling through the rank of his foes, stabbing one in the back and cutting the hamstrings of another. With a final, skull-splitting blow, he hacked through a fifth brute and once again stood before his awestruck wife, intent on protecting her with every sinew of his body, every drop of his blood. He danced forward, waving the blade, and the remaining attackers actually took a few steps backward.

Still, the ring of deadly warriors remained solid, fully enclosing the elves, though the enemy was a little more cautious about pressing in. When Porthios rushed forward, the brutes fell back quickly, this time stumbling out of reach of his lethal steel. From the corner of his eye, he saw that one of the monsters lunged toward Alhana when he advanced, and like lightning he whirled, cutting the thing down with a stab to the throat.

A red haze filmed his vision, and he vaguely wondered if he was wounded. But it was the heat of his own emotions, the rage possessing him, turning him into a lethal fighting machine. Rushing forward, he had enough control to bluff a charge to the right, then whip to the left and stab another brute before the creature could raise its weapon in a parry. Again he repeated the maneuver, and another monstrous attacker fell back, bellowing in anger and clutching hands over the deep cut in its belly.

Four more remained, and the next time he rushed forward, they stumbled backward in a frantic attempt to avoid his cutting steel. Now they were a dozen paces away from the tree, a loose ring that he could have dashed through with a sudden sprint. But still, there was Alhana and Silvanoshei—they couldn't run, and he couldn't leave them.

So he resolved to finish this fight with the same cold violence that the brutes had used to commence it. Porthios charged forward again, faster and farther, and this time he caught one of the brutes before it could retreat. A single slice ended that ugly warrior's life, and at the sight of the newest corpse the other three turned and raced away, smashing through the brush like panic-stricken cattle.

* * * * *

The jagged bluff known as Splintered Rock rose from the depths of the forest, the spiked promontories reminding Porthios of the towers of a distant elven city. As he and Alhana plodded closer, however, they clearly saw the frost-cut cracks in the face of the stone, the heaps of talus piled at the foot of each weather-beaten spire. The meeting place served its purpose well, for it was far from any roads or well-used trails, and yet the elves could see it from a long distance away.

Slowly, over the course of several days, the refugees from the bandit camp had trickled into the meeting place, gathering around the deep, clear lake at the foot of the bluff. Tarqualan and his griffon riders were already here as Porthios, now carrying Silvanoshei, and his wife dragged themselves wearily into the grassy meadow at the lakeshore.

The outlaw prince surprised many, even including himself, when he burst into tears at the sight of Stallyar. Many feathers of the griffon's right wing had been blasted by a dragon's lightning bolt, but the creature held his eagle's head up proudly, yellow eyes flashing as Porthios wrapped both arms around the strong neck. Stallyar dropped his beak into an affectionate peck on the elf's shoulder, then settled down to rest. Tarqualan told Porthios that the mighty creature had been tense and agitated until the moment when his master had appeared. Only then did it seem that Stallyar would allow himself to relax.

"My lord, you can well imagine the consternation we all felt upon your mount's arrival. There is not an elf here that did not pledge his life and his sword to avenge your death. Indeed, there are many parties of warriors in the woods, both searching for you and exacting whatever vengeance they can against the Dark Knights."

Porthios described his encounter with the brutes and learned that similar ambushes were experienced by many of the refugees. Samar had led dozens in a fighting retreat, running a gauntlet of attackers and wounding a blue dragon with his lance. Finally he had led the group here, arriving a few hours before Porthios with many wounded in tow.

"The attack plan was worked out with an eye toward strategy," the prince realized. "The enemy general only sent his dragons against our camp when his troops were already in place in the surrounding woods."

And, tragically, it was a tactic that had proven lethally successful, for even four days after the appointed time of the rendezvous, barely two-thirds of the elves who had fled the encampment had arrived at Splintered Rock.

It was with relief and delight, on that fourth evening, that Porthios and the rest greeted Dallatar and his band of Kagonesti. Not surprisingly, the wild elves had made their way around the enemy's traps, even turning the tables on several companies of brutes who had been lying in ambush alongside well-traveled trails.

But Porthios was surprised by the news Dallatar shared as the two of them sat around a small fire later that evening. Alhana reclined nearby, resting uncomfortably as she nursed her baby, still trying to recover from the rigors of the flight. Samar, too, was present, watchfully eyeing the dark forest. Porthios felt a pang of guilt as he saw that the warrior-mage seemed to take care to avoid sitting at Alhana's side.

Porthios asked the Kagonesti chieftain if he had made contact with his spies in Qualinost.

"Yes, I did. As you expected, they surrendered to the Dark Knights without a fight. The city has been occupied, though the senators and nobles have been allowed to keep their wealth and stations, except for a few of the more independent thinkers. The senators called Queralan and Anthelia, for example, have been arrested and imprisoned in a camp outside of the city."

"And what about the common people?" Porthios asked.

Dallatar shrugged. "There, again, those who have the courage to speak out against the occupation have been arrested, their property—such as it is—confiscated."

"Who is the ruler of the occupation forces?"

"A lord called Salladac. It was he who commanded the operation against your encampment. He was aided by Palthainon, who revealed the location of your band. Rumor has it that the lord knight is quite pleased with the attack. However, it might please you to know that another Lord— Haldian, I think they called him—who originally commanded the invasion of the west was sentenced to death, executed by order of Salladac."

"No great loss . . . he was a fool," Porthios declared grimly. "Better for us if he had been left in charge. Are your own agents safe?"

"My agent is my daughter . . . and, yes, thank you for the inquiry. She is well. In fact, in addition to a belated warning about Palthainon's treachery, she sends a message for you."

"A message?" Porthios felt so separated from his previous life in that place that he had somehow brought himself to believe that his own existence was no longer relevant to the elves of the city. "From whom?"

"From the Speaker of the Sun, your nephew, Gilthas."

Porthios spat scornfully, drawing a sizzle from the embers of the low fire. "What does he have to say to me?"

"He begs the honor of a meeting with you."

Now the outlaw sat up straight. "Why? So he can turn me over to his puppet master, this Lord Salladac?"

"I don't know why he wants to speak to you, but the question was phrased as though he asks you for a favor."

"And why should I grant that favor? This is a transparent attempt to trap me. After his dragons and his brutes failed, Lord Salladac is obviously turning to my own kinsman to use against me!"

Dallatar was noncommittal. "My . . . agent seems to feel that the young lord is sincere, that he feels genuine disgust at the betrayal of his homeland."

"He was a *part* of that betrayal!" Porthios declared passionately. "He wears the medallion that I gave up—gave up because a Qualinesti arrow was pointed at my wife's heart."

"Gilthas didn't know that!" Alhana, pushing herself awkwardly to a sitting position, spoke with surprising vehemence.

Porthios turned to his wife in anger and astonishment, but something in her direct gaze caused him to hold his temper in check. "You spoke with him about the matter?"

Alhana smiled, albeit a thin and bitter expression. "We were held prisoner in the same room for a time, until Rashas decided that I was a bad influence on him."

"What—what was he like?" For the first time, Porthios found himself thinking about his nephew in more than just superficial terms. "Why would he take the throne from me under those circumstances?"

"For much the same reason you gave up the medallion," Alhana explained gently. "He, too, knew of the arrow pointed at my heart. He is terribly young, not as wise as either you or I could wish. But I believe, my husband, that he has a good heart."

"I still say it would be madness to meet him!" Porthios declared, groping for the strength of will that had stiffened his resolve when first he had heard this harebrained idea.

"You can always take precautions," his wife noted. "Choose the place of the meeting yourself. Place plenty of guards around it."

"And what if he has a company of Dark Knights follow him to the rendezvous. Do you want to risk another ambush?"

"What about sending a griffon for him?" Alhana countered with maddening logic. "No one on foot or even horseback could follow, and if a dragon appears, you can cancel the meeting—even, if he betrays you, send the boy to his death," she added harshly.

"Boy?" asked Porthios. "This is the Speaker of the Sun, the ruler of Qualinesti, we're talking about!"

"And he's also the son of your sister and her husband, Tanis Half-Elven, in case you've forgotten. I think you should see him!"

"All right—all right!" Porthios snapped. He turned to Dallatar. "I'll see him as soon as you can arrange a rendezvous."

He was irritated at allowing himself to be persuaded, frustrated by this enforced isolation in the wilderness, galled by his dependence on others.

Even so, he was surprised by his certainty that, however reluctantly, he had made the right decision.

* * * * *

"And so the blues left you alone after you breathed in the face of one of them?" Silvanoshei asked.

"For a time, yes," Aeren replied. "I knew they would be back eventually, however."

"Were you afraid?"

The great serpent snorted in disdain. "I watched and I waited. I was ready to fight for my lair. But they were busy with the elves— and besides, along this shore the eating was very good."

Qualinost Enchained

Chapter Fifteen

Gilthas looked out from the upper floor of his house, studying the city sprawled across the landscape. He was purposely looking south and west, away from the Tower of the Sun. He saw the domed hill where the Hall of Audience lay under the open sky, and from his vantage on the third floor, he could even catch a glimpse through the treetops of the mosaic tiles of the great map, the detailed relief depiction of the nation and its surroundings that had been scribed right into the floor of the hall.

The arched bridges that framed the city were silvery threads against the sky, so fine that they might have been gossamer webbing, yet he knew them to be strong structures, made of elven steel and each capable of supporting a great weight. Trees were everywhere, and if their leafy crowns were a little parched and browned, that was no different than the surrounding forests—or, indeed, from anywhere else on the continent that sweltered under the oppression of this brutally hot, dry summer.

On the surface, this was the same elven city he had first glimpsed a year before, the halcyon place he had dreamed about all his life, had run away from home to visit. He had been welcomed here, and then imprisoned . . . threatened, and then raised to the highest office in the land, at least in name. Now heat shimmered from the landscape, and the sun blazed down from a sky that was only pale blue but lacked the hint of even a single wisp of cloud.

Gilthas fondled the medallion he wore over his breast, the golden disk that lay beside the Sunstone on its own chain. He thought about what that medallion was supposed to signify—the Speaker of the Sun! What could be more exalted? It was a title greater than king, loftier than any emperor.

And yet when it was wrapped around him, it was only a hollow shell.

At first he had been Rashas's puppet. Now he was a mere figurehead enforcing the rule of Lord Salladac. When would he get the chance—when would he find the courage—to be his own master?

He heard the shy knock at the door and knew that he was about to encounter the one bright spot in his life.

"Come in," he called, and Kerianseray entered. She held the neatly pressed folds of his Speaker's costume.

"Is my lord ready—that is, are you ready to don your robes?" The slave woman's voice was a musical charm in the room, and she blushed as she corrected the form of address that had been ingrained since her childhood.

"I suppose I am," Gilthas sighed. "At least this is going to be a small meeting. Only Rashas and a few senators, plus Lord Salladac, are going to be there."

Kerian said nothing as she laid his robe on the table and went to get the golden brushes that she used on his long hair. He flopped down onto the couch, then looked up as she returned.

"Has there been any word from . . . from the forest? Do you know if he will agree to see me?"

She shrugged, a tiny gesture. "I have heard nothing yet. I will tell you as soon as I know, of course."

"Yes . . . thank you," he said, feeling as if he had been chastised for being an impetuous youth. Of *course* she would tell him!

For a time he relaxed, eyes closed, letting her brush his hair. He relished the feel of the stiff bristles against his scalp, but even more pleasant was the touch of her fingers as they stroked through his golden locks, occasionally coming into contact with his skin. Each time they did, it was as though he felt an electric spark, and he tingled with a pleasure that he tried to conceal but felt certain that she must sense. How could she not feel an emotion that was so strong, so consuming, that sometimes it threatened to burst into real fire?

When she was finished, he rose, lifting his arms so that she could slide his robe onto him. His hands, still upraised, were extended over each of her shoulders, and impulsively he lowered them, letting his fingers come to rest against the soft silk of her gown.

She froze, drawing an almost inaudible gasp. He didn't move, though it felt as though his whole body was vibrating, buzzing like the wings of a bee or a hummingbird. Slowly she drew a breath. Her eyes were lowered, fixed upon his chest even though he looked searchingly into her face. Her mouth was slightly open, and he quivered at the sight of her tongue as it slipped forth just long enough to wet her lips.

He wanted desperately to kiss her, and he sensed in her stillness a willingness to accept his own lips against hers. Time stopped. Even his heart seemed not to beat as he yearned, longed, lusted for a further caress. Still her eyes remained lowered demurely, and he felt the thundering of his own pulse— or was it hers?—pounding in his ears.

But gradually, reluctantly, he knew that he couldn't pull her closer, couldn't move his mouth to hers. His exhalation was ragged as he dropped his arms, then turned slightly to allow her to pull his belt around him. Momentarily she looked up before once again lowering her eyes, and the look he saw in her face struck him deeply. Her emotions were powerful, shining from her eyes like bright sunlight, and for that second, they blazed into him, furious and unabashed.

Yet he couldn't read them, couldn't see what she was feeling. Was she hurt? Angry at his presumptuous embrace? Or was that scorn he saw there? Did she mock his cowardice, his hesitancy? Miserably he turned his back, analyzing that look over and over but failing to come to any closer understanding of what the woman was feeling.

She cinched the sash around his waist and then knelt to tie his golden sandals. Not once did her face rise to him. Instead, she pulled the straps and laced the bindings with firm, businesslike tugs. When at last he was dressed, she bowed deeply and took two steps back.

"Does my lord Speaker require anything else?" she asked, addressing the floor.

"Not now . . . Kerian. . . ." He spoke to her, but his voice trailed off as still she wouldn't lift her face to meet his gaze.

"Thank you . . . thanks for listening. For . . . everything," he concluded lamely.

"As you wish," she said. Finally she looked at him, but she had managed to wipe all trace of that blazing emotion from her gaze. Her eyes were dispassionate, her face devoid of any expression save dignified respect. "If there is nothing further . . . ?"

"Of course. You may go," he said.

He felt his knees shaking as she closed the door behind her. He put both hands upon the table and leaned there for a moment, breathing deeply, trying to understand the passions that were coming over him. By Paladine, by all the gods, he knew that he wanted her, craved her in a manner that was as sudden and frightening as it was irresistible and all-consuming. Perhaps that feeling had lingered in his subconscious over the past weeks and months, but never had it burst into open flame as it did this morning.

Guilt and confusion wracked him. She was a *slave*, bidden to do his will! And yet she was his master in ways he couldn't understand. Merely that flash of heat in her eyes had practically brought him to his knees. And now that she was gone, it was as though the room was colder, darker. The emptiness of his life surrounded him, and he almost called her back, summoning her into the room so that he could bask in the warmth of her presence.

But duty called, and so he trudged like a zombie to the lower floors of his house, where he fell into step with the honor guard of the four Qualinesti warriors who had been waiting there to escort him to the Tower of the Sun. Once there, he found Rashas and a few senators in the council chamber, awaiting the arrival of the Speaker and Lord Salladac.

"Are you ill?" asked the leader of the Thalas-Enthia, peering suspiciously into Gilthas's face. "You look pale. Did you eat something disagreeable?"

"I must have done so," the Speaker replied, ashamed that his feelings were so clearly displayed to these elves who really meant so little to him. "Give me a moment. I'm sure it will pass."

"Slave!" barked Rashas, summoning one of the attendants from the side of the round council chamber. "Bring the Speaker a stool and some water!"

Though he didn't want to admit it, Gilthas was grateful for the seat. His legs were still trembling, weakened by the wave of emotion. A few sips of cool springwater helped to restore him, however, and he looked around the chamber, identifying the dozen or so nobles who were attending this conference with their new conqueror. Idly, Gilthas was surprised to note that Guilderhand wasn't present. The spy had made a point of attaching himself to everything involving the city's new rulers.

The drink and the chance to catch his breath did their work, and Gilthas felt ready to fulfill his ceremonial role by the time Lord Salladac, escorted by two of his armored knights, was shown into the chamber.

As the men entered, Gilthas hastily rose so he could stand with the senators, anxious that the human conqueror see no sign of his weakness. But it seemed as though Lord Salladac took little notice of the elves who were here. Instead, he strode to the rostrum and seated himself upon the lone stool, the perch that Gilthas had just vacated. The lord's bearlike features were creased by a scowl that made him seem fierce and vaguely beastlike.

"How did your campaign in the west fare?" Rashas asked solicitously. "Surely you were able to destroy the outlaw camp."

"Aye . . . what there was of it, we trampled into the ground. Smashed the huts and burned the few wretched belongings they had there," growled Salladac. Still, he did not sound like a soldier who had won a great victory.

"Did you capture Porthios?" Gilthas asked, trying to keep his voice level. He knew that this had been one of Salladac's major objectives, though Kerian had convinced him that the elven prince would not be taken easily.

"The bastard got away, with most of his elves," declared the lord. "It's like the forest swallowed them up—and then spit out my brutes when they tried to follow!"

"Surely with his camp destroyed and his followers scattered to the four winds, you have drastically curtailed his operations," Rashas said smoothly.

"That we have," the lord of the Dark Knights admitted. "And we butchered a few of the wretches, those who weren't fast enough to disappear."

"Then it must be called a victory," Rashas replied. "Know that we elves of Qualinost are grateful to you for cleaning out the pests that dared to dwell in our midst."

"You should be," the lord retorted. "But the work's not done yet. Still, I'll have to wait a few weeks to finish it."

"It won't be long before the rest of the rebels are brought to heel," Rashas declared. "Perhaps we will even have some useful information for you soon."

Gilthas narrowed his eyes and looked at the elder senator, whose face was creased by a faint, private smile. The younger elf remembered how Palthainon had previously betrayed the position of Porthios's camp. Now he wondered what Rashas meant and made a mental note to try to find out.

"You have other business more pressing?" Gilthas wondered, speaking to the human lord.

"I'm staying here, but my dragons are off to Silvanesti tomorrow," the lord replied.

"Why are they going?" asked the Speaker.

"They're needed to assist in a campaign. The eastern elves have not proven to be as reasonable as you Qualinesti, and my colleagues anticipate a rather brutal campaign. Unfortunate, too. You know, you elves of the Thalas-Enthia are really a credit to civilization in the way you saw the practical solution here."

Gilthas flushed, deeply ashamed at the comparison. The other elves, he saw, nodded pleasantly, as if honestly pleased by the compliment. Couldn't they *see*? Were they really so shameless to believe that it was better to surrender to a powerful master than to even make a pretense of prideful resistance? Trying to conceal his own disgust, Gilthas allowed himself to be grateful that Porthios had escaped the lord's attack. He hoped that the rebel leader would contact him soon, would agree to meeting the Speaker who wore the medallion that Porthios once had claimed as his own.

Lord Salladac made his departure, leaving the elves to conclude matters of the city's governance among themselves. They discussed matters of food allocation, since though there were not that many knights living in the city garrison, the humans showed a capacity to eat far more than any individual elf.

"We should at least be glad that he marched those damn brutes out of here," a senator called Hortensal said, grimacing at the requirement that he give a valuable granary over to the Dark Knights.

"And the dragons," said another, smug because his holdings were in crystal and glass, for which the humans had thus far shown little interest. "Imagine how much they would eat if we had to take care of them."

"Let them eat rebels," Rashas said bitterly. "Porthios has been a thorn in our side long enough!"

"You mentioned that you might have information for Lord Salladac soon," Gilthas said casually. "What did you mean by that?"

Rashas looked at the young Speaker sharply. "That's a private matter, but it may prove that Porthios is not as clever, his movements not as mysterious, as he might think."

"May he rot in the Abyss!" declared one of the senators, a merchant who had lost a small fortune when the bandits had plundered an incoming caravan of steel coins.

"So we should pray," Rashas continued, his unblinking stare fixed upon Gilthas. "And let us remember that discussions in this chamber are the private matters of the elven state. They are not to be repeated, nor even speculated upon, beyond these walls."

Gilthas knew that he was being warned, and the thought was vaguely pleasing. He shrugged, adapting an air of unconcern. "Of course," he said agreeably. Still, he could not bring himself to join in the chorus of general condemnation that echoed from the elves who were still talking about Porthios.

"And what about Silvanesti?" Rashas asked. "Doesn't it seem foolish that they will subject themselves to a war without hope of victory?"

"They won't have a chance against the dragons," said Hortensal, with a dismissive shrug. "They were too stupid to follow our example, to realize the futility of resistance."

Gilthas grimaced at the words—he couldn't recall the Qualinesti offering any resistance at all—but he decided to hold his tongue. Instead, it was Rashas who spoke.

"At least the Silvanesti will be busy with war. They will have no time to meddle in our affairs."

"And thus the sanctity of elven purity is preserved!" cried Hortensal, with every appearance of enthusiasm.

"Indeed. Sometimes the greatest gifts come disguised in the most mysterious fashion," Rashas agreed.

* * * * *

Gilthas swam long strokes in the clear pool outside the Speaker's house. For an hour, he cut through the water, back and forth, alternately churning and gliding until he was exhausted. Then he went inside and had a bath in water so hot that it all but scalded his skin. When he got out of the tub, two matronly slaves toweled him with rough enthusiasm, so much so that it seemed as though they scraped away a whole layer of his skin.

Even so, he still felt unclean.

He went to his study, where he closed the door and, despite the late afternoon sun streaming in through the open window, lit an oil lantern and settled in a corner chair. He had a leather-bound tome in his hands, a volume he had recently discovered in the library of this great house. The book was entitled *The Vingaard Campaign*, and had been scribed by the renowned historian Foryth Teel, assistant to Astinus Lorekeeper himself.

More significant to Gilthas, it was a story about his mother. The events described in the book had occured only thirty years ago. Foryth Teel wrote a story of war, of a remarkable series of offensive battles during which the Knights of Solamnia had liberated the lands of Northern Ansalon, the territories that had over previous years been crushed under the heel of the dragon highlords.

He had been reading bits and pieces of the book over the last few days, perhaps to remind himself that there had really been a time—and not very long ago!—when the elves had fought for a just cause, battling with courage and heroism against the hordes of the Dark Queen, who sought to subjugate the world underneath a realm of violence, slavery, and savage conquest. At times, he was numbed by a sense of real grief as he thought about how far his people had fallen.

During other passages, he was staggered by a sense of bitter irony. The Emperor of Ansalon, the Highlord Ariakas, had fought for five years, slowly expanding the swath of his conquest across Krynn until, under the leadership of generals such as Gilthas's mother Laurana, the dragonarmies had been swept backward, finally scattered when their queen had deserted them and their foul temple. Now it was Ariakas's son, the Lord Ariakan, who led the Knights of Takhisis on a fast and efficient campaign. In a matter of weeks, he had conquered territories that his father had never been able to reach, and now held such firm sway on Ansalon that it was difficult to conceive of any kind of organized resistance.

And then there were times where Gilthas was simply lost in a story of high adventure, when he marveled at the exploits of dragons of gold and silver, of brave warriors—including not only his mother, but also his uncle, Gilthanas, and legendary heroes such as Flint Fireforge—and of the desperate battles that culminated in the magnificent victory at Margaard Ford, a key crossing of the Vingaard River. In the end, he admitted that this was the reason he enjoyed reading the book, for it carried him away with its epic sweep and its dazzling rendition of people, dragons, places, and events.

He wondered if his mother had received his invitation, if she planned to come here. He missed her, longed for her presence and her guidance. It was better for her safety, he told himself, though he realized that her presence would do more to ease his own loneliness than it would for Laurana's security.

An hour later Kerian knocked, and it was with a rush of pleasure that he closed the leather covers and called for her to enter.

"Hello," he said, rising and stretching his arms over his head. "I was reading . . . got lost in the past for a little while."

"I am glad," the Kagonesti woman said. "I came to see if you would like some wine before dinner."

"Yes, that would be splendid." He noticed that she had brought a pitcher, and she advanced into the room at his answer. "Would you care to have a glass with me?"

"Yes . . . I would."

He waited while she poured them each a mug of the pale liquid. When she brought his glass over to his chair, he took it, then followed her to sit beside her on the couch.

"I have had word from my . . . from the forest," Kerianseray said. "It arrived just this afternoon."

"Word from the wild elves? How?" Gilthas asked. He wasn't aware of any messengers coming to the house.

"I am sorry, my lord, but I am not permitted to discuss that part of my duties."

Gilthas was surprised by her refusal. Only then did he stop to consider the extraordinary trust she had placed in him merely by revealing the fact that she was able to maintain some sort of surreptitious contact with her tribe.

"Of course. Forgive me for asking," he said, though a part

of him was desperately curious and thought that, if she really *did* trust him, she should be willing to reveal the details he sought. Still, he decided to let the matter rest for now. "What did you learn?"

"Porthios Solostaran has agreed to meet with you, provided you come to the meeting alone."

"Yes, of course! That's wonderful!" he cried, elated.

"I'm glad you're pleased," Kerian said, looking happy herself.

Impulsively he put his hands on her shoulders, and this time pulled her close before she could lower her face. His lips found hers, and their kiss was like a bond sealed in fire. Her mouth was slightly open, and Gilthas felt a whirlwind of emotions, new experiences assaulting him, tantalizing him, reaching deep into his soul.

As if he were mired in a dream—a fantastic, wondrously arousing dream—he felt her arms reach around his shoulders, and then she was pulling him closer. She welcomed his kiss, reciprocated with warmth and fire.

And then that fire was everywhere, pouring through Gilthas's veins, clouding his thoughts, pounding a savage drumbeat in his heart. He drew a breath, the sweetest air he had ever tasted, and pressed harder against her, feeling her falling back as his weight bore her down upon the couch.

Their surroundings disappeared, and he was only aware of the two of them, each wrapped in the other, in bliss and warmth and desire. And for a time, too short a time, Gilthas forgot his throne, forgot the Thalas-Enthia, and was one with the woman he loved.

*   *   *   *   *

"Finally the blues did come again for me, three of them. They threatened to kill me if I did not leave."

"Did you have to fight them?" asked Silvanoshei.

Aeren puffed out his chest. "I was prepared to, as I told you. But they were too many, and they promised to kill me—a promise I knew they would keep.

"So instead, I claimed that I needed time to gather my hoard, that I would leave in a few days and let them have my cave."

"What happened then?"

"I emerged at the appointed time and flew high and wide, seeking the new tenants of my lair. The air was hot and thick by then, but I looked for a long time."

"But you didn't find them?"

"No. I searched, expecting to see them . . . but it seemed that the blues were gone."

Speakers of Past and Present

Chapter Sixteen

They left the Speaker's house in the predawn hours, when the night was at its darkest and activity in the city had almost completely ceased. There were a few patrols of Dark Knights wandering the streets, but by elven standards, these humans made so much noise and their night vision was so feeble that Gilthas and Kerianseray had no difficulty evading the sentries in the vicinity of the Tower of the Sun.

Of course, the magical lights that danced through the city during the night hours were still in evidence, but it seemed to Gilthas that their brilliance had somehow been muted since the coming of the conquerors. Whereas in the past the entire city had seemed to sparkle with brightness, now each lantern existed in a small island of illumination, but the contrast only served to heighten the shadows in the majority of the city that remained unlighted.

Once they had passed into the darkened reaches of elven homes, the pair hid in the shadows for several minutes while a party of armored men marched past. The young Speaker was acutely conscious of the woman's presence beside him. He placed a protective arm around her shoulders and relished the warmth as she seemed to melt into his side. Even so, she seemed considerably less frightened than he did, and he found himself wondering how many times she had left the house in the dark of the night to wander Qualinost on some mysterious purpose.

But those thoughts vanished as the guards turned a corner. Instantly she was up, pulling him by the hand, leading him in a sprint down a lane shaded by thick borders of overhanging aspen trees.

He tried to keep up, but he was embarrassed to realize that he was gasping for breath after a short run. Tugging on her hand, he tried to slow her headlong pace, but instead she pulled him along urgently, all but dragging him as he stumbled the last two dozen paces to the end of the lane. Here again she pushed him into the shelter of roadside shrubbery, still holding his hand as she knelt beside him and studied the wide roadway before them.

Gilthas sensed affection in the touch of her dry fingers on his moist hand, but he also felt the competence, the confidence of this woman he knew so little about. Though he strained to control his rasping breaths, she pressed a finger to his lips, and he forced himself to be utterly silent. Here, too, there were Dark Knights. Indeed, he was startled to find out how fully Qualinost was garrisoned by its new conquerors. His guess would have been that there were only a few dozen of the human warriors in the city, but if that were the case, they had seen half of them in the past few blocks—and that at the darkest hours of night!

Finally they were running again, around corners, through curving little streets that were barely wide enough for the two of them to pass side by side. Still they avoided the occasional patches of illumination, always choosing the darkest route when a pair of alternating paths presented themselves. They were going uphill, Gilthas noticed, and then suddenly the trees were finished and the dazzling night sky yawned overhead. He stumbled, shaken by the vast sense of openness after all the winding, narrow byways. His feet scuffed over flat tiles, and only then did he realize that she had brought him to the great Hall of Audience, the hilltop clearing with its mosaic map and broad clearing.

The great constellations sparkled overhead, gleaming from the moonless sky. He gaped at Paladine and Takhisis, as always in opposition, facing each other across the sky. Many times as a youth he had whiled away the nighttime hours by staring upward at the fabulous array of stars, but never had he seen them so perfectly, never had they seemed so close. He had to resist the childish notion that he could reach out and pluck them from the sky like sparkling cherries. Vaguely he noticed that even now, in the depths of the night, the air was as hot and stifling as normal for a midsummer day.

"Over here," she whispered, tugging him along the edge of the trees that fringed the clearing. They stayed low, moved like furtive creatures of the forest, though it seemed that here, at least, the Dark Knights had left the city of the elves to itself.

Then he gasped audibly as he saw white wings shimmering in the deep shadows. Two large creatures waited there, and even before he saw the eaglelike heads upraised, yellow eyes staring at the pair of elves, he knew these were griffons.

Only once had he ridden one of the magnificent creatures. That had been upon his first meeting with Rashas. How blind he had been then, how fooled by the venerable senator's gracious words, his elegant veneer. Gilthas had mounted the steed and ridden double with Rashas, his mind awhirl with nothing more than his first glimpse of Qualinesti. It had never occurred to him then that he was coming here to serve the senator's purposes, that indeed Rashas had lured him with the perfect bait: the chance for a stifled youngster to get out from beneath his parents' wings, to have a taste of freedom.

Freedom! The very notion left a bitter feeling in his memory as he thought of how fully he had been tricked. Within a matter of hours, he had learned he was virtually the prisoner of Rashas, and within days he had been installed as a figurehead on the throne of his mother's people.

"They will carry us," Kerianseray was saying, gesturing to the creatures. Both, Gilthas now saw, were saddled and apparently eager to fly.

Once again he had a feeling of his own wrongness, of the guilt and culpability that lay on his shoulders because he had unwittingly stepped into his crown. As a result of that conspiracy, which had included the holding of Alhana Starbreeze hostage, the griffons had stopped serving the Qualinesti. Yet obviously they still served Porthios.

He stepped up to one of the creatures, which regarded him with a glare that he thought was exceptionally cold and aloof. Gilthas bowed stiffly, not wanting to appear weak or indecisive in front of this proud creature. Yet he was embarrassed as he tried to slip his boot into the stirrup and found the silver bracket always dancing just beyond the reach of his toes. Finally Kerian stepped to his side, helped him plant his foot, then aided him to swing his other leg across the creature's leonine haunches.

Once he was astride the griffon, Gilthas noticed that the saddle felt very natural, almost as though it conformed to his body. The back was high and pressed close to his spine, which was good, because the griffon pounced forward with a sudden beat of its wings, and without that brace, the elf would certainly have slid right over the rump to sprawl gracelessly on the ground that was already receding beneath him.

He saw the treetops of Qualinost whirl past below, felt the creature bank as it followed a course over the densest of the city's vegetation. Like the two elves on foot, the griffons avoided those parts of the city where the magical lights danced. Soon they soared beneath one of the lofty arched bridges, and though Gilthas could clearly see the Dark Knights pacing their monotonous duty overhead, the twin fliers whisked through the shadows undetected.

Kerian, on the other griffon, was nearby. Somehow she looked relaxed as she leaned forward in the saddle, the reins held loosely in her left hand, golden hair trailing in a plume behind her. As they passed over the deep gorge that yawned to the west of the city, Gilthas was clutching the horn that rose from the forepart of his own saddle. Only after he glanced again at Kerian did he belatedly remembered the reins. Picking up the leather straps, he held them lightly, certain that the griffon did not need—and would not welcome—his steering or guidance.

The night air was surprisingly cool once they rose above the trees, but after the numbing heat of the last weeks, Gilthas relished the chill, enjoyed the sensation of his sweat drying from the force of the wind. He looked back, seeing the illumination of the city's lights fading through the woods. Within a few minutes, Qualinost had faded into the distance behind them, and the forest sprawled strangely dark to all the horizons below.

They were flying west, he knew from the position of the stars, though Gilthas found it impossible to calculate how far they had traveled. Strangely, he didn't feel any need to sleep. Instead, he absorbed the view of the starlit landscape, watched the occasional clouds wisp across the heavens, or stole surreptitious looks at Kerian, riding in silence just twenty or thirty feet off to the side.

A glance over his shoulder showed that dawn had begun to pink the horizon, but there was no distinguishing characteristic in all the vast forest to give him a clear idea of where he was. Slowly daylight filtered across the sky, and with the increasing illumination, the two griffons dived until they were flying just above the tops of the trees. He suspected that this was to avoid discovery by dragons, and the suspicion gave him a little thrill of adventure that soon translated into an acid churning of his stomach.

Finally the sun rose into the cloudless sky, and the heat of the direct rays on his back brought back awareness of this scorching summer. They coursed through dry air, and in the harsh light, he saw that many of the trees were withered, their leaves tinged with a brown that was utterly unnatural for the eternally lush forests of Qualinesti. They crossed over a small stream, and in the glimpses he got between the leaves, he saw that the water was still and muddy, more a series of stagnant pools around bone-dry rocks than any kind of fresh water flowage.

And then, at last, something broke the monotonous blanket of treetops. A bluff jutted before them, a conelike promontory formed by some ancient geological convulsion, or perhaps the work of some ultrapowerful wizard with a taste for altered landscapes. The sides of the elevation were thickly blanketed by trees, but the face was bare rock, a cliff worn ragged by weather, reduced to a series of tapered spires rising upward from the jagged summit. At the base of the cliff was a small lake, where the waters somehow remained clear and blue in the midst of the drought.

Here the griffons descended, gliding just above the lake's surface. Gilthas was enthralled by the sight of huge trout darting away from their swift shadows.

Finally he looked up and saw that they were angling toward the shore. And there, in the shadows beneath the lofty oaks and vallenwoods, he saw a number of people gathered, arrayed in a semicircle, clearly awaiting their arrival.

The griffons swept closer, and Gilthas could see that these were elves. In the woods beyond them, more griffons were at rest, though some of the creatures lifted their heads or made sharp squawks to acknowledge the arrival of their two fellows.

With a suddenness that almost pitched him from the saddle, Gilthas's steed swooped down and skidded to a halt on the dry ground at the edge of the lake. Immediately hard-faced elves raced forward, flanking him with swords drawn.

"Get down!" one of them barked. "Quickly!"

Gilthas did so, scrambling from the saddle, kicking out of the stirrups, and somehow coming to rest on his feet. He noticed that Kerianseray had dismounted smoothly and was welcoming the embrace of a tall, fierce Kagonesti. That warrior, whose face, chest, and limbs were covered with the whorls and leaves of black tattoos, stared over Kerian's head at Gilthas, his expression cold and unreadable.

Trying to summon what he could of his dignity, Gilthas straightened up and looked stiffly over the assembled elves.

These were a mix of wild elves and crudely dressed Qualinesti, the latter wearing leather leggings and cloth tunics to set them apart from the Kagonesti, who wore loincloths. One of the Qualinesti, a golden-haired male with stern features, his mouth locked in a harsh frown, stepped forward from the throng.

Gilthas was certain this was Porthios.

"Greetings, Uncle," began the young Speaker. "I am grateful that you have agreed to see me."

"You should be," Porthios snapped. "For by many accounts, you are the one who has stolen my medallion and my throne, who purports to lead my people but is really the tame lackey of the Thalas-Enthia!"

Gilthas felt the sting of the words, used all his willpower not to recoil. "I had no part in seeking this throne," he retorted, his eyes searching through the elves beyond Porthios, seeking one particular face. "Instead, it was thrust upon me—after it had already been taken from you!—and I donned the medallion to avoid an even darker alternative."

"What alternative is darker than betrayal? Than exile?" growled the former Speaker of the Sun.

"The murder of a princess . . . the loss of an unborn child's life," Gilthas said, his tone softening as he found the person he sought. "Hello, my queen. I am glad to see that you are well."

"Hello, Gilthas," Alhana replied with a smile. She stepped forward, taking her husband's arm in a gesture that seemed incongruously tender in contrast to Porthios's harsh words. "And I am glad to see you healthy as well."

"Tell me why you wanted to see me," Porthios demanded, clearly vexed by his wife's friendliness with the young elf.

"Because I admire what you have done, and I despise what has happened in Qualinesti. You might be interested to know that your victory over a wing of the Dark Knights' army resulted in a general's execution. I have heard that Lord Ariakan himself found your attack embarrassing and disconcerting."

"And who is Lord Ariakan? Is he your new master?" The outlaw captain seemed determined to be rude.

Gilthas stiffened. "My admiration was based on an account of your actions and a genuine interest in seeing if there was something, anything, I could do to help you. However, I have no interest in being insulted and ridiculed. I can leave right now!"

"No," Porthios growled, "you can't. Not unless you know how to persuade the griffons to obey you."

Gilthas felt a nervous surge in his gut and knew that the other elf spoke the truth. Still, he tried to cover his anxiety with bluster. "Am I your prisoner, then? This journey was a ruse on your part to work my capture?"

"Why should we take risks like this? You wouldn't be worth the trouble," Porthios said with a sneer.

"Then why am I here?" Gilthas retorted, getting hotter by the second. "Why did you let me come?"

"Because you know things about the Dark Knights . . . things that I need to know. You were right, in a sense. You might be able to help me."

"Come, Husband. This is not a matter to be discussed while we stand here and wait for the sun to reach its zenith," Alhana said gently. She had not let go of his arm, and now she gently pulled him through a half circle while she turned to Gilthas. "Join us for a bite of food . . . and we can sit, as conferring elves should." She looked chidingly back to Porthios. "Not stand around like human bulls getting ready to fight a duel."

Gilthas followed, aware that Kerian was walking behind him, still arm in arm with the glowering Kagonesti warrior. Lining their route into the forest were many other elves, and it did not escape the young Speaker's notice that there was not a friendly face in the lot.

All of which made Alhana's graciousness an exceptional relief. She led them to a small clearing, merely a bare patch of forest floor surrounded by the trunks of many massive trees. It was almost as though a natural room had been formed here in the woods. Stern warriors stood at the gaps between the trees, giving some measure of privacy to the elves who entered the enclosed space.

They included Porthios and Alhana, Gilthas, several other elven warriors, and Kerian and the Kagonesti brave who had not left her side since their arrival. Gilthas was further pleased to recognize the warrior-mage Samar, who with Tanis had aided Alhana's escape. So far as the Speaker had known, Samar had been killed during the queen's first, ill-fated attempt at escape.

"No . . . I was saved by healer magic," Samar explained easily. "And in our second attempt, we were more careful, though I regret that we were not able to get you away with us."

"Sometimes I wish you had," Gilthas admitted, allowing himself a moment of glum honesty.

"You tried to *escape?*" Porthios asked skeptically. "Rashas was holding his prospective Speaker prisoner?"

"I told you, Husband," Alhana interjected with a touch of exasperation. "It was only the threat against my life that forced Gilthas to take on the medallion and the throne of the Speaker."

"It's true," Gilthas insisted, trying to be pleasant, though he admitted to himself that he was tired of Porthios's scorn and irritated with the outlaw prince constantly questioning his motives. "Rashas showed me an archer, one of his Kagonesti slaves, who held a bow drawn, an arrow aimed at your wife's heart. He made it clear that he would give the order to shoot if I showed any hesitation."

A question suddenly occurred to the young elf, and he fixed his eyes upon Porthios with a hint of challenge. "And that medallion still bore the enchantment of the sun . . . that meant that you gave it up willingly! Why?"

The prince glowered and flushed, but finally shrugged in resignation. "Rashas used the same tactic against me," Porthios admitted. "I gave it up to spare Alhana's life."

"Then take it back!" Gilthas urged suddenly, impetuously. "I would willingly return it to you, and you can have the throne again!"

Porthios shook his head firmly. "I'm an outlaw, remember? My days of living in Qualinost, in any elven city, are behind me!"

228

"If that's the case—if you accept the judgment of the Thalas-Enthia that you've been exiled—then why do you choose to dwell in the Qualinesti forests?" Gilthas shot back, his chin jutting forward in challenge.

The older elf blinked, then allowed himself a tight smile. "I see the pup is finding his bark." His expression darkened. "But my reasons are my own, and I have no intention of justifying them to you."

Gilthas shrugged. "It's not necessary that you do. But I would have expected your actions to make a little more sense, that's all."

"They make sense to me."

"You said that I could help you, that you wanted information about the Dark Knights. What do you want to know?"

"This Lord Salladac . . . you have met him?"

"Yes."

"Tell me what he's like, his strengths, especially, and any weaknesses you might have observed."

Gilthas tried to comply. He listed the Dark Knight leader's grasp of strategy and tactics, his obvious mastery over his own troops. He described the speed with which the knightly army moved, the well-disciplined dragons, and the rank after rank of fierce-looking brutes, all apparently devoted to their lord. Gilthas also mentioned Salladac's utter ruthlessness in dealing with the incompetence of his own lieutenant, the soldier who had been executed for failing to guard his camp.

"That incompetence was highlighted only by our attack," Porthios interjected with no attempt to conceal his pride.

"Exactly. Salladac is a diplomat, too. In negotiations, he is unfailingly pleasant, yet he seems to get exactly what he wants."

"That's because he deals from a position of strength."

"Perhaps . . . and also because, in my experience, he's been negotiating with weaklings." Gilthas was startled by his own frankness.

"Do you include yourself in that assessment?" Porthios looked at him shrewdly.

The Speaker merely shrugged. "You can, if you want. I was

present, but—as I'm sure you could imagine—it was Rashas who did the talking."

"Gilthas—that is, the Speaker—tried to raise a company to defend the city!" Kerianseray, speaking for the first time, interrupted with surprising vehemence.

A warm flush of pleasure flowed through the young elf at her words, though he tried to mask his emotion from Porthios and from the fierce-looking Kagonesti who glowered at Kerian's side.

"This is true?" asked the outlaw captain.

Now Gilthas's emotions shifted again toward shame as he remembered his pathetic efforts. "I tried, that much is true. But the elves of the city showed no stomach for the fight. I was able to gather about fifty old warriors, half of them lamed during the War of the Lance."

"They had no stomach for the fight, or for their leader?" Porthios stabbed shrewdly.

Gilthas remained silent, biting his tongue as he glared at the outlaw.

Porthios snorted in contempt. "I would have expected more from the son of Tanis Half-Elven. Your father was impetuous, a fool in some ways, but at least he—"

Gilthas had heard enough. His features twisted into a snarl and he jumped to his feet. "Listen, damn you—leave my father out of this! Tanis has more wisdom in his big toe than you, a so-called elven prince, have in your whole body! You won't insult him in my presence, or I *will* fight you!"

He dropped his tone, his voice deliberately scornful, challenging. "Are you a complete fool? Can't you see that I don't have any more choice in these matters than you do? If you're too stupid to get that through your head, then send me away or kill me . . . whatever you plan to do."

With a glower of pure fury, he raised his fist—he had no weapon—and took what he assumed was a martial stance. "That is, you can *try* to kill me!"

Porthios stared at him, his face darkening to a furious crimson. Then, to Gilthas's immense chagrin and embarrassment, the outlaw prince threw back his head and laughed out loud. He bounced to his feet and, still laughing, reached forward to clasp the Speaker's clenched fist in both of his hands.

"Well said, young nephew. You are your mother's—and your father's—son after all. And you're right to talk to me like that. I apologize for my rudeness."

Utterly flustered now, Gilthas followed the other's lead and sat back down. He regarded Porthios warily, surprised to realize that the outlaw now seemed to be in a fine mood, for he was chuckling and shaking his head in amusement.

"You were telling me about this Dark Knight lord . . . painting a rather formidable picture, I must admit. Does he have *any* weaknesses?"

Gilthas had actually given this question some thought, and he had an answer prepared. "If he has a weakness, and I am not certain that he does, it is that Lord Salladac is convinced—is *too* convinced—that he cannot fail. He exhibits a sense of arrogance that might lead to his undoing."

"In what way?" Porthios was listening intently.

"He has been ordered to send his dragons and half his army to aid in the campaign against Silvanesti, for example, but he's decided to remain here, fully confident that he and his regime are safe."

"As to the city, is it true that the Thalas-Enthia is allowed to meet, to conduct business as usual?"

"Yes . . . up to a point. The most radical members have fled, and their houses have been given over to the knightly garrison. There is a curfew now, but of course that doesn't mean much to elves—it's not as if we carouse like dwarves until all hours—though the knights have many guards patrolling the city at night." He flashed a smile at the Kagonesti woman across the campfire. "Fortunately Kerianseray didn't seem to have much trouble in leading us past them."

"My daughter has been trained to know the stealth of the deer and the speed of the rabbit," declared the tattooed warrior who sat so protectively beside the wild elf maid.

"Your *daugh*—of course, yes," Gilthas said, flustered. Alhana's eyes sparkled at his discomfort, though he tried manfully to maintain his composure. Nevertheless, he was almost giddy with delight at the news. Though the wild elf brave was clearly mature, his tattooed elven face gave no hint that he was anything more than a grown male, so the Speaker had naturally formed a mistaken impression about him

"Forgive me," Porthios said. "This is Dallatar, chieftain of the Kagonesti in these woods. His warriors have allied themselves with ours in defense of our homeland."

"I'm glad," Gilthas said sincerely. "And you should know that there are those in the city who would be your allies as well."

"I believe you," the dark elf said, and Gilthas was surprised at the wave of relief those words sent through him.

"Now that we've gotten some of this business out of the way," Alhana suggested, with a pointed look at her husband, "why don't we move to the council fire. There we can eat—not a palace feast, of course, but we make do with the humble fare that the forest provides—and perhaps our guest might get a taste of our hospitality instead of our suspicions."

"Agreed," Porthios said cheerfully.

The elves made an informal procession as they left the enclosed space between the tree trunks. Gilthas was surprised to find, a few paces deeper in the forest, a wide, open space in which were gathered hundreds of elves and griffons. A few tall trees grew here and there, with broad upper branches sweeping outward, interconnecting enough to deny any glimpse of the sky. More significantly, he realized, this huge encampment was consequently invisible to discovery from the air.

The "humble fare" of the forest was a dazzling array of foods, centering around roast venison, stuffed game hens, and fish fillets spitted and grilled over hardwood coals. There were fruits and tubers in accompaniment, including berries that had been whipped into a light froth and then spread over thin strips of bread. The outlaws even had wine, though Porthios cheerfully admitted that it was not of their own making. Instead, they had taken it from an outbound caravan. Many jugs had been cached near here, so that when the blue dragons had driven them out of their previous camp, they had still maintained a ready supply of the beverage so favored by the elves.

The atmosphere was convivial, and Gilthas found himself envying these elves of the forest. In his opinion, they paid but a small price by sleeping on the ground, making do without the dancing lights, the elegant surroundings of Qualinost. Porthios tried to point out that a great deal of work went into gathering the food, and even more time was spent guarding themselves against attack, but even these deterrences seemed merely like an adventurous aspect to what must be an idyllic life.

These were the thoughts on Gilthas's mind as he rose to visit the latrine long after the meal had been supped. The wine left a pleasant taste on his tongue and a mild buzz in his head as he wandered through the woods.

It was so peaceful here, he thought as he heard birdcalls in the dark woods. He strolled through the dark, coming back to the firelit clearing by a roundabout path. At the edge of the illuminated swath, he almost stumbled over a figure crouching in the bushes.

"Excuse me," stammered Gilthas, embarrassed by his clumsiness. He assumed that this was merely another elf who, like himself, had wandered off to relieve himself in private. Then he caught a glimpse of the sharp, angry features.

"You!" gasped the young Speaker.

Immediately the other elf, who had recognized Gilthas at the same time, spat a curse and snatched at something he held in his hand. The Speaker saw a golden ring, twisted by frantic fingers. With a single muffled word, the figure disappeared. Gilthas lunged forward, groping through empty space, knowing that the other elf had teleported away.

"Porthios! Alhana!" he cried, lunging into the clearing, pointing to the place where the other elf had crouched.

"What? What's wrong."

"There, in the woods—a spy was watching!"

"How do you know he's a spy?" demanded the outlaw captain, drawing his sword and racing toward the empty patch of shrubbery.

"Because I recognized him. His name is Guilderhand, and he's loyal only to Rashas!"

* * * * *

"I'll have to return to the city immediately," Gilthas said. "Guilderhand is probably there already, but perhaps I can try to minimize the damage."

"How?' Porthios asked scathingly. "He saw you here, he knows the location of our camp, and you claim that he's loyal to our staunchest enemy. Our only alternative is to flee from here and take you with us!"

He looked at Gilthas closely. "Which is a shame, my young prince, because I had realized that with you on the Speaker's throne, we could in fact be very useful to each other."

"It might not be as bad as we fear," Samar reported as he came to join them. The warrior-mage had been investigating the place where Guilderhand had disappeared. "Perhaps we can send someone after him and get to him before he makes a report."

"How?" asked Porthios.

"I have a device of teleportation myself, which is the same enchantment that Guilderhand obviously had on his ring." Samar produced a small vial from his pouch. "It is contained here, in a bit of mint. It can be used to send someone to Qualinost, to try to intercept—and to silence—the spy."

"I'll go," Gilthas said quickly. "It has to be me. I can move around the city, and no one will be surprised to see me there."

"Then perhaps we do have time," the outlaw captain said. He looked at Gilthas. "Do you know what needs to be done?"

"To go after Guilderhand?" Gilthas asked, his mind still taut with the fear and excitement of the encounter.

"You'll have to kill him if you can find him before he reports to Rashas," Porthios declared grimly. "But if you're too late, then flee the city, or suffer the consequences of having the senator and the Thalas-Enthia know about our alliance."

"I understand," Gilthas said, and he did—up to a point.

The one thing he didn't know was how in Krynn he would go about trying to commit a murder.

PART III

CHAOS

Prologue

25 SC

"The blues left . . . and you stayed," said Silvanoshei, standing to stare directly into one of Aerensianic's huge, golden eyes. "When the storms came, you could have stayed hidden, remained in this lair your cherished so much. Samar has told me that you did not. But what is it that drew you out of your cave?"

The dragon snorted in amusement. "Something came to me—something that I could never have expected—but once I found it, I could never turn my back."

The dragon paused in his story for a moment, lifting his head and fixing his eyes toward the mouth of the cave. "Wait," he said.

The two elves watched as he lifted the great body onto his four legs and crept, catlike, out of the corner of his lair. Aeren's eyes were fixed upon the trough in the floor of the cave, where the tide had advanced in a gently surging wave of seawater. Something splashed in that wetness, and then a sleek body vanished beneath the surface.

"A seal," whispered Samar, holding up his hand to halt Silvanoshei as the younger elf started to move. Instead, they both sat still and watched.

The brown-furred animal popped its head above the surface again, and by this time, the green dragon had reached the edge of the water. With a single, practiced gesture, Aeren snapped down, lifted his prey upward, tilted back his head, and swallowed the animal in a massive gulp, a convulsion of emerald scales rippling along the length of his sinuous neck. He remained still for a few minutes, then uttered a contented sigh and returned to the pair of elves.

Samar still had his hand on the dragonlance, but although he kept his eyes upon the wyrm, watching for any sign of aggression, he didn't lower the weapon. Instead, Aerensianic settled to the ground over his meager treasure pile and nodded contentedly.

"There've always been seals in these waters—that's one of the things that attracted me here. Even in that summer, when the air was so hot and the sun seemed to scorch the sky, they came to the shore, and I ate well.

"I took to perching on a certain ledge on the face of the bluff over the sea. Even though it was scorching hot, especially as the summer moved on, the heat was somewhat mitigated by the sea breeze. Here, beyond the reach of the splashing surf, I could watch the rocks on which the waves crashed just below. Often the creatures would climb onto the perches, confident that they were safe from sea predators. Rare was the seal who could escape the strike of my jaws from above as I lashed down to snatch the hapless creature around the head.

"Thus I was content to watch and observe . . . or so I thought.

"On one of the warmest of the midsummer days, I was startled by a large winged shadow that flickered past. Of course, at first I though it was a blue dragon attack, and I lunged backward into the cave.

"Only then did I look up, and imagine my surprise at the sight of another green dragon, a splendid female! She was not as large as I, and she banked and came to rest on the ledge with a willingness that I found strangely enticing.

" 'Greetings, O strange clan dragon,' she said, politely dipping her neck. 'I am called Toxyria, and I am happy to find you here along a coast I thought had been abandoned by our kind.'

" 'Greetings, Beautiful Toxyria,' I returned, and I explained that I had lived there for but a single winter. 'And is your lair along here?' I asked.

" 'A half day's flight to the south,' she explained, purring at my flattery. 'And do you live here with your mate?' she inquired demurely.

"I admit that in my delight I huffed a plume of green mist from my nostrils, and Toxyria inhaled the gas with obvious relish. 'I have no mate,' I explained. 'I have flown here alone, from a forest a thousand miles and more away.'

" 'There is a plentitude of edibles in these seas,' she noted, which I interpreted to mean that she did not regard me as unfriendly competition for the local food supply. 'You will find that the winters are mild, for the sea is warmed by a northern current—that is, if you decide to stay.' She looked at me with an expression I can only describe as hopeful.

" 'I have never found better hunting, nor a finer cave,' I said. 'All that was missing was the companionship of my clan . . . and perhaps that lack may have been very recently addressed?'

"She moved into my lair the next day, bringing the few baubles of her treasures that she deemed worth saving. I confess that I was embarrassed about my own poor hoard, but I explained the lack by reason of my recent arrival, and Toxy proved quite understanding. In fact, I wondered if she had purposely left many of her treasures behind out of a wish to spare me humiliation. Her tender actions gave me a powerful resolve to plunder sailing ships, perhaps even raid a few castles on distant Ergoth, in order to quickly establish a trove that would make her proud."

The dragon's voice turned melancholy, and his expression

was far away as he stared toward the twilit entrance to the cave.

"She came here?" Silvanoshei pressed. "Then where is sh—?"

He stopped as Samar put a hand on his arm. The young elf looked annoyed for a moment, but he didn't press the question.

"That detail, I suspect, our friend will get to in good time. . . ."

The Truth About Treachery

Chapter Seventeen

High Summer, 383 AC

The crushed mint was sweet, hot, and biting on his tongue as Gilthas bit down on the vial of powder. As Samar had instructed, he tried to envision his destination. Magic surrounded him, and for a dizzying second, he thought he was dying. He had no sense of focus, of place . . . nothing surrounded him, and he couldn't picture that any solidity awaited him.

And in the next instant, that crazed sensation passed, and he was staggering, trying to regain his balance as he felt a floor underfoot, saw walls come into view around him. He lurched two steps to the side before he felt his footing level out, and then he stood still, blinking, holding his arms out to the sides as the sense of motion slowly receded.

He was standing within his own study, in the Speaker's House beside the Tower of the Sun. True to Samar's word, the magic had returned him to Qualinost. A look out the window showed that it was still the dark of night, so Gilthas assumed that the other part of the warrior-mage's statements were true, that virtually no time had passed while he was teleporting.

Still dazed, Gilthas reconstructed the magical journey, the hundreds of miles traveled in the blink of an eye. The warrior-mage had told him to carefully visualize his destination, and so he had chosen this room, the place he was most familiar with in all the city.

He thought with a pang about Kerianseray, who would be returning to Qualinost on the back of a griffon. Irrationally he feared for her because she had to travel alone, though when he paused to think about it, he knew that his presence had been more a liability than an asset when it came to safety.

But finally his agitation began to settle, and he started to focus his thoughts, knowing that he had work to do. He needed to find Guilderhand and . . . His mind balked at the implications of impending violence, but he realized immediately that he needed a weapon.

He immediately went into the formal receiving room, automatically chanting the magic word that brought the crystal chandeliers into blazing prominence. There, arrayed on the stone wall above the massive fireplace, were the weapons of elven heroes—several long swords, a pair of crossed arrows, and an odd collection including a scimitar, long-hafted halberds, and even a wicked and obviously very heavy battle-axe.

The long sword being the traditional weapon of the elven warrior, Gilthas automatically went to the smallest of those, lifting down the keen weapon, surprised by its weight. He touched a thumb to the blade and winced at the drop of blood that quickly welled from his skin. Clearly the weapon was sharp enough to kill. He tested the balance of the sword, wielding it back and forth in front of him, trying without success to imagine what it would feel like to plunge that steel tip into flesh.

But how would he carry it? Or conceal it, for that matter? It was not like the Speaker of the Sun to go armed about the city.

His first question was answered when he found an assortment of scabbards in a nearby closet. One of these easily fit the sword, and though it took him several minutes, he finally figured out how to suspend the weapon from his belt. As to his second worry, he decided to bluff it out. If anyone questioned him, he would haughtily reply that the Speaker of the Sun would carry whatever he damn well pleased when he went about the city. Somehow the grim determination evoked by his words gave him confidence as he stalked through the quiet house and carefully opened the front door to step into the stifling air of the night.

Only then did he remember the Dark Knight guards who had so diligently patrolled the nighttime streets of Qualinost. He knew that his arrogant declaration would carry very little weight with these humans who had seen the elves surrender like whipped puppies even before a blade had been drawn in anger. There was no alternative. He would have to evade the patrols and hope that, on his own, he could be as successful as Kerian had been proven herself to be.

And how would he find Guilderhand? Would the spy teleport himself directly to Rashas? If so, then of course Gilthas would already be too late—unless for some reason the senator had not been where the spy expected to find him.

It was a hope, and the only one Gilthas could arrive at. He trotted down the winding path to the street and then paused to look up and down, trying to spot the patrols that had been so frequent around the Tower of the Sun. Already he was sweating, though he forced himself to breathe quietly, not wanting to make any undue noise. Surprisingly, there were none of the Dark Knights in sight. He didn't waste time wondering where they were; instead, he darted along the shadows beside the road, hurrying to the nearest corner, where he ducked into a side lane.

Here the path was much darker than the main street, but he still tried to move quietly, loping along and holding the sword, which he quickly realized had a tendency to jangle. He dashed around another corner, trying to remember the street leading to Rashas's elegant manor. It should be familiar, he thought wryly. It had been the first place he had visited in Qualinost when he had ridden into town all wide-eyed and gawking, never even suspecting why he had been brought here or that he would soon be the senator's prisoner.

The side street angled back toward the main avenue, and the neighborhood looked familiar. He reached the edge of the wide route. There it was!

The large house, behind its sculpted hedge of lush blossoms, was unmistakable. He saw the lofty tower where Alhana had been held prisoner, and the other, lower wing where he himself had been reclused after Rashas had decided that he should be separated from the queen. He crouched in the shadows at the intersection, again studying the main avenue, alert for the presence of Dark Knight patrols.

Again he saw no sign of the city's human occupiers. He began to think that was strange, but he didn't waste any time wondering about his good luck. Instead, he started toward the gap in the hedge that led toward the front door.

Here he hesitated, however, as other questions began to assail him. What should he do about Rashas's Kagonesti guards? With the exception of Kerianseray, who had come with him when he had moved to the Speaker's house, the senator's slaves had seemed fanatically loyal, not to mention fierce and bloodthirsty. His hand came to rest on his sword, but Gilthas knew he'd be no match for one of these savage warriors if they met on hostile terms.

Studying the house, he was surprised to see that many lights were on. His heart sank, and he immediately suspected a reason: Guilderhand had returned here, and the senator was busy learning about the Speaker's meeting with the outlaw. It would be foolishness—almost suicide!—for him to walk into that conversation.

Before he could make up his mind to turn and flee into the night, however, the front door burst open and none other than Senator Rashas came rushing out, trailed by several of his wild elf bodyguards. The elder elf stumbled to a halt at the sight of the lone figure standing in his gateway. Rashas blinked, then uttered an oath as he rushed forward..

"Where in the Abyss have you been?" he demanded. He seemed ready to grab Gilthas by the arm and shake him, but apparently thought better of such a presumptuous action. Instead, he planted his hands on his hips and glared at the Speaker of the Sun. "We've been looking for you since this morning. There are things happening, and you were needed in the councils! And now with the summons—by Paladine, you know we were supposed to be there an hour ago!"

"Things happening?" Gilthas was stunned, his mind trying to keep up with the words. He had been prepared for the senator's anger, but his questions were merely mystifying.

"I ask you again, where have you been?"

"I—I went for a walk in the forest. I wanted to do some thinking by myself."

Rashas lowered his voice to a hiss, a strong, penetrating force that pushed its way into Gilthas's ears alone. "Don't ever do that again! Do you understand? We need to know where you are at all times!"

Through it all, the younger elf was realizing one thing: Rashas didn't know! He hadn't spoken to Guilderhand! Almost light-headed with relief, he nodded dumbly, made sounds of assurance with his dry mouth and clumsy tongue.

"Come on, then. At least you're dressed now, and I don't have to drag you out of bed." Rashas took hold of Gilthas's arm and pulled him along the street toward the Tower of the Sun. "We've got to get to Lord Salladac!"

The Speaker had enough presence of mind not to ask why they were going to see Lord Salladac. Instead, he trotted along beside the older elf, who was moving along at what would normally have been quite an unseemly pace. They hurried down the main avenue, and once again Gilthas took note of the absence of Dark Knight guards. It had not been his imagination. Clearly they had been ordered to other duties than the night patrols of Qualinost's streets.

As they approached his own house, the young elf flushed at the realization that he'd left the chandelier blazing in his receiving room. Bright light spilled from the windows across the garden, casting bright splashes of illumination through the shadowy street. Again Rashas made no remark about anything strange, so fixed was he on reaching the tower. Holding his sword to keep it from jangling, Gilthas was startled to realize that the senator hadn't even commented on the fact that he was armed.

They arrived at the Tower of the Sun at the same time that Lord Salladac, coming from the other direction, approached at the head of a small company of guards.

"Thank all the gods he's not been waiting for us," Rashas whispered. "I'd hate to think what would happen to your head if he'd been here on time!"

Gilthas merely nodded, further mystified.

Silent servants admitted them to the vast council chamber, which was illuminated by a few small candles, though the corners around the walls and the yawning space overhead all expanded into utter darkness. Salladac seemed to like it like this. He bade the two elves join him on the rostrum while the guards—Dark Knight and Kagonesti—all halted a discreet distance away.

While they settled themselves on three stools, Salladac's eyes fastened on Gilthas with a penetrating stare, and for an instant, the young elf was certain that he had been caught. He thought of the sword, knew beyond doubt that he could never draw it in time to strike, and he saw, too, that any damage he could do here was useless to the cause that had brought him back from Porthios's camp.

Then the lord sighed and seemed to relax, stretching his arms over his head and making a great show of working the kinks out of his back.

"These nights are too hot, and your elven mattresses are too thin," he said by way of introduction. "Even after a good night's sleep I wake up stiff, and now, with all this alarm in the wee hours, I swear I'm lucky I can even walk."

"What is the source of the alarm, my lord?" Rashas asked quickly.

"Urgent word from Lord Ariakan at the High Clerist's Tower," Salladac said bluntly. "I received a message, carried on dragonback, just after sunset."

"Word about what?" Gilthas blurted.

"It seems there's a new threat developing in the north," the human lord explained. "I don't doubt that it's something we'll be able to handle, though I admit there was a peculiar urgency to my lord's missive. The Silvanesti campaign has been indefinitely postponed. My dragons are being recalled as of this morning, likewise about half of my brutes."

"You're leaving Qualinesti?" asked the young Speaker, now totally mystified. Guilderhand was utterly forgotten in the midst of these startling developments.

"Only temporarily, I assure you," the lord said. He glowered sternly. "Don't get any ideas about changing the new order of things. I anticipate that I'll be back, *with* my dragons, in a matter of days."

"We have no such thoughts, I assure you," Rashas said. "But we would like to know about this threat. Is it a danger to Qualinesti as well?"

"I wish I knew," Salladac admitted. "But to tell the truth, I'm afraid it might be. There are reports of fires burning where they don't belong—over the ocean, to be precise. All Palanthas is in an uproar, and Ariakan wants all the talons of his dragon forces gathered in one place."

"Is it an invasion?" wondered Gilthas.

"Tough to say for certain, but it could be. My lord used the term 'Storms of Chaos' when he talked about the things he'd seen. It's not terribly specific, but it was the *tone* of his letter as much as anything else that has me worried."

Salladac let the elves digest this disturbing bit of news as he looked back and forth at them frankly. "If the worst comes, then Qualinesti will be attacked by forces more horrible than anything we've—either elf or human—ever faced before. And we'll have to fight it together if we are to have any chance. That's why I called you here—*both* of you."

"Of course," Rashas said, though he cast a sneering, sidelong glance at Gilthas.

"Rashas, if the unexpected happens, you will be in charge of maintaining calm in the city. Gilthas, my lord Speaker, you will need to muster a military force—all the elves who can hold a sword or shoot a bow. My knights and brutes, such as remain, will help you, but until I get back, you must take charge!"

"Me? I mean, of course," stammered Gilthas, utterly flabbergasted by this development.

"Is that . . . I mean, have you thought this through?" asked Rashas, his own eyes wide. "No offense to the young Speaker, but he has never been in battle before!"

"And you have?" The human's tone was biting. "Let's just say I like the young fellow's mettle."

Rashas frowned but clearly knew better than to forcefully argue with the lord who had conquered his city. Instead, he cleared his throat and waited for Salladac to invite him to speak.

"Speaking of enemies, there's the other matter," the senator began, with a hesitant look at Gilthas. "Perhaps we should speak in private?"

"Talk to me now," the human said brusquely. "Surely you can see we're in a hurry."

"Yes, well . . . about my agent, Guilderhand. I have yet to hear his report, but if he's successful, then we may have more enemies than just this 'Storm of Chaos' to deal with. If that's the case—"

"I've spoken to Guilderhand, just tonight," Salladac said breezily.

Despite the man's light tone, Gilthas felt his heart sink to his knees. He knows—and I'm doomed! Again he thought of the sword, weighed his chances, and knew he would be dead before he pulled the weapon halfway out of its scabbard. Vaguely, as though from a long distance away, he heard the lord continue to talk.

"Don't look so surprised," chided Salladac, speaking to Rashas. "And you certainly shouldn't be hurt by the fact that he didn't come directly to you. You see, there was a feature inherent to that ring of teleportation that he thought he stole from me. In reality, as I told you, I provided the thing to him, though I kept that feature a secret. No matter where he wanted to go, the magic would bring him directly into my presence."

"And he used the ring. . . . He found . . . that is, he made a report," pressed Rashas.

"And the ring took him to you?" added Gilthas, appalled at the implication and wondering why the lord hadn't already ordered him arrested or worse.

"Oh, yes," Salladac said smugly. He cast a meaningful look at the young Speaker, then shifted his attention back to Rashas. "He told me many things."

"Where is he now?" demanded the senator. "I have to see him, to talk to him myself!"

"I'm afraid that's quite impossible," the human replied.

"Why? *Why?*"

"Well, you see, I decided that the little weasel was giving me nothing but a pack of lies. You'll understand, of course, that I had no choice in what to do."

"What *did* you do?" gasped Rashas, the color draining from his face.

"The same thing I'd do to anyone who told me lies," Lord Salladac replied, rising from his stool and stretching again. "I had him hanged."

* * * * *

Rashas, too stunned for words, had departed with his Kagonesti guards. The senator would return to his house and begin making plans for keeping order in a city menaced by a hitherto unknown threat. Gilthas had started for his own house, but had been delayed by the subtle gesture of one of the human knights escorting Lord Salladac.

After Rashas had vanished down the street, he was led back into the tower, where the lord met him with a stern glare.

"Guilderhand's report was interesting, as I'm sure you can well imagine," Salladac said without preamble. "Aren't you going to thank me?"

"For what?" blurted the elf, whose head was still spinning.

"For killing him and saving your life. What do you think senators like Rashas would have done if they'd had the chance to talk to him?"

Gilthas didn't need to exercise his imagination too hard. Hadn't he been prepared to commit murder, just to prevent those conversations from occurring?

"Th-thank you," he said, realizing that he was indeed grateful to the man, even as he was powerfully mystified. "But why did you do it?"

"Frankly, I wondered a little bit about that myself," Salladac admitted. "And it comes down to a couple of reasons.

"One, it goes back to what I said before. I like your mettle. You haven't had a chance to show it much, and with that vulture staring over your shoulder, the queen knows you don't get much of a chance to do so. But I think you've got some good stuff in you, and what Guilderhand said didn't do anything to change my mind. At the same time, just between you and me, every time I talk to Rashas I come away with a bad taste in my mouth. Between giving you over to him or tightening a noose around his pet spy, it was a pretty easy decision."

"Then I thank you again sincerely," the elven Speaker said. He decided to be blunt and forthright. "But surely you know that I was seeking to undermine your rule, even to find a way to resist the Dark Knights' conquest."

"Certainly. But I think that mission has been overtaken by events. Another thing I meant: Lord Ariakan sounded damn worried, and he's not a man given over to worry. These Storms of Chaos are a real threat, and if they come here, it's not going to be Rashas and—I admit—not you, either, who'll put up a real fight."

"But Porthios . . . ?" Gilthas said. Finally he saw the reasoning, some reasoning, behind the knight's actions.

"Aye, lad. We will need fighters like Porthios on our side—on both our sides."

"You fear it will be that bad?"

"I fear it will be worse . . . a fight for our very lives, a battle for the survival and the future of the world."

Gilthas found it odd that he felt a greater respect for this human warlord, conqueror of his people, than he did for the elves like Rashas who had led Qualinesti into the place where it could so easily be overrun. His own pride made it difficult for him to acknowledge these truths, but he declared that he would do whatever he could to prepare his city for defense.

"And as to Porthios, I will try to reach him, to let him know of the danger . . . and to bring him into common cause," he pledged.

"That's all we can hope for," Salladac replied. "Good luck to you."

"Thank you, lord." Gilthas hesitated, then knew what he really felt. "And good luck to you as well."

Turning to go, the elf sensed a strange hesitancy, looked back to see that Salladac had something more he wanted to say.

"What is it?"

"There is more news from the Tower of the High Clerist . . . news of a personal nature. Grim news, I'm afraid."

Instantly Gilthas knew—he had sensed it, from the moment he learned about the Dark Knights' invasion. He knew that there were people, many people, who would resist that onslaught and that many people would pay with their lives.

"My father . . . ?" he said, his voice a dry rasp, hoping that he was wrong, yet knowing he was right.

"Tanis Half-Elven fought bravely. He almost won the struggle to hold the main gate," Salladac said, his voice devoid of emotion. "In the end, he died a warrior's death . . . a death that should make a son proud."

* * * * *

"I never did get to Ergoth," Aeren said softly, his thoughts returning to the present.

"You were caught up in the war?" Silvanoshei pressed.

"Yes, but it was not the war that I expected. . . ."

Storms of Chaos

Chapter Eighteen

The two green dragons passed a week in sublime relaxation. Toxyria's next season for mating was still several years away, which spared them the frantic, even savage passion of an immediate draconic rut. Instead, they hunted, feeding each other the plumpest seals, catching dolphins to share, and lolling on their bluff with leather-lidded eyes peeled, constantly studying the northwestern horizon in search of a promising sail. Aeren remained alert for danger from the forests, too, but his earlier observation seemed accurate: The blue dragons had apparently abandoned Qualinesti.

If not for the oppressive heat, it would have been an interval of splendid peace and rest. Yet the unnatural weather was too extreme to ignore, and the relentless presence of the baking sun, the utter lack of moisture in the air, caused the two dragons to share a lingering sense of unease. The sky remained devoid of clouds, but it never reached the depths of blue that normally would have characterized fine summer weather. Instead, the sun blazed relentlessly, trees wilted, and the world seemed to wait . . . for something.

And the green dragons watched.

The first sign of significance, noticed by both of them at the same time, was not the indication of a passing ship that Aeren had been hoping for. Instead, it was a glowing redness that, with startling rapidity, suffused the sky to the north and west.

"It looks like the reflection from a great fire," Aeren said worriedly.

"But there's nothing except ocean out there. It's almost a hundred miles to Ergoth!" Toxy, who had spent more time familiarizing herself with the area, explained.

"Then maybe Ergoth is burning," the male surmised. From his secluded ledge, he lifted his neck and head high, peering over the top of the bluff behind them, scanning the skies for signs of danger. But there was nothing else unusual, aside from the—by then—normal state of heat for that summer. Still, both dragons agreed that the bizarre redness was a strange and unsettling phenomenon.

"I'm going to fly over there and have a look," he announced, feeling very brave.

"We'll both go," Toxy said, fanning her wings beside him.

And so the pair of emerald dragons launched themselves from the cliff, gliding upward in the face of the stiff offshore breeze. Soon the coastline was a verdant fringe to the rear, and the waters of the wide strait expanded before them and to both sides below.

The sun was shining, but the surface of the sea had a curious, leaden quality; it was not the shimmering swath of diamond speckles that they had both become accustomed to. And the air had a strange taste—not like smoke, exactly, but as if an acrid scent somehow permeated everywhere. It reminded Aeren of the ozone aftermath of a lightning strike, though there were neither thunderclouds nor blue dragons in evidence.

The shore thinned farther behind them, and the strange swath of radiation grew more pronounced. Aerensianic was grateful for the female's company, and he couldn't deny that he was growing more and more afraid. Yet because of Toxyria, he was determined to put on a show of bravery. He flew with his neck and head fully extended, his tail trailing straight behind as he boldly glared at the distant sky.

"Look there!" gasped Toxy, banking and angling her head downward to point.

Aeren, who had been looking upward, ducked to see specks of brightness bubbling through the water, as if fires were somehow burning in the midst of the brine. They grew more intense, and he counted three patches of orange flame, churning and roiling toward the air with explosive force.

One broke from the surface in a hiss of steam and immediately angled upward. Squawking in astonishment and fear, Aeren saw that this was a fiery flier—a creature of flames, in the shape of a dragon! Moments later the other two burst from the sea, and there was no mistaking the nature and the threat. These were three dragons of pure fire, and they were rising rapidly, blazing wings stroking as they flew straight toward the pair of greens.

"Flee!" cried Toxy, obviously appalled at the horrific apparitions. She banked tightly and, wings driving powerfully, bore toward the Qualinesti coast.

Aeren was right behind. He cast a horror-stricken glance beneath his belly, confirming that the fiery monsters were indeed chasing them. They had altered their climb as the greens had turned and now were swerving after them in crackling, spark-trailing pursuit. Even worse, they were closing the distance!

"Faster!" he gasped, winging powerfully, wishing he could push Toxy through the skies. The larger of the pair, he was also the faster flier, and though he was nearly mad with fear, some deep and unsuspected reserve of courage wouldn't let him pull ahead of his companion. Instead, the two greens flew side by side, streaking through the air, riding the crest of the wind, instinctively racing toward the safety of their oceanside lair.

Once more Aeren looked back and saw that the fire dragons were even closer. Black, lightless eyes gaped like death from their orange faces. Everywhere a normal dragon would have been scaled, these monstrosities had surfaces of seething, boiling fire. Their wings were like flaming tendrils, somehow smooth and solid enough to bear the beast's weight. The green dragon couldn't imagine what it would be like to touch that flame. He pictured it searing his talons away, consuming his flesh with hungry fingers of pure heat. He saw that the leading fire dragon was only five or six lengths behind them, with its two mates a similar distance beyond.

"No good!" he gasped. "They're . . . too fast!"

His heart swelled, and in an instant of pure, furious decision, he did something more selfless than he had ever done before. "Keep going!" he cried to Toxy.

Then he curled through an upward loop and flew straight at the fire dragon, his emerald jaws spread wide in a cry of challenge and pure, unadulterated fear.

* * * * *

With the revelation that they'd had a spy in their midst, Porthios realized the elven outlaws would have to move camp again. Privately he placed little hope in Gilthas's attempt to prevent Guilderhand from reaching Rashas. At best, he hoped the young Speaker might be able to talk his way out of a dungeon, or to avoid an even grimmer fate.

But to the prince, that was a minor problem compared to the threat of blue dragons once again winging downward into the trees. At Splintered Rock, they lacked even the minimal defensive benefits of the ravine, so the elves' only hope of survival was to keep their location a secret. Despite the many comforts of the site at the base of the craggy bluff, the Qualinesti outlaws and their Kagonesti allies decided they once again had to pack their belongings and begin a trek through the forest.

The outlaw prince was becoming increasingly aware of the difficulties inherent in his status as an outlaw. Qualinesti was a vast forest, surely, but there were only a limited number of places where a large group of elves could find comfortable camp. They needed not only plenty of food, but also a steady supply of clean water—especially now, when summer's unnatural heat so oppressed them. Also, they had to have a tall canopy of leaves that was thick enough to screen them from aerial searchers, and ideally enough flat and open space between the trees for five hundred elves to camp in some semblance of comfort.

At the same time, he realized how perfect the Splintered Rock site was. A wide stream flowed into the lake, bringing a steady supply of fresh water. There was plenty of space, and ample types of wild game in the area. Both the lake and the stream were well stocked with fish, and since the tribe had arrived here, they had managed to eat very well.

Still, a day after his nephew's visit, Porthios was agitated and restless. He paced back and forth through the camp, looked around, saw the perfection of the locale . . . and knew that it was no good to stay there, not since the location was known by the spy called Guilderhand.

Late that afternoon he called a council of his most trusted lieutenants. Alhana, Samar, Dallatar, and Tarqualan all joined him in the snug grove where he had first met with Gilthas. They dispensed with the normal ritual of a fire, since the air was already superheated and the utter lack of wind would have insured that any smoke would merely have formed a haze around their heads.

"I'm thinking that we have to leave," said the prince. "I don't want to, but with our position discovered by the spy, it's too dangerous to stay here."

"I agree," Dallatar said. "Though in many ways our camp here is ideal, we have no real protection against an attack."

Samar and Tarqualan nodded, too, while Alhana, cradling a sleeping Silvanoshei, seemed too weary to make any kind of signal. Instead, she slumped against a tree trunk and watched the proceedings without expression. Porthios couldn't help but notice the dark circles under her eyes, the outline of her strong bones through the pale skin of her increasingly gaunt face.

The prince forced himself to concentrate on the matter at hand. He addressed Dallatar. "You know these forests better than any of us. Is there another place that might fulfill our needs?"

Alhana lifted herself to speak. "A place not terribly far away," she said. "The people are tired and many are wounded. They need rest and food, a chance to get their strength back."

The wild elf chieftain thought for a little while. Finally he gestured to the stream that flowed past the encampment. "We can follow that creek toward its headwaters in the southern highlands. Perhaps three days' march will take us into the hill country. There are many valleys there, still thickly forested, with plenty of game. However, the trail will climb steeply toward the end. It will not be an easy march."

"That's too far!" Samar interjected. "You heard the queen. Many of us cannot make a trek like that!"

The others looked at him, startled by his vehemence, while Alhana reached a restraining hand to his arm.

"It's all right," she said quietly. "I know we can do it. The strong will help those who are weaker, and the tribe can make it."

Porthios felt that increasingly familiar twinge of jealousy. He shook his head, angry at himself. Why did he let it bother him? He knew that his wife loved him, that she had given birth to his baby! Wasn't that enough?

Tarqualan was speaking. "I suggest we use the griffons to move those who are too weak to walk. It's even possible that we could get more of them to join us, though it would take a few days."

"I know there were many griffons in Qualinesti years ago," Porthios said. "Do you know where they've gone?"

"Most are dwelling in the valleys of the High Kharolis," said the scout, speaking of the lofty mountain range that sprawled over the dwarven kingdom of Thorbardin, miles to the south and east of Qualinesti.

"Do you think they would agree to help us?" wondered the prince.

Tarqualan nodded, but it was Alhana who spoke. "They abandoned the Qualinesti just a year ago, after Rashas ordered me imprisoned. It may be the knowledge that the prince has returned and I am now free could bring them to our assistance."

Porthios was somewhat heartened by this news. "For this move, I don't think we can count on more help than the griffons we have with us right now. But if we can make this march and reach a new camp, then we can send an emissary to the mountains to see if we can bring more griffons into our camp."

"That emissary would have to be you," Alhana said, addressing her husband.

"Why?"

"You are the symbol of Qualinesti, of the heritage that the griffons have served for so many centuries. If you were to go to them, to speak to them and show them our need, I think they'd follow you back here."

"Very well," Porthios agreed. "For now, we'll move out first thing in the morning, and as soon as we make a new camp, I'll see if I can enlist the aid of Stallyar's clan."

Later in the evening, with pickets posted on all sides of the camp, the tribe settled down to a night of rest. Sometime before dawn, Porthios awakened with an uneasy sense that something was amiss. He listened for the normal sounds of the nighttime forest and immediately realized that he could hear nothing except the rippling of the nearby stream and the soft breathing of Alhana who, with Silvanoshei wrapped in her arms, lay beside him. The stifling, muggy heat made it feel more like a midsummer day than the middle of the night.

But there should be soft birdcalls whistling through the woods, heralding the imminent arrival of dawn. Tiny mammals should be scurrying through the brush, looking for a last morsel of food before daylight once again sent them cowering into dens and burrows. Bats, too, were common in these forests, and their shrill, almost inaudible cries had been an accompaniment on every night spent out in the open.

Now there was none of that.

Instantly tense, though not yet alarmed, Porthios rose to his feet and silently made his way among the slumbering elves. He was holding his sword, only because the weapon gave him a sense of security, and he probed into the undergrowth beyond the clearing.

"Guards? Are you there?" he whispered, quietly approaching a sentry post. Odd . . . he had personally appointed all the pickets, but now he had no memory of the elf he had sent to watch this quadrant. The lapse in recollection was deeply disturbing, uncharacteristic of him and very unsettling in this strange, still night.

He stumbled over something. He looked down with a gasp to see a helmet and an empty shirt of leather armor. There was a sword, a longbow—This was the guard's equipment! But where was the man? He stared into the underbrush, trying to see through the thick swaths of darkness that gathered so closely beneath the trees.

And then, with a chill of icy horror, he realized that the shadows around him were alive.

* * * * *

Gilthas couldn't help but be pleased with the results of his second effort at recruiting. For some reason, now that they had already been conquered by the Knights of Takhisis, the elves seemed more inclined to realize that their kingdom could actually be facing an additional threat. Rumors and tales about the "Storms of Chaos" had spread through all strata of city society. In addition, the hot weather, the unnatural stillness of the air, and the thickening miasma that seemed to plague each breath all contributed to the feeling of impending disaster.

In any event, young elves, males and females both, came forth in the hundreds to join the ranks of the "Qualinost Legion," as the Speaker was calling his new command. They joined him on the hillcrest where the Hall of Audience spread under the open sky, and Gilthas found all his skills taxed as he tried to organize them into ranks, companies, and platoons.

In these efforts, he had the assistance of a burly Dark Knight sergeant named Fennalt, a man assigned by Lord Salladac as the elven commander's aide. Curling mustaches framed a square face with a stern, rocklike chin, making the veteran soldier a picture of strength and competence. Fennalt took charge of the actual organization and training, a fact that relieved Gilthas as soon as he heard the man's voice boom across the makeshift parade ground.

Still, the Speaker was kept busy with matters of procuring supply, continuing to gather recruits, and maintaining accurate records of the legion's formation and training. In fact, he was glad for the distractions created by this mountain of work, for it kept him from worrying about the thing that would otherwise have been at the forefront of his consciousness.

Kerianseray had yet to return from the camp of Porthios. Two days after his own arrival, the young elf had seen no sign of her, nor did any of his other servants admit to any knowledge of her whereabouts. Even when the workload was filling his head with facts and figures, he found his mind drifting away, occupied by concern for the beautiful wild elf slave who had risked so much for him.

Until he awakened in his house, the third day after his return from the forest, and was delighted to see Kerian enter his sleeping chamber to bring him his day's garments.

"I–I'm glad to see you!" he blurted. "I was afraid for you. I didn't know if you were safe."

"I stayed with my father and his tribe for a day. Last night I flew on the back of a griffon to the city. The elves are preparing to move again, for they feared that Guilderhand might have revealed their position—and I feared that you might have met difficulties when you got back here."

Gilthas quickly described the events following his return. "Thank you for taking me to Porthios . . . and for coming back to me."

"As you can see," she replied in a level tone, "I have willingly returned to slavery."

He flushed and shook his head. "No . . . you have your freedom. You shall do what you want with your life." His heart pounded, and he watched her carefully, wondering if she would immediately start for the door.

"Then I will stay here," she said simply. "Where I am needed, and where I can do some good."

She came to him and he reached out to her. This time their lovemaking was a slow process. Exploring and touching and teasing each other, they merged into a singleness that seemed to represent utter perfection. It was a long time before the Speaker of the Sun got out of bed.

Finally, refreshed and more invigorated than he had ever been in his life, he went to the Hall of Audience for the day's exercises. He was pleased to see that the elven recruits were learning to follow simple commands, to march, to wheel in response to an order. Gilthas, too, found himself feeling more and more comfortable with a blade in his hand. As he had previously, he joined in the drills and began to learn the rudiments of handling his weapon, the long sword he had removed from the wall in his house on the night when he had gone to seek Guilderhand.

Fennalt, for his part, had expressed appreciation bordering upon awe for the ancient long sword and had willingly showed the Speaker the proper techniques for wielding the light, supple blade for defense and attack. Like Gilthas, many of the recruits were armed with swords and often shields, while others bore spears, and of course many were skilled with the longbow that was such a staple of the elven armory. A few trained on horseback, though the vast majority worked as infantry.

Lord Salladac had gone back to his camp outside the city, where he was organizing the remnant of his army—the troops that were left after so many had been called away to campaigns in Silvanesti or Palanthas—into light companies. The blue dragons were gone from the city, and though the Dark Knights occasionally raised a cheer or clashed in a loud combat drill, they remained outside of Qualinost. At times, Gilthas even began to convince himself that he was the ruler here, the true master of the city.

Rashas came to the practice grounds late that morning, watching the drills for a while and then gesturing to Gilthas. Leaving his troops under the care of the knight, Fennalt, the Speaker walked over to the senator.

"There has been a message from your mother," Rashas said curtly. "The famous Lauralanthalasa of House Solostaran is on her way to Qualinesti."

"Good," Gilthas replied. "We must do everything in our power to make her feel welcome." Perhaps it was the new confidence he was feeling, or else he was relishing the feel of the sword in his hand. In any event, the young ruler spoke boldly to the senator who had placed him on his throne.

"This is the city of her ancestry. Undoubtedly her return will be greeted with joy. I want you to remember that I'm bringing her here for her protection."

"Of course. She no longer has authority over these elves, but she will be welcomed as a heroine."

Gilthas stared into the eyes of the elven senator. "I know you think to trap my mother when she comes here. Know this, Rashas: Should you make any move to harm her, I will fight you and all you represent. You will never more have your pliable youngster sitting on the throne."

"As you wish," declared the senator in a tone that lacked any sense of irony, at least so far as the younger elf could hear. "She will be treated as befits a former princess and a true heroine of Krynn."

It was shortly after the senator's departure that the practice was disrupted by shouts of alarm, screams bordering on hysteria. Neatly trimmed ranks broke in confusion, and horses whinnied, bucking and rearing wildly. Casting weapons to the ground, many of the young elves fled, screaming, from a threat that Gilthas couldn't see. The Speaker raced across the Hall of Audience to see Fennalt cursing, elves running in all directions.

And then a figure strode into view, swinging rock-hard fists, crushing those few elves too slow to get out of his way. Some swung their swords or stabbed with spears, but these weapons broke or bounced against the creature's skin. With a horrid laugh, the monster came onward, and Gilthas finally got a good look.

The attacker was cloaked in the body of a tall elf, but it was distorted by burning coals of fire where his eyes should have been. His mouth stretched wide to reveal sharp fangs, and his voice was a howl that seemed to rise from the darkest depths of the Abyss. No one could stand against him, and as he stalked through the parade grounds, the Qualinost Legion could only dissolve into panic.

* * * * *

"Only later did we learn that the Storms of Chaos broke everywhere upon Krynn, not just in Qualinesti, but across the entire world." Samar shook his head, grim with the memory of that horrible summer.

"Just like that?" Silvanoshei said, his voice hushed. "Creatures such as these came from the sea and the land and attacked?"

"All was under the threat of destruction," the dragon declared seriously. "The harbingers of chaos were like nothing we had ever faced before—the dragons of pure fire, whose flesh would burn your own should the creature even fly close—"

"Or the shadow wights," Samar agreed. "Their chill touch sucked not only the life of the victim, but all memories, all lingering effects that the slain one had left during the course of what might have been a very long life."

"And they were led by daemon warriors," the dragon added. "These were monsters made from the stuff of nightmares, and they appeared in the guise that would cause the most horror in their enemies."

"All were immune to weapons?" Silvanoshei asked, confirming what he already knew.

"To all weapons except those that had been blessed by the gods," Samar agreed, "and on this dark day, their attack was just getting started. . . ."

Fall of the Thalas-Enthia

Chapter Nineteen

"Rally to me! Stand and fight, you blackguards!" shouted Sergeant Fennalt. The knight's face was purple, his voice hoarse as he shouted at the fleeing elves. He swatted at his recruits with the flat of his broad blade, but the terrified warriors just broke around him and ran in panic away from the Hall of Audience.

Gilthas, too, shouted, cursed, and railed, but he was caught up in the wave of panic, running elves knocking into him, pushing, shouting, clawing at each other in mindless desperation to escape. Though he tried to push his way through the terrified recruits, the best he could do was hold his ground, watching as the human warrior faced the apparition from . . . from *where?*

The creature had the physical appearance and size of an elf, yet somehow it seemed much larger. Eyes of pure, bright fire glowed in its face, easily dissolving any suggestion of mortality. It stalked across the ground without pause or hesitation, reaching out and attacking on the move, striking at any elf too slow to get out of its way.

Like a demon from the Abyss, the monster bashed and howled, clearly enjoying the slaughter it was wreaking on these pathetic mortals. Abruptly it turned to the side, striding across the field, ignoring the horses, now riderless, that bolted past. With a lightning lunge, it reached out to grab a fallen elf by the foot, twirling the hapless fellow over its head and then casting him like a rag doll far across the ground.

The Dark Knight sergeant, apoplectic with rage, roared at his recruits, but even the fury of his loud voice couldn't control the panic. Indeed, headlong flight seemed like the only proper response, and the companies of Qualinesti recruits raced from the hilltop in all directions. One or two bold elves tried to slash at the creature with their weapons, but the being of chaos merely laughed as the blades snapped against his flesh, or bounced back with no visible effect. A few archers shot, and though their aim was accurate, the arrows merely sizzled into ash as they struck the monster's impervious skin.

"Who are you? How dare you come here!" demanded Sergeant Major Fennalt. "Now you'll taste a knight's steel!"

"Fennalt! Fall back—we can't fight that thing!" Gilthas clearly saw the futility of attack, realized that their weapons were useless against this horrible apparition. He shouted at the knight, urging him to flee.

But the burly sergeant would have none of it.

Instead, the knight raised his huge, two-handed sword and stalked forward, ready to face the fire-eyed horror that now stood atop the hill, in the center of the Hall of Audience. The elven figure paused, and then twisted and grew. Gilthas gaped, horror-stricken, as he saw an image of a leering giant, the bearded face distorted by the rot of death—and still marred by those hellish eyes. Then the monster changed again, growing into the visage of a draconic face and hulking, scale-covered body.

Fennalt paused for a moment, staring upward with his

sword raised. Then he drew a deep breath, shouted a battle cry, and charged. He stabbed, but his sword bounced back from the scaly flesh.

And that monstrous being reached out with hands that had suddenly sprouted cruel claws. It reached for the human, tore his arms from his torso, then gored him with a single sweep of those horrible claws.

The sergeant of the Dark Knights perished in an instant, and by then the rest of Gilthas's elves had raced for the streets of their city. Appalled, sickened, and horrified, the Speaker could only turn away and join in the flight.

* * * * *

Gilthas made his way to the Tower of the Sun. Everywhere he passed through streets filled with panicked elves, some crying out in fear, others angrily demanding explanations of the inexplicable events of which, finally, they were beginning to learn. But those who had seen the onslaught were too frightened to stop, too terrified and stunned to articulate what they had seen. Instead, they merely shrieked sounds of mindless terror, and fear swept through the city like an irresistible tide.

The sun remained high, baking the hapless metropolis, and in places Gilthas came upon truly bizarre scenes. He saw an elderly elven matron, utterly naked, run screaming from her house, crying that her nightmares had come to life. A few steps later, he saw a burly warrior, a large sword clutched in his hands, frantically dashing around his garden, slashing at the trees and bushes, wood chips and branches flying as he wailed aloud about the end of the world.

Finally the Speaker reached the base of the lofty tower, where he found a large crowd surging outside the doors to the great council chamber. He forced his way through the throng and saw that the golden doors were actually standing ajar. The chamber within was even more crowded than the street, but through sheer will and the considerable use of his elbows and fists, Gilthas managed to push his way farther and farther into the great, circular room.

"The world itself is aflame!" shouted one senator, his voice shrill with panic. "The knights have abandoned us. We have to flee!"

"Silence!" roared Rashas, his own visage pale, his mouth white-lipped and tense. He whirled to confront Gilthas, who was making his way toward the rostrum. "What have you seen? What's going on out there?" he demanded harshly.

The Speaker climbed the steps and shook his head in a mute admission of ignorance. "I wish I could tell you," he declared. "We're attacked by forces unlike anything ever seen in this realm or, I suspect, any other."

"It's the Storms of Chaos—they break upon us!" shouted the agitated senator who had previously, and hysterically, given voice to his panic.

"Please try to be calm!" Gilthas pleaded. "Such fears accomplish nothing save to fan the fires of their own making!"

He still wore the ancient sword that he had first taken off the wall in his house a week before. Now the young elf drew and raised the weapon, brandishing silver steel over his head.

"Listen to me!" he cried. "We can't let ourselves panic. We must try to understand what's happening!"

The crowd grew silent as Gilthas tried to make sense of the chaotic attack that had ripped through his legion, killed his sergeant, and sent the elven troops fleeing in panic through the streets of their city. And though he had, for the most part, kept his wits about him, he couldn't decide what had happened, nor could he make any guess as to the nature or homeland of the horrible attacker.

"What happened in the Hall of Audience?" Rashas asked. "We've heard reports of a fire-eyed warrior, a giant of unparalleled cruelty!"

The Speaker sighed and nodded grimly. "I saw the thing with my own eyes. It seemed to come from the city streets, walked right up the hill—though how it could have passed among us for long, I don't know. But when the bravest man of my legion turned to fight the thing, it tore him apart as though he was a child's toy."

"And the knights and their dragons?" demanded another elf. "Where are our conquerors now?"

"Lord Salladac is still outside the city," Gilthas snapped. "He told me his dragons had been summoned to Lord Ariakan, in preparation to face the threat that has now so savagely come upon us."

"We need him here!" shouted an ashen-faced senator.

"I agree," Gilthas said, the urgency of the situation overcoming his shame at seeking the human general's help. "I need volunteers, swift runners to race to his camp and let him know what's happening here!"

Six elves quickly offered to make the journey, and the crowd parted enough to allow them to leave the tower.

"Now, the rest of you . . . you need to go to your homes, arm yourselves and your families!" Gilthas ordered, even as he wondered what good weapons might be against the horror he had observed on the hilltop. "Gather everyone who can fight—sons, daughters, servants—everyone! And make haste!"

Some elves started to disperse to follow his bidding, but many members of the Thalas-Enthia milled around in the chamber, shouting at each other, demanding information and protection. Even when Rashas shouted his agreement with the Speaker's orders, these panicked elders could only wring their hands and cry.

Through the chamber's golden doors burst a panicked herald. "It's coming!" he cried, gesticulating wildly. "The demon approaches, and it brings in its wake serpents of pure fire!"

Immediate pandemonium rocked the chamber as the senators scrambled for the main door. Shrieks arose from outside, and through the open portal, Gilthas caught a glimpse of the crowd streaming away. Some of the cries rose to expressions of pure horror, and the air glowed red, as if a fire was showering from the skies themselves.

At the door, the herald disappeared, and in his place was the fiery monster Gilthas remembered from the Hall of Audience. Now it was in the guise of a Dark Knight—resembling the bold Sergeant Major Fennalt, in fact—though the fiery eyes dispelled any appearance of normalcy. Throwing back its head, the creature emitted a laugh of rock-shaking power and strode into the chamber.

The flood of fleeing senators broke back upon itself, but now the chaotic warrior was among them, picking up esteemed members of the Thalas-Enthia and tossing them into the air like rag dolls. The monster pulled some of the elves apart, crushed others with blows from hammerlike fists. All the while it uttered that ghastly laugh, crowing like a fiend from the Abyss, exulting as it spread horror, panic, pain, and death.

Other senators turned toward the two small side entrances to the tower, pulling open the doors and spilling out as fast as they could force their way through the narrow openings. Fear filled the room with an acrid stench as the formerly dignified elves clawed over each other in desperate attempts to escape. Shouts and screams echoed from everywhere, and the esteemed members of the Thalas-Enthia punched and tackled each other, tore mindlessly at robes and hair.

But now fires rose from beyond these doors, and the screams of dying elves, accompanied by the horrific stench of charred flesh, roiled into the chamber amid clouds of black, churning smoke. Heat blasted inward with the smoke, and beyond each door, orange flames glowed even brighter than daylight, radiating into the chamber in waves of searing heat.

"Dragons! Dragons of fire!" cried one senator, his face blackened and peeling from a blast of supernatural heat. "The city is burning—Qualinost dies!" he groaned, toppling to the floor and quivering in the throes of convulsion.

Gilthas watched, horrified, as death surrounded the chamber, wading through in the person of the fire-eyed warrior of Chaos, pouring into the side doors as beings of living, boiling flame. A dragon stuck its head through one of these smaller apertures, and the elves recoiled from a visage of gaping jaws and pure, roiling flame. A cloud of fire burst from those jaws, roaring through the chamber, crackling in greedy hunger, killing all the elves across a wide swath of the floor.

"What can we do?" Rashas demanded, staring wildly around, reaching forward to clutch Gilthas by the arms.

"This way!" the Speaker said, breaking away and racing toward the stairs that curled upward to the tower's higher reaches.

With Rashas at his side, Gilthas darted onto the steps, pounding upward, dashing away from the carnage in the main hall. He left the screams and cries below him, climbing until he was gasping for breath, until his lungs rasped desperately for air. Trying to think, he sought to make some sort of rational plan, but in the end, all he could do was run. Rashas, screaming for him to wait, was left far below.

On an upper level, he burst through a door to find himself on one of the side balconies, perhaps halfway up the thousand-foot spire of the Tower of the Sun. He gaped in horror at the scene of Qualinost spread below him. Immediately he saw that events had advanced rapidly, even in the relatively short time since he had entered the council chamber.

The rainbow bridges flanking the city had collapsed and now smoldered as twisted ruins to the west and south. The sun was still high, red and stark and unforgiving as it blasted downward from a sky of pure, roiling white. It seemed to the elf that it hadn't moved from its spot at the zenith of the heavens.

Flames broiled upward from many parts of the city as groves, gardens, and splendid buildings were consumed by fire. He noticed, with odd detachment, that even structures of marble and crystal were engulfed, tongues of orange licking along surfaces of solid stone, charring and melting the rock. One lofty spire, the mansion of a great and ancient noble family, shriveled and bent before his eyes. With a groan of helplessness, he watched the structure topple, crashing into the street to crush dozens of panic-stricken elves who fled this way and that.

Here and there he saw more of the fire dragons, at least a dozen creatures of pure, living flame. They seemed to frolic and cavort with monstrous cruelty, trailing sparks, bellowing hate, belching flame. Everything they touched was incinerated, and they howled in unworldly exultation when their fiery tails lashed around to consume the people of the city.

At the base of the Tower of the Sun were two of these creatures, eagerly pouncing on the few elves who had escaped the council chamber below. These wyrms paused only to raise their heads to the skies, roaring in triumph, blasting gouts of fire and sparks from their widespread jaws. Then they dropped to the ground again and resumed their murderous game.

White wings flashed before him, and Gilthas saw a griffon approaching, incongruous in this sky of fire and death. The creature's feathers were seared by fire, its flesh torn and bleeding, as the valiant animal crashed into the balcony.

Only then did Gilthas see that the creature had a passenger, an elf woman who had been clinging desperately to the saddle. She had long, golden hair, though some of it had been charred away. The skin of her arms was reddened by fire, and she moaned in pain as the Speaker helped her to slump down from the saddle. Only then did he get the shock of recognition.

"Mother!" he cried, taking her in his arms, easing her from the saddle.

Like the griffon, Laurana had been burned. Her skin was blistered, and some of her tunic had been singed away— clearly the griffon had barely evaded one of the fiery wyrms. She was weeping, and he laid her, as gently as possible, on the floor of the balcony. A low wall blocked their view of the tortured city, though Gilthas was keenly aware of the fires that had burned through marble and of the monsters still cavorting at the base of the Tower of the Sun.

The balcony's tower door burst open, and Rashas tumbled through, gasping for breath, his face streaked with lines of age and horror. Wiping the sweat from his brow, he dropped to one knee and drew deep, ragged breaths. He didn't seem to notice Gilthas or Laurana as he cowered against the wall, his eyes fixed upon the door that he had slammed behind him.

From within the tower came a sound that chilled the young Speaker's blood. It was the fire-eyed monster, climbing the stairs, and he could clearly picture it tossing back that grotesque head, mouth gaping as it once again gave voice to that cruel mockery of a laugh.

At that sound, Laurana groaned and opened her eyes. They fixed upon Gilthas, but then widened as the horrible laughter was repeated. Wincing in pain, she struggled to raise herself to a sitting position.

"Mother, what's happening?" asked Gilthas.

"The Storms of Chaos, my son. They have broken upon us, upon all of Krynn! I was on my way to you when I saw the first signs of war—fires everywhere, dark shadows writhing across the land. And these daemon warriors, such as that thing that we hear now, everywhere leading the forces of Chaos across the world."

Now the thudding crashes of the daemon warrior's footsteps boomed beyond the door and halted.

"You—you have a sword!" cried Rashas, suddenly pointing at Gilthas. "You must stand against that thing—fight it, slay it, or we're doomed."

Gilthas shook his head, denying the truth. He looked at the griffon, then at his mother. "Get back in the saddle. Fly away from here to safety!"

"Osprey will do no more flying," the elf woman said gently as the griffon struggled unsuccessfully to raise its proud head. "And in any event, there is no safety, no refuge save what we make for ourselves."

The door splintered outward, crushed by the impact of a mighty fist, and Gilthas scrambled to his feet, clumsily drawing his sword. This situation was absurd, he knew, remembering the way Fennalt's sword had bounced off this same creature's breast. He moaned, fighting back tears, afraid not so much for himself as at the thought of his mother similarly ripped by this unstoppable beast. She had come to him in answer to his summons, when he had called her here for her protection! Now she would die horribly in the hour of her arrival.

Yet somehow he found his feet carrying him forward, his hands—in the maneuvers that Fennalt had taught him only in the last few days—clutching the hilt of the long sword, raising the blade to slash warningly before the daemon warrior's laughing face.

And even now that face resembled the visage of the warrior the monster had slain, the curved mustache and blocky chin that had once represented such competence to Gilthas. The beast crowed with a cruel caricature of the arrogance that Fennalt had displayed toward the untrained elves he had sought to prepare. Yet now that hauteur had a sneer of real viciousness, and the look of contempt caused Gilthas's stomach to lurch and his knees to quiver.

But when the monster reached forward, enough of the young elf's instincts remained that he slashed the sword through a frantic, wheeling arc, driving the keen edge against the daemon warrior's arm even as he prepared for the aftershock when the blow bounced away. Closing his eyes, gritting his teeth, Gilthas put all of his strength into the attack, praying to every god. With fear and hate, he drove the weapon through the monster's flesh, lopping off one hand, continuing on to slash deeply into the second wrist. The daemon warrior howled, falling backward for a step as the stunned elf opened his eyes and looked at his bloodied blade, gagging in horror at the sight of the dismembered hand twitching on the floor at his feet.

A flush of energy overtook him, and Gilthas raised the blade, lunging toward the hissing daemon warrior. He saw the fiery light flare brightly in the wicked pools of the creature's eyes—and then he hesitated as the visage before him changed, shifted, sprouting a beard, the human's features lengthening into an image that was at least partially elven. The creature closed its eyes, and immediately that horrible presence was gone.

"Father . . ." whispered Gilthas, recognizing Tanis Half-Elven in that once-ghastly face. He looked down at the hand, shocked and grieving. "Forgive me. . . ."

The wounded image of Tanis bent double, moaning in pain.

"Kill it!" cried Laurana, pushing herself up to her knees and shouting. "It's not your father! It's a trick!"

Gilthas stared dumbly at the person he knew so well. He brought up the sword, but he couldn't drive it forward, couldn't force himself to attack. "It's Tanis, don't you see? Look!"

272

The half-elf was hunched over, his wounded hand clutching the stump of his bleeding wrist. "Help me!" he gasped, his voice taut with pain. It was the voice Gilthas knew so well, the sound of the man who had given him life, who had raised him from infancy until his destiny had brought him here.

"I'm . . . I'm sorry," he said, lowering the blade and stepping forward.

The bearded face came up a little more, but there was a flash of something there, and suddenly Gilthas saw the hateful fire burning in those eyes.

And all the force of his rage, of his frustration and betrayal, went into his arms and hands as he thrust the sword forward, driving the keen steel through the monster's breast, tearing away at the foul stuff of its innards.

The daemon warrior screamed, an unworldly howl, and stumbled backward, writhing on the steel blade, finally breaking free to tumble to the floor. Tanis's features disappeared. Instead, Gilthas was staring at a beast of unspeakable horror, a gaping maw bristling with sharp teeth, skin black as oily coal except for the hellish fires of its eyes.

Slowly those flames faded to dull embers, and then went dark.

* * * * *

"So that's how Chaos came to the city," said the dragon quietly as Samar, white-faced and sweating, stopped to catch his breath.

"And as it came to everywhere, all over Krynn," continued the elf grimly. "Like the Great Rift that opened in the Turbidus Ocean, the fires that burned across the crest of the Vingaard Mountains . . ."

Aeren nodded somberly. "And the horror that lived in my own skies. . . ."

Nightmare Woods

Chapter Twenty

Porthios tumbled back into the clearing, shouting an alarm, waving his sword, frantically stabbing . . . at *what*? Despite the aura of menace, the bone-chilling horror he felt, there was no substance, no mass of flesh to these attackers.

For the writhing shapes seemed to be nothing more than pure shadow, insubstantial patches of darkness that closed menacingly around him yet had no bodies, no physical form. But when he recalled the empty helm and cuirass, he knew that somehow these bizarre nothings had destroyed the life and the soul of at least one brave elven warrior. And they were relentlessly determined to close in, to kill again and again.

The steel long sword in his hand, hallowed weapon of his family and cherished artifact of elvenkind, tore through one of the shadows with a sound like water sucking down a drain.

Porthios felt the resistance, knew that he had gouged one of these shadows. But there were more, dozens more, oozing out of the darkness. They came at him from all sides, clearly attacking, though he could distinguish no details of face or body on any of them. At the same time, he knew they were real, and he sensed the deadly menace in the chilly and silent advance. They reached with tendrils of horrific darkness, lashing limbs that changed in shape or size as he dodged and retreated.

He shouted as loud as he could, desperately trying to raise an alarm in the camp. Then he stabbed and slashed again with his sword, lunging forward, dodging to the side, striking like a snake as he made sure than none of the tentacles of inky black could reach far enough to come into contact with his skin. Each time his sword cut through the tenuous shape of a shadow, he heard that awful gurgling death and saw the darkness wisp away.

But there were so many of them! They began to close a circle around him, and in seconds, his retreat was nearly cut off. Spinning frantically, slashing in every direction, he cut at the things, dissolving more of them, opening a gap in their ranks that allowed him to tumble past. Porthios rolled across the ground until he slammed against the trunk of a tree. Instinctively he knew that to be touched was to die. He was on his feet in a half a heartbeat, slashing and parrying, holding the eerie things back as once more he raised his voice in alarm.

"To arms, elves of Qualinesti! We're attacked!"

In the camp, the elves were already aroused, griffons growling and screeching, warriors raising their weapons, other elves streaming into the woods, fleeing the mysterious attackers that were now emerging from between the trees. Most of the outlaws abandoned what few possessions they had brought with them, splashing through the stream, racing through the woods around the base of the Splintered Rock bluff. Porthios saw that Alhana had already snatched up Silvanoshei and fallen back, joining the flight that threatened to become a panic. Only then did the elven prince turn back to the fight, brandishing his blade, striking at any of the shadows that came within range of his steel.

He saw a dozen brave elves charge, instinctively forming a battle line, but their blades sliced harmlessly through the looming shadows. A moment later the tendrils of darkness reached forth, and the elves were simply gone. In their places, weapons dropped to the ground, shirts and belts and boots still tumbling from the momentum of the charge, but of the flesh and the lives that had been there, Porthios saw nothing. It was as though the courageous warriors had never been there.

More shadows swirled toward him, and his blade cut through them, killing some and driving the others back. Already he was realizing an important truth: His weapon, blessed by ancient powers, was potent against these things, but the blades of nearly all of his warriors were utterly useless against these beings of foul magic. The elves as a whole had no means of fighting this unnatural enemy.

Another rank attacked before Porthios could call them back, and these, too, perished, vanished utterly except for the tools and clothing that they had carried into the fight. His elves did not lack in courage, but they had no effective tools for battling this foe. More of them were turning to run, overcome by fear and lacking any means of stopping the horrific assault. Griffons, too, were winging away after too many of them had flown at the shadows, only to vanish in utter, complete dissolution.

"Fall back!" the prince shouted, still wielding his own blade against a press of attackers. "Get out of here! We'll regroup on the far side of the bluff!"

Many of the warriors heeded his command, fleeing with the elders and children. But others stayed behind to wage the fruitless fight. Porthios recognized a brave warrior, silver sword flashing like lightning in his hand as he raced to defend his prince.

"Tarqualan!" cried Porthios, watching as that elven warrior came up against the rank of seething, squirming shadows.

And then the valiant fighter, veteran of so many of his

prince's battles, was gone, vanished in body and sight . . . and even, Porthios realized with a chill, in his very memory. He couldn't recall the name of the bold commander who had stood so staunchly in the face of a nightmarish attack, who had ridden at his side through twenty years of campaigns in Silvanesti.

And finally all the elves were running, stumbling through the undergrowth, fleeing in mindless panic through the dark, haunted woods.

* * * * *

Dawn broke as Porthios was still following at the rear of the band. He had no idea how many of his elves had been lost to the horror, though he took some minimal comfort from the observation that the shadows were not vigorous in their pursuit. Samar now fought beside the prince, the two of them forming a rear guard as the rest of the elves had crossed the stream and made their desperate way through the woods. The Silvanesti's dragonlance, like Porthios's sword, had proven to be lethal against the dark and insubstantial attackers.

Finally they pulled away, leaving the shadows lingering in the deep woods as the elves gathered around the far side of the Splintered Rock bluff. The sun was up, the heat already pressing downward like a sweltering blanket. Amid the milling band of wailing, crying elves Porthios found his wife clutching Silvanoshei. The baby was squalling loudly. The elven prince tried to think, but the shrieks of his son were driving daggers through his mind.

"Can't you make him stop crying?" he asked, fear and helplessness boiling over.

"He's terrified!" Alhana snapped back. "And so am I—so are we all!"

"I'm sorry. Here, let me hold him," Porthios said softly. "We're safe here, at least for a while."

"Do—do you think so?" she asked, trying bravely to conquer the quaver in her voice.

The baby fussed and twisted in his arms, and Porthios

couldn't lie to her. "I don't know," he admitted. "I don't know what attacked us, where they came from, or what they want."

All around him, elves were gasping for breath, lying in various states of exhaustion around the tree trunks and rocks at the base of the mountain. Somehow they had made their way here through the darkness, but now he had no idea of where to go, of what to do next. And through this panicky confusion, his son's distressed wails had pierced his awareness like a knife cutting through soft flesh.

"How many of us got away? And what about the others? They're just . . . *gone.*"

Alhana spoke numbly, but Porthios knew what she meant. He remembered acts of bravery, bold warriors lifting steel to stand against the shadowy attackers that had emerged so silently from the woods. But when he tried to recall individual battles, the last fights of brave elves, some of them warriors who had fought under his command for two decades, there was simply nothing there.

Desperately he tried to remember a name, to picture the stalwart face of a loyal lieutenant. It was as though the shadows, having killed an elf's body, had also sapped away any memory of his existence, any legacy he might have left behind.

The griffons, too, had fought the attackers valiantly. Many had perished during the battle, vanishing into space like the bodies of the elves who had been touched by shadow. The others had finally flown away, seeking the safety of the skies when the entire camp had been overrun. Now a few of them had returned to light on the upper slopes of the craggy bluff. Though Porthios looked upward, scrutinizing the heights for a sign of Stallyar, he had seen no indication of the familiar silver-feathered wings.

"My lord Porthios!" cried an elf, gliding low on the back of a griffon. Porthios recognized Darrian, a courageous and skilled archer and a veteran of the Silvanesti campaign.

"Here!" he shouted, waving from the ground.

The griffon came to rest on the forest floor, and Darrian leaped from the saddle and came stumbling toward him. The warrior looked haggard, his skin scratched and torn by brambles, though he didn't seem to be otherwise wounded. Indeed, Porthios reflected grimly, the shadowy attackers didn't seem to have injured any of his elves. Either the outlaws had escaped, terror-stricken but whole, or they had been touched by those chill tendrils and vanished utterly.

"What? Are we attacked again?" asked the leader of the ragged band.

"No, but soon! The shadows are coming around the bluff, blocking our flight. They'll hit us from the other side within the hour."

"How close?"

"A mile, no more. They move slowly, but deliberately. They don't seem to stop for anything!"

Porthios looked at Darrian's empty quiver. "Did you damage them, do any harm at all, with your arrows?"

The warrior shook his head. "Not at all—save once, when I used an arrow given to me by your father, the Speaker of the Sun."

"Was that missile unique?"

Now the elf nodded. "My king told me that its head was of purest steel and that the shaft had been blessed by Paladine himself."

"And what happened when you used it?"

"I shot into a mass of shadows, lord, and it seemed as though they were all torn, ripped into scraps of darkness. They made a hideous screeching, and then they vanished."

Porthios described the small success he had had with his own sword, and Samar with his dragonlance. "And those, too, are weapons blessed by the gods, imbued with powerful magic. As to the rest, even the keenest of elven steel seems useless against them."

The sun remained high, as if it was going to stay at zenith forever, and as the rays drove downward through the leaves, the forest grew hotter and hotter. Insects droned, and the sounds of grief and despair wailed even louder within the elven prince's mind.

"What are we going to do?" Alhana, who had been listening anxiously, asked.

"They've cut us off from the east and west," Samar noted. "We have the lake to our north and the mountain to our south. Do we stay and fight them here?"

"We'll have to climb the bluff," Porthios declared, instantly making up his mind. "I don't know how we'll stop these things, but we'll roll rocks down onto them if nothing else."

* * * * *

The stronger elves helped the weaker, and slowly the band of outlaws made its way up the steep, jagged boulders that lay scattered in profusion on the slope of Splintered Rock. As they gained altitude, they could look across the canopy of the forest, and they saw many places where smoke billowed up from the distant trees. The sun was a fiery orb, a searing spot of red in the white sky, and it blazed with merciless force onto the trapped elves.

By midday, the surviving outlaws had all gathered near the jagged summit, and Porthios wasted no time in appointing lookouts to hold stations around the entire perimeter. The deadly shadows seemed to move up the rocks behind them, though they came only very slowly, creeping a dozen paces over the course of an hour. Still, from the top of the bluff, the elves could see that it was only a matter of time before they were overwhelmed.

Dallatar, who had wielded an axe of legendary power against the shadows, found Porthios and reported that every ravine, every gully down the slopes seemed to be guarded by the slowly climbing shadows.

"There would seem to be no escape from here," he concluded grimly.

"Then we'll fight them," the prince replied with more determination than he felt.

"At least we will die as warriors . . . but still, I would prefer not to die at all, at least not yet," noted the wild elf, with a shake of his head.

"We can use the griffons to escape," Samar suggested.

"There are at least a hundred of them up here, and maybe four times that many elves. Over the course of half a day, they could carry all of us to safety, set us down somewhere in the woods where we can gather again."

"But who knows what we'll find there?" Porthios asked in despair. "We'd leave part of our band hopelessly exposed while the rest are being moved!" His mind quailed at the thought of Alhana and Silvanoshei exposed to these horrible attackers while he was off with another group, unable to protect them, to do anything to save them.

"The griffons in the High Kharolis!" his wife said suddenly. "You were talking about them just a little while ago—where they gathered after they left Qualinesti. You should fly there immediately, ask them—beg them if you have to, for help! If they came to our rescue, we could all fly at once, stay together, fly away from the shadows if they try to come after us in the forest."

"It's our only chance!" Samar agreed. "I saw where they laired when we flew here from Silvanesti. I can describe the spot to you."

"It's a chance, I admit," Porthios said. At the same time, he was thinking about this wonderful elf woman and about the son they had brought into the world. He remembered especially the long years in Silvanesti, while she had worked in Qualinesti, doing the work that was really his own legacy. How much of their current troubles had arisen because he had been willing to leave her for so long?

"But I can't go," he said firmly.

"Why?" demanded the Silvanesti warrior-mage.

"Too often I have neglected my wife for matters of state and leadership. Now we are in our worst danger, and I will not abandon her."

"But you'd be coming back!" Alhana tried to persuade him.

"No . . . because I won't be going." The prince turned to Samar. "You'll have to go in my stead. You know where the griffons are, and Stallyar will take you."

Samar looked at Alhana, then nodded slowly to Porthios.

"I understand . . . and I will do this, my prince," pledged the warrior-mage.

And the shadows crept closer from below.

* * * * *

"So it was you who flew to the High Kharolis?" Aerensianic asked.

Samar nodded. "I went on this quest with heavy heart, for I truly believed that I would never see my queen again."

Dragon War

Chapter Twenty-One

Aerensianic roared again, fury somehow overcoming his terror as he hurled himself toward the imminent collision with his blazing pursuer. He didn't look away, only hoped that Toxyria was winging with all speed toward the coast. Below him, the gray sea spread flat and metallic, and then the blazing image of the fire dragon filled his view.

Wyrms of fire and poison collided in a hissing tangle of green smoke and red fire, talons ripping, fangs slashing, and powerful wings driving the monsters together with headlong speed. Aeren felt his nostrils burning, sensed the scales ripped away from his flesh under the onslaught of that awful heat. But at the same time, he realized that the fire dragon was falling, that its flames sizzled and died within the billowing ball of the green's lethal exhalation. He expelled another cloud of deadly vapor, then plunged onto the still-burning back of the fire dragon, tearing with his claws, ignoring the heat that burned his mouth as he bit down on the other serpent's spine.

He tore into the fiery flesh, biting deep, driving his fangs with hissing fury into scalding flesh. With convulsive force, he ripped away a piece of the monster's backbone, spitting the smoking flesh to the side. At the same time, he felt a reflexive quiver in the great body beneath his talons, a shudder that convinced him that the other wyrm was dead. Spreading his wings, he felt those massive membranes crackle and strain where they had been scalded. Nevertheless, they bore his weight, pulling him away from the now lifeless hulk that tumbled toward the sea.

Aerensianic spun toward the fire dragon's two companions, both of whom dived toward him with widespread jaws and wings that left trails of smoke and sparks in the air. The green dragon knew he couldn't avoid the twin attackers, and so he spread his own jaws and belched a massive cloud of gas straight into the path of the nearest fire dragon. His wings cracked and blistered from the heat as he strained to hold himself aloft. Inwardly he quailed at the prospect of another clash with the unnatural monsters. Still, he held firm to his course, ready to fight and even prepared to die.

He was vaguely aware of another cloud of gas, a churning mist of green that enveloped the second fire dragon, and then Toxy was slashing into the fight. She screamed in pain as flames charred her body, but she bit and clawed and rent before belching another massive cloud of lethal gas. The supple body collided with his own, and then the two greens pushed off of each other, wheeling and snarling back into the fight.

The four mighty serpents whirled and dived and banked through the skies, surrounded by mixed clouds of fire and lethal gas. Teeth and talons tore at flesh of scale and fire, while cries of pain mingled with roars of fury. It seemed to Aerensianic as though the world was tilting on its axis, that the sun might have been standing still in the sky. The gray seascape was like a sheet of cold steel, as hard and firm and unforgiving as any metal shield.

Hellish heat blistered him, while chaotic sounds merged

into a cacophony of fury and pain. Cries of his own agony were mingled with bellows of ultimate fury. Numbed to the hurt of his own burns, Aeren slashed and whirled through the melee with howls of pure hatred, latching on to his enemy's fiery flesh, pressing and crushing with killing force. Ignoring the blistering heat, the agony that shivered through every portion of his being, he slashed another fire dragon to ribbons. Nearby, Toxy did the same to the last of the chaotic beings, and finally two more corpses plummeted into the gray sea.

The pair of green dragons, singed and scarred but alive, spread their wings and glided painfully toward their coast. Behind them, sizzling plumes of steam rose from the sea, while overhead sunlight slashed downward, cruel and blistering. Despite the heat, Aeren shivered, and he saw that Toxy was trembling beside him. He sensed intuitively, and knew that she shared his awareness, that something about their world had utterly, fundamentally changed.

* * * * *

Though Toxyria was even more badly burned than Aeren, she was able to make it back to the coastline, landing with a barely controlled crash before the sea cave that served as the green dragons' lair. Aerensianic, ignoring the pain of his own wounds, circled over the crashing surf, watching anxiously as his companion slithered out of sight, vanishing into the shady coolness of the cavern.

Only then did he lift his head, seeking through the air, looking to all horizons to see if there was any sign of more fire dragons. Only the sun shared the sky with him, and once again he had that eerie thought—the blazing orb remained directly overhead, stubbornly refusing to move from the zenith. Finally he too landed, creeping into the lair to curl up in a dark, moist alcove of the cave. Gently Aeren licked at the horrible wounds that scarred Toxy's flanks, while she lowered her head and breathed out a mournful sigh.

At last they slept, for how long Aeren couldn't tell. He awakened with a groggy return to consciousness, aching in every nerve. Despite the pain, he crawled to the entrance to peer outside. The sunlight still beat straight down outside the cave, though he found it hard to believe that they had slumbered through a full day. Still, he felt a little stronger, and the pain in his neck and wings had diminished considerably with the rest.

"Stay here," he whispered as his companion moaned.

She shook her head in reply, lifting her sinuous neck.

"We have to get help," she said. "This is a danger that is greater any we have ever seen, greater by far than the threats of metal dragons or of the lances that pierce and kill."

"What should we do?" Aeren asked.

"You go north . . . seek more greens, and the blues, too, if you can find them. Tell them of these fire dragons and bring them here."

"And you?"

"I will go south . . . there, too, I hope to find greens. And beyond that, there may be white dragons living in the realms of ice. I will bring them, and in all our numbers, we will fly against the Storms of Chaos."

Aeren wanted nothing more than to hide, to wait inside his lair and hope that the awful storm would pass. But somehow now, confronted by Toxyria's strength and determination, he couldn't allow himself to cower away from the world. The pain of his burns was a chorus of agony, seeming to penetrate everywhere through his body. Fear numbed, almost paralyzed him, but he would force himself to be strong for her.

"This is a good plan," Aeren agreed. "But be careful. Now that I have found you, I should grieve to lose you."

She blinked, leather lids drooping over her slitted eyes in a touching gesture of affection. "I will be careful—and you do the same, won't you?"

Aeren nodded and gently nuzzled the female's long snout. Finally the two dragons took to the air, soaring over the forests of Qualinesti. Toxyria disappeared, following the coastline south, and Aeren flew in the opposite direction. His goal was specific: He had seen the blue dragons rising from an encampment to the north, and now he went to seek them. Though they had not been in the sky recently, they could certainly have been waiting, hiding on the ground. Distrustful and admittedly afraid of his kin-dragons, he had not been bold enough to check as far as their lair.

Now, for Toxy, he would.

All the while the sun stood high in the sky, red and implacable, shining downward with radiation of powerful, unforgiving heat. The vault of the heavens was an expanse of deathlike pallor, white, hot, and dead. The pain in Aeren's burned limbs soon returned, but he ignored the discomfort, emboldened by the knowledge that Toxy, who had been hurt even worse than he, had somehow found the courage to fly forth.

At times the green dragon bellowed aloud, braying the distress call of a chromatic dragon, a cry that should have brought any of his kin-dragons in earshot flying to the rescue. But he saw no sign of scale nor wing, nothing to disturb the relentless sameness of the forest. In the distance, plumes of smoke rose from the woodland and seemed to promise that elsewhere, too, there were attackers of chaos and fire wreaking their destruction upon the helpless world. Once, far away, he saw a conical mountain, spires of jagged rock rising from the steep slopes, while a curious swath of darkness seemed to seethe and writhe around its base. The place had an eerie sense of menace, and he circled wide, giving it a broad berth as he continued his search.

He found several camps of the blue dragons, but these were abandoned and—judging from the dried droppings the green dragon inspected—looked to have been vacated several days earlier. Of the human knights who had brought these dragons here, there was no sign, and Aeren concluded that the dragons and their riders had all departed in response to some command from their distant and unknown masters. They had gone, leaving this part of the world to the mercies of the Chaos storm. It seemed obvious that if this forest was to survive, Aeren himself would have to play a large role in protecting it.

The green dragon calculated that he searched for many hours, even for more than a day, but always the sun remained immobile, fixed and glaring as it scorched him, scalded the

poor forest even as it seared the wounded flesh on the green
dragon's back, neck, and shoulders. Sometimes Aerensianic
wondered if the fires he saw in the distance were caused merely
by the dryness of the woods, the helpless tinder yielding to
conflagration upon the first spark. But he readily recalled the
unnatural horror inspired by the blazing, spark-trailing
dragons, and in his heart, he knew this was not the case, knew
that the forces that had attacked Toxy and himself were striking
everywhere upon the world.

Finally he circled back, winging southward again, flying
toward the rendezvous at the oceanside lair. His course again
took him within sight of the same conical peak he had seen
earlier, and once more he noticed the broad swath of unnatural darkness. Biting back his fear, Aeren cast his spell of invisibility over himself and resolved to investigate the strange
phenomenon.

Unseen by anyone on the ground, he soared close to the
jagged bluff and noticed that the sides of the mountain were
teeming with elves. Still cloaked by concealing magic, he
winged through a wide circle, looking around. He noticed griffons flying through the air, circling over the summit . . . and
among those fliers, he was startled to see a creature of silver-
feathered wings, a griffon unlike any other in the world.

More frightening, and unnatural in the same bizarre
manner as the dragons of fire, he saw that the shadows at the
base of the hill were thick and alive, seething with a motion like
angry waves. Aeren's blood chilled at the sight of them, and he
knew that these were beings of Chaos, every bit as deadly and
unnatural as the burning serpents. The dark shapes swarmed
around the hill, thick in the woods, projecting an unmistakable
aura of chill and death.

And like the fire dragons, they seemed to indicate nothing
so much as the very end of the world.

* * * * *

Finally Aerensianic glided southward, following the coastline back to the lair he had found in the sea cave. In places, he

passed forests that had been decimated by fires, and then he would fly beside long swaths of still pristine woodlands. So far as he could tell, he was the only dragon in this part of Krynn.

Eventually he recognized the spit of land just north of his cave, and he dived, anxious to return to the lair, hoping that Toxyria would be here as well. He came to rest on the rocks of the shoreline and ducked his head into the cavern.

"Toxy?" he asked with a hopeful snort.

Only then did he catch a whiff of the sulfurous taint of soot and smoke, unnatural evidence of flame in this moist environment. With a reflexive leap, he sprang into the air, barely avoiding the gout of fire that exploded outward from his lair. Straining his huge wings, the green dragon rose, desperately gaining altitude, pulling away from the ambush that had been laid for him.

He banked and flew along the coastline for a few strokes, then caught an updraft and rose higher, away from the surf and beyond the crest of the coastal bluff. His mind was torn by fear, anguished by one question: Had Toxyria returned and been slain in the lair by the hateful wyrms of fire?

He looked below, seeing that no fewer than three fire dragons had emerged from the cavern. Trailing sparks and smoke, they were flapping after him in determined pursuit. If she had been in the cave, she was certainly dead.

Rage clouded his senses, driving him into a battle fury as he tried to imagine the fate of the female that, he had hoped, would someday become his mate. His own forlorn flight and fruitless search only aggravated his bitterness. If they had killed her, he vowed that he would not allow them to survive.

The fire dragons swept upward from the cave, and with a bellow of rage, Aerensianic turned about and dived toward his fiery pursuers. He roared, a wave of sound that echoed off the cliff and thrummed through the air. Jaws gaping, he spewed his breath of green gas at the first of his pursuers.

The first burning serpent shriveled and steamed, then tumbled from the sky. The next wyrms came after him, and once again Aeren flew into a conflagration of hellish heat. His claws ripped at fiery skin as he felt the membranes of his wings curl and tear from the onslaught.

And then there was more gas around him, and the last two fire dragons were plunging toward the ground. He felt a blast of cold against his wings and actually relished the chill as it soothed the pain of his burns. He saw white dragons diving past, breathing their icy breath to douse the last of the fire dragons. The lifeless bodies of the Chaos wyrms plunged, sizzling, into the sea, and the dragons of ice and poison soared side by side over the western cliffs of the Qualinesti shore. Aeren banked, ignoring the pain that shrieked through his torn and scalded wings. Proudly he nodded his thanks to these kin-dragons, ice-breathing cousins who dwelled on the vast glacial reaches to the south.

Finally he saw the green shape that he had missed, that he had feared for. Toxyria fell into pace beside him, and he saw that she had returned with several more greens as well as a trio of white dragons. The serpents came to rest on the bluff overlooking the sea, and for a moment they were silent, observing the three pillars of steam that marked the graves of the fire dragons.

"What news from the north?" Toxy asked after they had nuzzled snouts long enough to ensure that each was relatively unharmed.

"No dragons to be found there, but it seems as though all Krynn is aflame," Aerensianic reported grimly. "I saw great forests burning across the land of the elves. Also there were living shadows, deadly and hungry. They were battling with elves, including one called Porthios, whom I once tried to kill."

"As to finding our kin-dragons, I had better luck," Toxyria reported, indicating the greens and whites that had come to rest around them. "I flew far, and our kin-dragons were glad to see me, for they had heard strange tales of events here and across the world. They were willing to fly to our lair to seek your advice and wisdom."

These serpents, none of whom was as large as either of the mature greens, watched respectfully, and Aeren sensed that they were hoping for his approval.

"Thank you for your assistance," he said gravely. "Not only

did you help Toxyria, but your arrival no doubt saved my life."

"There is other news, brought by our kin-dragons," the female green dragon added. "As you surmise, this storm wracks the whole of our world."

"Are the chromatics all battling in the cause of our queen?" Aeren asked.

"Not just the dragons of our own kin and clan," Toxy said, surprising the big male. "But even silvers and golds have joined with blues and reds, all of them battling the Storms of Chaos that have struck so many places at once."

"Together?" asked Aerensianic, truly stunned.

"Everywhere," Toxy declared, fixing him with a look that he found curiously compelling, even as it made him feel just a little bit trapped.

"What should we do?" asked the male.

"You are the biggest, the mightiest of us all," Toxyria replied in a tone that informed him that her mind was already made up.

Aeren slumped. In point of fact, he wanted nothing more than to fly away from here, to find some shore where the Storms of Chaos had not yet broken. Yet even more than that, he wanted to be with Toxyria, and he clearly understood what that entailed.

"I think we should go and fight these attackers wherever they can be encountered," he found himself saying.

"I do, too," the female said, obviously pleased. "And you told me that some of the creatures of Chaos have come as shadows and make their attack upon elves."

"Then," Aerensianic declared, making it sound as though it was his idea, "we should go there as well!"

* * * * *

"So that's why you came to us," Samar said.

"Yes . . . I fear that, if not for Toxy, I would have hidden away, and Fate would have found me in good time."

"Then we all owe her a great deal," said the elf warrior-mage, "for our situation by then was dire indeed. . . ."

Flames Across the Forest

Chapter <u>Twenty-Two</u>

Gilthas helped his mother toward the doors of his own house. Laurana, burned from her encounter with the fire dragon and bruised from the crash into the tower, limped bravely beside him, but he sensed that without his support, she would have fallen. Still, though she was white-lipped with pain, she made no complaint nor any sound except an occasional gasp for breath.

It had taken them more than an hour to make it down from the Tower of the Sun and across two hundred paces of the besieged city. For some reason, probably nothing more than the luck, good or evil, that seemed to mark the chaotic progress of the attackers, the Speaker's residence had been spared the damage that had scorched so much of Qualinost. Everywhere across the city, however, the vista was scarred by evidence of the onslaught. Ruined houses and yards, sometimes a whole block of utter destruction, smoldered next to other structures that had been untouched by violence. Across the street, a garden bloomed and a small fountain sprayed merrily in ironic contrast to the shattered house just beyond. Pillars of smoke rose into the sky, marking the destructive swaths of the fire dragons, while panic-stricken elves sought shelter in many of the remaining buildings.

Rashas, trembling with fear, trailed right behind Gilthas. The senator had refused to leave his side since the younger elf had slain the daemon warrior. Indeed, the elder had literally clung to Gilthas's arm as they had made their way through the charnel house that had once been the chamber of the Thalas-Enthia. The rostrum and the circular floor were covered with charred bodies. The golden doors had been twisted off their hinges, and one had even melted into a puddle of now-hardened metal. Here and there, one of the blackened elven shapes twitched pitifully or stretched open a mouth to draw a rasping breath.

Escorting his wounded and weakened mother, Gilthas had roughly pushed Rashas away, ordering him to go to the aid of some of the elves who moaned so piteously in the ruins. Instead, the senator had slunk along behind him, ultimately darting through the door of the Speaker's house as if he feared that Gilthas intended to lock him outside.

Kerian and the other terror-stricken members of the household were there to greet them, and swiftly Laurana was carried to a nearby couch, where she was given water and fruit while the young Kagonesti maiden went to fetch some of the poultices she had made up as an antidote to burns. The house was crowded with refugees, many of them burned, others bleeding, and all of them dirty and frightened.

All looked to him with hopeful eyes, and Gilthas felt a bitter sense of irony—now they turned to him for help, when there was nothing he could do for them.

"What's happening?" Kerian asked quietly after Laurana had been made as comfortable as possible. "I saw dragons. They looked like they were on fire!"

Gilthas described the attack in as much detail as he could

bear. "My mother called these the Storms of Chaos. They sweep across the world, and they have struck our city with unspeakable violence."

"What can we do?"

Here the Speaker could only shake his head and groan in despair. "Nothing, so far as I can see, except fight them where we can and probably die."

* * * * *

"The shadows are starting to come up faster," Darrian said, moving back from the crest of the bluff to Porthios and Alhana. "What do you want us to do?"

"If nothing else, we'll do what I said before—roll rocks down on them," the prince said, even though he found it hard to imagine that such crude defenses could have any effect on the lethal, yet insubstantial, attackers.

Still, he and Dallatar rousted the weary elves who had sought respite and shelter amid the scraggly trees growing across the mountaintop. Besides the two leaders, he had identified a few—no more than a dozen—who possessed weapons of ancient power, swords that had proven to have some effect against the shadows, and these went to the tops of many of the ravines that scored the mountainside. There were other routes that were left undefended, but Porthios couldn't bring himself to expose a defender whose weapon would be useless against these things.

Other elves pried at some of the great rocks that lay precariously balanced at the edge of the bluff, though they waited for a signal from Porthios before pushing them all the way free. He skirted the full perimeter and saw that the shadows were in fact seething and slipping up the slopes of the mountain more quickly than they had before. They curled over rocks, oozed up sheer faces, and slipped through the rough gaps between the many obstacles dotting the slopes of Splintered Rock.

Completing his circuit, he found himself again beside his wife, who held their baby against her breast and stood at the edge of the bluff, looking down with a hard, unflinching expression. He touched her arm and she looked at him, and still her expression was devoid of fear. Porthios was profoundly moved by her strength and deeply aggrieved at his own inability to protect her or to shield all the elves from this unspeakable onslaught.

"How long ago do you think Samar left?" asked the prince, knowing it would take at least two days for the Silvanesti to reach the griffon aeries in the Kharolis and return.

With a look at the still stationary sun, Alhana shook her head, yielding to a measure of discouragement. "Not more than twenty-four, maybe thirty hours at the most," she said. She didn't voice the obvious conclusion, but Porthios knew that she understood as well as he did: Even if they answered the elven plea for help, the griffons would never get here in time to save them from this onslaught.

"My prince, they approach quickly, right below here!"

Darrian spoke urgently from nearby, and Porthios ran to look over the edge. He saw that several of the shadows had surged above the rest, slithering across the rough surface to ascend the steepest portions of the bluff.

"Drop some rocks on them," he ordered curtly, and immediately the elves pushed and prodded, breaking loose several of the granite spires that jutted from the edge of the precipice.

Slowly, grudgingly, the rocks worked free of their foundations. First one, then several, and finally a cascade of boulders tumbled down the slope, bouncing, cracking, breaking into smaller pieces, sending fragments shooting far away from the face of the bluff. Sounds of collision echoed and pounded through the air, rising into a rumble like a constant thunder, shaking the ground under their feet. Debris showered through the shadows, and then the first of the rocks smashed into the attackers with crushing force.

A cloud of dust obscured the slope. Porthios squinted, trying to see through the murk, to determine if the shadows had been affected at all by the crushing rockslide. Finally the cloud settled lower, and the elves raised a cheer when they saw that the heights of the slope had been swept free of shadows.

But the cheers quickly faded as the dust continued to blow away. Far below, among the jumbled boulders near the base of the slope, the shadows still seethed. They crawled over jagged stones, swept through the gaps between large rocks, and once again resumed their inexorable progress up the hill. It was impossible to tell if their numbers had been thinned by the rockslide. As far as Porthios could tell, the shadows still seemed to cover the whole slope.

Still, the rocks had delayed the onslaught. Porthios sprinted around the top of the bluff, telling all of his elves of their success, encouraging them to wait until the shadows were very close. On the far side of the mountain, the attackers had crept far up the slope, and here the rocks began to fall immediately. Soon they were tumbling from all around the rim of the summit, as everywhere elves worked to loosen stones, continued to send an avalanche of granite into the unnatural shades.

For long hours, the elves battled, sweating under the merciless sun, prying loose every rock that showed any signs of instability. And when those were gone, they set to work on the more firmly footed stones, chopping with weapons, digging and scraping with swords, and working makeshift levers quickly whittled from some of the mountaintop tree trunks. They threw smaller stones by hand, even dumped clods of dirt and loose tree trunks into the creeping darkness.

But finally it was clear that the deadly shadows were not going to be stopped by any such onslaught. Each time they were bombarded, they came back more quickly than before, sweeping across the increasingly barren slope with relentless, lethal purpose. Porthios imagined that the mountain was sinking into a morass of darkness. The black outline completely masked the bottom of the slopes and rose inexorably up the sides.

Some of the shadows slithered through the ravines that led straight to the top, and the few elves with magical weapons held out valiantly but were gradually forced to fall back to prevent themselves from being surrounded and overwhelmed. Porthios ran from one position to another, stabbing and slashing with his sword, exhorting his elves to greater effort. He rushed to a place where the shadows began to creep over the crest of the bluff, chopping and hacking, surrounding himself with the horrible gurgling sounds of the creatures' death throes. His arm was leaden with fatigue, and sweat ran unimpeded into his eyes. He knew he couldn't last much longer.

"Look to the west!" At first the cry was voiced by a lone elven child, standing and pointing through the hazy sky.

Others took up the cry, and Porthios squinted, making out huge winged shapes soaring toward them. These were dragons, he saw immediately, and he soon discerned that their colors were green and white. The relentless approach of these ancient enemies sent a shiver of terror through his body. Groans of fear rose from the elves, who now all but collapsed underneath a wave of hopelessness. How could the gods abandon them so thoroughly?

"Fall back! Form a ring in the middle of the summit!" cried the prince. Why had he allowed Samar to leave and take his dragonlance with him? He shook away the regret, knowing it was a petty reaction and understanding that a lone lance, however bravely wielded, would have no chance of stopping a force like this, numbering at least six or eight dragons.

And now the wyrms were sweeping into an aggressive dive, swirling around to encircle the upper slopes. The tactic startled the prince, who thought the dragons would have merely swept forward in level flight. They banked along the face of the bluff, apparently ignoring the terrified elves who huddled so miserably on the crest.

Even more surprising was the target of the dragons' attack as they dived down to sweep the slopes of the bluff with blasts of frost and gaseous breath. Icy gusts of cold roared across the rocks, leaving the granite ice-limned and slippery, sweeping away the shadows in the fury of chilly death. Clouds of green gas billowed across the mountainside, permeating through the shadows, sending the horrid darkness recoiling rapidly downward.

"They're here to help us!" Alhana cried in delight, the first elf to vocalize the stunning truth.

And then all the elves were cheering as the chromatic

dragons, clans that had been regarded as evil throughout all the ages of elven history, relentlessly attacked the lethal shades. Porthios killed a few of the shadows that moved up to escape the dragons, but most of the dark forms abandoned the attack to slip hastily, soundlessly down the mountain. Some of the shadows withered under the brutal onslaught of dragon breath, while most retreated, slipping and sliding down the slope to finally gather in the shelter of the forests clustering close around the mountain's base.

Finally the dragons rose to circle overhead while one, a massive green, came to rest on the summit of Splintered Rock. Porthios was struck by a sense of familiarity, especially when the wyrm opened its mouth and spoke in smooth, cultured tones.

"Porthios of the elves, I am pleased that at last we meet."

The prince tried to calm the quaking of his knees as the dragonawe swept over him. "I . . . we are all grateful for your assistance," he said. "And I am surprised that you know me."

"I came from Silvanesti. There I tried to kill you," the dragon said, without any tone of apology or regret. "I must say, it seems a good thing that I failed."

"*I*, for one, am glad," said Alhana smoothly, stepping forward to take Porthios by the arm. "And what is the name of this dragon who has rendered us such crucial aid?"

"I am called Aerensianic, lady elf."

Another green dragon, slightly smaller and more graceful than this huge serpent, came to rest beside the first. "And this is Toxyria."

"We are grateful for your timely assistance. As you saw, we were on the brink of complete disaster," Porthios said, bowing formally to the female dragon.

"These attackers are strange," said the second serpent, nodding her head politely. "We breathe on them and they retreat, but they do not die."

Indeed, the shadows still seemed thick at the base of the mountain, though at least they made no pretense of attacking. They lurked among the trees, occasionally creeping onto the jumbled rocks at the foot of the mountain, but then falling back as soon as one of the dragons soared near.

But the shadows did not vanish entirely. Instead, they skulked through the forests, still completely encircling the mountain. Their presence would block any attempt by the elves to climb down, to make an escape on foot.

For several hours, the elves and their ancient enemies rested together on the mountaintop, exchanging tales of the chaos storm, warily watching the shadows that lurked below. Porthios learned that Aerensianic was in fact the dragon he had battled in Silvanesti. He wanted to ask the serpent more about that campaign and about his reasons for coming to the western realm of the elves, but his thoughts were interrupted by a cry from across the mountaintop.

"Look, it must be Samar!" shouted a sentry, pointing into the distant sky.

The elves rushed to see what at first looked like a massive flock of geese, hundreds of dark specks in the sky winging closer to Splintered Rock. But as the forms got bigger and bigger, the feline legs trailing to the rear became visible, and finally it was clear that one of the griffons—a silver feathered male in the lead—was bearing a rider who carried a long, slender lance.

And then the skies were full of griffons, led by Stallyar and Samar. They were startled and cautious when they spotted the dragons and circled warily until the shouts and cheers of the elves coaxed them down. Finally they came to rest among the others on the mountaintop. Many griffons settled among the rocks on the high slopes, while others remained circling overhead, cawing and screeching.

"The griffons knew about the Chaos storms," Samar explained. "They were willing to come, especially when I explained that it was you who called for help."

Porthios was touched. "I thank you," he said to Stallyar. The proud eagle's head dipped in a polite response.

"Now we can get away from here," said the prince, gesturing to the thousand or more griffons around them.

"But it is not enough to flee," said Toxyria as Aeren nodded his head sagely in agreement.

"No," Alhana chimed in. "We know that the whole world is imperiled. We have to do what we can to save it."

* * * * *

"Lord Salladac is coming. He attacks across the east bridge, bringing a company toward the center of the city."

The report came from an exhausted sentry, who had obviously run all the way to the Speaker's house. Alerted by the elf's shouts, Gilthas met him in the front garden.

"When will he get here?" The Speaker felt a momentary flash of hope, until the sentry continued.

"He can't come any closer. His company was surrounded as soon as he got into the streets. There are more of those daemon warriors, and now the fire dragons are moving in that direction."

Gilthas shook his head, wanting to deny the report, to curse the messenger. All around him, the city was dying, fires and destruction spreading as far as he could see. A few minutes earlier he'd heard reports of a new threat, vile shadows that slipped silently through the streets and sucked the life from anyone they touched. More daemon warriors, too, had emerged from the forests to smash and destroy. Knowing that one of the monsters had been enough to rout his entire legion, he couldn't face the thought of fighting a multitude of the beings.

"By the gods, we're doomed," he whispered, his voice a groan that barely reached his own ears.

"Be strong, my son."

He heard Laurana speaking behind him, and somehow her voice gave him strength. He straightened and raised his voice to address the elves, several hundred in number by now, who had gathered before his house. Many of these were warriors who had been training in the legion, while others included nobles and slaves, merchants and laborers. All were armed in some fashion or another, and all looked to him for guidance, for leadership.

"We have to take the city back," Gilthas declared, hoping

that he looked stronger and more confidant than he felt. "First we'll need to arm as many of us as possible with weapons that will do some good against these forces of Chaos."

"I have three swords here, ancient relics of Kith-Kanan that have been held in my family for generations," declared one elf, a male the Speaker recognized as the young senator Quaralan. He had been exiled from the city upon the Dark Knights' arrival, but now he had obviously returned to fight for his homeland.

"I'm grateful to see you here," Gilthas said. "Use one blade yourself, and give the others to warriors who know how to use them."

Queralan quickly found a pair of willing volunteers, while Gilthas led many of the warriors into the house. There he proceeded to hand out the hallowed artifacts that decorated the wall of the formal gathering room. Some of the fine blades he gave to veteran elves, while the larger weapons, such as the axes and halberds, he bestowed upon the brawniest of his warriors. There were two dragonlances as well, and these he gave to a pair of warriors who had served under Laurana during the War of the Lance.

"You cannot do this—you have no right!" Rashas insisted, whispering to him from the shadows near the fireplace. "These are sacred relics of our people."

"And I will give them to the fighters who have the greatest chance of returning our city to elven control," Gilthas snapped. He wanted to say more, but Rashas bit his tongue and backed away, so the Speaker contented himself with this minor victory.

At the same time, he resolved that he would have more to say to the elder senator—much, much more. He was through answering to the commands of this craven elf, a creature whom he realized was as much a servant of the Dark Queen as any red dragon or any Knight of Takhisis. But the time for that accounting would come later.

Finally he led the force of elves out of the house, moving them along the street at a trot. Laurana had been remarkably aided by Kerian's potions, and she came along at his side, bearing a slender blade of shimmering steel. The wild elf maid, similarly armed, advanced at his other side.

"We'll go down the main avenue," Gilthas decided, "and try to fight our way to Lord Salladac." He thought for a moment about the irony—now the elves were advancing to the rescue of their conquerors—but then his mind quickly focused on more practical concerns.

In line they advanced, those bearing the enchanted weapons in the front rank. They jogged past smoking buildings, stepping over rubble and even bodies that were scattered through the street. Almost immediately they encountered a swath of the seething shadows, and the defenders of Qualinost charged into the battle. Gilthas led the way, chopping to his right and left, exulting at the feel of his sword cutting through the dark harbingers of Chaos. With each slashing cut, one of the shadows disappeared, dissolving in a gurgle of surreal agony.

Laurana and Kerian used their weapons with unfailing courage to strike at the supernatural shadows that now began to melt away before the advancing elves and humans. Everywhere the chaos creatures swept backward, recoiling from the startling assault until finally they retreated to either side. The road once again lay unobstructed before Gilthas and his elves.

Soon the bold company was moving on, charging toward a block of burning buildings. Cheers and battle cries rose from all the ranks as the hope of victory sank in. These elves were ready to fight, and believed that they could win. Once Gilthas noticed that Rashas, apparently frightened of being left behind, was accompanying them, though he stayed in the middle of the group, well back from any actual fighting. Quaralan, in contrast, led a band of young swordsmen who alertly guarded the rear of the formation.

Finally they saw the knights, the pennant of the Dark Queen rising above a small knot of men embattled in the center of a wide intersection. The elves advanced with more cries, but then shadows came forward from the buildings on both sides. Looming daemon warriors led them, and dragons of fire howled in exultant fury as they swarmed toward the elven company. The attackers came from before and behind and closed in quickly from both sides.

It was then that Gilthas realized that he had led his elves, including his mother and his lover, into a deadly trap.

* * * * *

"It was a simple matter to mount all the elves on the griffons," Samar said, while Aeren nodded at the memory. "You were carried by your mother, and Porthios, on Stallyar, took the lead."

"And we flew to the place where the battle raged," the dragon added. "I remember Toxyria in the lead, proud and beautiful and brave."

"To the city, then? To Qualinost?" asked the young elf.

"It was where the matter would be decided," agreed Samar.

Chapter Twenty-Three

"Stand fast, there!" Gilthas shouted as the elves on the left flank of his impromptu line started to back away in the face of the charging fire dragons. "Quaralan, look to the left!" he called, drawing the attention of the young senator.

Immediately Quaralan led his swordsmen to stabilize that part of the line, drawing the two elves bearing dragonlances with him. The first fire dragon roared forward in a blaze of flame and sparks, but the lancers stood with admirable courage, planting the butts of their weapons on the road and allowing the monster to impale itself on the silvery heads. With an unworldly howl, the serpent disintegrated into a cloud of smoldering ash.

Coughing and choking, slashing at the fires that scorched their faces and arms, the elves fell back, but the following fire dragons veered up and away, apparently daunted by the fate met by their comrade.

Gilthas looked to the front, where the street was black with the deadly shadow wights, the creatures milling and surging in the gap between the elf company and the Dark Knights. The monsters slithered closer, and though several were slashed and destroyed by the magic weapons of the elven company, others reached forward with their lethal tendrils, sucking vitality, even flesh itself, from any victim in reach. The line was quickly fragmented, and Gilthas was horrified at the prospect of the shadows slipping into the mass of elves, striking and killing in every direction.

He wanted to shout a warning, but his tongue, even his mind, seemed frozen by indecision. What could he say that wouldn't add even more to the confusion?

It was his mother who came to the rescue.

"There!" Laurana called, tugging at his arm, pointing to a walled courtyard at the side of the road. "We should take cover there—bring the dragonlances around to cover against attack from the skies."

"Yes—go!" shouted Gilthas, immediately seizing on the plan. He raised his voice to a shout that penetrated above the din of battle. "Fall back to the right, behind the wall. Quickly!"

Instinct compelling the move toward safety, the elves instantly obeyed. Gilthas felt a flush of pride as he saw that even under this horrifying scourge they did not yield to panic. Many of them poured through the gates, while others scrambled over the shoulder-high wall.

Gilthas, Kerian, Quaralan, and the two lancers were the last to fall back, and they stood at the open gates for several moments, slashing at a couple of shadows that came close, stabbing the lances to drive back a fire dragon that padded across the street. Only after the dragon once again took to the air did the Speaker and his companions enter the courtyard, allowing the gates to be slammed behind them.

Gilthas quickly saw that they had found a fairly effective defensive position. The courtyard was attached to several other gardens and yards, and the elves had rapidly spread out to garrison all these interconnected areas. He wasted no time in scrambling up to a small tower that overlooked the street.

Many shadows, eerie and silent, swirled about at the base of the wall. Apparently immune to the effects of gravity, some of the swaths of darkness slipped up the wall and reared over the top. Elven blades slashed, and most of these fell back or gurgled into dissolution.

The Speaker of the Sun looked across the avenue of chaos and saw that the company of Dark Knights had formed into a hollow square for defense, but that formation was sorely besieged. Shadows sucked at the fringes of the unit, draining away man after man in lethal attacks. Apparently a few of the knights were armed with weapons that were effective against the chaos creatures, but many of the others seemed utterly vulnerable. Gilthas saw Lord Salladac wielding a massive two-handed sword, standing at one corner of the square and chopping a huge daemon warrior in two with a single slash of the weapon.

"Salladac—over here!" cried the elven leader, his voice once again booming over the ground. He saw the human meet his gaze. With a gesture to the nearby gate, Gilthas urged the lord to bring his company into the makeshift fortress.

With a grim nod, Salladac shouted at his standard-bearer, raised his sword, and led his men into the mass of shadows. The banner of the Dark Queen surged forward, and the knights came after, a hoarse cry bellowing over the field.

Gilthas jumped down from the tower and raced to the gates. "Open them!" he shouted. "Elves of Qualinost, charge with me!"

"No!" cried Rashas, who had been cowering behind the wall nearby. "You're mad! You'll let those shadows in here—they'll kill us all!"

"Get out of the way," growled the Speaker. "We've got to get the knights in here. Together, we have a chance!"

"Don't listen to him!" cried Rashas, throwing himself against the elves who were beginning to unbar the gate.

Gilthas roughly pushed the senator out of the way, and the gates swung open. A surge of willing elves charged with the Speaker into the street, and the wailing Rashas was borne along in the front of the rank.

"Stop!" he screamed. "Let me go!" Desperately Rashas squirmed to the side, finally tumbling free from the press of attacking elves. Almost immediately a shadow loomed right behind him, dark tendrils extended.

"Look out!" cried Gilthas, horrified at the soulless, flesh-less apparition that seemed to rise higher than the gibbering senator's head.

Rashas stared at the horrifying image but seemed unable to move his feet. Gilthas reached out and grabbed the senator by the shoulder, pulling him away from the shadow. Another elf, one of those armed with a dragonlance, stabbed with his weapon, and the black shape dissolved into tattered remnants of darkness.

Stumbling away from the rank of attacking elves, Rashas looked at Gilthas with wide, staring eyes. Abruptly he turned and raced away, running along the wall of the courtyard— *outside* the barrier that was protecting the rest of the elves.

The fire dragon had been circling overhead, and this lone elf created a tempting target. With a shriek of triumph, the creature tucked its wings and dived, leaving a cloud of sparks trailing through the air.

Rashas heard the serpent's bellow and looked up, his mouth jabbering soundlessly. The senator fell to the ground and tried to claw his way through the quartz paving stones along the road. The flaming dragon fell on him, crouching firmly on the writhing elf, and Rashas's screams rose to a fevered pitch before abruptly ceasing.

"Kill that dragon!" shouted Gilthas, perversely enraged by the sight of the serpent's triumphant bellow. With the lancer beside him, he rushed forward, and the twin weapons slashed into the blazing flesh. With a writhing lash of its fiery tail, the wyrm toppled over and thrashed its last.

Only then did Gilthas notice that the knights had fought their way out of the intersection and were charging toward the elves. The vanguard of the Qualinesti stood aside, fighting as a rear guard as Salladac's men spilled through the gates.

Finally the elves, too, fell back, and once again the gates were closed and barred.

"Good work," declared the Dark Knight lord, gasping for breath and wiping the soot from his brow. "I thought we were lost out there."

"What's the use?" growled Gilthas, still horrified by the gruesome end of the man who had brought him to Qualinesti. He had hated Rashas on some level, but in another sense, the elder senator's demise was profoundly unsettling. "We're trapped in here. It just might take a little longer to reach the end."

"Then at least we can die with honor," declared Lord Salladac.

* * * * *

Great swaths of the forests were burned and blackened, with destruction spreading to the far horizon. The vast formation of griffons, dragons, and elves flew above tortured, blistered landscapes, often veering away from the plumes of smoke rising from the still-smoldering ground. In other places, trees had been felled as if by an angry giant, a great swath of shattered timber that had been plowed through the woods by a force of unimaginable and unspeakably chaotic power.

Scouts on griffon-back reported that the shadowy attackers at the base of Splintered Rock were not pursuing. Even so, Porthios maintained the vigorous speed of his flight. He felt a deep, fundamental fear for his land, even for the city elves who had branded him an outlaw.

Alhana, still bearing Silvanoshei in his *tai-thall*, flew beside him, her face an image of taciturn strength and desperate determination. Every time he looked at her, Porthios felt his heart breaking as guilt assailed him with the knowledge of the trials his wife and child were subjected to. Samar flew just beyond, his silver-tipped lance extended.

Porthios used his knees to guide Stallyar over, until the silver-feathered griffon flew right beside the warrior-mage. The prince looked over his shoulder, saw that Alhana was some distance away, and spoke to his old comrade in a low voice.

"My friend, I want to talk to you before this battle."

"Speak, my prince," Samar replied, raising an eyebrow in surprise but keeping his own voice quiet as well.

"If this fight goes wrong—for me, that is—if I am lost, I want you to pledge your protection to your queen. Please protect her with all the loyalty you have displayed through the years—and please extend that loyalty and protection to my son as well."

Samar's eyes widened, but he quickly nodded. "Aye, my prince. You have my pledge."

Porthios rode along in silence, wrestling with the rest of what he wanted to say. Finally he cleared his throat. "It may be that I have been unfair to you . . . that I have allowed unworthy suspicions to color my feelings and my actions. If so, I am sorry. I know that your affection for my wife has been noble and pure."

Now it was Samar's turn to be flustered. He looked down at his saddle, then back to Porthios. "I told you once that before you came to Silvanesti I think I was a little bit in love with her. Perhaps that has not changed in all these years."

The prince nodded. "Even so, I know that your actions have always been those of an honorable man."

"You are correct, my lord, and I thank you for your trust."

"You are worth far more," Porthios replied, once more clearing his throat awkwardly. "Now let us go to war."

Finally they reached Qualinost, and they found the city all but engulfed in flames. Columns of smoke rose into the sky from many places, and the skyline of the elven metropolis had been altered almost beyond recognition. Many of the silver and marble towers had been felled, and the bridges that had flanked the edges of the city now lay as twisted wreckage in the deep ravines.

At least the Tower of the Sun still stood, though several fires burned nearby. Sounds of battle rang throughout the city, and with frantic haste, the elves of the outlaw force soared over the deep ravines, winging into the polluted air over the city.

"There!" cried Dallatar, pointing toward a cluster of walled courtyards near the city's fringe. They saw a battle raging, with elves trapped in the crude fortifications while shadows seethed outside and fire dragons surged through the air overhead.

Porthios led Stallyar and the other griffon riders through the air. The formation, bright with white wings, spread across the sky, angling downward into the besieged city.

* * * * *

"Look, we have new hope!" cried Kerian, seizing Gilthas by the arm and pointing upward.

He gaped as the sky overhead filled with griffons, many of them ridden by elves. The fliers soared into battle, slashing through the fire dragons. One of the elves bore a dragonlance, and with the silver-tipped weapon, he speared one of the flaming serpents, ripping the creature into two pieces.

Then there were more dragons there, wyrms of white and green diving from the clouds, rending the fire dragons with breath of lethal frost and thick, toxic clouds of emerald smoke. These serpents roared and attacked in vengeful fury, diving into the aerial melee without hesitation.

Other griffons came to rest within the walls of the courtyard. Elves, including many Kagonesti, dismounted from them. Another flier came to rest nearby, and Gilthas saw a familiar figure on the creature's back.

"Alhana!" cried Laurana, recognizing the elf woman at the same time. She helped the queen to dismount, gingerly assisting with the baby, who rode silent and wide-eyed in his *taithall*.

The two females hugged in teary relief as Gilthas joined them. "I'm glad you're safe," he said. "Did the prince come with you?"

The Queen of Silvanesti pointed to the skies, where griffons wheeled and screeched between dragons of fire and scale. "There—he leads the warriors."

"I see!" cried Gilthas as a silver-feathered griffon slashed into combat with a blazing dragon. Horrified, he gasped, then whispered to himself. "By Paladine, be careful, Uncle!"

Alhana, with Silvanoshei held against her heart, gasped as her husband rode his griffon into the attack. She scarcely seemed to breathe as she watched the spectacle of horror and destruction that sprawled through the skies above the once-splendid city. The griffons dived and whirled, aided by chromatics breathing frost and clouds of lethal gas.

From below, a serpent of flame arose, trailing sparks, vengefully roaring as it gained altitude, and the elven prince on his griffon turned to do battle. Arrows flicked through the sky, apparently vanishing into the fiery aura of the dragon's burning nature.

The dragon opened its mouth, and a blossom of fire erupted. Alhana screamed as the fire surrounded the silver-feathered griffon. Porthios and Stallyar disappeared into the hellish cloud. The flames crackled and boiled, roaring with the heat of a coal furnace, lingering in the air for a long time.

Moments later the limp forms of a griffon and an elf tumbled out of the flames, falling toward the ground in a lifeless plummet. The queen's scream was still echoing around her as the charred body of her husband vanished into the smoldering heat of the ravine beyond the city.

* * * * *

Aerensianic saw the silver-feathered griffon perish in the grasp of the blazing serpent, and the green dragon was filled with a rage as powerful as it was inexplicable. He flew into the battle with a roar, ignoring the pain as his talons and fangs ripped through the fire dragon. He wanted to avenge the elven prince, to hurt this Chaos dragon who had slain the enemy that Aeren had once tried, and failed, to kill.

Toxyria flew at his side, and she, too, slashed at the wyrm of flame. The creature, lethally torn, tumbled lifelessly to the ground.

Two more fire dragons dived from above, and Aeren bellowed in fear as he saw the female vanish in a cloud of boiling, churning flame. With a white dragon flying at his side, he flew against the diving pair, and in moments both wyrms fell, their flames permanently doused by the violent attacks of the vengeful chromatics.

But it was too late for Toxy. Her wings charred to ash, she tumbled from the sky. Her yellow eyes fastened one last time upon Aerensianic. In bleak and helpless horror, he watched her smash into the ground with bone-crushing force.

He plummeted after, coming to rest beside her shattered form. She lay broken and battered, sprawled across a wide street, and he nuzzled her neck, her nostrils, desperate for some hint of breath, of vitality.

But he was too late. She was already dead.

* * * * *

Charging humans and elves swept forward, and the last of the shadows vanished under magical steel. At last Gilthas looked at a sky that was vacant of fiery serpents. A final daemon warrior wailed, pierced by lance and sword, and then the creatures of Chaos were gone.

Humans and elves gasped for breath and looked at each other as if mystified by the end of the battle. Griffons began to land all around them, and even dragons of green and white came to rest in the city of the elves. Those serpents, Gilthas saw, were gathered around a motionless green shape that had tumbled to the ground about a block away.

Of Porthios Solostaran, there was no sign.

A few minutes later Samar landed. His dragonlance was seared and scorched but, like the elven warrior-mage himself, intact.

"The prince apparently fell into the stream in the bed of the ravine," he said grimly. "I fear that his body was washed away."

Alhana pressed a hand to her mouth but made no sound. Laurana wrapped her arms around her brother's widow, pulling her close, and for long moments, the two women stared wordlessly at the sky, at the expanse of the ruined city.

"He died for us all," said the queen.

"And he will be remembered as a hero of elvenkind," Laurana added, "who sacrificed his life in our darkest hour."

The Dark Knight lord came over to the elves, stopping to face Gilthas.

"We have won—the day is ours," Salladac said, placing a hand on the elf's shoulder. "You are a hero of Krynn. Word of your deeds this day shall be carried to Lord Ariakan at once."

"Perhaps our battle, and the loss of Porthios and all those brave warriors, will not be in vain. Perhaps the Storms of Chaos have been halted, held at bay."

"No doubt my lord will send word about matters in the rest of Krynn," agreed Salladac.

"Your Lord . . . Ariakan. He still fancies himself the master of Qualinesti, no doubt," Gilthas replied.

"Fancies himself, and is that master in fact," Salladac said. "We have a treaty, you may recall."

Gilthas gestured to the ruins that lay scattered about the base of the Tower of the Sun. "A treaty signed by a senate that no longer exists," he observed.

"But a treaty signed, nonetheless," declared the lord, still calm. His dark eyes remained focused, unblinking, on the Speaker of the Sun.

In contrast, the young elf felt his temper slipping. They were surrounded by hundreds of elves and only a fraction that many Dark Knights, and he couldn't abide this man talking to him as if Qualinesti was still a conquered realm. "Perhaps this is the time to overthrow the invaders," he said, trying to bluster.

Salladac sighed. He, too, made a gesture, one that encompassed the green and white dragons who lolled, licking their wounds but still an obvious presence, up the street. "They, as well as we humble knights, are servants of her Dark Majesty. Would you care to ignite another battle so soon on the heels of the last?"

"Please, man and elf," said Laurana, quietly advancing to take her son's arm. "This is not the time for starting a new war. Look around you, at the devastation and the death. Look even to the sky."

313

Gilthas did, and he saw that the scorching sun had barely begun to inch its way toward the horizon.

"Can't you see?" Laurana continued. "Krynn is entering a new age. Would you have the histories record that you two welcomed that age with an act of war? Our survival has been attained because you worked and fought together. Surely you can continue that cooperation, make it your legacy for the future!"

The Speaker of the Sun looked at the human lord and heard his mother's words. There would be room for both of them in Qualinesti, he saw. There would have to be, for he could not bring his nation into another war.

Salladac, too, felt the same, for he extended his hand in a gesture of peace.

Gilthas reached forward and took that hand, and the new age of the world began.

Epilogue

"It is time I returned to my homeland," Alhana said. She bore the baby in the *tai-thall*. She and Samar were prepared to mount their griffons as the animals pranced restlessly on the outskirts of the city.

"If we find Porthios . . . his remains, I mean," Laurana said tenderly, "he will be buried with honors, and we'll let you know."

"Thank you, Sister." Alhana sighed."Silvanesti will be suffering under Konnal, I fear. With my husband dead, there remains nothing for me here—and it may be that I can do some good in the land of my birth."

"I bid you farewell, my queen," Gilthas said.

"And may good fortune greet you in the land of your father," Laurana added.

The two watched the griffons as they soared into the sky, finally vanishing into the east. Kerian's arm tightened around Gilthas, and he turned toward the city and his new life as the king of the elves.

* * * * *

The wild elf warrior found the charred body in the stream. Aided by the poultices prepared by his wife, he carried the badly injured prince back to a streamside cave. For long weeks, he tended him, nursing him first to consciousness, and then to the point where the elven prince could move.

"My face," groaned the prince, staring with horror at his reflection in the stream. "I am a freak, a monster."

"Come," Dallatar said, helping Porthios to make his way onto the winding, shaded trail. "Your home is in the forest now."

* * * * *

"And I turned my back on that world and came here to live out my life in solitude and peace," Aeren said. "I crept into my cave and slept"—he looked at Samar with narrowed eyes—"and slept well, until you poked me with that accursed spear."

"We shall leave you to that peace, dragon," said Silvanoshei. "I thank you for your story."

He reached forward and touched a talon of the great foot. "I am sorry for the loss of Toxyria," he added quietly.

"I, too," said Aeren, lowering his head.

Only after a long pause, many heartbeats of reflection, did the two elves rise and make their way out of the cavern, back to the world of sun and sky and sea.